Ҫһє

DIVIDED KINGDOM

BOOK 1

MASKED

SHARI CROSS

To my grandpa,
You believed in me from day one.
Though you were never able to read the book you were so proud of,
you were with me through every page.

"ONE THREAD PULL'D
UNRAVELS THE REST."
-Bianca Barela, *The Wheel, 2019*

Chapter 1

Sweat beads at my hairline, making me instantly regret wearing my cloak. Pushing it off my shoulders, I welcome the hesitant breeze that whispers along my skin. It's hot today, too hot for early spring. I glance up at the sky and have to search for a cloud. When I find one, it's peeking behind the snow-capped mountains in the west.

"Addalynne, are you listening to me?"

I turn to my brother, Gregory. He looks irritated. I wonder how long he's been trying to get my attention.

"I didn't hear you. You mustn't have been talking loud enough," I answer with a shrug.

"Yep. It was definitely that I wasn't loud enough. It had nothing to do with you being completely oblivious to everything around you."

"I'm not oblivious. You're just not very interesting."

Gregory tugs my hair. I turn and try to shove him, but he jumps to the side, out of my reach.

"You got lucky that time!" I shout at him as he runs ahead of me, laughing. I run after him, through the wild grass of the field, a fistful of dirt in my hand. He's fast, but the tree line is approaching and so is the wall in front of it, which means he has to slow down, and within seconds I'm upon him. I reach up and rub the dirt in his hair. It falls like dust around us.

"I yield! I yield!" He laughs, and I smile with my victory. "You're vicious today. It's a good thing I'm not going into the woods with you."

"Why not?" I practically whine as a scowl imprints on my face. If he doesn't come, we can't play King's Schild.

"I told Walter I'd meet him at the Barren Fields," he replies as he continues to shake dirt from his head.

"Fine," I shrug, letting my gaze linger on the branches overhanging the uneven grey stone wall that separates the forest from the village. I wonder if that wall is as old as Sir Alsius. I imagine that the branches are wisps of his hair, the larger cracks in the stones his eyes: watching us and warning us to stay away.

"But you better not go any closer to the river than the Grey Tree," Gregory again tugs on a strand of my black hair to get my attention.

I turn toward him. His eyebrows are drawn tightly over the concern in his brown eyes. "I won't, but you know nothing ever happens."

"Then why do you always insist on going there?"

"Because if anything does come close to the river, I am going to be the one to see it."

I move through the forest breathlessly, trying to make no sound. I have to stay quiet or the enemy will hear me approaching. If they see me before I get to them, I'll be killed.

I step around an oak tree and see them beyond the trunks of several willows. I reach behind me and grab the hilt of my sword, pulling it from its sheath. Holding it firmly in front of me, I creep toward them, marking the largest one as my target. If I can take him down, the rest will be easy.

His back is to me, and with the cover of branches and my quiet steps, he doesn't sense me approaching. So close . . . one more step . . . I lunge forward, thrusting my sword into his back, and watch as the disturbed leaves rustle before falling to the ground.

The long branch I fashioned into a sword sticks awkwardly out of the defeated blackberry bush. Playing King's Schild isn't as much fun without Gregory.

I turn and head deeper into the forest, brushing my fingers along the trunks of the trees as I pass. The sound of leaves crunching under my feet fills the silence: a greeting from an old friend.

After several more minutes, the shimmering line of the Glass River emerges. My gaze settles on the Grey Tree, its dark branches reaching toward the river like long, crooked arms. Others think the Grey Tree is strange, with its tangled roots that grow above ground and its bare branches. It's not dead, it grows this way, and that makes others superstitious of it. But not me. To me, it's beautiful. Besides, it sits right on the edge of the Glass River, offering a great lookout point of the south.

I carefully walk across the roots, get a good grip, and make my way up the tree, settling onto a branch that provides the perfect spot for me to sit and watch. I set my gaze on the Faenomen Forest, fixating on the budding green leaves of the trees that line its entrance, blurred, but dancing in the breeze behind the fog. The fog is always there, pressed up against the southern bank —a thin veil between our kingdom of Silveria and the forbidden kingdom of Incarnadine.

The hellions are supposed to live in the Faenomen Forest of Incarnadine, but I've never seen a sign of one. Regardless, it's the warnings that make Incarnadine forbidden. And the fact that it's forbidden makes me curious.

Just like every other day, I wait in the tree, but nothing happens. After the sun is far in the west, I begin to make my way down. That's when I see it—a shadow in the fog. I stop moving, my breath stuck in my throat as I stare out over the river at the dark silhouette that's beginning to take shape. My pulse races while I watch it stagger forward. *A hellion. I'm going to see a hellion.*

But an ordinary boy emerges from the mist.

He stumbles to the river and falls to his knees, his trembling arms extending toward the water. That's when I notice something thick and red covering his hands and sleeves. *Blood.* I press the back of my hand against my mouth, cutting off the scream that's trying to escape.

His reflection in the water is as clear as if he were in front of a mirror. Through it I can see the wrinkles in his ivory tunic, which is stained with dirt, grass and more blood. His wavy, dark brown hair is falling around the pale skin of his face.

As his hands touch the water, his reflection shatters into thousands of red-streaked shards. Suddenly, the boy goes oddly still, his gaze fixing on the water. *Does he see me?* My heart thrashes with panic. But just as I realize I'm too far away to be visible, the boy falls forward, headfirst into the river.

Within seconds I'm out of the tree and running toward the water. Before I give myself too much time to think about what I'm about to do, I jump into the river.

A million needles pierce my skin as my body meets the icy water. My feet hit the bottom and slip on the mud causing me to sink down further. For a moment, all I can think about is the cold, dark water that's burying me in its frozen embrace, but as the shock wears off, I'm able to plant my feet on the bottom and stand, breaking the surface.

Blinking against the drops of water that are holding onto my lashes, I look around and see the boy several feet away, floating with his face down in the river. Thankfully, the water isn't too deep and I'm able to walk toward him by grasping the scattered rocks which keep me from slipping. When I reach him, I grab his arm and drape it over my shoulder.

It's difficult and takes all my strength, but I manage to walk us to the northern shore and pull him up on the bank. I look down at the boy, my chest heaving. He's lying on his stomach, unconscious, but the slight rise and fall of his back tells me that he's at least breathing. I have no idea how to help him. But I know my mother can.

I bend down and again drape his arm over my shoulder. He's bigger than me, probably around my brothers age, making it difficult to stand. Somehow, I manage to make it to my feet and drag the boy, as fast as I can, back to the village.

The clearing peaks through the trees, and the long grass beckons like a warm bed. My body is past exhaustion and, as I cross the line of the woods and step into the grass field, my knees buckle and I collapse. Lying on my stomach, I gasp for air. The boy is partially on top of me and, using my last bit of strength, I roll out from under him.

This is impossible! I wrap my fingers around several strands of grass and try to rip them from the ground in frustration, but my fingers slip right off. I'm too weak to even throw a proper fit.

Get up, Addalynne! If you don't, he's going to die. I push myself up and stagger to my feet. My arms are shaking, but I grab his wrists and try to pull him. He doesn't budge, and again I fall to the ground.

"Gregory!" I shout and again push myself to my feet. Hopefully, he'll be on his way home and he'll hear me.

"Gregory!"

The sound of rustling grass pulls my attention to the east and I see the familiar light brown hair and scattered freckles of Gregory's friend, Walter, running toward me.

"Addalynne?" His widespread eyes are filled with bewilderment as he approaches. "What's wrong? Are you hurt?" His hand instinctively goes to the dagger at his hip, his eyes scanning the area around me.

"No. I'm fine." I speak through sharp breaths, my lungs burning with each word. "But I need Gregory." I really don't want to explain this to Walter.

"Gregory's in the market. I can go get . . ." His words trail off, his attention falling to the body beside my feet. "What's that?"

"A boy."

"I . . . I know it's a boy," he stammers, pink blossoms growing on his cheeks. "Who is he?"

"I don't know."

He raises an eyebrow as he takes in the water dripping from my sleeves and pooling around the skirt of my dress and the boy. "Did you drown him?"

"No! I found him floating in the river." I'm definitely not going to tell Walter that he came from Incarnadine. At this point, I don't think I'm going to tell anyone that he came from the forbidden kingdom.

"Why is he covered in blood?"

"I don't know."

"Is he dead?

"No!" But he's going to be if I don't get him home. I let out an exasperated breath. "Walter, I need your help."

Chapter 2

HER

Walter and I reach the walled entry of my home and simultaneously let go of the boy. I drop to the ground and pull in several deep breaths, trying to slow my rapidly beating heart.

"Now what?" Walter says through gasps of air, his hands on his knees.

"I have to get my parents," I push the words out, each one fighting its way around my labored breaths. "And you have to leave."

Walter's eyes widen. "I can help—"

"No, Walter. I'm going to be in trouble for going to the river no matter what. There's no point in you having to answer questions, too."

I can tell he wants to argue, but after a minute he nods in agreement and begins to leave.

"Walter!" I call and he turns to face me. "Don't tell

anyone about this. *Please.*"

"I won't. I promise."

Walter walks away, and I run inside and get my parents.

Of course, Mother immediately begins asking questions, but I ignore her and watch my father, who's already outside, lifting the boy in his arms. I trail my father, my fingers wrapping around the fabric of my dress, as he carries the boy inside and lays him on the wooden table in the kitchen. We stand in silence, watching the beads of water drip from the boy's hair onto the table.

"Is he dead?" I ask hesitantly, my voice shaking, terrified of the answer.

Mother lays her fingers against his neck. "No."

She uses a dagger to cut his tunic up the middle. Warmth instantly burns across my cheeks. I know I should turn away, but my gaze travels along the pale, damp skin that covers his chest and stomach. It seems unharmed. Mother tilts his head to the side to examine the back of his neck. A charcoal colored marking lingers just beneath his hairline. Mother brushes up his hair with her fingers to look closer, and her red hair falls between his neck and my line of sight, creating a curtain between us.

"What is it?" I ask. My teeth grab hold of my lip as I wait for her answer.

"A birthmark."

"Are you sure?"

"Yes, see for yourself." Mother lifts her head and lets

me lean in. She's right: a birthmark. Though it's unlike any birthmark I've ever seen. Most are random splotches of color, but this one holds the shape of a perfect crescent moon. Mother lets go of his hair and most of the birthmark disappears, leaving just the bottom curve exposed.

Mother continues to check him for several more minutes. "I don't see any other injuries aside from this," she says as she lifts up his hair and points to a strawberry-sized lump with an inch long gash high on his forehead.

"But what about all the blood on his clothes?" Father asks.

Mother pauses, and I get the feeling that her hesitation is not from lack of knowledge.

"Could all that blood have been from this cut?" I ask, prodding her to answer.

"Well, head injuries can bleed quite a bit, and he may have used the shirt at some point to try and stop the bleeding."

I nod my head. "That's probably what he did," I say, but in my heart something tells me the blood on his shirt isn't his.

"It doesn't seem infected," she says, her gaze on the cut. "But I would still prefer to burn some rosemary and thyme to help keep it that way."

I run to the kitchen and fling open the cupboard. Purple, yellow, green, and black herbs hang from the tops of the shelves, taunting me as I search for the right ones. Finally, my hands wrap around the bushy green herbs and I begin crushing them in an iron bowl. I run back to mother and watch as she twists her hair into a braid before kneeling by the fire to light the herbs.

Once lit, Mother places the bowl by the boys head and begins to clean the wound. I watch her carefully and am ready to hand her the thread she needs to sew his stitches. Then I run back to the cupboard and search for the yellow flowers of the yarrow and the wood-like cloves. She'll want them to treat the wound. Sure enough, when she's done with her mending, she asks for the yarrow and cloves and I'm ready. I'm willing to do anything to stay with the boy, and as long as I'm helping, Mother won't make me leave. After treating the wound and bandaging it with cloth, she says all we can do is wait for him to wake up. I watch as Father moves the unconscious boy into the extra chambers and out of my sight, leaving me feeling completely helpless.

Mother turns to me and I know it's my turn. I'm so exhausted that I don't even argue when she has me take an overly warm bath, during which she checks me again to ensure I have no injuries. After the bath, she tells me to sit by the fire and makes me drink a chamomile tea with a dash of mint to help calm me. I slowly sip the steaming liquid and feel it burn its way down my throat. I wait for the calm to come. I take another sip and wait again. Nope. Not working.

"What happened, Addalynne?" she asks. Father quietly steps into the room and takes a seat across from me.

I have no idea what to say. Instead, I stare blankly at

my parents, taking in the deep red of Mother's hair, which reminds me of the blood on the boy's hands. I repress a shudder and look toward my Father. His face contains more patience than Mother's, but there's a noticeable trace of anxiety in his brown eyes. I'm out of time. I obviously can't lie about being near the river. But I have to lie about how I found the boy. No one will let him stay in Faygrene if they know where he came from.

"When we were walking to the forest, I told Gregory that I wanted to go to the Glass River," I begin, trying my best to ignore the already disappointed look on Mother's face. "He didn't want to go, so I ran from him and hid in the forest until I knew he wouldn't find me."

"Oh, Addalynne," Mother groans.

I pretend not to hear her and continue with my lie. "I went to the Glass River and walked along the bank for a little while . . ." and then what? . . . "and then I saw the boy. He was floating face down on a log." There, that should work. "I was afraid he would drown if I didn't do something, so I jumped in and pulled him out." At least that part is true.

My parents are quiet while they process my deception, their faces seemingly calm. I almost let myself relax. Maybe the tea is working. But then the yelling starts.

"How could you be so irresponsible, Addalynne?" Mother paces in front of me, her braid as unraveled as she seems to be.

"I know you're careless at times," she continues. "But this? Completely disregarding everything you've been told and going to that river is unacceptable!"

Father drags his fingers roughly along his brow. "You never listen, Addalynne! If you would only learn to listen!"

I swallow against my suddenly dry throat, the tears building. I hate that I disappointed them, but I don't regret what I did.

Mother and Father stop yelling, and a silent minute passes as I wipe at the traitorous tears that continue to sneak their way past my lids.

"You need to understand that you can never go there again," Father finally says, his voice much calmer than before. "However, I must say that I'm proud of you."

Proud of me? I look up at my father. His eyes are fixed on my mother and her face looks more bewildered than mine.

"Proud of her? For what? For being reckless? She could have been hurt or . . . worse!" She can't bring herself to say killed, though we all know it's what she was thinking.

"Yes, Genoveve, she was reckless. But she also saved a boy's life. He would have drowned had she not been there to pull him out of the water, and though I'm upset that she was near the river, I'm proud that she was brave enough to rescue the boy." Father moves his gaze to me. "But it doesn't change the fact that you disregarded our wishes, and because of that, you will not be allowed to leave our home unless your mother or I am with you."

"That's completely unfair!" I shout, rising to my feet. If I can only leave with one of them, I won't be able to go to the Grey Tree. And something finally happened! I can't stop going now!

"Unfair?" Disbelief blooms in Mother's voice. "Unfair would be locking you in your chambers for the rest of your life, and believe me, Addalynne, I'm tempted to do just that. Father's consequence is more than fair."

"Can I at least ride my horse?"

"No!" They both reply.

"That's not fair to Freyja! She can't be locked in the stables all day!"

"Gregory can alternate between riding her and Sejant. She'll be fine."

Breathe, Addalynne. Arguing will get you nowhere. I swipe at my tears. "And how long is this punishment going to last?

"Until further notice," Father replies.

* * *

Sitting in the entry, I hypnotize myself with the dancing flames in the hearth, each second passing like a drop of water falling from a block of ice. The smell of rosemary and thyme has permeated our home, settling into my hair and clothes. Every time I breathe, it fills my nostrils with its once pleasant, but now suffocating scent. The herbs have been burning constantly since Walter and I dragged the boy home from the river. That was two days ago, and he still hasn't woken up. I keep asking Mother if the boy is dead. He seems dead; he never moves. She assures me he's alive and says, "Hopefully, he'll wake up soon." I just wish I knew when soon was going to be because waiting around like this is driving me mad.

The groaning of the kitchen door pulls me from my thoughts. I turn and see Mother walking toward me.

"You can't keep moping around, Addalynne. Do something."

"What can I do? You and father took away my freedom."

Mother's aggravated laugh cuts the air between us. "Always so dramatic."

"I'm not being dramatic, Mother. I'm simply stating a fact. You're the ones who said I can't leave unless one of you is with me, so what am I supposed to do? Father's working at Lord Berrenger's, and Gregory took Elizabeth riding, so it's not as though I can spend time with them."

"You can study."

I drop my head into my hands and groan.

"I want you to be well-read, Addalynne."

"I read every day."

"Yes. But I'm not talking about your silly books. I'm talking about poetry."

"But I don't like poetry."

Mother sighs and turns to face me. "You don't have to like it; you have to learn it."

"Why can't I read about the kingdoms?"

"Because you know everything you need to know about the kingdoms already."

"That's hardly anything!"

"Yes, and it's better that way!" She pauses for a deep breath, something I see her do often, especially when she's talking to me. "Addalynne, please, for once do what I'm asking without an argument."

But I want to keep arguing. Gregory was allowed to read the book of the kingdoms when he was twelve, and I'm almost thirteen. Why can't I? It's completely unfair! But the look on Mother's face steals the fight from me. She looks . . . sad, frustrated. And no matter how unfair I think this is, I don't want to be the cause of that face.

"Fine, Mother. I'm sorry."

> *Mine Lady weaves*
> *color'd thread*
> *through the Wheel of Fortune*
> *what sayeth thou*
> *not of death*
> *one thread pull'd*
> *unravels the rest*

I'll admit, the poem is beautiful, but something about it leaves me feeling unnerved: as though it's warning me somehow. I can almost imagine Sir Alsius reciting the last line and then looking at me; *Don't pull the thread, Addalynne.*

I close the book, place it back on my father's desk, and study the bookshelf behind it. My eyes scan the books until they land on one bound in red leather, the words The Divided Kingdom etched in black script on its spine. Stepping around his desk, I move toward the book and my fingers trail along the title. I spare a nervous glance at the door and then slowly begin to pull the book from the shelf: pulling that thread. It's not yet half way off when the door swings open. I shove it back in place, my heart a hummingbird in my chest as I spin to face the intruder.

Gregory laughs quietly and then shuts the door behind him. "What are you doing?" he asks and drops down lazily in Father's brown leather armchair.

"Nothing." I look at the skirt of my dress, my hands running along the creases.

"Come on, Addalynne, I know that face. Besides, I saw you."

I glance up at Gregory. His face is calm, but expectant, waiting for my answer.

"I want to know about the kingdoms."

"You already know about the kingdoms."

"No. All I know is that Faygrene is in the Kingdom of Silveria, and the Kingdom of Incarnadine is on the southern side of the Glass River."

"That's not all you know. You know about the hellions." He wiggles his fingers toward me as he says, 'hellions', and I laugh in response, both of us remembering with skepticism the warnings Sir Alsius annually passes down.

I move around my father's desk and sit on top of it, my legs swinging off the side. "Fifty years ago our village had an encounter with one of the hellions that lives in the Faenomen Forest," I mimic, in my best impersonation of Sir Alsius, Faygrene's village elder.

Gregory laughs. "What did the hellion look like, Sir

Alsius?"

"Oh, we do not speak of it. No. That may draw it near. We must never speak of it."

"I don't think they know what it looked like," Gregory says, ending our impersonations.

"Of course not. Think about it, Gregory. The story always starts with fifty years ago. How old were you when you first heard the story?"

"Five."

"And now you're fourteen. Shouldn't the story now say, fifty-nine years ago?"

Gregory chuckles. "You're right." His smile leaves his face and his eyes study me with contemplation.

"What?" I ask, not liking his scrutiny.

"I'll tell you what I can about the kingdoms, Addalynne, but honestly the book doesn't say much."

I wait expectantly for him to continue.

"According to the book," he begins, his voice a hushed whisper. "Silveria and Incarnadine used to be one kingdom—Alomeria. The queen of Alomeria had twin sons, Alderon and Ceris. The brothers were inseparable, until they realized that only one of them would be king. Alderon was born first which meant that he was next in line. But one day he had some sort of accident."

"What kind of accident?" I interrupt.

"I don't remember. He fell off a horse or something. It doesn't matter, what matters is that it left him barely able to move. And, because of the accident, the King named Ceris heir to the throne instead. Alderon was obviously furious because becoming king was his birth right. Anyway, some more boring stuff happened, and then, several years later, Alderon found a way to cure himself." Gregory turns to me with a wide smile, the narrow gap in his front teeth on full display. "Now this is where it gets good," he says and leans forward, his elbows resting on his knees. "The cure he found also gave him powers. At first, he was careful with his powers and didn't use them much, but that changed as soon as the King died. Within a fortnight of their father's death, the brothers were at war. Ceris had most of the kingdom's army under his command, so that forced Alderon to rely on the few thousand men that were loyal to him and, of course, on his powers. Somehow, Alderon was able to use his powers to open the threshold into other realms."

"What other realms?"

"It didn't say. It just said, 'other realms,' but those realms are where the hellions came from. Once Alderon brought them through, he sealed them in Alomeria and tried to use the hellions to fight on his side. But he couldn't control them, and soon both armies were almost completely annihilated." He sweeps his arm in front of him as though it's made of iron, not flesh, as he says, 'annihilated.' "To end the war and save the few people they had left, the brothers decided to divide the kingdom and somehow contain the hellions in the Faenomen Forest. And that leaves us with Silveria and Incarnadine, separated by nothing more than the Glass River."

"And the Faenomen Forest," I add.

"Well, the Faenomen Forest is part of Incarnadine,

Addalynne."

"Did the book say what the hellions were?"

"No."

"Did it say how Alderon cured himself and received the powers?"

"No."

I ponder this for a moment and decide he's telling me the truth. Gregory wouldn't lie to me, not about this. "Thanks for telling me."

"Just don't tell our parents that I told you."

"You know I won't."

Gregory leans back in the chair again. "Is the boy still sleeping?"

"Yes. I honestly don't know if he's ever going to wake up."

"He will," Gregory says confidently and rises to his feet.

"How do you know?"

"I don't. But I tend to believe things will work out. I guess, you just have to have faith."

Faith? Do I have faith? I would like to think so, but wanting something and actually having it are very separate things. Regardless, I hope Gregory's right and he wakes up soon. I want to know all his secrets, now more than ever.

Chapter 3

HER

"Did you see Becky's new dress?" The delicate voice of my little sister interrupts my thoughts, which are sparring between worrying about the boy and thinking about what Gregory told me. Elizabeth is sitting in front of the window, her small ivory hand lifting up the doll, her eyes hopeful for my approval and attention. I place a look of pure admiration on my face and move to sit beside her.

"Wow! It's lovely, Lizzy!" I run my fingers along the navy fabric of the doll's new dress. "Becky will be the prettiest girl in Faygrene."

A soft smile paints Elizabeth's young face. She looks so much like our mother; the same curly red hair, the same blue eyes. I share the same black hair as my father and Gregory. But where their eyes are the deepest of browns, mine are the color of amber. Mother says I have the same hair and eyes as my grandmother. I wish I could have met her. I have never seen anyone with eyes like mine.

"Mother made it for her," Elizabeth says adoringly, her concentration still set on her favorite toy. She received it for her sixth birthday and it hasn't left her side since.

"Addalynne!" Mother's voice calls from the kitchen. I kiss Elizabeth's head and push myself to my feet.

When I open the door to the kitchen, I'm met with the smell of boiling onions. Mother is standing in front of the pot, stirring the broth. She glances at me and then nods toward a bowl and cloth that are on the table. "I need you to take that into the boy's chambers and lay it on his forehead, however, before you do that, be sure to check his wound. If you see a sign of infection, come get me immediately," she says, and turns back to her stew.

I make my way down the dim hallway, lit only by a flickering torch on its last breath, and stop in front of the door. Since the moment my father moved him into this room, I have been anxious to see him, but now that the moment is here, I only have one thought terrorizing my mind: what if he's dead? My hand trembles as I turn the doorknob, my nerves jumping frantically. I hold my breath and push the door open.

The boy is lying on the bed, his pale face illuminated by the ivory candle flickering on the table next to him. Other than the small light from the candle, the space is almost completely engulfed in darkness. I look over at the fireplace and see that the fire has burned down to embers sizzling against the blackened logs. I stoke the fire and, once I have the flames burning again, make my way to the side of his bed.

The boy's eyes are closed and his brown hair is falling along his forehead, blocking my view of his cut. I move my fingers gently to his face, my heart pounding, and brush his hair away from his forehead. It's difficult to see in the dim light, making me lean in close to get a better look. I'm so close that, though my mother has cleaned him as best she could and changed him into some of Gregory's clothes, I can still smell faint traces of the river on him—dirt and stale water, mixed with lavender soap and a scent that could only belong to the woods. The black stitches are still perfectly in place, the skin underneath a little red and bruised, but it doesn't look infected.

I drag the back of my fingers along his hair line, which is warm, but thankfully, not feverish, and his eyes open. My breath catches and I go completely still, as though his wide, green eyes won't see me if I don't move. He blinks rapidly, and I jerk my head back and take a step away from the bed.

"Who . . . who are you?" he stammers, his eyes ignited with panic as he searches my face. I'm too shocked to respond, and after several seconds, he warily examines the room around him. "Where am I?"

I suck in a breath and push out the words. "I'm Addalynne Troyer. You're in my home." His gaze returns to me.

"Addalynne?" His eyebrows pinch together. "Am I

supposed to know you?"

"No. We've never met before." My words cause him to slightly lean away and fear returns to his eyes. "I saved your life," I add, hoping to show him he has nothing to fear. He takes several deep breaths and looks at his hands which are twisting their way through the fur of the blanket.

"What do you mean you saved my life?" he asks, his voice filling with what sounds like a mixture of doubt and . . . irritation? I risked everything to save him and he's bothered by it?

"Well, a thank you would be nice, but . . ."

"Thank you." He lifts his head, his eyes locking onto mine. "I'm sorry. That was rude of me. I'm very grateful, but I don't understand . . ."

Heat spreads to my cheeks and continues down my neck and chest. Clearly he's confused and scared, and I let my inability to hold my tongue make him feel bad.

"I'm sorry, too. I should have explained better." I stop and think about my next words. He didn't see me in the woods, so he doesn't know when I came along and found him. And, what if he's not someone I can trust? I don't know anything about him, other than where he came from. Which means I shouldn't tell him that I saw him stumbling through the fog in Incarnadine. He can be the one to tell me where he came from. And then, for his safety, I'll convince him not to tell anyone else. "I found you floating face down on a log in the Glass River. I jumped in and pulled you out." More confusion passes over his features. "Do you remember how you got into the river?" I whisper, hoping he'll do the same.

The boy's breaths accelerate, pushing through his mouth in short, strained bursts, his eyes becoming lost, unfocused. "No. I . . . I don't remember anything."

He's in worse condition than I thought. I need to get my mother. But I can't bring myself to leave him. "Don't worry. I'm sure you'll remember. You seem to have hit your head." I lightly place my fingers above his cut. "And that's probably making you forget what happened." I try my best to calm him, but my words do nothing.

"No! You don't understand! I don't remember anything! I don't know who I am! I don't even know my name!" His voice breaks with his words and he drops his head into his hands, his fingers fisting tightly in his hair. My heart jumps and I grab hold of the wooden arms of the chair for support. *Pull yourself together, Addalynne.* He's allowed to be afraid right now, not you.

"Don't worry. I'm sure you'll remember." I force out the words as I move away from his bed. "I'll be right back," I continue. "I just need to get my mother." With a deep breath, I run from his chambers.

I sleep fitfully in my bed for several hours, remembering the look on my mother's face when I brought her to check on the boy. She was frightened, I could tell, though she said otherwise. I wanted to stay with him, but he told her he was tired and wanted to sleep, so she pulled me from the room and insisted I go to bed as well. But I can't sleep. I can't shake the feeling that something's wrong. The thought that he's going to leave flickers across my mind and makes its way to a painful burning in my chest. I don't want him to leave. Nothing like this has ever happened before. Everyone I know, apart from Sir Alsius, was born here in Faygrene. And this boy is from Incarnadine. Once he gets his memories back, he can tell me all about Incarnadine, and I will finally know the truth.

I turn to my side and close my eyes, willing myself to sleep, but the fear that the boy will leave continues to plague me. I grab the thin, ivory candle on the wooden table next to my bed and move across my chambers to the fire. I light the candle with the dimming flames and carefully make my way to his chambers.

Stepping inside the dark space, the fear that has been haunting me is immediately confirmed. His bed is empty, the blankets thrown to the bottom. A lonely breeze blows through the open window.

A restricting ache takes hold of my throat and I have to blink back the tears that are pooling in my eyes. I move toward his bed and place my hand on it—still warm. He hasn't been gone long. I move around his bed and don't let myself hesitate before climbing out the window.

The chilling night air slams into me as my bare feet touch the cold, hard ground. I look down at my thin chemise and think longingly of my cloak hanging by the door in the entry of our home, but I keep walking, the frozen rocks grinding into my bare feet.

I make my way around the side of our home and through the gate in the center of the surrounding stone wall. After I close the gate behind me, I try to force my eyes to adjust to the darkness that's thankfully lessened by the brightness of the moon. My gaze travels to the road, squinting into the silver, damp night, and I see him, a dark figure, moving silently before the trees. I run, ignoring the stabs of pain in my feet. When I'm close enough to him and far enough from home, I yell.

"Stop, please!"

At the sound of my voice he stops and turns toward me, the look on his face uncertain.

"Where are you going?" I ask.

He lets out an anxious huff of air and I watch it form in front of him. "I don't know. I just felt as though I . . . I thought that if I could find this river you say you found me in, something would come back to me."

The conflict pulls inside me, a tug of war between the honorable truth and the self-serving lie. I know I have to help him. It's evident in the desperation and emptiness in his face and voice that he's hurting. But how far should I go? Part of me is glad he doesn't remember. It means he'll be safe and able to stay, but another part of me is disappointed. If he can't remember Incarnadine, he can't tell me about it.

"I'll take you to the river, but you have to promise you'll come back home with me. Promise you won't leave." There, a compromise. Mother's always telling me to learn to compromise.

"Where would I go?" he asks, his voice drained of emotion, but he's not looking for an answer. And, though I feel sorry for him, I can't help but feel comforted as I realize that, at least for now, he has no reason to leave.

With new determination, I run to the stables. Once inside, I take two of the spare cloaks and one pair of boots. I hand him one of the cloaks, knowing he must be freezing in his thin tunic and breeches, and drape the other cloak around my back. Then I slip on the boots. They're much too big for me, but it's preferable to being barefoot and cold.

As I lead him to the river, an awkward silence falls between us. I search my mind, trying to find something clever to say, but nothing comes to me. Instead, I decide to ask the questions that have been pacing on my tongue.

"So, you don't remember anything?"

"No."

"Not even bits and pieces—there's nothing at all?"

"No."

"What's the first thing you do remember?"

He stops walking, his head tilting to the side, his bottom lip pulling into his mouth. I can't help but smile at the gesture—it's the same thing I do when I'm lost in thought.

"The first thing I remember is opening my eyes and seeing your face. It's as though that's where my life began. There's nothing before that moment."

My heart breaks for him and the pain he's feeling. I don't know what to say, though, so I say nothing, and continue toward the river. It's the best I can do for him.

We step into the forest, a place that's as familiar to

me as my own skin. But tonight I don't recognize it. Everything is bathed in a silver glow, like a place that until now only existed in dreams. I may have to sneak into the woods at night more often.

After several minutes of uninterrupted walking, the river comes into view. The water is eerily calm and still, a sheet of black glass reflecting the pale light of the moon. It seems as though I could walk out onto it and stand on its surface, bathing myself in the kiss of the moon. I pull my gaze away from the river and move it to his face, which is lined with thoughts, and not happy ones.

"This is it. This is where I pulled you out."

We stand in silence for several minutes as he stares out at the water. Without warning, his hand grabs hold of mine, his icy fingers tangling with my own. I look up at him, startled, but he's still staring at the river. I have never held a boy's hand before, other than my brother's. I imagined it would be strange, but there's nothing strange about the feel of his hand in mine. I let my gaze drift over to the southern bank. The fog is there, its tendrils reaching toward the river as if offering it a loving embrace. A shiver spreads down my spine.

"Is there anything else you can tell me about how you found me?" he asks, breaking my reverie of the fog.

Guilt washes over me. Should I tell him the truth? Yes. But if I do, it will only make things worse. I'm not worried about being able to trust him, not anymore. It's just that I can only trust myself to keep this secret and this secret must be kept. If anyone ever finds out he came from Incarnadine, they will banish him, or worse.

They'll consider him forbidden, perhaps even cursed. I can't let that happen to him.

"No, there's nothing else. I'm sorry."

And I am sorry, more than he knows, but I saved him, and now I have to protect him. I don't know why I'm so drawn to this sad, lost boy, but it's as though part of him has crawled inside me and locked the doors. I can't let anything happen to him. In this moment, I vow to do whatever it takes to keep him safe.

Chapter 4

HIM

"Come now! We're going to be late!" Genoveve calls from down the hallway, her voice echoing off the stones and making its way toward us. Addalynne doesn't waver from the worn pages of the book she's reading. She hasn't put her book down for what seems like hours, and from the intense look of concentration on her face, I'm not entirely sure she heard her mother. She's lost in her head, a place I'm learning she likes to go frequently. I don't know the girl well, but I know she spends most of her time looking for an escape. She wants a different life, and I only want to remember mine.

"Addalynne," I say her name quietly, hesitant of pulling her from her story.

"Hmmm."

"I think your mother is getting anxious."

"She's always anxious." Her eyes don't leave the page

as she speaks, and with a flick of her finger she turns to the next one.

"What are you reading, anyway?"

She places the book on her lap and sets her amber eyes on me. "The Siren's Call. It's about mermaids."

"Mermaids. I've heard about mermaids before." But just like all the other times I try to access a memory, a door slams shut on me. I can picture the mermaids, I can remember details from stories told about them, but I don't know how I know them or why. Sometimes I hear a soft voice speaking to me, a voice from my past, but after a few seconds the voice becomes contorted and then dissolves into a vacant echo. It doesn't stop me from trying to remember, but it's like trying to scratch my way through metal.

"Do you think they're real?' Addalynne questions excitedly.

"Maybe," I reply with a shrug. "Do you want them to be?"

"Yes. I want all the stories to be real." Her eyes burn with her words and, though I don't want to turn away from her, the way she's looking at me makes me . . . nervous . . . shy? I'm not sure, but it's not a feeling I'm familiar with.

"Addalynne!" Genoveve calls again. "We're leaving now, with or without you both!"

Addalynne gently nudges the book off her lap, letting it slide onto the bed. With a sigh, she stands and extends her hand to me. I unhesitatingly grasp her hand with my own. A mischievous smile tugs on her lips. "We better go," she says. "If we're late, we'll miss Sir Alsius's warnings. and believe me, you don't want to miss them."

The walk to the market is quiet, and I must admit, a little tense. Genoveve keeps turning back to look at Addalynne, her eyebrows tightened with what seems to be a mixture of irritation and anxiety. Addalynne either takes no notice or has perfected the art of avoidance.

We turn the corner and come down a row of small, wooden houses. People are stepping out of their doorways, their arms filled with food to bring to the feast.

"Relax now, Genoveve. I told you we wouldn't be late," Robert speaks quietly, his free hand rubbing soothing circles on Genoveve's back. My stomach knots. Do I have a mother and father somewhere? Is my mother worried about me? Is my father comforting her?

We step into the market square and my footsteps falter. I'm not sure what I expected, but it wasn't this.

Rows upon rows of wooden tables line half of the square. The tables are lit with candles and filled with wine, bread, meat, fruit, and pots of stew. People are scattered about, some eating and drinking, others laughing and dancing. Children are running around, chasing each other through the maze of villagers, while their mothers shout at them to not get too close to the fire.

The fire is burning brightly on the other half of the market square, casting long shadows behind it. There are three empty chairs behind the fire and a stack of logs waiting to be tossed into the flames.

"We're going to go sit with Walter and John," Gregory says.

"Very well," Genoveve replies, and Gregory begins to walk away. I hesitate, my gaze shifting between Gregory and Addalynne. But Addalynne begins to follow Gregory as well, making my decision easier.

"Where are you going, Addalynne?" Genoveve asks, and we both turn to face her.

"With Gregory and . . . him," she says, motioning toward me. I try to ignore the pain her words bring, knowing that my name is lost somewhere in the darkness of my mind, along with the mother and father who gave it to me.

"Shouldn't you be asking permission to go with Gregory as opposed to telling us what you'll be doing?"

"But Gregory didn't ask."

"Gregory's not in trouble for disobeying us."

Addalynne takes a deep breath. "Mother, may I please go with Gregory?" she asks, her jaw clenched so tightly I'm surprised she could get the words out.

I suppress a chuckle and look the other way, knowing that if I look at Addalynne, I'll laugh.

"I suppose you may."

Addalynne turns and walks away, and I follow.

I swallow the last drop of stew and bite into the warm bread, savoring every crumb.

"No! It's going to be Wesley Gaunt. He'll be the one to be knighted by the King," Gregory says in what I'm learning is his argumentative voice.

"Wesley Gaunt?" John counters with a laugh. "Wesley the Weak is what he should be called."

Gregory tosses a chicken bone on his plate and lets out an irritated huff. "Have you gone completely mad? He's the strongest Schild the King has. He can take on ten men and leave them all bloodied and dismembered without receiving a scratch."

"But he's never been to Incarnadine," Walter adds. "And Terryn Mowbray has."

"No, he hasn't!" Gregory shouts with a laugh, his head shaking in disbelief.

"Yes, he has. He even wrote a journal about it, detailing how he fought trolls," Walter argues.

"Oh, yeah? What's it called?" John counters, now seemingly siding with Gregory.

"It's called the . . . the uh . . . the Tale of . . ."

"He doesn't know," John laughs.

"The Tale of Walter the Gullible," Gregory adds. We all laugh at this, myself included, though I do feel a little bad for Walter, whose face is beginning to resemble an apple.

"Just because I don't remember doesn't mean it's not true."

Walter's words stop my laughter. "He's right," I say, because he can't remember, and I can't let that be the reason he loses.

"See," Walter says with a smile, "even he agrees with me."

"Yeah, but he doesn't know his elbow from his ass,"

Gregory says jokingly, and playfully tosses a small bone in my direction. I toss one right back, hitting him square in the chest. The hit cuts off his laughter, but makes the rest of us laugh more. "I'm joking. I'm joking," he says with a gasp. "Clearly you haven't forgotten how to throw."

"No," I reply with a smile. "That's all instinct."

The others begin to reach for seconds and I return to my bread. I take a bite and look down the length of the table, to the opposite end, where Addalynne is sitting with her friend Mary.

When we arrived at the table, Mary was sitting here with John and Walter. She quickly jumped up to embrace Addalynne before glancing over at Gregory, a subtle pink hue growing on her cheeks. As I watch her now, I notice that every few seconds she looks over at Gregory. But Gregory refuses to look at her. When he first saw her, he said hello, but his eyes never left the ground.

"Hey, umm, New One, did you want more lamb?" John asks me, and I can't help but laugh. I've heard boy, kid, and even orphan, but I've yet to be called 'new one.' "Sorry," John says, "It's hard to address someone with no name."

"He has a name," Gregory intervenes.

"He does?" Walter questions.

"Of course he does," Gregory continues. "The problem is that no one knows it."

"Sure we do. It's Orphan," says a boy with hair so fair it's practically white, as he approaches the table. He stops on the opposite side, directly across from me, and grabs a roll from the basket between us.

"Samuel, your ability to suddenly appear even though no one wants you here is truly amazing," Gregory replies, his voice bleeding sarcasm.

Samuel Hunt. Addalynne told me about him. He has an older sister, Matilda, and his family works for the Lord of Faygrene, Lord Berrenger. Addalynne told me that Samuel and Matilda's father do the farming for Lord and Lady Berrenger, and that their mother cooks and cleans for the Berrengers. Addalynne's father works for Lord Berrenger as well, but he's Lord Berrenger's Bailiff, a much higher position than that of Samuel's family, which explains Samuel's tattered clothes and rough demeanor toward Gregory.

"Nice dagger, Orphan." Samuel's chin motions to the dagger at my waist. "Who gave it to you? Your father? Oh, wait, I forgot you don't have one."

I pull in a breath, my body tensing slightly.

"Did you not understand me before?" Gregory rises to his feet. "That was me telling you to leave."

"It's all right, Gregory," I say. "He can stay. He doesn't bother me." I turn toward Samuel. "Why don't you have a seat and join us."

Samuel places his palms on the table, leaning toward me. "I don't need your pity, Orphan. You're no better than me. You're nothin' and you don't belong here."

A burning takes hold of my chest. I close my eyes, my hands curling into fists, and try to calm my anger. The last thing I need is to get into a fight. That would upset Genoveve and then she might make me leave. And if I can't stay here, I'll really have nothing left. I open my eyes. Samuel is still leaning toward me, and John, Walter, and Gregory have risen to their feet, ready to watch or intervene, I'm not sure.

"Ignore him," John says to me. "He's just mad that you get to spend so much time with Addalynne."

Addalynne? What does this have to do with her? Samuel glares at John, and Gregory looks as confused as I feel, but his confusion quickly switches to anger.

"Are you after my sister, Samuel?" Gregory takes an aggressive step in Samuel's direction.

Samuel looks down the table at Addalynne, just as she glances in our direction. Her eyes meet mine and she smiles just as Samuel says, "Not at the moment. But when her titties grow, I'll be the first one to see 'em."

I jump to my feet and lunge for Samuel. Hands grab hold of me, keeping me back. I struggle against them as Samuel laughs and walks away.

"Let go of me!" I shout.

"Calm down first," Gregory says.

"Didn't you hear what he said? You should be angrier than I am!"

"Yeah, I heard him, but I also know that this is exactly what he was wanting from you, so calm down." I turn to look at Gregory, but instead my eyes find Addalynne. She has risen to her feet and is watching me. I stop struggling. The look of fear on her face takes all the fight from me.

Once the others realize I'm not going to struggle

anymore, they let go.

Addalynne and Mary slowly make their way over to us, Addalynne's gaze still weary. She stops a few feet away from me. "Are you alright?" she asks.

"I'm fine."

"What did he say to you?"

"Nothing worth repeating."

She turns to Gregory. "What did Samuel say to him?"

Gregory runs a hand through his hair and shrugs. "Like he said, nothing worth repeating. Come on, the council's about to start."

We take our seats in front of the fire. Genoveve and Robert are only a few rows of people behind us, and I can feel Genoveve's eyes on us. Addalynne is looking at her mother with minimally tamed irritation. I turn toward Genoveve. She's mouthing something at Addalynne, something that looks like, "Not tonight." I turn away, letting my gaze settle again on Addalynne. Now she appears to be suppressing a laugh, and that laugh is dancing with the mischief in her eyes.

A cool breeze runs across my face. I lift the hood of my cloak just as Sir Alsius takes his place across the fire, facing the awaiting people. He's old, much older than anyone I've seen in this village. The texture of his pale skin looks as thin as fine parchment, ready to blow away with the next breeze. Maybe the only thing holding it in place is his flour-white beard that hangs, long and stiff, down to his chest. His eyes haven't lifted to ours yet;

they're pointed to the ground. His lips are moving slowly, and though the crowd is completely silent, no sound reaches us. Suddenly, he raises his eyes and their steel grey glare lands directly on me. I want to look away, but I can't. It's as though I'm as mobile as a statue, and I'm immediately struck with an image of myself unable to move, inside someplace dark and damp. It's not until his gaze travels from mine that the memory dissipates, leaving me hollow.

"Is it time already?" he says quietly, his voice a dry whisper. "Time . . . it is the one thing that will continue to evade us and confound us. I see there is a new face among us this evening. Tell me, my boy . . ." He's staring into the fire, but I know he's speaking to me. "Do you intend to remain among us?"

Intend? Do I have much of a choice? If my intention is to survive and not live my life alone or as a nomad then yes, I intend to stay. But, if my family comes for me, that will change things. Or should I leave? Should I travel to other villages and search for my family? Addalynne's hand wraps around mine. I look at her, watching the tension settle in her features.

"Yes, I intend to stay."

Sir Alsius nods his head. "Robert," he moves on to Addalynne's father, speaking slowly and deliberately. "Are you prepared to care for the boy?"

"Yes, Sir Alsius. The boy is no trouble."

"We shall see."

We shall see? What does he mean by that?

"Pay no attention to him," Addalynne says, leaning

close enough to speak without being heard by anyone other than me. "I told you how they fear anything not from Faygrene. *He* is the reason for that fear. *He* creates it."

"Sir Alsius." A man with wavy, shoulder-length, brown hair; dressed in a fine navy cloak rises from a chair behind Sir Alsius. I hadn't taken notice of him before, but from the way he carries himself, I can only assume that he's Lord Berrenger. Next to him is a beautiful woman with a waterfall of golden curls—Lady Berrenger.

"My Lord," Sir Alsius says with a nod, though he doesn't turn to look at Lord Berrenger.

"I have already addressed the matter of the boy with Robert. Let us now move along to the reason for this council."

"As you wish, my Lord." Sir Alsius closes his eyes, and Lord Berrenger returns to his seat. "Many of you know the story I'm about to tell. And though I tell it every spring, it does not change the level of importance it holds. We must constantly be reminded of the danger that looms in the shadows of the Faenomen Forest." He opens his eyes, and again stares directly at me. "Besides, if we're going to have a new face in our village, we must be certain he understands. After all, the safety of every one of us depends on it." He pauses for a moment.

"Fifty years ago, our village had an encounter with one of the hellions that lives in the Faenomen Forest," Sir Alsius continues emphatically. I have to suppress a laugh, because I can hear Addalynne whispering his words with him.

"What did the hellion look like, Sir Alsius?" Addalynne asks.

"Addalynne!" Genoveve scolds, but Addalynne ignores her.

"As I have told you before, child, we must not speak of it, for that may draw it near."

"But, Sir, you're speaking of it now."

I force out a cough to hide my laugh.

"Addalynne, stop now," Genoveve whispers.

Sir Alsius looks at Addalynne and then shifts his gaze to me. He shakes his head as he lets out a sigh. "I tell you this for your safety, and for the safety of others. It is not my place to describe the hellion to you, for a description of that sort only builds in the imagination, and imagination is a dangerous thing for children to have. It leads to curiosity, and curiosity is not allowed, not if we are to remain safe. All you need to know is that there is magic in this world, magic that you cannot even begin to imagine, magic that is dark and dangerous. But as long as we stay in Silveria, we will be safe. Neither the magic nor the hellions can reach us here, and we must keep it that way by staying away from their territory of Incarnadine. Other villages in Silveria have little need to worry, but our village of Faygrene borders the edge of safety. We cannot ignore Incarnadine's existence, as other far away villages so easily can, but we can avoid it. And avoid it we must. You see, the legends surrounding the forest came long before me. The warnings have been whispered and passed down for hundreds of years, and people heeded them. This is the one thing that allowed them to live in peace. But then the day came that several people decided to challenge the warnings."

Sir Alsius stares intently at Addalynne as he says, "They went to the river and disturbed the water by throwing stones and calling the hellion's name. It didn't take long for the hellion to hear its call and make its presence known. What happened after is too horrifying to tell, but those who dared call out to the hellion were never seen again. For when you search for the secrets of the Faenomen Forest, the secrets of the Faenomen Forest search for you, and it won't be long before they find you. Magic is on their side, dark magic, and once it finds you, there's no running from it. So if temptation settles within you, remember these words, and stay away from the Glass River."

The council then continues, with Lord Berrenger addressing the people about village matters. I hardly listen. My mind is like sap on a tree, stuck on Sir Alsius's story and the things Addalynne and Gregory have shared with me. What is in the Faenomen Forest? Is there truth to the stories they speak of or are the tales merely lies to keep people bound to one kingdom—a way to keep betrayal at bay?

Someone accidentally bumps into my shoulder. The people around me are rising and gathering their belongings. The council must be over. It's freezing out, and the moon is hidden behind the clouds, making the sky as black as a sea of crows. Robert picks up a torch that's lying near the fire and lights it.

I stand and dust the dirt from my legs, but the

feeling of someone watching me stops my movement. Glancing around myself, I finally find where the stare is coming from—Sir Alsius is waiting near Dahlia's sewing shop, a lit torch in one hand, his other beckoning me. I look back for Addalynne, but she's busy being scolded by Genoveve. Gregory is busy not looking at Mary, and Robert is speaking with Lord Berrenger.

I make my way toward Sir Alsius, curiosity and apprehension dueling within me. As I approach, he silently walks around the corner, and I follow him until he stops in the doorway of a boarded-up shop.

"Sir," I say with a nod.

He assesses me for a moment, his eyes turning gold in the light of the flame he holds. "You are not from here."

"No, sir. I'm not." Everyone knows this, but the way he's looking at me makes me feel as though I'm hiding something. "I don't know where I'm from," I continue, rambling now. "I assume I must be from a village upstream, though I don't know how far."

"No, Boy, you misunderstand me. I am not saying that you're not from Faygrene, I am saying that you're not from Silveria."

Not from Silveria, then that would mean . . . "Incarnadine?" I say, though it comes out as more of a breath than a word.

"Shhh. I did not say that and neither will you. I simply said that you're not from Silveria." He reaches out and places his hand on my chest while closing his eyes. Should I walk away from him? Surely he's mad. What other explanation could there be?

He opens his eyes again and the flame from the torch blows out. "No matter what happens, you cannot go back. Not yet. This is your home now. There's a reason you have forgotten your past. Leave it forgotten. Do not try to remember. And if by chance you do, forget it again and never mention it." He turns to walk away, but I can't let him leave, not after that.

"Why are you saying this? What do you know?" I ask him as I follow him into the field.

He turns around and faces me, a look of fear and confusion on his weathered face. "Who are you? Why are you following me? I don't have anything for you. Go away."

"But, sir . . . you just spoke with me."

"I've done no such thing. Now let an old man be." With that, he walks away, and this time I let him.

Making my way back to the market, I try to shake off his words. I can't be from Incarnadine. Surely, I would know if I were. Even though I can't remember my past, I would feel it. I know I would. There is no truth to his words. They are just the mad ramblings of an old man. Like Addalynne said, he spreads the fear of Incarnadine by telling stories he probably knows nothing of. He doesn't trust me because I'm unknown to him. There's nothing I need to forget except his words. And that's exactly what I'm going to do.

Chapter 5

HER

"Do you think they're looking for me?"

The boy's words whisper through the darkness. I open my eyes and try to adjust to the black shadow that has spread through my chambers. He came in here to talk earlier, as he does every night, but I thought he had fallen asleep. I sit up and wrap my arms around my legs, pulling them against my chest and resting my chin on my knees.

"Who?"

"My family."

"Oh." I blink again and this time his frame comes into view—hunched shoulders, fingers twisting through the fur of the blankets. "I'm sure they are." Could they be? And if they are, what would it mean for us? What if they come here?

"Sometimes I wonder if I even have a family."

46

"Of course you have a family."

"You don't know that."

"Well, you exist, which means you have a family."

"Have and had are very different, Addalynne." He lets out a frustrated breath, but I know the feeling isn't because of me. "I may have *had* a family, and they're dead or I may *have* a family and they don't want me."

"Or you may *have* a family that loves you and is looking for you as we speak." For his sake I want this to be true, but I saw the blood he was covered in, and I know that nothing good waits for him in Incarnadine. He was meant to come here, somewhere safe.

"It doesn't matter anyway. Even if they are alive and looking for me, they'll never find me. Who knows how long I was floating in that river? I've been here for weeks and there's been no sign of anyone looking for a missing boy."

He was in the river about two minutes, but I can't tell him that. He'll want to go back to Incarnadine, and I can't let him. "You still don't remember anything?"

"No."

Several minutes pass while I struggle with my guilt, and he struggles with his empty memories. I keep telling myself that I'm doing this for him, for his safety, but underneath I know the truth; my motives are mostly selfish.

"Do you want to know what I fear most?" His voice trembles.

I glance at his shadowed form and wait for him to continue. He doesn't look at me when he does.

"I'm terrified that I'll never remember . . . that I'll never know who I truly am. How can I be anyone when I've lost fourteen, maybe fifteen years of my life? How can I build a life with no foundation? It's like trying to plant a tree that has no roots."

I wish Gregory were here. He would know what to say. He would find a way to calm him and make him laugh. Instead, he has me and my tangled tongue.

"You don't need roots to grow," I begin. "Every week, my mother brings home new flowers from the market. They don't have roots, but they grow and thrive. All they need is a little . . . water. And you received plenty of that."

His laughter cuts through the dark and brings a smile to my face. "I'm going to be a gentleman and refrain from pointing out the holes in that argument."

"What holes? There are no holes in my argument. It makes perfect sense."

"Of course it does," he continues with a laugh. After a few seconds, silence settles over us once more, clinging to us like fresh fallen snow. "What are you afraid of?" he asks.

"Spiders."

"Then I guess I shouldn't tell you that I saw one go right under your bed a few minutes ago."

"I can't even see my own hand. There's no way you saw a spider."

"Fair point. But I don't believe you're really afraid of spiders."

"What makes you say that?"

"Because your favorite place to be is in the woods, preferably in your Grey Tree, and the few times I've climbed with you, I've seen plenty of spiders."

"Fair point. I'm not afraid of anything"

"Everyone is afraid of something." His words come out slower this time. He shared a true fear with me and I turned it into a joke.

"I'm afraid I'll never leave Faygrene," I begin, offering him my honesty. "That I'll spend my entire life behind the village walls, never seeing what lies beyond them, never knowing the truth. All those things they speak of . . . the hellions, the magic . . . I want to see it all."

He nods. "So you want to go to Incarnadine?"

Incarnadine. That word coming from his lips holds more meaning than he knows. Do I want to go to Incarnadine? The thought fills me with nervous excitement, but I don't even want to put the thought of going to Incarnadine in his head. "No, I just want to know the truth, maybe see something from the Grey Tree." Like I saw you. "Mostly, I want to leave Faygrene. I can't bear the thought of being trapped here my entire life."

"If you could go anywhere, where would it be?"

Incarnadine. "The ocean. I've seen pictures of it and can only imagine what it's like in person. Besides, I would love to meet a mermaid."

His laughter is louder this time, startling me from my imagination. "I could see that. You splashing around with a mermaid." His laughter slows. "One day we'll go.

We'll find a way. I promise."

The thought brings a smile to my face as I lay back down.

After a few minutes, I feel his weight leave the bed. I open my eyes and watch him make his way to the door. "Goodnight, Addalynne," he says and then leaves my room. A singe of disappointment burns through me, so I close my eyes and picture us far away, sailing on a ship across the sea.

I help prepare supper by stirring a large pot of potatoes, the aroma of garlic and onions watering my eyes and mouth. Mother is giving Elizabeth a much needed bath, Father is tending to the horses, and Gregory and the boy are at the market. This leaves me with my uncle Geoffrey, who arrived from Artania early this morning. He's been gone for a little over a year, so he spent the day getting re-settled in his home here in Faygrene and talking with my parents about everything he missed while he was away.

I steal a glance in his direction and watch him pace nervously across the kitchen. His peppered, grey curls are sticking to the back of his neck, damp with sweat, and his blue eyes are darting back and forth toward the door.

"What's wrong?" I ask. He stops pacing and turns to face me, a smile on his face.

"Nothing, my dear."

"Are you sure?"

"Yes, Addalynne. I'm fine. It's just strange to be back after so long."

I don't believe him, but I know it would be rude of me to continue questioning him so I reluctantly return my attention to the potatoes.

At that moment we both hear the front door open, followed by the loud laughter of the boys. I turn and once again look at my uncle. His eyebrows are drawn into a worried crease.

While we eat, Uncle Geoffrey's apprehension is palpable. His hands fidget with his napkin and his bread roll as he asks the boy questions ranging from what he hopes to do in the future, to his favorite food and color.

I glance around the table and see that Mother and Father have pleased and understanding smiles on their faces. Gregory looks slightly confused. Elizabeth is poking her carrots with the wrong end of her fork and watching them jump across her plate with a laugh. I want so badly to ask my parents and uncle what's going on, so I stuff food in my mouth. If it's full, I won't be able to say something that will get me in trouble.

After supper, the boy, Gregory, and I stay to clear the table while Mother, Father, Uncle Geoffrey, and Elizabeth go back into the study. We clean in silence, letting the sound of our families' murmured voices drift toward us. My heart is pounding with anxiety, and I force myself to focus on piling the plates and bowls in order to keep from fidgeting. After several long minutes, the door to the kitchen swings open and Mother walks briskly in, her red hair tumbling loose from its braid.

"My dear," Mother begins, her words directed at the boy. "We would like to have a word with you."

"Why do you want to see him?" I ask.

Mother faces me. "Because, as I said, we want to speak with him."

I set down the plates. "Can I come too?"

"No."

"But—"

"Addalynne," Gregory says, cutting off my argument. I turn toward him, and he shakes his head. I look back at the boy, and his eyes find mine. The rag he was wiping the table with is clutched tightly in his fist, and there's a trace of fear in his eyes. But after a few seconds he offers me a reassuring smile and, after taking a deep breath, follows my mother out of the kitchen.

"Why are you so jittery?" Gregory mumbles around the mint leaf that's pressed between his teeth as he leans against the wall, his arms crossed in front of him.

"Because there's something going on that they're not telling us, and it's obviously about the boy."

Gregory shrugs. "You're probably right. But getting worked up over it won't help anything. Besides I'm sure it's nothing bad."

He can't be sure about that. What if they somehow found out he's from Incarnadine? Is that why my uncle was so apprehensive? I nervously glance around and then make my way out of the kitchen and into the front room.

"Where are you going?" Gregory whispers.

"To listen." I open the front door and step out into the night. I try to pull the door shut behind me, but Gregory is there to stop it. I turn toward him expecting him to make me go back inside, but instead he steps out as well and shuts the door behind us.

We quietly make our way around the side of our home, ducking under branches and stepping around shrubs. The open window of the study is just ahead. I can see the golden glow pouring through the window, inviting us toward it. We slow as we approach and drop to a crouch. My fingers grab onto the sill and I lift my head up high enough to peek in.

Elizabeth is playing in front of the fire while the others are sitting in the chairs. The boy's hands are in his lap, his fingers folding and unfolding nervously, his attention set on my uncle.

I strain my ears to listen.

". . . know you have been happy here," my uncle is saying. "But I promise you would be happy living with me as well. You will have your very own room and . . ."

I stop listening, my mind swirling around Uncle's words. He wants the boy to live with him? That means he doesn't know he's from Incarnadine. But that also means the boy wouldn't be here with me. I pull myself out of my head and focus again on my uncle. There's a trace of hope in his eyes that I haven't seen in five years, and that hope immediately pulls me back to the past.

I'm standing in the front room of our home. It's dark, and the fire in the hearth seems menacing. My heart is pounding, and I'm clutching a doll that I rarely touch. But Aunt Lucinda gave it to me, so I want it with me now. My uncle's shout of pure agony pierces the air. I'm scared and I only want my mother.

"Mama," I call, but the word comes out smaller than a whisper. Fear has eaten away my voice. But somehow arms find me, my brother's arms. He pulls me onto his lap and holds me by the fire, but I don't like the fire, not tonight, so I bury my face in his shoulder.

I pull myself out of the memory. I don't want to relive the day my uncle lost my aunt Lucinda and their newborn daughter. Looking again at my uncle's face, I see the hard lines that trace his eyes and mouth. The sorrow aged him, painting his hair grey and leaving his face lined with sadness. But there's something different about him today. His blue eyes are still clouded and bereaved, but there's a light in them, one that hasn't been there in a very long time. I can't continue to be selfish. The boy would be happy living with my uncle and my uncle needs someone. He can't be alone forever, besides my uncle's cottage is just down the road so—

"Addalynne!" My mother's shout startles me away from my thoughts. I look toward her and at first I'm confused by the look of shock and anger on her face, but then I remember where I am: crouching outside the window, eavesdropping on a conversation I'm not supposed to hear.

I jump to my feet and turn to run, but something hard slams into my head. Pain shoots through me and my vision blurs. My body sways slightly before falling to the ground.

"Addalynne, are you okay?" Gregory is crouching

over me, but my vision is still spinning and I can't bring myself to answer.

After several dizzying seconds, the sound of footsteps rushes toward us. The boy gets to me first and kneels down next to me, his fingers gently brushing aside the hair from my forehead. It stings when he touches me and I wince in pain.

"You're bleeding," he says, his green eyes darkening with concern.

"What are you doing out here?" Father asks as Mother takes her place by my side. Gregory and I look at each other. I don't know what to say. I don't want to be in trouble again, but I should be honest. I open my mouth to speak, but Gregory's words come first.

"I wanted to hear what you were talking about," he begins with a shrug. "Addalynne only followed me out because I asked her too. I'm sorry, but we're part of this family too and we should have been included."

The look on Mother's face is suspicious, but it doesn't matter. She may not believe Gregory's lie, but neither of us are going to contradict it. He owes me for taking all the blame for being at the Glass River and he knows it.

"You're right. We should have included you, but eavesdropping is not a solution," Mother responds and I'm surprised that I don't completely pass out. She would have never conceded to me in such a manner.

"I'm sorry," Gregory says with more sincerity than I've ever been able to fake. "But right now we should just get Addalynne inside before she runs into any more trees."

I lie on my back and pull the fur blankets up to my neck. The orange light of the fire illuminates most of my chambers, leaving only the top of my bed engrossed in shadow. I turn to my side, my head aching in protest, and stare at my reflection in the mirror near the door. My face looks pale, but my cheeks are still flushed. My black hair is tangled, falling like snakes around my head, and the white bandage, that mother wrapped around my forehead, is stained with a small line of blood.

After a few minutes of silence, my door creaks open. I raise my drowsy eyelids and see the boy standing in the doorway. He makes his way to the side of my bed and stops near the table where he begins to shift his weight from one foot to the other while staring down at me in awkward silence.

"How are you feeling?" he finally asks, his eyes traveling to the cut on my forehead.

"Better. My head hurts, but I'll be fine."

He averts his gaze to the floor and runs a hand through his hair.

"I'm leaving tonight," he says quietly. "I'm going to live with your uncle. But I think you already knew that."

"Yeah, I heard."

He chuckles slightly, but doesn't lift his head.

"I'm sad you're leaving," I admit. I want him to know the truth.

He looks up, his expression slightly guarded. "You are?"

My stomach tightens with nerves and my face burns. This time I look down. "Of course I am."

"I can say no. I can tell him I want to stay here."

A lump rises into my throat. I swallow it down and shake my head. "No. You'll love it there. My uncle's a very kind man. He'll be good to you. Besides, there you'll have your own belongings, instead of sharing with Gregory."

"He said I would have my own loft and my own horse. He also said he would train me to become a blacksmith and teach me archery."

I look back up at him. He's smiling, his dimples barely visible with his head directed toward the ground. "That's wonderful," I reply. "Because then you can teach me archery, too."

"I think I can agree to that," he says with a small laugh as he finally lifts his head to look at me again. He brushes his hair back from his forehead, exposing his fresh scar and making his hair stick up in disarray. A blend of uncertainty and doubt sinks onto his face. "He said he wants to call me Drake. What do you think?"

Drake. "I like it. I read in a book that Drake means 'dragon.' Dragons are . . . mysterious." My lips twist into a smile, hoping he'll find humor in my words. The answering curve of his lips tells me he does, and it gives me the courage to continue. "They're also strong. It's a perfect name for you."

"So, you like it?"

"Yes, I already told you I like it. Plus it will be much better than calling you 'boy.'"

He laughs, "You're right, I like it too." A few seconds of silence stand between us before he continues. "I have to leave now, but I'll see you tomorrow." His words come as a question, and there's a trace of uncertainty in his eyes.

"Of course, Drake," I say with a smile. He returns my smile with one of his own, and this time it reaches his eyes, showing the deep dimples in his cheeks. As he leaves my chambers, I close my eyes and let sleep pull me in. Tomorrow can't come soon enough.

Chapter 6

W*here are they?* I lean against the stone wall that surrounds the woods, twirling the tips of my hair with my fingers as the sun travels farther across the sky. I hate waiting. It's boring and I don't have the patience for it. I bend down, pick up a stick from the ground and toss it in the air a few times before grabbing it with both hands and snapping it in half.

"What did that stick ever do to you?"

I jump at the sound of Drake's voice, dropping the stick halves on the ground. "You know I hate it when you sneak up on me!" I spin around to face him. He's only a few feet away, his black tunic rolled up to the elbows, his arms crossed over his chest.

"It's not my fault," he chuckles. "You're so lost in your own head, a troll could sneak up on you." He walks

59

toward me and I have to tilt my head back to look up and meet his gaze. His green eyes are bright with humor, and his dark brown hair is falling carelessly across his forehead. I want to brush it out of the way, but refrain, as I always do.

"Where's Gregory?" I ask, not bothering to mask the annoyance in my voice.

"He's not coming. He was in the middle of a game of skittles and didn't want to leave."

Typical. "Were you playing too?"

"Yes."

"Why did you leave? Didn't you want to stay and finish the game?" I lean back against the wall and cross my arms in front of me.

"I did, but I knew that would make you angry, and you're pretty scary when you're angry." He offers me a crooked smirk, only one of his dimples showing. That face may work on other girls, but it's not going to work on me.

"Well, if you would rather be there, then go. I don't need you to keep me company." I turn my back to him, walking through the gate and into the woods. My aggravated footsteps press heavier into the ground, causing the birds to scatter from the trees. Within seconds Drake is smirking by my side.

"I'm joking, Addy. Well, not about the angry part, because you can be rather frightening. But I left because I wanted to come meet you. Besides, now that I've left, someone else may actually have a chance at winning, and it's only fair that I give them that chance," he says with a slight shrug and a tone of mock sincerity. I begin to laugh, but stop myself. I'm still mad and I don't feel like letting go of my anger yet. I know it doesn't make sense to be mad that he was a little late, but no matter how much time has passed, I'm still afraid the day will come that I'll be waiting for him and he'll never show, that he'll disappear and go back to the life he has forgotten.

Drake nudges my side with his elbow. "Come on, Addy, if you stay mad at me then I can't teach you to shoot the bow today."

I stop walking and turn to face him. Sure enough, the leather strap of his hunting bag is strung across his shoulder.

"Are you really going to teach me to shoot today?" I ask, the excitement erasing most of my anger.

"I am, but I can't teach you if you're still mad. You have to be calm and level-headed to hold a bow." He raises an eyebrow. "Two things I'm not sure you're capable of."

"I wish you were capable of keeping your thoughts about my temperament to yourself."

His shoulders shake with his laughter. "Is that your way of asking me to stay?"

I try to hold back my smile, but fail miserably. "Maybe."

"Fine, I'll stay, but I know you only want me to because of the bow." He playfully ruffles my hair and then continues down the path, heading farther into the woods, knowing I'll follow.

"That's true," I call out as I follow him. "Did you tell

Uncle Geoffrey?" I hope he didn't. If my uncle knows, he'll feel obligated to tell my parents, and they'll never allow it.

"No. Don't worry."

Good. I shudder to think of what Mother would say if she knew. She already disapproves of my going into the woods. "It's as though I had two sons instead of two daughters," she always says with a deep sigh. Over the years I've learned to ignore this comment, knowing she's only looking for me to pity her and start acting like a "proper young lady."

Drake stops several feet ahead of me. We're in a small, oblong clearing. Thin grass brushes against my feet and gives way to random clusters of yellow wild flowers. My favorite part of the clearing, though, is the overturned tree. The trunk is broken at about a foot from the ground. The remainder of the trunk lies next to the stump, moss clinging to it like snow. I take a seat on the trunk and watch Drake as he carefully places the bag on the ground.

"First, I'm going to show you how to hold the bow. Once you can do that correctly, I'll bring out the arrows," he says as he retrieves the bow from the bag. He gently strokes it with his fingers and then beckons me forward with a curl of his hand, his attention still on the bow.

Once I'm standing next to him, he begins his instruction, starting first with all the safety precautions. I try my best to listen while he rambles on about how to properly hold the bow, how to never aim anywhere near any bystanders, how to always remain calm. But all I can think about is getting my hands on the bow.

Finally, after what feels like hours, he carefully places the bow in my arms. It's surprisingly heavy. Drake watches me, the corner of his mouth curved with amusement, while I struggle to lift it to its proper position. He really is annoying sometimes. Thankfully, it doesn't take long for me to learn how to hold it, and after another short lecture, he lets me shoot my first arrow.

I pull the arrow out of the quiver and carefully load the bow, keeping it aimed firmly on my target, a large oak tree about twenty feet away. With the hemp string from the bow pulled back and pressing against the right side of my face, I count to three, release the arrow, and watch it sail straight past the tree and lodge itself into the ground.

"That was good, Addy. It takes time to learn to hit your target. You can't expect to have perfect aim on your first try." Drake walks toward my shameful arrow.

"Were you able to hit the target on your first day?"

He laughs while bending to retrieve the arrow. "Not in the center."

Not in the center? Then that means . . . "But you were able to hit it?"

He rises to his feet and turns to face me. There's a small smile turning up the corners of his mouth. He shrugs and moves toward me. "I think so, Addy, but I can't really remember. That was a long time ago."

"I know you remember, Drake. Tell me."

I look up at his face and see that he's clearly trying to

suppress a laugh. "Why does it matter?" He reaches forward and brushes several stray hairs away from my forehead. He tucks them behind my ear, before dropping his hand back down to his side.

I don't respond. I just wait for him to tell me because I know he will.

"*If* I remember correctly, I hit my target on the first day, but it took me several days of practice before I was able to hit the center. Archery takes time to master, and you'll get no closer to hitting your mark by wasting your time questioning me." He hands me the arrow and we continue practicing, but while he hits every tree directly in its center, I get no closer to hitting any part of one. After several more hours, I'm completely frustrated, and my arms are aching.

"Can we stop now?" I ask, wiping the sweat off my brow and looking at another arrow that missed its mark by at least three feet.

"Giving up so quickly?" he teases while again retrieving my misguided arrow. My only response is a glare, which he of course laughs at. I'm glad he finds me so amusing. "Do you want to go to the Grey Tree?" he asks with his crooked, half dimpled smile, knowing I won't resist. I open my mouth to respond, but my stomach makes a strange rumbling sound, reminding me how long it's been since I've eaten. "We can pick some berries along the way," he adds. I nod, and after packing his bag, we begin to walk toward the Glass River. It's been three years since I've seen anything strange at the river, three years since I pulled him out. But still, almost everyday I watch, hoping I'll see something that shows me the truth of the Faenomen Forest.

When we arrive at the Grey Tree, I climb up first and settle myself on my favorite branch, letting one leg dangle over each side.

He comes up after me and sits on the branch next to mine. He extends his long legs out in front of him, crossing them at the ankles, and leans against the trunk as his eyes slide closed.

Though the Grey Tree is bare, the leaves on the trees around us are beginning to bud, filling in the lifelessness of the past winter. It's spring, and that means it's almost his birthday. In our minds he'll be turning seventeen, since we figure him to be the same age as Gregory. I turn toward him, a smile twisting my lips, the wind blowing several wild strands of hair across my face.

"It's almost your birthday. What do you want to do to celebrate?" I ask excitedly.

He slowly opens his eyes, looking sideways at me. "It's not my birthday, Addy. I really don't understand why you insist on celebrating it." He's trying to sound irritated, but I can sense the amusement in his tone and face.

"Because it's the day you came into our lives, and *that* is worth celebrating." I could recite this argument from memory because we have it every year. I was the one who originally thought of celebrating his birthday on the day I found him, and everyone else wholeheartedly agreed, except for him, and so this moment repeats.

"Well, since it seems to be more important to you that we celebrate, why don't you tell me what you want to do," he says and lazily turns his head toward me.

"No, Drake, it doesn't work that way. You don't get to back out of this."

"I'm not backing out, I'm just asking what you want to do. Whatever you choose will be fine with me. You know that."

"I'll choose in a couple months, on my birthday. I'm not choosing on yours." I cross my arms in front of me and raise an eyebrow. A laugh escapes his lips, though he tried to hold it in.

"Then I choose to do nothing."

"You can't do that!"

"Why not? You're the one who said that since it's my birthday, I get to choose. And I'm choosing to do nothing." He once again leans back on the tree, his eyes closing and his lips turning up in a satisfied grin.

"Fine! I'll choose then!"

"Too late." He shrugs.

"Drake!"

His eyes open. "Addalynne!" he yells back, mimicking my tone.

Sometimes I honestly don't know why I like to spend so much time with him. I turn away, setting my sight on the tree nearest us. I hear him laughing beside me and the slow burn of frustration spreads through me. "All right. All right. I surrender. You choose."

"Does that mean I win?" I set my chin, still refusing

to look at him.

"Win what?"

"This argument."

His laughter picks up again. I look down at the ground, contemplating whether or not I'm too high up to jump.

"Sure, Addy. You win."

I know he's only giving in out of amusement, but it's good enough for me. I settle back against the trunk and turn to face him. "We can ride our horses around the outskirts of the village. Then we can go into the market and I'll buy you one of those fancy pies at the bakery." The thought of the peach one makes my mouth water. "Then my mother will make you and Uncle Geoffrey supper."

"Sounds perfect." He gives me a crooked smile, his right dimple pressing in. "Are your parents going to the Floret Ball? It's in a few weeks, isn't it?" He asks, successfully changing the subject.

"Yes. It's all Mother can talk about." I, of course, will be at home watching Elizabeth. You have to be seventeen to attend the Ball, and I'll be turning sixteen a little over a month after the Ball, which means I won't be able to attend this year or next year. But he . . . "Are you going?" The question comes out paranoid and high-pitched, startling us both.

He studies me for a moment, his head slightly tilting to the side. I turn away, pretending to be distracted by the grey bark, my heart beating dizzyingly fast.

"No," he finally replies. I release a breath, and my

body relaxes. I begin to turn back toward him. "You seem relieved," he continues. The bark once again becomes incredibly interesting.

"No. I'm not relieved. I just don't think you would have fun at the Ball."

"Oh, really? And why is that?"

Because I won't be there. "Because Gregory won't be there. He's not going this year because Mary isn't of age yet, and in case you haven't noticed, he's rather taken with her."

"Believe me, I've noticed," he says, and I finally feel secure enough to look at him. His green eyes are fixed on me. "But John and Walter are attending. I could always go with them." He continues to look at me, clearly waiting for my reaction, but I set my shoulders and keep my expression completely blank.

"You could." Yes, he could, and it doesn't matter if he does. He doesn't have to experience everything with me. And maybe if I continue to tell myself this enough times, I'll believe it, and the thought of him going will stop hurting.

"I'm not going. I already have plans," he says.

"Oh?" My heart picks up again. Plans with who?

"I'm going to spend the evening relaxing at the Troyers' home, watching a girl named Addalynne read while her sister plays with dolls."

I let a laugh escape, sending the tension with it. "I don't remember inviting you over."

"I don't remember ever needing an invitation. But for arguments sake . . . Addalynne Troyer, may I please come to your home on the evening of the Floret Ball, because I will not be attending. Oh, and to save us time in the future, I would also like to ask your permission to come to your home on the night of the Ball next year, as I don't plan to attend then either."

I lean back on the tree, my eyes closed, a full smile on my face. "I'll have to think about it."

We spend the rest of the afternoon talking and laughing while we toss berries back and forth. Drake teases me about my shooting, but I remind him that I'm a much better rider. Whenever we race, I always win. He says this is only because I'm lighter than him, but we both know it's not.

All too soon the sun is hovering in the west, reminding us that it's time to head back.

We climb down from the tree and Drake slowly walks to the bank of the river. His face tightens, the way it does when his mind is consumed with thoughts.

"What are you thinking about?"

"My past," he replies quietly.

"Do you remember something?" I stand beside him, my chest clenching with fear.

"No. But I get a strange feeling when I'm here, especially when I'm close to the river." His fingers tug through his hair. "Something inside tells me that these woods aren't safe, and it's not because of the warnings. It's something else, something much deeper than that. I feel it in my bones." As he speaks, he stares across the river and into the fog on the southern side, his mind entirely consumed. "Do you feel it, too?"

I shake my head while I pull at my thoughts, trying to think of something to say. His mind may not remember, but his body is clearly reacting to whatever happened to him before he fell into the river. But that's not something I can share with him.

"It's probably because this is where you almost drowned, and you're reliving that fear." There. It's the partial truth. "This side of the forest is safe." I speak in the most reassuring voice I can manage, hoping we can move on from this.

"I don't know that you're right, Addy." He moves along the edge of the river, and I have to quicken my pace to keep up, trailing several feet behind him.

"You won't stop coming in here with me, though, will you?" I call out. He stops walking and turns to face me. His eyes are dark and intent, his cheeks slightly flushed.

"No. I'll still come with you, but you have to promise me that you will always wait for me." His eyes search mine. "Do not come here without me." His voice is stern and unwavering, leaving me no room to argue with him, even if I wanted to, which I don't.

"I'll always wait for you, by the gate. I won't come into the woods alone. I promise."

His shoulders visibly relax, but his attention goes back to the river. I know him well enough to see the inner battle that's still waging inside him.

"There's something else you're not saying." Fears grasp muffles my words, making them come out as little more than a whisper.

"I just wish I could remember something, anything, about my past. Why was I in the river? Did I run away from home? Did I have some sort of accident? Did someone . . ."

I place my hand on his shoulder. He turns his head and his eyes find mine. The sorrow and desperation in them almost makes me tell him the truth about that day, but then I remember what that truth means and where it will lead him, so I shove the temptation back down inside me and close the door.

"You can't think that way, Drake. Just focus on what you have. You're happy here, aren't you?" I say, hoping he wants the life he has more than the life he lost.

"I am, but . . ."

"But what?"

"But sometimes this life feels like a lie."

My hand drops from his shoulder and I take an involuntary step back. "How could you say that? All the love we give you, all the time we spend together. None of that is a lie."

"All of that may be real, Addy, but I'm taking on a life that isn't really mine. I'm joining a family that isn't blood. And the fact that I'm so happy here makes it even worse."

"How could that make it worse?"

"Because it makes me never want to leave. And when I find myself lying awake at night, smiling about something that happened that day, I can't help but think about the mother and father I left behind. I'm happy and smiling, and they could still be miserable and worried about me. How can I accept a brand new life when I don't know what I left behind in the old one?"

My heart races, as though it's searching for a resolution, one that will calm him and keep him here. "Because what if you left the old one behind for a reason?" I begin. "What if you ran away? What if your real family was hurting you?"

"What if they loved me?"

We stand in silence for what feels like an eternity. "I can't speak for them, Drake," I finally say, praying my words are enough. That *I* am enough. "But I love you, my parents love you, Gregory loves you, Elizabeth loves you, Uncle Geoffrey loves you. He's taken you into his home and has raised you as his own son, loving you just as much as he would love his own blood. Isn't that enough?"

Drake closes the space between us and takes my face in his hands. His eyes are burning with emotions, and after several agonizing seconds, he finally speaks. "It's more than enough. And that's why it scares me."

"Don't let it scare you! Don't let this fear take you away from me!"

He drops his hands from my face and wraps his arms around me, pulling me against him. "I'm not going anywhere. Like I've told you before. There's nowhere for me to go. I wouldn't even know where to start. I just have to battle with my guilt occasionally, but don't worry. I'm fine." He pulls back and looks into my eyes. His face is wearing a smile, but I can't tell if it's a mask.

"Now let's get you home."

"You're sure you're all right?" I ask.

"I just spent the day watching you fail horribly at shooting a bow for the first time. How could I possibly be any better?"

I shove him playfully. He wraps his hand around mine and gives it a comforting squeeze before leading us toward the village.

As we approach the grey stone wall in front of my home, Drake pulls me into his arms. He hugs me tightly and rests his chin on top of my head.

"I'll meet you at the wall in front of the woods again tomorrow morning," he says before slowly pulling away. He takes a slight step back and his gaze settles on my face. He raises his arm up to ruffle the top of my hair, as he always does, but as his hand reaches up, he pauses. Something resembling confusion or worry passes along his features and instead, his hand gently cups my cheek, his thumb tracing along my skin. "Good night, Addy," he says quietly, his gaze drifting to the ground.

Before I have a chance to respond, he drops his hand and turns away. I watch him walk toward the road, his hands stiff at his sides, my cheek tingling, my heart unsteady.

"Good night," passes through my lips on the current of a shivering breath.

Chapter 7

HER

"Ouch!" I jump as the needle pierces my skin.

"Are you all right?" Mother asks while she rubs the side of my stomach.

"I'm fine. It didn't really hurt. It just startled me."

"Good. I'm sorry, but I did tell you to keep still. You're always fidgeting." She sighs and continues sewing the side of my dress.

I glance down at her and watch her work. The needle is pressed between her pursed lips as her blue eyes study the seam she's working on, her eyebrows pulled together in concentration. Several delicate braids wrap around her head, entwining her red curls in an elaborate spiral. Just imagining the time it took exhausts me.

Mother grabs the light blue fabric of the dress with one hand and removes the needle from her mouth with the other.

"Now don't move, Addalynne. I'm going to sew the last few stitches. If you need to take a breath, now is the time to do it."

I laugh and take one last breath before letting it out and holding my body as still as a statue. After a few seconds, Mother pats me on the back.

"There. It's all done. Now take it off."

I watch as Mother flips it around, so that the seams are on the inside, before pulling it back over my head and walking me toward the mirror.

It really is beautiful. The color matches the blue of the sky and compliments my fair skin. The wide sleeves fall past my wrists, the material draping several inches beyond my hands. The fitted top has a square neckline that sits rather low and hugs my curves, displaying the fact that I'm no longer a little girl. The top leads down to my lower hips where the dress slightly billows out into a full skirt. Around my hips there's a thin, silver rope acting as a belt. A dagger would sit so nicely there.

"Thank you, Mother. It's beautiful."

"You're the one who makes it beautiful," she says with a smile. "Now tell me, have you given some thought to our conversation?"

I move away from the mirror and walk toward the window, feeling the early stirrings of agitation.

"You'll be of age in less than a year, Addalynne."

"I know, Mother. You never fail to remind me." I reply curtly while staring toward the trees, counting the green leaves that are dancing in the wind. Anything is better than having this conversation.

"That's because this is important, Addalynne. Marriage is not like one of your books that you can just discard when you get bored."

Marriage. How can I possibly even think about marriage. "I know it's important, Mother."

"And yet you continue to put me off."

"Well, I don't know why you're pushing me about this. As you said, I have almost a year."

"That's little time if you want much of a choice."

A humorless chuckle escapes my lips. "I was under the impression that women weren't given much choice in this."

"That's not always true. I chose your father."

"After he chose you."

"Well, yes, but I still chose him in return. And I was lucky. You shouldn't wait until there's no time left. Then you will be left with little choice. Unless . . . unless you've already made it."

"What would possibly give you the impression that I've made it?"

"Come now, Addalynne. I'm not that naive. You and Drake . . ."

I spin around to face her. She's sitting on my bed, her hands folded calmly in her lap, one eyebrow raised in speculation. I cross my arms in front of me. "What are you implying?"

"You spend every day together and—"

"We do not! I spend plenty of time with Mary!" This isn't entirely true, but I won't give her the satisfaction of being right. Besides, it doesn't matter if we spend every day together.

"Oh, I wasn't aware you were still spending time with the Bradlock girl," Mother replies, her face pinching with surprise. Good. Maybe now I can keep the conversation off me, and on the relationship between Gregory and Mary, which my mother is not yet aware of. I open my mouth to tell her, but she speaks first. "How does Drake feel about her diverting your time away from him?"

"He doesn't care. Why would he?"

Mother shakes her head and laughs to herself. It would be nice if she let me in on her joke.

"You and Drake are more than friends, are you not?"

My sharp intake of breath causes me to choke. My eyes water and my throat burns as the coughs battle through me.

Mother rushes toward me with a metal goblet of water. I drink the water and take slow breaths as the coughing finally subsides.

"No!" I say when I regain my voice, but the word holds little conviction, and in my heart I feel the doubt, though I don't know why. We *are* only friends. He's never tried to be more, and I've never really thought about how I would respond if he did. I close my eyes and think of the way his hand caressed my cheek after we shot the bow together a few months ago, but this time, in my imagination, his thumb begins lifting my chin toward his face. My pulse quickens and then the Drake of my imagination drops my chin and laughs as he ruffles my hair, returning to the Drake I know. And the

Drake I know would never kiss me because, if he wanted to, he would have done it already. He's hardly even touched me since that day. "No," I say again. "He's my friend. There's nothing more between us." The words come out quiet, but this time they have their conviction.

"Oh, I just assumed . . ."

"Well, you assumed wrong," I reply bitterly, heat spreading across my face and chest. She returns to the bed, her back facing me. I shouldn't have spoken to her so harshly. With a deep breath, I move toward the bed and sit down next to her, placing my hand on top of hers.

"I'm not trying to rush you, Addalynne. But if you and Drake are truly not more than friends, then you have some thinking to do. I know that in your mind eleven months is a long time, but it's not. Not for something this important. All I ask is that you give some of your attention to the young men in the village. I'm sure many have tried giving you their attention already and you just didn't notice. For now, all I'm asking you to do is notice." She places a kiss on my forehead and then leaves my chambers.

I stay on my bed and let myself think about her words. I've never given much thought to my future, other than how badly I want to see anyplace that's not Faygrene. But I think about it now. Can I really see myself getting married so soon? It seems unlikely. I'm nowhere near ready. Besides, she's wrong. I would have noticed if any of the boys in Faygrene were taking interest in me. They aren't. At least, I don't think they are. But would it really be so terrible if one of them did? The thought leaves me flustered, and my mind returns to Drake. How would he react to someone courting me? Would he be jealous? The thought makes me smile, but I quickly shake it off. I don't want Drake to be jealous. I want him to be happy. Besides, there's no reason for him to be jealous. We have both known that this day would come. And if Drake didn't want me to be with someone else then he would have done something about it. I know he would have. Drake's not timid. He doesn't want me in that way, and I don't want him in that way either, so I'm not going to think about it anymore. And as much as I hate it, maybe Mother's right. Maybe I haven't been paying enough attention, and maybe I should start. I don't want to be forced into saying, 'yes' to someone I hardly know.

My head aches with my thoughts and the anxiety they bring. Today I'll try to notice the other boys, to see if they do seem interested. If I do this, though, I'm going to have to cancel my plans with Drake. There's no way I can focus on them if I have him distracting me. I'll go see Mary instead. She can help me through this.

Freyja's trot is steady, allowing the breeze to brush through her golden hair as I make my way to Uncle Geoffrey's. I move east, cutting through a crop of willows and bypassing the road. On the other side of several cascading branches, I see the familiar, weathered, wooden fence surrounding their small stone cottage. Drake's horse, Bear, is still there, tied to the post. I climb off Freyja and tie her to the post as well.

My body noticeably warms and my stomach tightens as I knock on the door. Why am I so nervous? I'm never nervous to see him. The coppery taste of blood fills my mouth, coming from the cut I made by biting my lip. The door opens and I release my bleeding lip from my mouth and look up at my uncle.

"Addalynne, my dear girl." He smiles as he pulls me in for a hug. He's filled out over these last few years, making it difficult for me to wrap my arms around his full belly.

"Hello, Uncle. How are you?" There's a slight tremble in my voice, my jitters still dominating me.

"Wonderful, my dear. And yourself?"

"Very well."

"How about your father? I suppose things are rather tense at the Berrengers' with Lady Berrenger missing."

"*Missing?* When did she go missing?" I think back on the last few conversations with my father, but he never mentioned this.

"It only happened yesterday morning. Your father told me that the Lord awoke and found his wife's chambers empty. He called on the guards to search, but she was no where to be found. Later in the day they discovered her horse was missing as well."

"Do they think she was taken?"

"Taken? Possibly. Or she may have left."

"Why would she leave?"

"Well, my dear, I'm not one to make assumptions, and you are here to see Drake, not to talk to an old man about curious village matters," he says with a sideways smile, barely visible under his peppered beard, getting straight to what he knows is the point of my visit.

"I always enjoy talking to you and you're not that old, but I was hoping to see Drake." I reply, knowing our conversation is over anyway. If I want to know more about Lady Berrenger's disappearance, I'll have to ask someone else.

"He's at the shop, finishing up a sword. When he left, he mentioned he had to meet you at noon. I was on my way to relieve him now."

"But his horse . . . ?"

"He decided to walk today. Would you like to walk with me? Freyja can stay here."

I nod and we walk to the market together in amiable silence, my mind completely preoccupied. What if Lady Berrenger crossed the river? What if something crossed the river and took her?

When we arrive, Uncle Geoffrey tells me to go on in, stating that he needs to stop at the bakery and will be back soon. I slowly make my way through the doors and into Uncle Geoffrey's blacksmith shop.

Daylight floods through the two open windows, causing reflections to cascade around the shop, bouncing off the swords, shields, axes, and spears that line the black stone walls. There's an array of daggers on a wooden table in the center. I move toward them and gently drag my fingers along the hilts, decorative stones, and blades.

With a sigh, I pull my hand away and venture to the

door in the back. It leads to the forge, where Drake will be. The sharp clanging and grinding sounds coming from the forge greet me as soon as I step into the stone hallway. The entrance is slightly up ahead and the door is already open, letting the orange light of the flames flicker into the dark space. I stop when I reach the open doorway, where I have a clear view of Drake.

The flames of the fire beneath the sword he's working on bathe his face in shades of red and orange. The sleeves of his black tunic are rolled up past the elbow, making the strength in his arms visible as he works. The way his arms move along the sword cause the fitted tunic to pull tightly across his chest, exposing the muscle there as well. I've always known he was tall, as the top of my head barely reaches his collar bone, but I hadn't noticed the change in his body before. I see now how much his body has filled out. When did that happen?

I reluctantly let my gaze travel to his face. His dark brown hair is falling across his forehead, tousled with its subtle waves. The ends of his hair, grazing his neck, are damp with sweat and curl more than the rest. His fair skin has a slightly bronze hue to it, and his cheeks are flushed with the heat of the flames. As he works, his lips are pursed, causing his strong jawline to appear tense. There are slight indentations of his dimples on his cheeks, strained in the studiousness of his face. He really is handsome. Suddenly, he looks up, his dark green eyes landing on me. I look away, and warmth floods my face.

"How long have you been here, Addy?"

I shift uncomfortably and try to swallow back my

embarrassment.

"A few seconds," I lie. By this point, it feels as though most of the heat has left my face and I hesitantly allow myself to look at him again. He's staring at me, but it takes me a moment to realize that his eyes aren't on my face. They're moving slowly along my body. The warmth returns instantly.

When Drake's eyes meet mine, he clears his throat. "New dress?".

"Yes," I reply quietly, a tremor still present in my voice.

"You're beautiful. I mean, the dress, it's beautiful. The dress is beautiful on you." He looks to the floor, his grip on the hilt of the sword tightening to the point of his knuckles turning white.

"Thank you," I reply weakly, my heart fluttering, as my gaze also travels to the floor. I can practically taste the awkward tension hanging in the air. I try to think of something to say, but all I can do is replay his words in my mind. *He thinks I'm beautiful.*

"Hey kids, will you be leaving now?" Uncle Geoffrey's voice makes me jump, startling me out of my trance. Thankfully though, his presence shatters most of the tension. With a much needed exhale, I lift my head, and watch him as he moves toward the sword Drake has finished. "This is perfect! Wonderful job, son." He pats Drake on the back and then takes it from his hands.

Drake moves stiffly toward the door, looking completely over my head. I inadvertently hold my breath as he moves sideways around me and steps into the hallway.

"I'll be back tonight, Father," he calls, and continues to make his way out the door. I glance back at my uncle, unsure of whether I should follow. Uncle Geoffrey simply nods and waves a dismissive hand, already lost in his work. With one last steadying breath, I follow Drake out of the shop and into the now excessively warm late spring air.

"Did you want to go into the woods or stay in the market today?" he asks, while meticulously keeping his back to me.

"Actually, I came here to tell you that I'm going to spend the day with Mary," I offer reluctantly. He turns to face me, confusion tightening his features. I look away.

"Why?"

"I haven't seen her in a while and . . ."

"You saw her two days ago," he interrupts. His eyes are on me, but I continue to keep mine on the rock I'm pushing around with the tip of my brown boot. "What's this really about, Addalynne? If you really wanted to spend time with Mary I'd understand, but we both know that's not what's going on."

As usual, he sees right through me. I take in an exasperated breath. "For a while now, Mother has been saying that it's time I consider potential suitors. And though I'm not entirely pleased with the notion, it's becoming increasingly more difficult to put it off." I tell him the truth, feeling utterly ridiculous as I do. His first response to my honesty is complete silence. Then . . .

"You don't have to do anything you're not ready for." His voice is so low, I have to strain my ears to hear him. "Besides, I don't see what this has to do with Mary."

"I want to spend the day with Mary to see if I'm ready. When I'm with you I . . ." I what? "I'm too distracted."

I don't look up to see him move, but I feel and hear him take a step closer to me. "Why are you distracted when you're with me?" His question comes out slow and deliberate, and for a moment, all words evade me. He takes another step. He's so close that I can feel his breath blowing across the top of my head. I try to concentrate on a response, but I'm too dizzy and hot, much too hot. Maybe I'm coming down with something. That would explain the strange feeling in my head and stomach, and my inability to form a clear thought. After taking several deep breaths, I steady myself enough to speak.

"I'm distracted when I'm with you because we're always going off on our own, leaving no time for me to notice anyone else. Besides, our going off together has created another problem."

"And what could that possibly be?" He takes a step back, and my head clears slightly.

"My mother thinks we're more than friends, and I assume she's not the only one." Numbing silence stains the air around us. I wait a solid minute for him to speak. When he doesn't, I let myself look at him. Now he's the one looking at the ground.

"And that's a problem?" Though his words are quiet, they're loud enough for me to hear the anger in them.

Why would he be angry? Surely he sees why this would be a problem. We're only friends, nothing more.

"Yes, Drake. It's a problem because it will make others think that I'm not available for courtship, and Mother wants me to be available."

"And we both know you always listen to your mother."

"Why does this bother you so much? Maybe I'm curious too, Drake! I'm not a little girl anymore! Besides, you knew this day would come!"

He looks up at me, his shoulders set, his eyes sparkling with what seems to be anger, but there's something else there as well, and though I can't place it, it breaks my heart.

"I'm not bothered. In fact, I would love to have some time to myself. Contrary to what you may believe, I don't need to spend every day with you. So go ahead. We certainly don't want others to think you're being romanced by me. Imagine how inappropriate that would be; the orphaned blacksmith and Addalynne Troyer, the village princess."

I pull my bottom lip into my mouth and bite down until I taste blood, desperate to focus the pain of his words elsewhere. *Don't cry.* My hands clench into fists at my side, anger settling in along with the pain. *Don't cry.* "I'm *not* the village princess."

"No, but you may as well be. Your family is the second wealthiest in Faygrene. Girls like you are meant for lords, not orphans. Besides, as I said, it will be nice to have some time to myself, instead of having to follow you around for Gregory."

For Gregory? "What do you mean you follow me around for Gregory?"

"Gregory wants me to make sure you're safe. He knows you wouldn't let him follow you around every day, so he asked me to."

I try to breathe, but my breath keeps getting stuck in my throat. The dizziness returns, leaving me unbalanced and nauseous. I can't look at him anymore. "So you only spend time with me because Gregory asked you to?" The idea is too painful to comprehend. He doesn't answer, but he doesn't need to. Now I know the truth. "Then we should stop spending time together. I don't want to be the burden you bear for your friendship with Gregory."

"That's fine with me, Addalynne, but what about you? If Mary is with Gregory, who are you going to spend your time with?"

"There are other girls I can spend time with apart from Mary."

A single, sharp laugh escapes his lips. "No, there's not. Mary is the only girl in Faygrene who even likes you. All the other girls in the village want nothing to do with you."

I suck in a breath. How did we end up here? He has never spoken to me like this. He has never looked at me this way.

All of this hurts entirely too much and there are absolutely no words I can find to say to him. All I can do now is put distance between us before he sees the tears that are forcing their way down my face. Without another second's thought, I turn and run as fast as I can, not bothering to pay attention to where I'm headed.

After several minutes, I find myself on the opposite side of the village, as far away from him as I can get without leaving Faygrene. I look around, taking in my surroundings. The end of the village lies to my left and a thick forest stands to my right. On the edge of the forest there's a large tree with ideal branches for climbing. It's not my tree or my part of the woods, but I don't care. It will be good enough for now, and he won't find me here —not that he's going to try to find me anyway.

After perching myself on top of one of the branches, I lean my back against the trunk and tuck my legs up to my chest, my arms wrapping around them. Within seconds my body is shaking with sobs. Everything between us has been a lie. He's the most important person to me, and I'm only a task to him. Something inside me tries to argue, to tell me that it isn't true. But what if it is? What if all our time together has just been an act, a way for him to keep me happy and safe, because that's surely what Gregory would have wanted him to do.

Stop, Addalynne! You have to stop! Pull yourself together! You're stronger than this! I tell myself this over and over, but the tears don't listen. I close my eyes and try to think of something else, anything else, but every image I pull into my mind has him there. And I'm tired, I'm so tired. I know I shouldn't sleep up here, but I can't help it and soon I'm fading in and out of sleep. Both my dreams and my waking thoughts are filled with him, and when I finally commit my eyes to stay open, I'm left with endless questions.

What will Drake do now? Will he spend more time with Gregory and Walter, or will he start spending time with other girls? What if he starts spending time with Antoinette or Jacqueline? He said all the other girls want nothing to do with me, and though I'm not sure about all the girls, I know that Antoinette and Jacqueline hate me. They would love nothing more than to take him away from me. I think about how they laugh and stare at me, how they tell me I should have been born a boy. Maybe he'll join them and laugh at the jokes they make at my expense. Well, that's fine. I can find other ways to spend my time, starting with climbing down from this tree, finding Mary, and finding a boy who notices me. The thought is much more appealing to me now than it was this morning. I'll find someone else to walk through the woods with, someone who wants to be there.

With new resolve, I make my way down the tree, being mindful of not ripping my new dress. As I jump to the ground, I look toward the village, scanning the deserted streets. Dark shadows extend across the ground, painting their silhouettes on the stones. I was in that tree much longer than I thought. My parents are going to be furious. I break into a run, trying to get home before night chases away the final traces of the day.

As I turn the corner and approach the road that lies in front of my home, I see my mother and sister walking toward me.

"Where have you been?" Mother yells, relief and anger stirring in her voice.

"I'm sorry. I was in the market and didn't notice the time. It won't happen again," I reply through gasps of air, my chest burning from running. Mother eyes me speculatively.

"Your brother was in the market all day. He said he never saw you there."

I didn't think this out very well, did I? The truth it is then.

"I had a fight with Drake this morning and didn't want to be around anyone. So I went and sat in a tree on the edge of town. I was always in view of the village and was perfectly safe. I didn't realize how long I was there. I'm sorry."

"What did you and Drake fight about?" Elizabeth asks at the same time that Mother says, "That explains it."

"Explains what?" I ask, ignoring Elizabeth's question.

"It explains why Drake has been pacing in your chambers, refusing to go home until he sees you," Mother replies, a touch of annoyance in her voice.

My heart stutters. "He's here now?"

"Yes. He rode Freyja back for you and then insisted on staying."

"What did you fight about?" Elizabeth asks again before I can respond to my Mother.

"It's not your concern, Elizabeth!"

Elizabeth turns on her heel and walks away, likely on her way to pout in her chambers.

"Just because you're upset doesn't mean you need to speak to your sister that way." Mother frowns.

"I'm not upset." I cross my arms and look away from her, wishing I could sink back into the trees and avoid this entire conversation.

"Clearly you are." She waits for me to respond, but once she realizes I'm not going to, she continues. "Do you want me to tell him you don't want to speak with him?"

If I tell her "Yes," she'll definitely make him leave. I try to clear my head so I can think, but there's nothing to think about. I'm still angry and incredibly hurt, but I want to see him.

The light from my open doorway flickers into the dimly lit hall. My hands shake and my heart drums painfully. With a deep breath, I walk in.

He's sitting on my bed, my sapphire hairpin between his fingers. His head is down and his shoulders are hunched with defeat. Seeing him here only reminds me of what I lost, and that makes it entirely too painful. My tears rush to the surface, but I thankfully manage to push them down by telling myself that he doesn't look happy, and I must admit, that makes me feel a little better.

He looks up and stands, his eyes locking on mine for several seconds, the rigid intensity of his gaze unnerving me.

"Addy, I . . ." He runs a hand through his hair, something he's been doing a lot based on its appearance. "I saw Mary in the market. You weren't with her." He pauses, clearly waiting for me to say something. A muscle jumps in his jaw, but I continue to stand silently. "I asked her where you were and she said she hadn't seen you."

I set my shoulders. "I decided not to go to the market."

"Where did you go then?"

"It doesn't matter."

"It does matter! You can't go off on your own and tell no one where you are."

"I most certainly can! I'm not a child, and I'm not your responsibility! And if you came here to yell at me, then please feel free to leave." I'm too exhausted to fight again and am starting to regret my decision to not have Mother make him leave.

He slowly rakes his fingers across his face, leaving one hand cupping the back of his neck. "I . . . did . . . not . . . come . . . here . . . to . . . yell . . . at . . . you," he says slowly, clearly struggling for patience. "I was worried about you." He takes several apprehensive steps toward me, my hairpin still in his hands. He stops with a couple feet between us.

"It's not your job to worry about me."

"It was never my job." He holds my gaze, his eyes searching mine. "I'm sorry, Addy. I should have never spoken to you the way I did."

"You meant what you said though, didn't you?"

"No," he responds firmly. "Gregory has never asked me to follow you. Being with you has always been my choice."

"Then, why . . ."

"I said those things because I wanted to hurt you. And I'm sorry. I'm so sorry."

The look he's giving me makes me desperate to move closer to him, to tell him I forgive him, but the uncertainty and pain I still feel holds me back.

"Why did you want to hurt me?"

He inhales roughly and blows out a trembling breath. "I don't know," he says quietly, his gaze dropping to the floor. "I guess I was afraid I was about to lose you and I let my pride get the better of me."

"You could never lose me, Drake."

He looks up, a sad smile on his face. "Well, that's good because I honestly don't know what I'd do without you."

In this moment it's as though there's an invisible force in the air, pushing us together. The need to have his arms around me is overwhelming, and leaves me breathless.

"What about the girls?" I ask, and the intensity of the moment dissipates.

"The girls?"

"Yes. What about what you said about the other girls?"

He glances up and a playful smirk develops on his face. "Oh, that part was true. They really don't like you." A laugh escapes my lips before I have a chance to hold it back.

At the sound of my laugh he closes the rest of the distance between us, hooks one arm around my waist, and pulls me against his chest. I wrap my arms around his neck, inhaling the scents of mint, leather, and smoke. He continues to hold me, slowly running his hands through my hair.

"Don't take it personally, Addy. It's only because they're jealous that you get to spend so much time with me." He laughs as I take a step back and push him away, but I laugh too, mostly with relief.

"Is that what you think, that all the girls in the village are desperate to spend time with you?"

"Of course they are," he says with mock arrogance. For several seconds we say nothing and I watch as the smile slowly leaves his face. He reaches his hand out and tucks my hair behind my ear. I close my eyes and lean into his hand, letting the sturdiness of it calm me. "Will I see you tomorrow?" he asks as he drops his hand back down, leaving me startlingly empty and unsatisfied.

"Yes." I open my eyes and watch him as he turns away and moves toward my open window. "But I still want to spend part of the day with Mary." It's true that I want to see her and talk to her, but I also want to protect myself. I have to stop needing him so much. Today showed me that. Because right now I know, without a doubt, that if I truly lost him, it would kill me.

He turns his head toward me, giving me a mischievous, dimpled smile. "She can have you in the morning, but in the afternoon you're mine."

He turns back to the window and climbs onto the open stone frame.

"You do realize that you can go through the front door?"

"Where's the fun in that?" He laughs and jumps down before I can respond. He lands on the ground below and his footsteps fade into the night. I make my way across the floor and catch a glimpse of something reflecting back at me through the mirror. I turn and see my sapphire pin settled in my hair, just above my ear.

Chapter 8

HER
1 YEAR LATER

Travelers, merchants, items from far away villages. It's all part of the summer festival. Every year the event is something I look forward to. But, over the last few months, I have been dreading this day. Well, in all honesty, it's not this day in particular, but what this day represents—summer.

Every summer knights from the King's Schild travel to Faygrene. They speak to the young men about joining the Schild, enticing them with descriptions of our kingdom's capital, Synereal—its spiraled streets and bustling market, the tall, ivory castle nestled amongst the trees, the glistening lake so clear they say it seems to be a painting of the sky. All of this is very enticing. The catch, though, is that most men who join the Schild stay in it for the rest of their lives, never seeing their families again, never being able to marry or have children of their own. This reality holds many back. It's not that King Theoderic forces them to stay—he gives them the freedom to leave at any time—but most don't choose this. They settle into their life in Synereal and enjoy the honor that comes with being a member of the Schild. They strive for knighthood and finish off their days protecting the kingdom.

At the end of last summer, knights of the King's Schild came and spoke with Gregory. Gregory wanted to join the Schild then, but he was worried about leaving us, and especially about leaving Mary. He thought about it for several months, but I knew he was going to join. He has wanted to become a guardsmen of the Schild since we were children. We both dreamt of it. And here was his chance to turn his childhood game into reality.

Of course I was right, and by winter, Gregory was certain he would join. He ended things with Mary, and told me that, although he loved her, he couldn't ask her to wait for him. Mary told me that she would have stayed with him until he left, but Gregory didn't want that. Apparently he told her he didn't want her to waste any more time on him. She cried when she told me and my heart broke for both of us.

Then, under the blanket of snow, summer still seemed far away, a precipice lingering in the future. Now it's here, and he'll be leaving in a little over a month.

The thought of his leaving devastates me, but I placate myself with the hope that he'll eventually choose to return home, or that I'll somehow have the chance to visit him in Synereal. Besides, I can't be angry with him for following his dreams. If I were able to, I know I would, but being a woman comes with its own set of rules. I can't leave on adventures, I can't join the Schild. I wonder if Lady Berrenger had dreams of adventure. Maybe that's why she left last year, never to return to the life she once knew.

I put on my black riding boots and turn toward the open window. Under the heavy branches of the tree I see Gregory and Drake.

The sight of Drake tightens my stomach with knots. Ever since our fight last year, it's as though we haven't fully regained our balance. We have days that are wonderful and easy. We fall into our friendship and it's as natural as breathing. Then there are days where things become tense and unsure. And things have only gotten worse since I officially came of age a couple of months ago. Now there's a tug of war between our awkward tension and his overprotection. I don't know which one upsets me more.

I glare at them through my open window. Gregory has of course joined Drake in watching my every move. They always happen to be going where I am and, on the rare occasion that they actually leave my side, they seem to keep me in their line of sight. It drives me completely mad. Their constant vigilance is suffocating and insulting. I'm seventeen years old! I'm capable of taking care of myself!

Well, they can't stay out there all morning. They'll eventually give up and go into the market, and that's when I'll leave.

"Addalynne!" Elizabeth calls, running into my chambers, her body a blur of red and green as she darts in front of me and lands gracefully on my bed. She sits on the edge with her legs dangling in front of her, a hopeful smile spread across her innocent face. The top of her curly red hair is loosely pulled back with a star-shaped, emerald pin, leaving the bottom half falling around her shoulders in long, perfect spirals. I lift my hand up and play with the tips of my own dark hair. It's usually straight and untamable, but last night Elizabeth convinced me to let her roll my hair in fabric. Now I have delicate curls blanketing me as well. They're beautiful, but unlike hers, they won't last.

"Do you like my dress?" she asks, as she stands and spins, letting the skirt flare out around her. At first I just see a beautiful green dress, making her look like a rose, but as I look closer, I realize that it's no ordinary dress, and I'm instantly pulled back into the memory it invokes; I'm twelve and struggling to pull an unconscious boy out of a river.

She stops spinning, but the skirt continues to sway at her feet.

"I thought it had been destroyed by the river," I say.

"Mother fixed it up for me. It was always one of my favorites." The look on her face makes it clear that she's looking for my approval.

I walk over to her and plant a delicate kiss on her forehead. "You look beautiful, much better than I ever looked in it." She's taller than I was at that age; the top of her head already reaches my nose, and though she's younger than I was when I wore it, the dress fits her perfectly.

"Thank you," she says, while reaching out and brushing her hand along the material of my skirt. "You look beautiful today, too."

I'm wearing the dress Mother made me for my seventeenth birthday. The top is a white blouse that falls off my shoulders and ties loosely in the center of my chest. A black corset that strings together gracefully down my back, is situated over the top. The skirt is dark green and falls to my feet, where I'm wearing black knee-length riding boots. It's not my most elegant dress, but it's flattering. The corset definitely emphasizes my curves.

I look back out the window and see nothing but the trees. "I'm sorry, Elizabeth, but I have to go now." I make my way toward the door.

"Well, I was hoping I could go with you today," she says quietly, her eyes pleading.

"Fine, I'll take you with me, but I'm going to find Mary. Maybe you can find some friends to run around with when we get there."

Crowds of people converge around us as we make our way into the market. Some people I recognize, but many are wealthy visitors; dressed in vibrantly colored tunics, dresses, cloaks and turbans. The summer festival always brings hundreds of people from other villages in Silveria to sell and purchase goods.

The vendors are set up outlining the square shape of

the market, selling everything from cloth, armor, swords, shields, fruits, vegetables, grains, livestock, ribbons and jewelry. Faygrene's permanent shops are a little ways behind them, their doors open wide as people pour through them as well. In the center of the market, minstrels are playing flutes, harps and violins. Their smiling faces are red, and shining with sweat. The walls of the market are draped with black and gold tapestries that are adorned with the Berrenger family crest: a winged lion.

Elizabeth and I continue to make our way past several booths along the eastern wall. We pass a toothless elderly woman, draped in a pale grey shawl that matches her thinning hair. Grains in every shade of brown and gold imaginable stand before her on a splintered wooden table. A smile contorts her face as we pass, drool slipping down the side of her open mouth. I smile back, but keep walking.

The next booth is selling chickens and goats. The chickens are held three to a cage and the goats are tied to the wooden legs of the booth. They look broken down, defeated. I wish I could cut their ties. My eyes land on their vendor. He's sitting on a cracking, wooden stool with his back leaning against the stone wall and his legs propped up on the booth. One of his hands is resting on his dirt-stained, white tunic, which is barely covering his bloated stomach. The other scarred and weather-beaten hand holds a turkey leg to his bearded mouth. He chews on the meat and the grease drips down his face, dampening the strands of his light brown beard. His blue eyes follow me as I pass. I turn my head and move us diagonally to the northern wall of vendors.

The first booth we approach is filled with jewelry. Elizabeth stops to examine an onyx hairpin. Though it's beautiful, I don't feel drawn to the jewelry and want to keep moving, but Elizabeth could stay at this booth all day.

"I'm going to walk around. I won't go far. Stay in the market," I tell her. She nods, her attention completely absorbed in the gold, silver, and gems in front of her. I leave her with her decorations and make my way farther down the line of vendors.

A streak of light shines toward my eyes, momentarily blinding me. I turn and find myself captivated by the most stunning dagger I've ever seen. Intricate vines are carved into the delicate silver blade, making it seem as though they're growing around the blade. The vining pattern continues on the silver handle, along with shining emeralds, shaped like green leaves. I reach my hand out and slowly run my fingers along the length of the blade.

"Careful. Though it looks delicate, it's rather sharp."

I glance up and find myself staring into the face of a young man with sandy blond hair and dark brown eyes. He's very handsome and startlingly familiar. He gives me a flirtatious smile as he casually leans next to me, against the counter of the booth.

"Do I know you?" I blurt, without thinking.

The young man laughs while running his fingers along a spiraled shield. "No, but I know of you,

Addalynne Troyer."

"How do you know my name?" I ask, feeling completely caught off guard.

"My father has told me about you. He did a decent job of describing you. Although, I have to admit, you're much more beautiful than I imagined."

I feel the blush spread along my face and fight the urge to look away.

"I'm Charles Berrenger, Lord and . . ." he pauses and his face momentarily pulls with pain, but as quickly as it comes, it's replaced with a relaxed smile. "Lady Berrenger's son."

I remember hearing about Lord and Lady Berrenger's son. He left Faygrene thirteen years ago, at the age of ten, in order to be educated in the capitol. I was only four when he left, and have no memory of the boy he was, though Gregory may remember him.

Charles reaches out his hand to me. I place my hand in his and he slowly brings it up to his mouth. He kisses my hand, and keeps his brown eyes on mine, his gaze piercing.

"Well, that explains why you look so familiar. You resemble your father," I say. Though he has his mother's fair hair, but that's not something I think I should mention. "But I thought you lived in Synereal."

He releases my hand. I drop it down to my side and discreetly wipe the back of it off on my skirt.

"I did. But I finished my schooling and decided to return to Faygrene. I must admit, I'm beginning to think it was a very wise choice." A sideways smile follows his words.

The sound of someone clearing their throat saves me from coming up with a response. I turn in the direction of the noise and see Drake standing on the opposite side of the booth.

"Ah. You must be the young man who owns this booth. We were admiring your craftsmanship. I'm Charles Berrenger." Charles extends his hand to Drake.

Drake reluctantly turns his gaze from me and sets it on Charles. He stares at Charles for a moment, his eyes weary and somewhat dismissive, before finally reaching forward and shaking his hand.

"Drake Walton, and yes, this is my booth." Drake doesn't bother to mask the irritation in his voice.

Why didn't he tell me he was going to have a booth in the festival this year? I open my mouth to ask him, but close it. Now doesn't feel like the right time.

I stretch my hand back over to the dagger, my fingers itching to hold it, while I try to think of something to say to help break the heavy tension that has settled over us. Animosity is pouring off Drake, and it's making me flushed and uncomfortable.

"How much is this dagger of yours?" Charles asks, his voice light and friendly. "This beautiful young lady is rather enamored with it and I would like to purchase it for her."

Drake swiftly takes hold of the dagger and looks it over for a moment before setting his cold, green eyes back on Charles. "This dagger's not for sale," he says firmly, and he begins to flip it through the air, catching it by its handle.

"Oh, I believe everything can be bought for the right price."

Drake continues to flip the dagger in the air, his gaze never leaving Charles. "Perhaps where you're from that's true, but here in Faygrene some things can't be bought, no matter the price offered." He stops flipping the dagger and pushes it down into his belt, his arms crossing over his chest.

They stare at each other in silence for several long seconds. Charles's gaze is no longer kind and inviting—it has turned cold and calculating. I'm half expecting them to begin comparing sword lengths when Charles speaks.

"I see." Charles turns to me and plants a charming smile on his face while he reaches for my hand once more.

"Addalynne, it was a pleasure to meet you. I'm sure I'll see you again very soon." He raises my hand to his lips and kisses it again. But this time he's not looking at me as he kisses my hand. He's looking sideways at Drake, and his eyes are filled with an unspoken challenge. I'm more than relieved when he lets go of my hand, turns on his heel and walks away.

Drake's eyes are on me when I slowly turn to face him and they're filled with questions. I watch as the questions fade from his eyes, replaced instead by a distant look that sends shivers down my spine. He averts his gaze to the people behind me while brushing his hand through his hair.

"I thought you weren't going to come to the market

today. I waited for you, but you never came." His hands move to grip the edge of the booth, causing the muscles in his arms to stand out, tense and firm.

"I wasn't going to come, but Elizabeth convinced me and I brought her," I lie, feeling guilty about deceiving him, especially now with that look in his eyes. "Why didn't you tell me you were going to have a booth?"

"Maybe I would have told you if you would have stopped avoiding me."

"I'm not avoiding you."

He raises one eyebrow in question, but doesn't pursue the topic. My half-hearted response tells him the truth. I have been avoiding him, but it's only because I hate being made to feel like a vulnerable maiden in need of protection. And though I know he didn't mean what he said when we had our fight last year, his actions continue to bring back those words. I want him to be with me because he wants my company, not because he thinks I need protection.

Drake moves his hand to his side and grasps the hilt of the dagger. He pulls it out of his belt and places it in a black leather sheath. "Here, it's yours," he says as he extends it to me.

"But, you said . . ."

"I said that it wasn't for sale and it's not. I made it for you. Father must have accidentally brought it out here with the rest of the daggers." He moves around the side of the booth and comes to a stop directly in front of me. His gaze remains locked on mine as he reaches down and grabs my hand. He holds it in his for a moment, his expression unreadable. A rush of heat and anticipation sears through my body. All I can think about is his hand and my hand and how I don't want to let go. I involuntarily lean toward him, wanting to be closer, needing to be closer. He looks down, breaking my trance, and gently places the hilt of the dagger in my hand. With one last distant look, he drops my hand and walks away.

I stay where I am, feeling stunned and hollow. I don't know what to think about my relationship with Drake anymore. It has become so strained. Frustration and angst seem to dominate the comfort we used to bring each other, and I often find myself fighting for air and control.

With a drawn-out breath, I reach down, lift the bottom of my skirt, and place my dagger in the top of my boot. I didn't even thank him for it.

I straighten myself out and force myself to make my way through the packed market, trying to focus on finding Elizabeth. But she's no longer at the jewelry stand where I left her. I turn back to Drake's booth. My uncle is there now, conversing with a group of men in vibrantly colored turbans. Again, the look Drake had in his eyes before he walked away from me flashes in my mind, and I feel nauseous. I have a growing fear that he's slipping away from me. I have to find him. I have to try to replace the distant look in his eyes with the look of affection and trust I'm so used to seeing in them.

My new resolve allows me to move through the crowd with more determination. But then the bells in the market begin to toll, and I stop. Three tolls means there's an important announcement to be made by the Squire. Six tolls means there's been an arrest, and a prisoner is going to be brought to the center stage of the market for sentencing. Ten tolls means there's a village meeting being called. I count the tolls now, as they ring. One . . . two . . . three . . . four . . . five . . . six . . . silence. The minstrels are forced off the stage by several guardsmen, who are ushering up a filthy, elderly man, dressed in rags and covered in dirt. Behind him is Lord Berrenger, dressed in his navy silk cloak, his graying hair covered by a feathered cap, preparing to address the crowd.

"Ladies and Gentlemen of Faygrene, this man has been caught stealing. It's up to you to decide how he shall be punished." Many people call out their recommendations. I block them out as I search through the crowd, looking for Drake. Out of the corner of my eye, I see red hair. Elizabeth is with Mother and Father, moving closer to the stage. I feel guilty for not finding her sooner, but at least she's not wandering around on her own. I look away from my family and continue on my mission to find Drake. I'm sure he hasn't stayed to watch the sentencing of the prisoner, and I don't want to either. I've seen enough in my seventeen years to know that these things rarely end well.

I make my way out of the crowded market place and head toward the woods. I don't know where else to look for him and can only hope he's gone there. Even with the uncertainty that seems to have grown between us, the woods have remained our place, and I have kept my promise to never go in without him.

As I approach the woods and our gate, I see a dark figure leaning against it. I break into a run, hoping with everything in me that it's him. Once I'm closer, I recognize the familiar dark, tousled hair, and the stiff but still casual stance that could only belong to Drake. Relief streams through me. He wouldn't have come here if he didn't want me to find him. Maybe he hasn't left me yet.

His head flies up and his eyes widen with surprise when he sees me running toward him. I run into his arms, crashing into his body, but he's strong and steady, and his arms are ready to catch me. We stay there for an immeasurable moment, rooted in a crushing embrace.

"I'm so sorry," I whisper.

"What do you have to be sorry for?" He gently pulls away from me, just enough to look into my face.

"I . . . I don't know really, but you seemed upset with me and I don't want you to be." I speak honestly, a tear slowly slipping from my eye. He releases a humorless laugh and gently wipes my tear with his thumb, his hand lingering on my cheek.

"Addy, you did nothing wrong. It's me. I'm the one who's been wrong, and I'm sorry." His face is filled with sorrow.

"What could you have possibly been wrong about? You have done nothing wrong. You have always been there for me, protecting me, going along with all my ridiculous plans." I offer him a small smile, and get a crooked one in return but it seems forced.

"Not always," he says quietly, and I know he's remembering what he said to me when we fought and how much it hurt me.

"Both of us have made mistakes, Drake. I just . . . I just want us back."

"Addy," he says with a shake of his head and a sad laugh. "If you only knew."

"If I only knew what?"

He rubs his palms across his face. "Nothing. Just . . . don't worry about it. From now on things will return to normal between us. I promise." He drops his hands to his side and a small smile forms on his lips. His eyes are still weary, but at least they're no longer distant.

"Good, because when Gregory leaves next month it's going to be hard for me and I'm going to need my friend," I say as I lean my head against his chest. I hear him murmur something that sounds like the word "friend," but it's hard to tell. He lets out a breath and rhythmically runs his fingers through my hair. I close my eyes and let the strong beat of his heart comfort me while I try to push away the sense of unease. Too soon he pulls away.

"We need to get back to the market. People have probably been looking for us." He grabs hold of my hand and intertwines his fingers in mine.

"All right, but I want to stop by my home first to grab a few extra coins to buy Elizabeth something nice." My mind drifts to the onyx hairpin. "I feel bad about leaving her."

Drake nods his head, and we begin walking toward

my home.

"Thank you, by the way, for the dagger. It's perfect."

"You're welcome," he says, giving my hand a gentle squeeze. "It will give you a way to protect yourself, in case I'm not there." *Why wouldn't he be there?* I feel the trepidation returning, but tell myself I'm being foolish.

"So is this your way of telling me that you're no longer going to follow me everywhere?" I say with a forced laugh, and gently nudge him with my shoulder. He smiles back, but it doesn't reach his eyes.

"I have to let you go sometime," he says, mostly to himself, as we approach my front door. "Go on in. I'll wait here for you."

I hesitantly walk into my home, haunted by his words, hating what they imply. As soon as I walk into my chambers, I open my window and try to breathe in some fresh air and clear my head. *You're overreacting. They're only words. He doesn't mean anything by them. Everything will be fine.*

After several deep breaths, I gather some coins from my table and tuck them into a hidden pocket in my skirt. Next, I carefully remove the dagger from my boot. My hands are trembling while I remove it from its sheath and rotate it, examining every precious detail. It must have taken him months to perfect the intricate pattern of the vines. I study the pattern and watch it lead up to the emerald leaves. The color of the stones matches his eyes and leaves me with a feeling of longing so deep it takes my breath away.

"Drake! How are you, my boy?" My father's voice

carries into my chambers through the open window, startling me. I move closer, straining my ears to listen.

"I'm well, thank you. How are you, sir?"

"I'm wonderful! Especially now that I've spoken with Gregory," my father replies joyfully. "He told me you and Walter are joining the Schild with him. Is this true?"

What's my father talking about? Drake isn't leaving! He can't be! He would have told me if he were! I gasp for air. *No! My father has to be wrong!* I drop the dagger onto the bed and grab the wall for support, forcing myself to listen, waiting for Drake to tell my father that Gregory's wrong, that he's not leaving.

"Yes, sir. Gregory was very happy when I told him."

I can't listen anymore. I push myself out the window and when my feet land on the ground, I run, heading for the only place I can find peace.

Chapter 9

HER

Alone. I haven't been alone in these woods for what feels like a lifetime. I need it now. I need to feel the presence of the trees and nothing else.

I try to slow my breathing and push the haze out of my head.

He's leaving. In six weeks, both of them will be gone. The thought is painful enough to bring me to my knees, but I force myself to keep moving. I push the pain away and focus instead on the anger. Anger is easier to deal with, and I'm not just angry, I'm furious.

I'm furious that he hasn't told me. I feel completely betrayed. I thought he was my best friend, but how do you keep something like this from someone who's supposed to be that important to you? We have all known for half a year about my brother's plans to leave, and we all knew Walter was considering it, but Drake never mentioned any interest in leaving.

This means that Gregory has been lying to me as well. He's known for who knows how long that Drake was going to go with him. Maybe he's the one who convinced him to go. And now they've told my parents. Why have I been the one kept in the dark about all this?

"Addy!" The sound of Drake's voice leaves me feeling as though all the breath has been taken from me. "Addalynne, where are you?"

There's distinct desperation in his voice, and a searing pain throbs in my chest. I didn't know it was actually possible to feel your heart break. My eyes burn and I swallow back the lump in my throat. Everything in me wants to answer him, but I can't. I don't think I would be able to look at him without breaking down completely.

"Addy, I know you're in here and I know you can hear me! I'm not leaving! I'll look for you all day if I have to!"

I look around for a good place to hide. But I'm at the Glass River now, near the Grey Tree, so there really isn't one. I sit down and lean my back against a large oak that's about twenty feet away from the Grey Tree.

Calm down. I need to calm down. I close my eyes and picture myself at the ocean. I imagine the feel of the moist breeze blowing gently across my face. I breathe in the smell of salt water and watch dolphins jump through the waves. I dig my fingers into the warm sand and wish the pain away.

The warmth of the sand sweeps across my fingers,

bringing with it an instant calm. It feels incredibly real. I let out a sigh, knowing I've succeeded in pushing back the tears and gaining control. I let the ocean fade away, but the warmth and light pressure on my left hand is still there. I can't be imagining it. It's far too real.

My eyes open. Drake is next to me, leaning against the same tree, his hand on top of mine, radiating a warmth so endearing it breaks my heart. His eyes are closed, his face a blank mask. I'll never understand how he can move so silently. If I weren't so accustomed to the strong beat of his heart, I would think he was a ghost.

"Why didn't you come to me when I called you?" he asks cautiously, his eyes still closed. I don't trust myself to speak, so I wait for him to continue. "You should have come. It's not safe for you to be in here alone, especially this close to the river." He opens his eyes and turns his head toward me.

"I've been coming into these woods my entire life and nothing has ever happened. Besides, I'm going to have no choice but to come in here alone once you leave. Isn't that why you made me the dagger?" I fix my gaze on him, my eyes telling him not to lie to me.

He moves from my side and comes to a crouch directly in front of me. The green leaves of the trees blow in the breeze behind him, their trunks surrounding us like legs of giants waiting to stomp us into the ground.

His dark hair is stuck to his forehead, damp with sweat, his full lips pursed in thought, his eyebrows scrunched together in consternation. The green of his eyes is made all the more striking by the flush of his cheeks, and it's to those burning emeralds that I'm drawn now.

"What do you know about my leaving?"

I take a deep breath and consider my answer. I could avoid his question and walk away, or I could confront him about his plans to leave. I may as well get the pain over with. Besides, just because someone is afraid of looking directly into the flames of a fire, doesn't mean it will stop burning.

"You're leaving with my brother and Walter to join the King's Schild. I won't see you for years, if I ever see you again at all, and you didn't even tell me." I wait for him to respond, searching his face, but it's carefully arranged to give nothing away.

"What did you overhear?"

"It doesn't matter. It's true, isn't it?" Please tell me it's not true, that somehow this is all a terrible misunderstanding.

"Yes. It's true."

My body begins to tremble. I don't want him to notice, so I push myself off the ground and walk away, wrapping my arms protectively around myself, trying to physically keep myself from falling apart.

"I'm sorry I didn't tell you," he calls after me. "The truth is, I didn't know how to tell you, but on some level you had to have known I was considering it. You know how badly I want to learn about my past, about who I am. If I travel to Synereal, I may see something that triggers my memory, or I might be able to talk to someone who can give me answers." His voice is replete with urgency, pleading with me to understand. "If I could go without joining, I would, but you know I can't. I could never afford to travel that far on my own."

I think about his words and about how desperate he is to discover his past. I could help him. I could tell him what I know, and maybe then he would stay. But then he would hate me for never telling him the truth before. I really am the biggest hypocrite. Here I am, angry with him for not telling me about his decision to join the King's Schild, yet I have lied to him for over four years.

I stop walking. My body is facing the Glass River, facing the exact spot from where I saw him stagger out of the fog. He approaches and stands behind me, close enough for me to feel his breath on my cheek.

"Can you really blame me for taking a chance to go somewhere that may be able to help me? You know if I stay here I'll never learn about my past. I'll never be able to remember, and no one will be able to help me."

His words hit me like a slap across my face. This time I can't stop the tears. I keep my back to him, not wanting him to see me cry. I don't think I could handle his pity right now. His hand slowly brushes my hair off the back of my neck, sending a shiver down my spine. He grabs hold of my shoulder and turns me to face him. Though my body is facing his now, I keep my sight on the ground, staring at the leaves and rocks that mix together in an erratic pattern of brown, grey, and green. He places his fingers under my chin and gently draws my head up to look at him. In his eyes I see the same sadness and guilt that I feel reflected back at me.

"Please don't be angry with me," he pleads, while reaching out and brushing my hair behind my ear. He's hurting because he hurt me. I'm hurting because he's leaving me. He feels guilty because he didn't tell me. I feel guilty because I have kept my own secrets from him.

I try to smile. "I'm not angry with you. I understand why you want to leave. I just wish you would have told me."

"I know I should have told you and I am sorry." His eyes burn with sincerity. He's desperate for my forgiveness, just as I will be desperate for his if I tell him the truth I've been hiding.

Looking up at him, I think about him leaving me and I can't stand it. The thought of not being able to look into his face every day, or hear his voice, or feel the sturdiness of his arms, is more than I can take. But he doesn't have to leave. Maybe, if he knew the truth about how I found him, it would be enough to keep him here. It would give him a clue to his past and show him that most of his answers probably lie in Incarnadine. He'll have to understand that going there isn't an option, not when it's so dangerous. And, though I know he'll be angry with me, he can't stay mad at me forever. Besides, if it makes him stay, it will be worth it.

"What if I could tell you more about where you came from? What if some of your answers lie here? Would you still leave?" I force out the words before I can convince myself otherwise.

"What are you talking about? He asks, his face taking on a look of confusion.

I turn my back to him again. I'll never be able to tell him the truth if I'm looking at him. "I haven't been completely honest with you about how I found you," I say very quietly. But he heard me. I know he did, because his breathing completely stops. My heart races. I don't think it has ever beaten this fast before. I wonder how much it can take before it gives out.

After what feels like an eternity, he finds his voice.

"What do you mean you haven't been honest with me? What haven't you been honest about?" There's a tremble in his voice, but I can't tell if it's from fear or anger. *Please don't hate me.*

"I'll tell you everything, but please don't say anything until I'm finished." I stare out across the river, into the fog, and start to relive that day.

"I was sitting in the Grey Tree, looking out over the southern bank of the river, when I saw you. You weren't floating on a log in the river. You were walking through the fog on the southern side, on the forbidden side, in Incarnadine. You were stumbling and dazed. When you reached the river, you fell to your knees and dunked your arms in. They were covered in blood and so was your tunic. After a few seconds, you fell over, unconscious, into the water. I jumped in and pulled you out."

I wait for him to speak, to say anything. My body is trembling and I don't know how much longer my legs will hold me.

"Why did you lie to me?" His voice slightly breaks with his words, and another tear slides down my face. "You know how desperate I've been to find out about my past, about who I am. You have known better than anyone how much it hurts me to not remember, and you lied to me." His voice is drenched in complete fury. The least I can do is show him the dignity of looking him in the eye. I owe him that much.

I slowly make my body turn to face his and his eyes meet mine. The pupils have taken over most of his beautiful green irises, consuming them in darkness.

"How many times did I ask you, Addalynne, if there was anything else, anything at all that you remembered? How could you lie to me for all these years?" His voice is low, rough, and flooded with hurt and anger. The pain tears through me. I feel as though I'm a piece of glass with a crack spreading across me, spidering off in all directions, waiting to shatter me completely. I have to make him understand.

"I had to! If I hadn't lied, they would have taken you away from me! They would have never let you stay if they knew you came from Incarnadine, and I couldn't stand the thought of you leaving me! I couldn't let them take you away, so I lied! I lied so I could keep you, so I would never have to lose you!" Our eyes are locked on each other, our chests heaving with our breaths.

"And now?" he asks, his eyes blazing.

"And now what?" My voice cracks with desperation and pain.

"Now do you still feel the same way? About me leaving?" His eyes are no longer angry. They still hold a deep intensity, but there's another emotion there as well, one I cannot place. I know now that I can't lie to him again. I have to start being honest with him, and myself.

"Of course I do. From the very first moment I saw you, a part of you crawled its way inside me and never left. I can't begin to think about what life would be like without you here. I didn't want to lose you then and I cannot bear to lose you now."

I watch his face change, igniting with hope and determination. He moves forward, closing the space between us, and comes to a stop inches away from me. The setting sun creates a cascade of shadows across his face. He's so beautiful it hurts. I realize now how much I've been lying to myself. My feelings for Drake haven't been feelings of only friendship for a long time. I was just too naive to recognize it. I know now why no other boys ever interested me. The only boy I've ever been interested in is him, and everyone else saw it, except for me. But I see it now. And maybe, just maybe, he wants me too.

He slowly reaches his hand up to my face. His fingers brush along my cheekbone and down to my jaw. They continue to brush down the length of my neck and down my side, stopping only when his hand is resting on my hip. His breath is unsteady as he stares down at me, and my body ignites with a yearning stronger than I could have ever imagined. I love him. And that means I have to let him go. My heart breaks with my realization.

He slowly leans down, his lips moving closer to mine. I turn as fast as I can and walk away.

What did I just do? The only thing I want is to run back into his arms and kiss him myself, but I can't. I can't give in to what I want because it would hold him back. He deserves to know who he is. He'll never be completely happy until he remembers his past, and maybe King Theoderic will be able to help him. He knows about Incarnadine, he might be able to help Drake get answers. He has to go to Synereal. I can't make him stay here for me any longer. Now that I've fully realized how much I love him, I can no longer let myself be selfish.

I turn back to him. His hand is still extended in front of him, where I was standing, and the look on his face is one of pure despair. It kills me to know that I'm the one who caused it. I have to stop hurting him.

He drops his head into his hands. "What are you doing to me, Addalynne?"

I'm trying to save you from my horribly selfish ways.

Finally, he lowers his hands and looks at me. His cheeks are still slightly flushed, but the emptiness has returned to his eyes.

"What do you want from me, Addalynne? Just tell me. I need to know what you see when you look at me. Do you only see a friend that you don't want to lose, or do you see more? I need to know, because I see more in you. I have seen more in you for a long time. But now . . . now I don't know what to feel anymore."

I see more, so much more. I see something I never knew I wanted—a life with Drake, not as my friend, but as my everything. But I can't tell him because it would only make things worse. Instead, I focus on answering his first question as I stare at the trunk of a nearby tree.

It's all I can do to keep from falling apart. "I want you to go to Synereal. I want you to try to find out more about who you are. King Theoderic can give you answers. I don't think you should tell him you're from Incarnadine. He seems kind, but there's no way to know how he would react to that information. Still, though, he can tell you much more about Incarnadine than any book can, and maybe it will help you piece something together."

"And what about us, Addalynne? If I leave, what happens to us?"

I should have realized he wouldn't let that part go. I can no longer avoid his gaze or his question. I let myself look at him, hoping I can find the words to say, but no words come. The look on his face erases everything from my mind. All the color has drained from him, leaving him ashy and pale. His eyes are filled with complete terror. But he's not looking at me. He's looking over me, at the southern side of the river. I open my mouth to ask what's wrong, but he cuts me off.

"RUN! RUN, Addalynne!"

I look across the river, squinting into the fog on the southern side. There's something headed toward the river, and it's something massive.

I run, but not toward him like he wants me to. I run to the Grey Tree. The only thing on my mind is finally seeing what it is that everyone has been warning me about all these years.

"Where are you going? We have to get out of here!" Drake chases after me. I reach the trunk of the Grey Tree and start to climb. He gets to the trunk seconds after me and his hands wrap firmly around my hips. I try to hold on, but he pulls me down and restrains me in his arms. I shove him as hard as I can, but his grip doesn't loosen.

"Let go of me!" I shout and continue to push against him.

He responds by readjusting his grip and walking us backward.

"I have waited my entire life to see what's on the other side of that river. I'm not leaving. If you're so afraid you can leave but . . ." his hand clamps down over my mouth, cutting off the rest of my words. He pushes me back against the tree, his body pressed firmly against mine.

"Shhh, don't make a sound," he whispers.

It's close now. Its heavy footsteps and the sound of something dragging fills the air. I have to see it.

I carefully reach my hand down to his belt and wrap my fingers around the hilt of his sword. I begin to pull it out of its sheath, and his body stiffens. He reaches down, grabs hold of my hand and stops my progress. I plead with my eyes, wanting him to understand that I only want to see. He looks at me with contemplation for several seconds. Then he gives a subtle nod, and together we pull out the sword. He lifts it up and angles it in just the right way for me to be able to look into the reflection of the blade.

Nothing could have prepared me for what's mirroring back at me from the sword. Though the image of the hellion on the other side of the river is slightly diluted by the fog, it's still frighteningly clear and far beyond anything I could have ever imagined. It's at least fifteen feet tall, with pale, grey skin that's covered in what appears to be oozing scabs. Bones protrude out of its sunken-in body, and a single, pale, ice blue eye scans the woods around it. Its nose is long and hooked, its teeth pointy as needles. Long arms hang down to the ground, followed by fingers that have claws as large and sharp as the blades of most daggers.

The hellion walks down the bank of the river, moving farther away from us. When we can no longer see it, Drake leans into me, his lips brushing my ear. My body reacts immediately, sending chills down the length of my spine and a tightening in my stomach.

"Now's our chance. We need to move quickly and quietly."

I nod, and we begin to move away from the river.

We have only moved a few feet when my foot presses down on a stick, inevitably causing it to snap. We both freeze. Drake stares at my immobile form, his face paling. The hellion's heavy footsteps hasten, the sound growing louder as it moves straight for us. Drake pulls on my hand, forcing me to run.

Suddenly, a shot of pain stabs my ankle and I'm swiftly swung off my feet. I scream as my body flies into the air, the branches of the trees blurring past my vision. Seconds later, my body slams back into the ground. Pain shoots through me and I gasp for air.

"Addalynne!" Drake shouts. I try to stand, but something is wrapped around my ankle and it's pulling me back toward the river. I dig my fingers into the dirt on the ground, trying to find something, anything, to anchor me, but there's nothing, and my fingers rake painfully through the dirt as I'm pulled.

Hands wrap around mine and I see Drake. He pulls me toward him, making my body the rope in a game of tug of war that Drake is quickly losing. My hands slip completely out of his grasp, and his face contorts into pure terror and rage. I scream for him, and he yells something in return, but I can't make out what it is.

I manage to flip my body around. A grey, snake-like vine is wrapped around my ankle. Its inch long thorns have already cut through my boot and are piercing into my skin, sending stabs of pain into my flesh. I wrap my fingers around the vine and pull as hard as I can manage, but it's covered in a thick slime, causing my fingers to slip off. My gaze follows the vine all the way through the fog and into the hazy opening of the hellion's mouth. With utter horror, I realize that it's not a vine at all; it's the hellion's tongue. I scream louder, completely overcome with terror. Out of the corner of my eye I see a tree branch that's hanging low to the ground. I reach out and grab onto it, desperately trying to hold myself in place. The hellion pulls harder, its tongue cutting deeper into my ankle, sending a burning pain through my entire body. I grip the branch as tightly as I can, but the skin on my palms tears, and my hold on the branch is ripped away.

Drake sprints past me and comes to a stop in front of me, his sword raised. He swiftly brings the sword down, stabbing it into the hellion's tongue. The agonized screams of the hellion fills the sky with the most abominable screeching I've ever heard. I place my hands over my ears and watch as blood flows from its tongue. It seeps through the ground, like thin red snakes slithering toward me. The blood reaches my foot and burns through my boot, melting the leather away. When the blood reaches my skin, I scream in agony. It feels as though my flesh and bone are being eaten away by a thousand razor-teethed insects. I blink against the pain and watch Drake sever the rest of the tongue. Then, he runs toward me and lifts me in his arms.

I feel my body moving through the forest, but there's a strange weightlessness taking hold. I stare up at the tops of the trees as I try to stay conscious, but my vision is blurring. All I see around me are tendrils of vines crawling down the trees, through a dark grey fog, trying to pull me back in. I hear Drake speaking and myself screaming, and I feel my body thrashing in his arms, but my mind feels separated from it. I try to find the sunlight to calm myself, but when I look up, I see that it's starting to rain. As the rain falls, I realize that it's not rain at all. It's blood and it's burning me, sending searing pain all over my body. I wish for death as the darkness pulls me under.

* * *

Hands, more hands touching me, pulling me, moving me. Most of them I don't want. There's one set of hands though, one set that I feel on me. These hands are welcome. They calm me in a way no one else's do. But I don't know whose they are. Recognition pulls at me, but as quickly as it comes rushing in, it slips away. The only thing I'm aware of is the pain, the constant pain. I gratefully slip back into the darkness.

* * *

"I don't know if she's going to make it," someone is speaking now, but I don't recognize the voice.

"She's a fighter. If anyone can survive this, she can," a female replies. She sounds familiar, but I'm not sure who she is.

"She's not going to die!" a third voice yells. It's a voice I know very well. I try to turn toward it, but as soon as I move, a burning pain flashes through my body. An awful wailing noise is around me now. I don't know who's making it, but I wish they would stop. Hands again, more hands touching me, but those hands are there, too, the ones that I want. Those hands go with the voice I heard, except now it's not angry. Now it's telling me that I'm safe, that I'm going to be fine. The wailing noise stops, and my body begins to relax. I fall back into a deep sleep.

* * *

I'm walking through the woods, but a heavy fog is

pressing in on me, making it difficult to see. Every step I take is eerily silent—no leaves stirring the wind, no birds sending their song into the air. These are not my woods; these woods offer no comfort. I feel empty here. Loneliness pours in from every direction.

I'm looking for someone, but I can't remember who. I turn around, hoping that if I head in the opposite direction, I'll find whoever it is I'm looking for. But my path is blocked by others. I don't know who they are, but their presence sends biting chills down my spine. Their lifeless black eyes are fixed on my face and they begin to move around me, their grey, skeletal arms reaching for me. All at once, they start calling my name in a wailing chorus. I try to back away from them, but there are more of them behind me, trapping me. Suddenly, there's movement in the trees above. I look up and see his face looking down at me, but just as quickly, he's gone.

"Drake!" I scream, as I wrap my arms protectively around myself. The others are moving closer to me now. "Go away!" I shout, and I break into a run, trying desperately to find a way through them. Their fingers brush against my skin, burning my flesh. "Leave me alone!"

They're grabbing me now, pressing against me, forcing me down onto the hard ground. Their weight suffocates me as my body sinks farther. "Drake," I call his name one last time, before the dirt fills my mouth, choking me. My vision disappears, sending me into darkness.

Chapter 10

HIM

She looks so lifeless. If it weren't for the flush of pink in her cheeks and her shallow breaths, I would think she was . . . no . . . I refuse to finish the thought. Lowering my head to her chest, I listen to her heartbeat. The sound of it beating is my only salvation. What she has been through would have killed most people, but not Addalynne. She *will* get through this.

I take her hand between mine. Her body is clearly still burning with fever, which makes me sick. This is my fault. If it weren't for me, she would have never gone into the woods. Instead, my carelessness and stupidity once again got the better of me, and she paid the price. I'll never forgive myself for not keeping her safe.

I let go of her hand and drop my head into my own, trying to make myself breathe. She's been in and out of consciousness for over a month, her mind clouded with hallucinations brought on by the poison and fever. Doctor Ellers says she's out of the worst of it and that she'll fully recover, but when? Every time she wakes up, I pray she'll stay conscious, that she'll fully return to us, to me. But she always slips back into the darkness.

"Please wake up, Addy," I plead. "You can be angry with me. I deserve it. But wake up. Let me hear your voice. You can scream at me, call me names. It doesn't matter, as long as I get to hear your voice." I lift my head and stare into her dormant face.

"Gregory and Walter are leaving in two days," I continue. "I'm not going with them. I'm staying here, with you. I'm going to be here for you, in whatever form you need. If you only want a friend, I'll be that for you. I won't push you to be more and I won't let my jealousy get in the way anymore. I'll do and be whatever you want. Just come back to me. You told me that you were going to need your friend when Gregory leaves. Well, I need my friend, too. I can't do this without you, Addy." I close my eyes and lean my head against the edge of her bed, trying to find any feelings of regret about my decision to no longer leave, but there are none. I know I'm making the right decision. The only thing Synereal holds for me are possible keys to my past, but my past can't compete with my present or my future, and Addalynne is both. I won't leave her.

A quiet moan escapes her lips. My head snaps up, my heart hammering in my chest. I wait for her lips to move again, my breath turning to dust in my throat, but she's as still as one of Elizabeth's dolls, her mind pulled back into a dream. I release my breath and notice that her black hair has begun to stick to her face. I gently brush it away and reach for the cloth her mother has been putting on her forehead to help with the fever. I dunk it in the cold water, ring out the excess, and place it on her forehead. Then I pick up her hand, and continue to wait.

Several minutes later, the door opens behind me.

"I heard you'll no longer be leaving with Gregory and Walter" The voice of Addalynne's father, Robert, drifts toward me, followed by his heavy footsteps. I keep my gaze fixed on Addalynne, refusing to look away from her.

"Yes, sir. I've decided to stay."

"I understand your decision," he says as he sits on the edge of Addalynne's bed. I glance over at him and watch his eyes linger on his daughter. He's trying to hide his fear, but I see it as clearly as I feel my own.

"You love my daughter," he continues, and I return my gaze to Addalynne's face. "That has been obvious to me for a few years."

This takes me by surprise. "How is that possible when I didn't even realize it myself until last year?"

"It was always clear from the way you looked at her. It was like you were seeing her for the first time every time. And then there's the way you watched over her. So protective. You were constantly aware of what she was doing, where she was going. Not to mention how mindful you were of others who began to show interest in her. I'm an observant man, Drake. Especially when it comes to my children."

I think back on all our years together. Sure, I

watched over her, but so did Gregory. Being protective doesn't mean I was in love with her. Then I think about me being "aware." I did always try to know where she was, or what she was doing. And when our friend, John, began to express interest in her, I became overwhelmed with what I thought was anger, but now realize was jealousy. I all but forced him to find someone else to pursue.

Robert's right. I have been in love with her for years. I just didn't know it until the day of our fight; when I realized that I could lose her to someone else. Every day since then I have watched her converse with other men, knowing they wanted more than her words. Every time one of them kissed her hand, or leaned in too close, complete rage burned inside me. The feelings I had stirring in me were no longer near that of an over-protective friend. I was dominated by jealousy.

I wanted to be the one to wrap my arms around her and never let go, to press my mouth against hers, and place my entire life in the curve of her lips. There have been so many times over the last year that I have looked at her and wanted to tell her how much I love her. If only I had been able to, would we be here now, with her fighting for her life, and me helpless to save her?

"I do love your daughter, sir. And I swear to you that I will never let any harm come to her, ever again," I finally respond to Robert. I already failed her once, but I will never fail her again.

"I know you wouldn't, Drake. I would never have to worry about her well-being if she were with you, but do you really believe this decision of yours is a wise one? I know my daughter loves you. She has always loved you and has always been fiercely protective of you, but you have to ask yourself if it's the same love you have for her. My daughter is loyal, brave, strong and kind, but she's also easily distracted and always looking for something new to excite her. When you came around, it was the most fascinating thing this village had seen in a very long time. And she was the one who found you, so she claimed you as hers immediately. You were her new, mysterious toy, and no one else could have you." He chuckles sadly and then shakes his head. "Tell me Drake, what will happen when that mystery wears off? What will happen when someone new comes around? Will she stay with you, or will she abandon you for someone or something more exciting?

"Now, I love my daughter, you know that, and I love you as well. You're family to me, and there's nothing I want more than your happiness. That's why I want you to be cautious."

I look over at Robert and his eyes meet mine.

"I could be wrong, Drake. She may love you as much as you love her. But these things I speak of are possibilities. You know her better than anyone. So ask yourself if you're positive that she'll stay by your side forever. If you're not, don't give up this opportunity to possibly find some answers about your past."

Robert's words spread like ice through my veins. He stands and moves around the side of the bed and places his hand on Addalynne's cheek.

I swallow against my discomfort. "I understand what you're saying, sir, but I have already accepted the fact that she may not return my feelings. If friendship is all she wants from me, that's what I'll give her."

Robert turns toward me, his face skeptical, but sympathetic, as though he's watching a fatally wounded deer struggle to stand. "Think about what you're saying, Drake. Picture her with someone else. Would you be content to stand in the background, being her 'friend' while she falls in love with him, marries him? Don't sacrifice something as important as your past for an uncertain future. Besides, you can always join the Schild and, after you find your answers, you can return. She's stabilized now, but it may take time for her to fully awaken. Why not spend that time in Synereal? And when you come back, if she's still waiting for you, then you'll know that she loves you as much as you love her." He moves toward me and places his hand on my shoulder. It's meant to be comforting, but it feels like iron. "Whatever you decide, all I ask is that you be sure it's the best decision for both of you." He gives my shoulder a gentle squeeze before turning to leave the room.

"Oh, I almost forgot," Robert says as he opens the door, and I turn around to face him. "Did Gregory tell you about the prisoner?"

"No. What prisoner?"

"The one from Incarnadine."

His words swim in my head like a rough current, beating against me. "Incarnadine?"

"Yes. They found him hiding in the woods on the outskirts of the capital. He's being held in Synereal for questioning. Addalynne would have been so excited." He smiles, but there's a deep sorrow to it. "Anyway, I thought maybe you could tell her. If she could listen to anyone while in this state, it would be you. And maybe it will give her a reason to wake up." With that he turns and leaves the room. I wait until he shuts the door behind him, then let out a breath and drop my head into my hands. My hands wrap around my hair, pulling.

What am I going to do? If the prisoner is really from Incarnadine, he could have answers for me, but the only way I can get those answers is to join the Schild and go to Synereal with Gregory and Walter. But if I join the Schild then I have to leave Addalynne. Then there's what Robert said. Would Addalynne leave me if someone new and exciting came along? Would she turn her back on me at the promise of adventure?

No, she would never do that. She loves me. I know she does. I saw it in her eyes and I heard it in her voice when she told me she didn't want to lose me.

But then I tried to kiss her, and she pulled away and told me I should leave. Then, when the hellion came, I called for her, but it wasn't my arms she ran to, she ran toward the Grey Tree, toward adventure. Dread courses through me. I could be wrong. What am I supposed to do? I lay my head down and press it against our intertwined hands, breathing in her scent.

Robert wants me to make the best decision for both of us? But how can I possibly know what that would be?

I hope that it would be my staying, and our being together. At the first sign of her reciprocating my feelings, I would ask Robert for her hand in marriage. But is that what she would want? What kind of a life can I offer her? I will never be known as anything more than, "the orphan." Besides, the life she wants is not one that confines her within the walls of Faygrene. Can I give her the escape she's always searching for? As a blacksmith, I can surely provide for her, but to travel would be difficult. I don't have the proper status or wealth.

And again, if I stay, I'll lose all hope of learning about my past.

But how can I walk away from her and let go of everything I've wanted for so long? I don't know if I can. But I don't have to leave forever. I can go to Synereal, get my answers and come back to her. Robert said it himself. I can always come back.

My body trembles as I force myself to stand. I have to leave. I have to take this chance to get answers. I owe it to not only myself, but to Addalynne. If we want a chance at a real future together, we have to know the truth of my past.

I look down at Addalynne, taking in every feature of her sleeping form. I memorize the raven-like color of her long, full hair. I trace my fingers along the fair skin of her face, lingering where a few freckles play across her cheeks. They're so light that most people don't notice them, but I've known they were there from the first moment I saw her. I can picture her now, her face inches from mine, her young, amber eyes wide and filled with excitement. Each freckle like a burst of energy. I store each one into memory.

My gaze then travels to her lips, soft and full. Every part of me aches to press my lips against hers. For over a year I have dreamt about what it would be like to part her lips with my own and feel her breath mix with mine. It kills me to think about how close I came to having that dream become a reality, only to watch it disappear. I place the curve of her lips into another part of my mind, where I'll protect it forever.

Lastly, I look at her closed eyes. Her eyelashes are brushing against her cheeks, sealing her eyes off from me. More than anything, I wish I could see them one last time before I leave, but I know it's impossible.

Leaning down, I gently press my lips to her forehead. "Goodbye, Addy," I whisper, forcing myself to let go. Because the truth is, though I know I'll return, I don't know when. I don't know how long this journey will take. All I can do is pray that she'll wait for me.

I don't let myself look back while I walk toward the door. If I do, I'll never be able to leave. My hand reaches for the door knob. I close my eyes and focus on breathing, pushing back every instinct I have that's telling me to go back to her. It takes all my strength, but I manage to open the door.

I slowly make my way to the front room where Addalynne's family is sitting. "Robert, may I speak with you?"

"Of course, my boy." Robert rises from his chair and walks toward me.

I turn and head to the kitchen, where we can have some privacy. "I've decided to leave with Gregory and Walter," I say as soon as we walk into the kitchen. Robert's face is carefully composed. "But," I continue. "I want you to tell Addalynne that I *will* return. I'm only leaving long enough to get some answers. Then I'll come back to be with her, if she'll have me. I'm going to write her a letter, explaining everything, but I want to make sure she knows. Please tell her."

Robert nods his head in understanding. "It will be the first thing I do when she wakes up."

"Thank you, Robert." I reach my hand out to shake his, but he pulls me in for a hug instead.

"Take care of yourself, Drake."

"I will."

As we walk out of the kitchen, Genoveve and Elizabeth rise to their feet, their faces tightened with confusion.

I walk toward Elizabeth and wrap my arms around her. "You be careful, all right. Don't go running around with any boys." I try to laugh, but it gets stuck in my throat.

"Why are you saying that?" she asks, but I can't answer. Instead, I plant a gentle kiss on her forehead and then turn toward Genoveve. She wraps her arms around me with the comfort and understanding only a mother can provide. I don't need to say anything to her. She already knows what my decision is.

After a few seconds, I drop my arms from around Genoveve and make my way toward the door. Elizabeth calls after me, asking me where I'm going, but I still can't answer her. All I can do is focus on walking, telling myself over and over that I *will* see them again. I *will* see Addalynne again. But if that's true, why does this feel so final?

Chapter 11

HER

Lilies . . . their aromatic scent drifts in with the breeze. I take a deep breath, enjoying the absence of pain. Keeping my eyes closed, I wait for it to come back. It will. It always does. One . . . two . . . three . . . no pain. I count to 90. Still nothing. One at a time, I let my eyes slowly open. Everything is blurry and bright, much too bright.

As my eyes adjust, I look at my surroundings. It takes me a moment, but I finally realize that I'm in my own chambers. To my left, the window is open, allowing a light breeze to blow through. To my right, my little sister is asleep in the chair with an ivory cloth draped across the skirt of her dark blue dress. Her red hair is pulled back into a loose braid, and curls are breaking through, escaping down her face. Her eyebrows are scrunched together, her lips tightened in thought as she sleeps.

"Elizabeth," I try to say her name, but my voice is raw and it comes out as a muted whisper. Still, it was enough to wake her, and I watch her eyes fly open, her body rocking forward in bewilderment. She blinks several times, as though she's trying to determine if what she's seeing is real. Then a full smile blossoms on her face. She pushes herself off the chair and drops to her knees at my side, grasping my hand.

"Addalynne, you're awake!"

"What . . ."

"Shhh. Don't try to talk too much. You need to save your energy." She rises to her feet, moves hastily across the floor and grabs a pail of water, all the while prattling on about fever and worry and something about Gerwyn Ellers, the village doctor. I try to process what she's saying, but her words seem jumbled and make little sense. Why would Gerwyn Ellers come here? Mother's a skilled enough healer; she never calls on him. When Elizabeth gets back to me, she raises a spoonful of water to my mouth, urging me to drink.

"This is so much easier now that you're *really* awake," she says with a smile. Her words confuse me further, but I don't bother to ask what they mean. After I take a few sips, she puts the pail down and rushes out of my chambers saying something about getting the others.

I try to focus on what's happening, but everything feels fuzzy, as though there's wool stuffed inside my head keeping me from composing a clear thought. I push myself to remember something, anything about why I'm in bed and being nursed, but the last thing I remember is being in the woods with Drake.

At the memory of him, my heart races. Elizabeth said she was going to get the others. Will he be with them? I desperately hope he'll come through my door. I need to see him. I need to hear his voice and feel his touch.

The door groans as it's pushed open, signaling the appearance of the "others." My fingers dig into the blankets. Mother and Father rush in with Elizabeth. No one else is with them.

A stab of disappointment pierces through me, but it's lessened by the happiness on my parents' faces. They rush to my side with tears of joy spilling down their cheeks. They hold me as they cry and kiss my forehead, telling me over and over how relieved and happy they are that I'm finally awake. *He* still hasn't come in, and neither has my brother.

"Where's Gregory?" I ask weakly as I regard them. It's now that I notice the dark circles under their eyes and the wrinkles in their clothes. All three of them glance at each other, clearly uncomfortable, waiting for someone else to answer. "Where is he?" This time my voice is much stronger and demanding, but its hoarseness grates in my ears. With an exhale, Mother finally answers me.

"He's in Synereal. He left with the Schild."

"No, he's not supposed to leave for six weeks. Why would he leave early?" They glance at each other again, hesitation and concern draining their faces.

"You have been in and out of consciousness for a little over three months, Addalynne. Gregory left two months ago," Father answers slowly. They watch me with guarded expressions as his words sink in. At the moment, I don't know what's worse: what they have said or the way they're watching me, as though they're waiting for me to go completely mad. I turn away from them and look out the window.

Three months. I have been asleep for three months. This seems completely impossible and yet I see it's true. The evidence is right in front of me, scattered in shades of red and yellow on the leaves that should be completely green. Besides, I can feel bits and pieces of the last three months pulling on my mind—whispers of memories that dance to the forefront of my brain. There's something else, too, something that's demanding my attention, but every time I'm close to remembering it, it slips away. There's a gnawing in my chest though, telling me something's wrong. There's something they're keeping from me. What aren't they saying?

I close my eyes and try to clear out the fog in my brain. I have to make myself remember what my mind has tried to forget . . . I see Drake, he's in our woods and he's staring at me with a hauntingly broken expression.

It all comes back, crashing in on me like a wave so powerful that I forget to breathe. I remember the anger. I remember the pain. I remember what my mind fought to conceal. Now I know why they're being so cautious with their words. It's not only my brother who joined the King's Schild. If my brother is gone, so is Drake.

* * *

* * *

My family continues nursing me back to health as the weeks slowly pass. My entire body aches, and it takes quite some time for me to be able to perform the simplest of movements. I still can't walk on my own, which is the most frustrating aspect of this entire ordeal. I have to rely on everyone else to help me get through my day, something I don't think I'll ever get used to. But at least Dr. Ellers says I won't have to get used to it. He says I'll be able to walk on my own eventually, that I just need time for my legs to get stronger.

Over the last few weeks, there's been a constant rotation of visitors, all of them wanting to do the same thing: hover over me and repeatedly ask how I'm doing. The most frequent visitors are Uncle Geoffrey and Mary. I don't mind their visits, but I still wish they wouldn't come. My uncle's eyes again linger in sadness, which only amplifies the pain of Drake's absence. Mary's visits are better, but I can see the grief she's in because of Gregory, which only reminds me that I lost them both.

She asked about Gregory the other day, wanting to know if we had heard from him. I told her that my parents wrote to him, informing him of my recovery, but they had yet to receive a response. Thankfully, she didn't press the issue, nor did she ask about Drake. But I could tell she wanted to. I don't know what I'll say if she ever does.

The most surprising visitors I've had were Lord Vernold Berrenger and his son, Charles. They were kind and thankfully, didn't stay long, but seeing Charles instantly brought back the memories and discomfort of the day of the Summer Festival. I hope they don't come back.

All of my visitors and family tell me that I'm making great progress, but in my opinion it's not enough. I'm tired of being a prisoner in my own body. Day after day, I'm left with nothing to do besides repeat the information they've given me. I sort it out piece by piece, trying to put it together in an arrangement that makes sense, but no matter how hard I try, it never does.

I think again about what they've told me. About how Drake rushed into our home that day, my limp body hanging in his arms, his face stricken with panic. He told them what happened in the woods with the hellion, which I now remember clearly, while my mother dressed my wounds. My body was badly cut and bruised, due to being dragged across the forest floor. But the wound that concerned them most, the one that made my mother call Gerwyn Ellers, was the one around my ankle. The skin around my ankle had been shredded and was causing me to lose large amounts of blood. It took many stitches and herbs to heal my wounds, and there were times they thought I wouldn't make it. But my body persevered, even though my mind remained trapped.

Apparently, I faded in and out of semi-consciousness enough for them to consistently force soup and water down my throat, but my mind never broke the surface of awareness until a few weeks ago. They said this was likely due to the poison. They believe the hellion's blood was poisonous and, since the blood had reached the open wound on my ankle, it was able to burn its way through my body, giving me a very high fever, and causing hallucinations. It was only recently that the poison finally made its way out of my system, allowing me to recover.

Certain images come back to me from time to time and I have to decipher them, determining if the memory is a real one or one of a vivid hallucination. Unfortunately, the memory that brings the most pain, the one I can't recover from, is completely real.

I look down at my visible wounds, the ones that have healed, as I think about my invisible wounds that never will. The light scars on my arms look like someone etched them into me, creating an erratic pattern of lines. My ankle is much worse, and the scarred skin around it is rough and wrinkled, reminding me of old leather. But this I can live with.

It's my thoughts and questions that torment me, and I have nothing to distract me from them, nothing to ease their bitter sting. I can't help but feel incredibly angry and betrayed that Drake would leave me. If he had been hurt, and possibly on the verge of death, I would never have left his side. Did he even care that I had been injured? Did he visit me at all? I have a memory that tugs on my mind, telling me he was here, that he checked on me, talked to me, but maybe these were hallucinations as well.

The sound of my door opening momentarily pulls me from my thoughts, and I watch Elizabeth come in and fill my water before moving to light the fire.

I push myself into a sitting position, with my back leaning against the wall, and stare out the window.

"Did anyone tell you about the man from Incarnadine?" Elizabeth asks. "They found him in Synereal and arrested him."

I feel the blood drain down my body. I turn to face her, but my fear makes even that simple movement difficult. "When?"

"A few months ago."

"After Drake and Gregory left?" My heart sprints ahead with my question as though its frantically searching for the answer.

"No. It happened just before they left. You were unconscious."

I drop my face into my hands and breathe. *He's okay. It wasn't him.* But he's still in Synereal, which means he could still be in danger if anyone finds out where he's from. "Has the man said anything about Incarnadine or why he's here?" I ask. What if he's here for Drake? Is that why Drake left?

"No, not that I know of, but it has everyone even more uneasy. Between the hellion's attack on you and now someone from Incarnadine crossing over, there are a lot of rumors."

"What kind of rumors?"

Elizabeth rings out a cloth in the wash bowl. "Different ones, but mostly people think that the Incarnadians are testing our borders for weakness."

"What do you think?"

Elizabeth shrugs. "I don't know. Maybe they are, but maybe it's just a coincidence. The man they arrested seems crazy. I don't think he's part of some big plan. I think he's just someone who got lost or ran away."

Is that what happened to Drake before I found him in the river? Did he get lost or run away?

"Maybe people from Incarnadine have crossed our border before and we just didn't know it," I say, wanting to offer a piece of the truth.

"Maybe," Elizabeth agrees and heads toward the fire.

"Did Drake know? About the prisoner?"

Elizabeth pokes the fire with a rod, but the flames stay minimal. "I think so. All of us did."

Dread mingles in my heart. More questions, more thoughts to torment me.

"He was going to stay, you know." Elizabeth says as she stands and moves toward me. My eyes follow her, feeling taken aback by her words. She sits on my bed. "He told everyone that he was no longer going to leave with Gregory and Walter. He said he was going to stay here with you. Then one day he came out of your chambers, spoke briefly with Father, and left. Father said that Drake told him that he had changed his mind and would be going with them after all."

This leaves me feeling more unsettled than before. He was going to stay with me, but decided not to. Why? Why would he do that? Was it the prisoner? Or was it because of me? I remember telling him that he should go to Synereal. But that was before the attack. The fact that he still left, after what happened, leaves me completely heartbroken. The tears sting my skin as they fall down my cheeks. Elizabeth wipes them away, but soon realizes that they're not going to stop anytime soon. She gives up the battle and instead crawls up on the bed and pulls me into her arms. I return the embrace and curl myself against her, eventually laying my head in her lap.

"Why? Why did he leave me?" I ask through my sobs.

"I don't know. It took everyone by surprise. I'm sorry you're hurting. I know you love him, but believe me when I say that I truly believe he loves you, too."

I push myself up and wrap my arms around my knees.

Her words frustrate me. I can't possibly allow myself to believe that he loves me. If he did, he never would have left. It's selfish to feel this way, to feel he should have stayed and given up everything for me, but if the roles had been reversed, I would have done it for him. I never would have left him.

Suddenly his words from that day in the woods echo through my mind: *'I don't know what to feel anymore.'* And I know why he left.

Once he realized I was going to live, his anger with me for lying to him must have resurfaced. He realized that he couldn't love me, that he was better off without someone as selfish as I am. I don't blame him. I am selfish, and I don't deserve him.

I don't know what to feel anymore.

Any love he may have had for me is gone. I made sure of that when I lied to him for four years. And now he's gone. He left to find out about his past so that he can have a different life, one away from me. I curl up on my bed and close my eyes. "Go, Elizabeth. Please. I want to be alone."

Without a question or breath of hesitation, my sister leaves. I think of being that cracking glass again, only this time the pressure of the pain shatters me.

Chapter 12

HER

I tie Freyja to the village stables and lift the hood of my cloak, hoping this time it's covering enough of my face to keep the stares away. Even though I've been to the market several times, I can't seem to escape the looks of surprise, curiosity, and even distrust that come from the people around me. It's even worse now that Samuel Hunt has disappeared. Lord Berrenger led a search for Samuel, but all that was found was a torn piece of his clothing, dangling on a branch near the river. The thought makes me shudder. Everyone's afraid, including me. We all know that the hellion probably took Samuel, and the accusing stares from the people around me make me feel somehow responsible. I mentioned this to Elizabeth the other day and she told me I was being ridiculous, that no one blamed me, but I could tell she was lying. After much more prying, Elizabeth finally caved and told me that some of the villagers are frightened of me. They think that I have somehow been cursed by the hellion. Maybe I have.

> *"Do you hear the crunch of leaves,*
> *Following behind you?*
> *When you turn what will it be?*
> *The Hellion's come to find you."*

The song is followed by the high pitched screams of several children. The first time I heard it it startled me, but now I recognize it and it's lyrics have become familiar enough to accompany my nightmares.

I turn the corner and see the baker's son, Winston, moving sluggishly behind the other children, chasing them, pretending to be the hellion. He's always the hellion. Probably because he towers over the other kids his age. Isobel's little brother, Thomas, is hiding behind the wall, watching Winston, a wooden sword in his hand. "Kill the Hellion!" he shouts, and jumps forward, lunging for Winston. I move down the next street and away from their game.

When I step into the market, I see almost everyone in Faygrene scurrying about, like mice searching for the only piece of cheese. Everywhere I look there are people perusing fabrics, sorting ribbons, sniffing flowers and inspecting jewelry. Too distracted to notice me or their fear, I think to myself with a smile. I guess I do have a reason to be thankful for the Ball that's a couple of weeks away.

As I shop for the items on Mother's list, my mind drifts to the conversation I once had with Drake about the annual Floret Masquerade Ball. He was true to his word and didn't attend the last two. Instead he stayed with Elizabeth and me, like he promised. But this year was supposed to be different. This year I'm eligible to attend, and he should have been going with me. But circumstances have clearly changed, and instead of going with Drake, I'll be accompanying my mother and father.

It's been seven months since the boys left. We've received several letters from Gregory. He says he's doing well and that he misses us. He says that Walter's adjusting well to the Schild. He never mentions Drake. Still, it doesn't stop me from scanning every new letter for Drake's name before reading the rest with a harrowing mixture of sorrow, disappointment, and anxiety. I don't understand why Gregory never mentions him, but it's probably better this way. Hearing about Drake would only make this harder than it already is. I don't need any more reminders that he left.

No. No more. I have to stop thinking about him. I push the thoughts of him away, refusing to be heartsick today.

I exit the bakery and stop dead in my tracks. Charles Berrenger is making his way through the crowd, heading straight toward me. I pull my hood tighter, turn and quicken my pace.

Mary thinks that Charles is going to present his jonquil to me at the Ball. At the Floret Ball, every young man who's not yet married is given a white jonquil.

During the Ball, they present that obnoxious little flower to the woman they most admire. If she accepts, she's accepting more than a flower, she's accepting a courtship that usually leads to marriage. The idea of Charles giving me his jonquil should make me happy. Any other girl would be thrilled to have the young Lord's attention, but I just hope Mary's wrong. I know I shouldn't feel this way. Charles is kind and he really is handsome, but I don't want him. I don't want anyone except the one person I can't have. At least Mother has stopped badgering me about it all. I guess my accident had one positive outcome.

I duck inside one of the open shops and watch through the doorway as Charles passes by. I'm not in the mood to talk to him right now or anyone for that matter. I stay inside, my fingers brushing over the spring flowers and leaves that decorate the shop. My fingers linger on several strands of wild grass as I delay, waiting until I'm sure I can leave without a run-in. After several minutes, I tell myself that it's been long enough and cautiously step outside.

"Excuse me, Miss, can you tell me where the bakery is?"

I turn around and my breath catches in my throat. Gregory is standing in front of me, a full smile on his face.

This can't be real.

Suddenly, he lifts me off the ground and spins me around. His laughter booms in my ears and I feel his heart beating, rapid with excitement. I've dreamt of this moment so many times, and now he's here, he's really here! He's no longer just a shadowed memory of what I lost. I wrap my arms around his neck while he continues to spin me, holding onto him with everything I have. He finally comes to a stop and sets me down on my feet.

The time in the Schild has changed him. He's at least an inch taller and his already broad stature has filled out with more muscle. His fair skin has darkened from the warm sun of Synereal, and his hair is slightly longer, falling near his shoulders and almost covering his brown eyes.

"Why are you home? I mean, I'm ecstatic that you are, but how did it happen?" I ask when I finally find my voice. I force myself to push the thought of anyone else who may have returned with him far from my mind. I can't allow myself to feel that kind of hope.

"I decided to leave."

"Why?"

"You want the honest answer?"

"Don't I always?"

Gregory takes a deep breath. "I couldn't rid myself of the feeling that I abandoned you."

"Gregory . . ."

"No, Addalynne, let me say this." He stops and looks at the people around us, their footsteps halting as they stare. He grabs my hand and starts walking us away from the market. We exit the center square and his pace slows, but he keeps his hand in mine. "At first, I thought that my loneliness and uncertainty were due to missing all of you and my worries about your health," he says as we continue to walk, leaving the villagers' stares behind us. "I reminded myself that all my life I had wanted to be a member of the King's Schild. You of all people know this," he says with a laugh. I smile at the memory of us running around with our wooden swords, pretending to be members of the Schild. "When the opportunity came, I thought about it for a long time, but I didn't really need to think about it. I knew I wanted to join. I've always known.

"The Schild taught me a lot, as did King Theoderic. I gained insight and experience that were invaluable, and I never would have attained them if I had stayed here. But once I was there, I constantly wished that I hadn't left. All I could think about was you and the rest of our family. I worried about your safety, the safety of all of you. Synereal has plenty of Schilds to protect it, but who was here to protect you?"

We reach the village stables and I stop in front of Freyja. "Gregory, you don't need to worry about me. I'm capable of protecting myself. I hope your reasons for leaving weren't only based on that," I say as I put the bread and soap I bought at the market into the saddle bag. I fasten it and turn back to Gregory. He's staring down at me, his eyes narrowed in thought. I know what he's thinking about: my accident with the hellion. But that could have happened to anyone. The frustration slowly spreads through me, but I take a deep breath and push it back. My brother's home, his reasons for being here don't matter. Besides, now is definitely not the time to argue with him. I can always pick a fight later if I still want to.

"They weren't only based on that, Addalynne, but it was a factor. You're stronger and braver than any girl I know, and than most boys for that matter. But you're my sister. My *younger* sister." He waits for me to respond, surely expecting me to argue again, but I bite back my tongue. He gives a soft chuckle and, with a slight shake of his head, he continues. "Anyway, after word reached the capital about Samuel's disappearance, I told the King that I wanted to go home, that I needed to be here to protect my family. I also told him that if he ever needs my service to send for me.

"He understood and said he was actually grateful to have someone he could trust keeping an eye on things in Faygrene. He asked me to notify him if any other attacks or disappearances happen. Then he thanked me for my service, told me I was always welcome to return, and wished me well." After a moment, his mouth turns up into a satisfied smile. I smile back while tears sting the bottom of my eyes and throw my arms around him.

His arms wrap around me, too, and he rubs his hand along my back: the way he used to when we were young and I had a bad dream. The tears pour down my face. Having him here makes me realize how much I've missed him. I've been so heartbroken over Drake that I didn't fully recognize the emptiness Gregory's absence left in me as well. Now that he's here, it feels as though a piece of myself has been returned to me. I'm nowhere near complete, and in all actuality, I probably never will be, but in this moment it's easier to breathe.

"I'm happy to see you're not angry with me," he says, his body shaking with laughter.

"I could never be angry with you, Gregory." I rest my head on his shoulder, tears trickling down my face. His body shakes more now, his laughter deepening. He pulls back from me and takes my face in his hands, wiping my tears with his thumbs.

"I'm going to remind you of that the next time you look at me like you're about to strangle me."

"I'm sure you will," I say with a laugh.

"You've really grown up. When I left, you were still a girl, now you're a beautiful young lady. Well, lady, might be an over-statement."

"haha," I say as I lightly hit his arm. His face holds a smile, but there's concern and worry stealing its warmth.

"Have you really made a full recovery?"

I take a deep breath. "Yes. My injuries have healed. I'm completely back to normal." This of course is a lie. I'll never be the same again, but that has nothing to do with my injuries and everything to do with Drake. I want so badly to ask about him, but I don't have the courage. He lets out a breath and some of the concern leaves his face.

"Just before I left Faygrene, Doctor Ellers assured me that the worst was over, that you were going to be fine, but I was still terrified. I don't know if you fully understand the extent of your injuries," he says with a slight grimace. I don't think he does either. "The day I got the letter from Mother and Father, telling me that you had finally fully awakened, was the best day of my life, but I still needed to see you healthy and healed before I could completely be at ease."

"Are you at ease?"

"Yes," he says with another laugh, and again pulls me tightly into his arms. Now that I'm not looking at his face, I find a trace of bravery.

"Did anyone else come home with you?" I ask, before I have the chance to stop myself. His body stiffens. He knows who I'm asking about.

"No. I came alone."

I untangle myself from his arms, and turn to face Freyja. I run my hands along the saddle and pretend to fasten it, even though it's already set for me. I don't want Gregory to see how much his words hurt me. But of course he knows exactly what I'm avoiding and within seconds he gently turns me around and pulls me back into his arms.

I want to ask Gregory why Drake didn't come home with him. I want to ask if Drake ever spoke of me, if he missed me as much as I miss him, but the way Gregory is slightly rocking me from side to side, clearly trying to comfort me, tells me that he already knows all too well how much I care about Drake. I don't want to make it even more obvious by asking questions that, despite their answers, will change nothing. Another round of tears fights its way to my eyes, but I push them back. I won't cry over Drake again. He made his choice, and it wasn't me.

"I'm so happy you're home. I missed you so much."

"I missed you, too. More than you could know."

I rise onto my toes and kiss his cheek. "I'm going to go home and rest. Are you coming home now, too?"

"No. I have . . . other business I need to attend to."

I nod. "I'll see you at supper, and after you can tell me about how your visit with Mary goes." He laughs and helps me onto Freyja. But his laughter soon fades.

"Do you think she'll still have me?" He asks, his voice quiet and apprehensive.

I look down at him and somehow manage a small smile. "Of course she will. You have nothing to worry about."

I turn Freyja around and head to the road. But I don't go home. Instead I ride Freyja along the outskirts of the village. I need time alone to breathe and to process everything. I need time to force myself to accept the fact that Drake is never coming back.

* * *

The next couple of weeks pass by in a blur. Everyone in Faygrene is completely preoccupied with Gregory's return and will speak of nothing else, which has at least taken some of their attention off of what happened to me and to Samuel. But now no one in our family can go anywhere without at least a dozen people stopping us to ask about Gregory and what he has said about Synereal and King Theoderic. I don't know how Gregory is able to so gracefully handle all the attention. He says he doesn't mind, that he understands their curiosity, but still, I can't see how it doesn't irritate him.

The worst part though, is the girls. Everywhere I go, groups of girls gossip excitedly in corners. When they see me pass, they run up to me and link their arms in mine, as though we've been lifelong friends, when in reality none of them have ever wanted anything to do with me, unless they were laughing at the jokes Jacqueline used to make at my expense. So I know they're only being friendly with me because they want me to put in a good word for them with Gregory. He'll be presenting someone with a jonquil at the Floret Ball, and they all want it to be them. Some of them ask me if I know who he's giving the jonquil to. I shrug my shoulders and tell them that we don't talk about girls. This usually gets them to go away.

But this, of course, is a lie. I know he'll be giving the jonquil to Mary. Though Gregory didn't give me many details about their visit, he did say that he felt "hopeful" after seeing her. I also saw Mary a few days ago, and she confirmed that he had been by to see her several times. She wouldn't give much detail either, but the subtle blush on her cheeks made it obvious that things were definitely not over between them.

Other than our chance meeting, Mary and I haven't seen much of each other lately, and I'll admit that I'm the one to blame. We're still friends, but being around her has become too difficult for me. Before Gregory came home it was still hard, but it was hard for both of us. For her, having to come to Gregory's home and be reminded of his absence was extremely painful, but she still endured it. The gods know I wouldn't have. I haven't stepped foot inside Uncle Geoffrey's home. Everything already reminds me of Drake. I don't need to see his empty loft. But Mary's stronger than I am, and she continued to visit. But now that Gregory's back, every time I see her I'm reminded that the person she loves came back to her, and I'm still alone and incomplete. I know it's selfish of me to pull away from her, but the truth is that lately I've pulled away from everyone. I don't have the energy to pretend that everything's fine, that nothing has changed.

But the reality is I can't keep going on this way. I have to move on with my life, no matter how impossible it seems. Maybe it can start with a trip into the market, a simple enough feat, but one that I have completely avoided this week so that I wouldn't have to talk to anyone about Gregory or jonquils or Balls. However, Mother needs thread for an alteration on my gown. She was going to go later, but I'll offer to go for her. I need to get out of here. As much as I try to deny it, my body craves the fresh air.

As I walk to the market, I can't help but glance at my woods. Sometimes I see several of Lord Berringer's guards patrolling the tree line, but not today. "No sign of any hellions," they'll say after they've taken a quick walk through the woods, and people will go about their day, comforted by the blanket of security the guards provide.

The wind is blowing through the new leaves and scattering the dead ones along the ground in a chaotic dance. I desperately want to go back into the forest, but I can't bring myself to do it. I haven't been there since the day of my attack, and every time I move in that direction, my body becomes paralyzed with anxiety. I'm not sure if it's the memories of the hellion or of Drake that keep me away. Maybe it's both.

I turn the corner and go down a narrow street. Jacqueline, Antoinette and Isobel are huddled together against the stone wall. Here we go again. I know they're going to ask about Gregory.

Jacqueline's annoyingly shrill voice drifts over me as I get closer. "If only Drake had come home. I would have done anything to receive a jonquil from him."

Drake. Why are they talking about Drake? I duck behind an abandoned street cart before they can see me. My heart is frantic as I strain my ears to listen to their conversation.

"I know. He's so handsome." It's Antoinette's voice I hear now. "It doesn't even bother me that he's an orphan. I would still let him into my bed." They all laugh at this, their giggles cutting through me, each one its own blade. My hands clench into fists around the hem of my cloak, and I have to remind myself to breathe.

"I thought he wanted Addalynne, with the way he always followed her around. But I guess I was wrong. He would have stayed with her if that were true."

There it is, the same thing I've been thinking. Only this time, hearing it come from Antoinette is debilitating.

"Maybe he did love her and she rejected him. That

could be why he left, too," Isobel says quietly. I always did like her best.

"No." Jacqueline is quick in her response. "Don't be absurd, Isobel. Addalynne is strange, but even she wouldn't reject Drake. He didn't want her." Jacqueline's voice is dismissive. "She probably threw herself at him, desperate to keep his attention. That's why he followed her into the woods every day. What other reason would he have for wanting to be around *her* all the time? Only the gods and the birds know what went on in those woods." Jacqueline's shrill laugh grates inside my ears and I have to fight every urge in me not to run toward her and rip her hair out. "Besides, if he was in love with Addalynne, then he wouldn't have kissed me."

I feel myself trembling as I struggle to push back the onslaught of emotions. This can't be true. He never would have kissed her.

"When did he kiss you?" Antoinette asks, jealousy sharpening her words.

"When I went with my father to visit my aunt in Synereal. I saw him in the capital's market. We started talking and he was *very* flirtatious, couldn't keep his hands off me." More giggles, more knives piercing my heart. "He walked me back to my aunt's house and when we got there, he pulled me into his arms and kissed me. Then, he told me he hoped he would see me again someday."

Jacqueline's confession leaves me drowning with anger and betrayal. In this moment, the only thing I'm aware of is the feel of the pebble in my fingers. I pull myself up, throw it as hard as I can in her direction and then turn and run. Their shouts follow me, and a voice inside my head tells me that what I did was cowardly and childish. I shouldn't have run. I should have stayed and confronted her. But all I care about is getting as far away from Jacqueline as I can.

I run into Dahlia's sewing shop, grab the thread and throw the coins on the counter, likely overpaying, but I don't bother to stay and find out. I feel stares on me as I rush through the market square. The oncoming tears are already stinging the back of my eyes, and the vomit that has risen into my throat leaves a bitter aftertaste when I swallow it back down. I grab my hood and pull it up, not wanting the prying eyes of the people around me to witness my tears, but they don't come. My eyes remain dry as I blink against the cold, spring wind. Maybe I've cried all I can for him, or maybe I'm too angry to cry. I was sick and recovering from my attack, wanting nothing more than Drake, and he was off in Synereal, kissing Jacqueline.

I'm such a fool. In my mind, all I see is him wrapping his arms around her, brushing his lips against hers, and whispering in her ear as she tosses her head back and laughs. These images repeat themselves over and over, making my stomach lurch, and before I know it, I'm vomiting in the bushes. As I stagger to my feet, I tell myself that I really can't go on like this. I have to move on, and tomorrow night is the perfect opportunity.

Chapter 13

HER

I stare at the floor-length mirror, mesmerized by the girl staring back at me. Though this is the same face I have seen every day of my life, there's something oddly different tonight. The top half of my dark hair is softly pulled away from my face by a circular ruby hair-pin, leaving the rest falling down my back in loose curls. My eyes are lined with a smudge of black charcoal, making their color striking behind thick, long eyelashes. My cheeks are flushed pink with my nerves, and my lips appear fuller, stained a vibrant red. Even as I pull my bottom lip into my mouth and nervously nip at it, the color doesn't fade.

Framing my eyes is a delicate golden mask. It's made from a thin wire that curves and twists to create the appearance of vines. The mask fits so well that it seems as though gold vines have been painted around my eyes and across the top of my cheekbones.

But it's not my face, mask, or hair that holds my attention—it's the dress.

The silky red fabric presses flush and low against my chest and is followed by a red fitted bodice that fits tightly on my waist and leads down to a full red skirt. Long, red sleeves drape off my shoulders and cascade well past my wrists. Gold thread is sewn into a swirling pattern along the bottom of my skirt and the cuffs of my sleeves. It's a gorgeous dress, and it's hard to believe I'm the girl wearing it.

"Charles won't be able to take his eyes off you tonight," Mother says excitedly, as she walks around me, taking in every detail she worked so hard to create. Charles . . . I had forgotten about him. "He won't be the only one either. There'll be quite a few young men who want you on their arm."

Mother really wants me to receive a jonquil. Maybe now I will. The thought makes me sick with anxiety, but I try to tell myself that this is something I want, something I need. Mother stops directly in front of me, holding my face between her hands. "I'm so glad Gregory will be there to look after you."

"You and Father aren't coming?"

"No. This night is about you and Gregory." She drops her hands to her sides and turns to her bed stand. "Your father and I have been to plenty of Balls. Now it's your turn to enjoy one, without your parents' prying eyes." She chuckles while she flips open the lid of her silver jewelry box and rummages through it. "Besides, we don't want to leave Elizabeth alone."

"You should go. I can stay with her. I really don't have to go."

"Don't be absurd, Addalynne. Your father and I would never dream of it." She shuts the lid of the box and turns to face me. "Besides, you look far too beautiful to stay home." She moves toward me, a coy smile on her lips. "Now turn around."

I do as she asks and feel something cold and heavy fall against my chest. My mother grabs hold of my shoulders and steers me back toward the mirror. A gold necklace now hangs down my chest, ending with a ruby pendant that sits on top of the curve of my bust. I watch as the scarlet gem rises and falls with my breaths.

"It was your grandmother's. I wore it to my first Floret Ball. My parents arranged for your uncle and I to visit Faygrene, sending us all the way from Artania in hopes that we would find a match. That was the night I met your father," she says quietly, her eyes shimmering with unshed tears. I turn to face her and she cups my face in her hand. "You have grown into such a beautiful young lady. How did I get so lucky?"

I try to find something to say to her, a way to tell her how much she means to me and how grateful I am to her, but before I get a chance, she gives me a quick kiss on the cheek and ushers me out the front door, insisting I can't be late.

My stomach spins with trepidation while I wait for the carriage to arrive, my fingers fiddling with the hem of my sleeves. It's a perfectly clear night, with stars lining the path to the full moon that illuminates the ground with its silver light.

"Gregory hurry!" I shout. I can't stand waiting out here alone.

Several seconds later the front door finally opens and Gregory walks out. He's wearing a white shirt underneath a long black leather vest. His black breeches are met at the knee by new, black leather riding boots. There are silver ribbons tied around his elbows, in order to add the right amount of decoration for the festivities.

"Well, if the time I spent away accomplished one thing, it made me forget how impatient you are."

"Where's your mask?" I ask, ignoring his words.

Instead of answering me, he pulls his silver mask out of his pocket and secures it to his face, where it covers the area from his eyebrows to his cheekbones, framing his dark eyes.

"I don't think I've ever seen you fidget like this," he laughs, as he adjusts his mask. I smile at him and try to take a deep breath.

"I'm honestly fighting the urge to run off and climb a tree right now." My words make him laugh harder.

"I'd like to see that," he says, his chuckles slowing down. "Don't worry. You're going to have a great time, and if you need me at all, I'll be there. Don't hesitate to come to me."

The carriage pulls up and Gregory helps me inside. Lord Berrenger's manor is rather close to our home, and on the short ride there, Gregory has to constantly remind me to breathe.

We pull into the drive and my eyes graze over the looming brick manor, though manor might be the wrong word, as its size makes it more akin to a castle. Its grey brick towers stand at least three times taller than the trees, and the manor itself is wider than the entire market of Faygrene.

Every tree in front of the manor is lit with glass lanterns that have been molded into the shape of birds. The candles inside them are flickering, making it seem as though the birds are lightly flapping their wings as they hover in the trees, their lifeless glass eyes set on us.

It's difficult, but I manage to peel my gaze away from the glass birds and fix it on the grey stone walkway. The edges of the walkway are lined by small, white candles, creating the illusion of stars that have fallen from the night sky. It's like a dream, and part of me definitely wishes it was.

We climb down from the carriage and make our way to the wooden front doors. Guards stand at attention beside the entrance. Gregory offers them a slight nod as we pass through the doors, and a young, formally dressed servant secures a white jonquil to Gregory's vest before allowing us to enter.

The scent of cinnamon floats over us as we step into the Great Hall, and the sound of whimsical music: a mixture of flutes and violins, greets us. A twirling mix of silver and white cloths drape across the high vaulted ceiling and cascade down the tall grey walls. Silver candlelit chandeliers, which are draped with strings of pearls, illuminate the Great Hall, creating a soft glow. I feel as though I've stepped into a cloud.

"Are you doing okay?" Gregory leans down and asks. He must sense my unease. I've read about lavish parties in books, but I never pictured myself at one. And now that I'm here, I'm not sure what I think. It's beautiful, but it's not something I could surround myself with often. It doesn't make me comfortable, and though it's crowded with people, I'm left with a feeling of loneliness. If it weren't for Gregory, I would have a hard time moving forward into the overwhelming extravagance of it all. But his presence gives me the reassurance I need.

"I'm fine." I answer and we begin to weave our way around familiar and unfamiliar faces. Everywhere we turn there are people spinning, laughing, and drinking, all of them dressed in their most formal garments.

We come to a stop at the edge of the dance floor and I notice that some of the more prestigious men have capes draped over their backs, symbolizing their higher status. I suppose one of them is Charles, though which one I don't know.

The song changes and the sound draws my attention to an elevated stage, where minstrels are playing their harmonic tunes. The stage stands along the far wall, in front of an immense stone fireplace. Between the minstrel's cloaks and the oversized flames behind them, they must be uncomfortably warm.

"Should we get some wine?" I ask Gregory, but there's no response. I look to where he was last standing and find the space empty. I glance through the crowd and see him in the center of the dance floor, holding a girl with long blond hair against his chest. Her back is to me, displaying only her navy dress and her curled hair, but I know it's Mary. At least one of us will be happy tonight.

Well, Gregory may not be able to join me, but that doesn't mean I can't have some wine. I move once again through the crowd, making my way toward the long banquet tables that are assembled around the dance floor. Silver cloths are draped across them, and ivory candles and bouquets of white lilies stand among the fruit, deserts, and wine filled goblets.

I see a goblet that's filled more than the rest and head straight for it, but just before I'm able to reach it a cold hand grabs mine. Startled by the contact, I spin around.

Charles is standing in front of me, his brown eyes stirring behind an ivory mask as he offers me an admittedly handsome smile. He's leaning down in a half bow, making his sandy-blond hair fall forward. An ivory cape and vest are situated over his white shirt, along with ivory breaches, leading down to blindingly white stockings. The King of the Clouds, I think to myself and almost laugh, but then I see his hands and the urge to laugh fades into unease. Both of his hands are extended out in front of him, one is suspended in the air, waiting for me to take hold of it. The other is holding a single white jonquil. This moment could change everything. I should feel excitement, but I can't rid myself of the gnawing pain in my chest.

Seconds tick by, and his eyes begin to question me. But before he lowers his hand in withdrawal, I extend mine and place it in his. The smile returns to his face and he secures his jonquil in my hair and leads me to the dance floor.

What did I just do? By accepting his jonquil, I'm accepting a promise of courtship and potentially marriage. Am I ready for that? The queasiness returns, but I swallow it back. I need to push these thoughts and unsure feelings away, at least for now. I can think about them later. Right now I want to try to enjoy myself.

"What do you think of the Ball?" Charles interrupts my fretting and begins to lead us through the current dance.

"It's lovely."

"But . . ." he prompts. *Does he see through me that easily?*

"But it's a bit overwhelming."

"Is that a bad thing?" He twirls me around and then stops my movement by pulling me against his chest. His mouth curls up into a lopsided smile. Feel something, Addalynne. This handsome man is looking at you with desire and holding you against his chest. This is your chance to move on.

But no matter how hard I try, I feel nothing apart from the familiar ache in my chest.

"It's not bad, just . . . different. I'm not accustomed to such ostentation."

"A lady of your status and beauty should be surrounded with such ostentation on a daily basis."

"I'm sure even you aren't surrounded with such ostentation on a daily basis."

He laughs and sends my body into another twirl. "Well, that's probably true."

We dance to several more songs, and to my surprise, I actually find myself laughing with him a little. As the current song comes to an end, Charles bends down and kisses my hand. When he looks up at me, the look on his face is joyful and carefree.

"I'm going to get us some wine. I'll be back soon," he says, before kissing my hand once more.

Another song begins, and the couples on the dance floor start to move around me, pressing against me. I make my way to the edge of the dance floor, somewhere Charles will still be able to find me, but where I'm not in danger of being trampled by the dancers.

Just a little way off, I see a silver fountain. If it's meant to resemble something, I don't know what it is, but the erratic swerves, turns and drops are mesmerizing. I stop in front of it, my fingers catching droplets of the cascading water. I watch the way it pours off the curves and arches, as though it's involved in its own dance.

A few minutes later, I feel Charles moving behind me. He's close enough for me to feel his breath on my neck and shoulder, stirring my curls against my skin.

"That was fa—" I begin as I turn around, but the rest of my words dissolve in my throat. It's not Charles who's standing in front of me.

Chapter 14

HER

My heart falters as I stare into piercing green eyes, framed by a black mask. These are the eyes that have haunted my dreams for the past eight months. These are the eyes that are as familiar to me as my own soul. And they're staring at me now, filled with a tangle of hope and fear. I let my eyes move away from his and glance down to see what he's holding in his hand. It's a single white jonquil.

I bring my gaze back to his face while my trembling fingers reach forward and take the jonquil from his hand. The numbing shock makes my movement slow, but not hesitant.

All the fear vanishes from his face, replaced instead with hope and determination. Without delay, he slips his hand into my hair and gently pulls Charles's jonquil from it. He turns it over in his fingers, looking at it with a mixture of curiosity and disdain before tossing it to the floor. Saying nothing, he grabs hold of my hand and pulls me with him into the sea of bodies dancing and forming promises.

The feel of his hand in mine sends a burning shiver along my skin and waves of confusion through my body. This is impossible. He can't be here. He's hundreds of miles away.

A growing sense of fear builds within me, starting in my chest and working its way through my body, weakening and numbing me. What if I'm imagining this? What if my mind was damaged in the accident and now I'm hallucinating when I'm awake? I close my eyes and breathe steadily, trying to sort through what I know is real. My body following his, bumping and stumbling around people, the fabric of their clothes scratching against me definitely feels real. His hand, tightly wrapped around mine, guiding me and warming me from the inside feels too perfect, too familiar to not be real. I let my eyes re-open. He's still here, his back facing me. I study the casual wave of his tousled dark brown hair, the ends touching his neck, where the bottom half of his familiar crescent-shaped birth mark is visible. My heart contracts. The hallucinations were never as sharp and tangible as this. *Could he really be here?*

Reaching under the sleeve of my dress, I pinch my arm as hard as I can. A sharp pulse of pain radiates where I pinched my skin, which confirms that I'm neither dreaming nor hallucinating. I wait for the excitement to come, but instead I'm overwhelmed by a suffocating sense of disquiet. Having him here is all I wanted, but now that he's here, I'm scared and confused.

He comes to a stop in an area of the dance floor that the chandeliers don't quite illuminate. He turns to face me, and his mouth draws up into a half smile with only one of his dimples showing.

He lets go of my hand and wraps his arm around me, placing one hand on the small of my back. The contact vanishes the hollow feeling and leaves me wanting more, needing more. His eyelids partially drop down and his fixed gaze burns through me as he pulls me even closer.

The feel of his body against mine leaves me flustered, and I pull my bottom lip into my mouth. He looks down at my mouth and slowly lifts his other hand to my face. He gently strokes his thumb along my bottom lip, extracting it from between my teeth. He looks into my eyes and reaches back down, grabbing hold of my hand once more. We move together now, in a slow dance, a contradiction to the fast, upbeat song that's being played.

I don't know how much more of this I can take. His closeness is overwhelming, making me increasingly lightheaded with every touch, every glance. I can't think straight with him so close to me, and I need to be able to think.

The dance continues in the most torturous sort of pleasure. We begin a sensual tug of war, Drake always trying to pull me closer, me constantly pushing farther away. His gaze never leaves my face, but I try to look everywhere but at him. Being near him again is more than I could have ever hoped for, but it's also incredibly painful. I want so badly to reach out and pull him closer to me, but I can't.

I look toward the crowded dance floor and see a girl with dark brown hair moving toward us. Her purple velvet dress is stretched tight and low across her chest, exposing her voluptuous curves, and her hooded grey eyes are fixed on Drake. The sight of Jacqueline leaves me debilitated, bringing back a flood of unpleasant memories—their passionate kiss, his telling her he hoped to see her again, and lastly, his walking away from me. Although this last one is not a real memory, it's an image I've conjured up in my mind enough times to become palpable and bitter.

I pull away from him and the feeling of emptiness instantly pours through me as his hand drops from mine. I push my way through the crowd of people, desperate to put distance between us and clear my head.

"Addy!" The sound of his voice, real and here, almost stops me, but I force myself to keep moving. Suddenly, his fingers are on my back. My steps falter and my breath solidifies in my throat, turning to a painful lump. I can't do it. My need for him is too deep.

I start to turn back to him, giving in, but Jacqueline reaches him before I do. Her presence brings back my resolve and I cut around her, knowing this will likely be my only chance to get away. After several seconds, I let myself glance back. Jacqueline has successfully blocked his progress and has her hands gripped firmly around his black vest. He's looking over her head, directly at me, his masked eyes filled with questions and pain. I turn away and quicken my pace. Someone else calls my name as I brush by, but I don't stop to see who it is. I have to get out of here and I have to do it now.

I reach the end of the dance floor and see a set of wooden double doors. I push through them and find myself on a candlelit veranda. There's a marble staircase to my right, which leads down to the garden. I head down the stairs, taking two at a time, and run toward the safety of the green grass and tall trees.

Once I'm far enough into the garden, I stop running. I inhale the fresh air in an attempt to fill my lungs and clear the dizziness from my head. Just ahead there's a pond with a grey, stone bridge running across it. I walk toward it, my head clearing with each step I take.

When I get to the bridge, I stop and lean over the stone railing. The reflection of the full moon is dancing on the water, creating a second luminous sky. My rippled reflection is there in the water as well. Strands of my hair have made their way out of my pin and are falling around my face. My cheeks feel warm and flushed, and my eyes seem crazed behind my gold mask.

I pull off my mask and hold it in one hand while I spin Drake's jonquil with the other. Closing my eyes, I try to slow my breathing. I picture the ocean, the one I let my mind wander to when I need to get away from reality. I imagine the blue waves splashing on the grey rocks, the sun setting over the horizon, a siren singing the most beautifully bitter song.

As she finishes her song, I hear the faint sound of footsteps slowing next to me, and I know exactly what

I'm going to see when I open my eyes. I don't understand how he always knows where to find me, and tonight this little ability of his is driving me mad with equal measures of elation and annoyance.

I delay for a while, letting myself count to one hundred. I do this partly to give myself more time to prepare, but mostly to irritate him. As I get closer to one hundred, my mind races with thoughts.

Ninety-five . . . what am I going to say to him? Ninety-six . . . I won't say anything. I'll let him be the one to speak. Ninety-seven . . . I can't believe he's here. Ninety-eight . . . I missed him so much. Ninety-nine . . . He probably won't stay. One hundred . . . I really hope he stays. I slowly open my eyes and gaze into the pond.

Another reflection is there now, staring back at me through the surface of the water. He's no longer wearing the black mask, and the moonlight is shimmering across his face, bathing it in a silver glow. He looks older: a young man now, instead of the boy from my memories. And somehow, he's even more beautiful. His dark hair is disheveled and his emerald eyes are intently set on my reflection. I look away from the reflection of his eyes. It will do me no good to look there. Instead, I study his dark clothes, and notice the wrinkles in his black long sleeve shirt and his black breeches.

Having him here shows me how completely lost I've been without him. When Gregory came home, I felt as though a part of me had returned, but I was still incomplete. Now that Drake is back, it's as though the rest of myself has returned to me as well—like the missing piece has finally been found. But even though I've found it, I feel as though it no longer belongs to me. I can see it lingering in front of me, but I don't know how to reach it.

I set my mask and jonquil on the railing of the bridge, then I turn and lean my hip against it, crossing my arms in front of me, making myself face him. He's leaning on his forearms, along the same railing about five feet away from me. His face is unreadable. Our eyes lock on each other and my heart races so quickly that I feel my pulse jumping in my throat. He pushes himself off the railing and turns to face me, his body stiff and apprehensive.

"Um . . . It's really good to see you," he says hesitantly, as he warily studies my face.

After almost a year apart, *that* is the first thing he's going to say to me? A scoff escapes my throat, and I turn away from him, again facing the water.

"You look beautiful," he says, his voice stronger and more determined. "Then again, you always do," he continues, returning to the quiet, unsure voice. "Will you *please* say something?"

No, I won't, because I don't know what to say, and even if I did, it would probably come out wrong. Besides, I refuse to shatter what's left of my heart. That's what I want to say.

"What would you have me say?" I ask instead.

"Something. Anything. Scream at me. Tell me how much you hate me. Only don't walk away from me again."

"I don't hate you," I whisper. And it's true, I could never hate him. He could spit in my face and tell me he never wanted to see me again and I would still love him with everything in me. I'm pathetic.

I walk to the end of the bridge and head toward the trees. The sound of his footsteps tells me he's crossing the bridge as well, following my lead. When I reach the tree line, I turn and face him. His eyes are dark and he's staring down at me with an intensity that stops my breath. Without warning, he takes one determined stride, successfully closing the distance between us.

His hands grab my face, and then his lips press against mine. The taste of his mouth and the way his breath mixes with mine clouds my head and sends my heart into a frenzy. I should resist, but there's not a single part of me that can.

I wrap my arms around his neck and pull him to me, twisting my fingers in his hair. A grunt escapes his throat as he feels me respond. One of his hands moves to the back of my head, tangling in my hair, while the other hand travels down my back and pulls me forward, pressing me firmly against him. Both of us are fighting for control, pushing and pulling, trying to take as much of each other in as we possibly can, trying to make up for all the time that was lost to us. His arm curls around my waist and he walks us backward, until he has me flush against the trunk of a tree.

He lets go of my waist and places his hands on either side of my head, his lips moving away from my mouth. He brushes them along the surface of my cheek before trailing them to my jaw and then down to the base of my neck. I struggle to catch my breath and gain control of my thoughts, of my body. I shouldn't be doing this. I have too many doubts. Too many questions. His teeth graze lightly against my neck. I'm angry with him, aren't I? But I can't remember why. All I can think about is his lips and how they're doing things to me that no one has ever done before.

My first kiss—this is my first kiss. But it's not his. He has done this before. His lips have done this before, and not to me. I untangle my fingers from his hair and move my hands to the center of his chest. His heart pounds beneath my palms as his lips caress my shoulder blade. My knees shake, but I manage to find my resolve and shove him as hard as I can. He stumbles backward, but quickly manages to steady himself.

"What was that for?" he asks, his voice shaky and breathless.

"You shouldn't have kissed me like that!"

"Well you didn't seem opposed to it." He straightens himself out and runs an unsteady hand through his hair.

"Was Jacqueline opposed to it when you kissed her like that too?" I attack, feigning mock interest. His hand drops to his side. He looks completely stunned. I wait for him to respond, hoping with everything in me that he'll deny it. That he'll tell me I'm mistaken.

"How . . . who . . . who told you that?" he stammers. My stomach drops.

"I overheard her talking with her friends and she told them all about it. How you saw her in Synereal and went on a walk with her. Then you passionately kissed her and told her how much you hoped you would see her again someday."

His face is a carefully composed mask. Clearly, I'm not mistaken. If I were, he would have refuted it by now. The fact that he doesn't deny my accusation sickens me.

"You know what the worst part of it is . . . ?" I say while fighting back the tears that are threatening to spill over, hoping my words will hurt him as much as his actions hurt me. ". . . that while you were over in the capital, going on walks and kissing Jacqueline, I was at home, sick and injured, and the only thing I wanted was you."

His eyes flash to mine, as sharp as cut emeralds. "That's a lie! You didn't want me!"

"How could you say that? Of course I wanted you!" I still do, despite everything. That has never been a lie.

"You didn't want me!" He repeats, his chest rising and falling with his angered breaths. "*I* am the one who wanted you! You are all I ever wanted! Everything I did was *for you* and I chose you! I was going to come back to you! *You* are the one who didn't want me." As he says this, all the anger leaves his face, replaced instead with pain.

"That's not true! I . . ." I try to argue, but stop myself because even though I want to tell him he's wrong, I know that I'm the one who's wrong. I was the one that pulled away from him before I was attacked, but that was only because I was trying to do what was best for him. He doesn't know that though. I have to be honest with him. Lying and trying to protect my feelings is getting me nowhere. "That day in the woods, I only pulled away from you and told you I wanted you to leave because I didn't want you to feel pressured into staying in Faygrene for me. It would have been completely unfair of me to ask you to stay, especially when I knew how much you wanted to go. I wanted you to stay more than anything, but I couldn't do that to you."

He seems to calm slightly, but then he shakes his head while crossing his arms defiantly over his chest, his eyes burning with an emotion I can't place.

"That was my decision to make, not yours. You should have been honest with me and let me decide what to do. Besides, that's not what I'm talking about. I decided to stay after all that anyway."

"Then why did you leave?"

His eyebrows scrunch with confusion. "Because of the prisoner. I had to leave and try to talk to him, to get some sort of answers from him about Incarnadine. And I told your father and you, in the letter I wrote you, that I was going to come back to you as soon as I had answers."

A letter . . . My father . . . I don't understand.

"Then your father wrote me and told me not to write you anymore. He said you were moving on and that you wanted me to move on too and that getting letters from me just hurt you more." The pain is clear in his voice as he speaks, but what he's saying doesn't make sense. He looks at the grass at his feet, his voice slightly lowering. "When I read those words, my whole world came crashing in on me. I never felt so much pain in my life, but I did what you wanted. I stopped sending you letters and I canceled my plans to leave the Schild. Then, one day I was in the capital's market and I saw Jacqueline and . . . obviously, you know the rest, but I didn't want her. I just wanted to see if I could feel anything for another girl."

"Did you?" I ask before I can stop myself. There are so many other questions I have about what he's said. But this is the one that matters the most. And though I'm terrified of the answer, I have to know the truth. His eyes flash to my face, looking at me as though I've gone completely mad.

"Of course not. All I felt when I kissed her was disappointment and heartache because she wasn't you. I didn't want to be disrespectful, so I told her that I hoped to see her again, but that was a lie." He pauses for a moment, as if considering his next words. He lets out a breath and looks me straight in the eye. "You are the only girl I have *ever* wanted. Every time I looked at you or thought of you, I knew that this," he gestures between us, "was the only thing that mattered. It was the only thing I needed. But I also thought that you didn't feel the same way, so I convinced myself that it would be better for both of us if I stayed in Synereal."

"Better for both of us," I repeat his words back to him with a frustrated chuckle. "It wasn't."

He doesn't respond to my words, and I take some time to try and wrap my head around what he's said, but it's too overwhelming. He said he wrote me telling me he was going to come back and that my father knew he was going to come back, but that's not true. It can't be. Then he said that my father told him I had moved on, but that's definitely not true. Sure, Charles had come to see me, but my father knew I didn't reciprocate his feelings. So he wouldn't have told Drake I had moved on. But why would Drake lie about that? And if Drake's not lying, then it's my father who has lied. But why would my father do that?

"I know I was sick, but once I woke up I was aware enough to know if I had received a letter from you. I didn't get any letters. And I definitely didn't tell my father to tell you not to write me or to tell you that I had moved on."

"So you think I'm lying to you?" he asks defiantly.

Maybe he is lying. Maybe he's trying to cover the fact that he wanted to stay in Synereal. But everything about his demeanor tells me he's not.

"I don't know what to think, Drake." And I don't, I'm too overwhelmed to think right now.

He moves toward me, his eyes guarded. He reaches inside his vest and pulls out a pile of what must be at least twenty letters. "Maybe these will help."

"I thought you said you stopped writing me."

"I said I stopped sending you letters, not that I stopped writing them." His voice is distant as he places the letters in my hands. He gives me one last unsure look before turning away and walking farther into the woods. I want to call out to him and tell him to stay with me, but instead I watch him walk away.

Chapter 15

HER

I wait outside the manor for Gregory, sitting underneath the glass birds, their flickering eyes watching me as my fingers drift absentmindedly to my lips, remembering the feel of Drake's kiss. My heart quickens at the memory, and I have to slow it by thinking about his words. Is he lying to me or is it my father who's lied? I'm not sure which deception would be worse.

After what feels like an eternity, Gregory finally makes his way out, arm in arm with Mary. His mask is now on her face, and hers is in her hand. They're joking and laughing playfully so it takes several seconds for him to see me, but when he does, he whispers something in Mary's ear, kisses her gently on the cheek, and rushes to my side.

"What happened? Did Charles hurt you?" he asks anxiously, crouching down next to me.

Charles. I almost forgot about him. He's probably looking for me. I feel instantly guilty, but I can't deal with turning down Charles's courtship right now.

"Drake's back," is the only thing I can manage to say. Gregory doesn't seem surprised.

"I assumed he'd eventually come back. He wasn't doing very well over there."

"What makes you say that?" *And why didn't you tell me?*

Gregory shrugs. "He was a great Schild, but he wasn't himself while we were there. Well, in the beginning he was. He even talked about coming back to you. But then one day he said he would be staying in Synereal. I asked him why, but he wouldn't explain. After that day he focused solely on his duties and hardly spoke to anyone, including me."

Our carriage arrives, and Gregory takes my hand to help me up. "What are those?" he asks, his chin motioning toward the letters. I ignore his question and take my seat. I can feel Gregory watching me, waiting for me to speak, but I remain silent and watch the trees pass. When we arrive home, I jump down from the carriage and run to the front door.

When I step inside, Mother's footsteps rush down the hallway, eager to find out how our night went. When she turns the corner, her gaze falls upon me and she stops.

"What happened?"

"Drake's back." Thankfully, Gregory answers for me while closing the door behind him. Mother nods and steps aside, allowing me to pass.

Once I'm in my chambers, I light the candles around my bed and peel off my dress, throwing it in a disheveled pile on the floor, leaving me in my chemise. I climb into bed with the letters and Drake's jonquil gripped tightly in my hands. I take a deep breath as I set them down on the nightstand, and take the top letter in my hands. With trembling fingers and a rapidly beating heart, I open the first letter.

Addy,

Another sleepless night passes by. I don't even try to sleep anymore. Instead, I come to the lake. The stillness of the water and the surrounding trees remind me of you. You would love it here. So quiet. Nothing but the sound of the leaves rustling in the wind and the water lapping at the shore. I can picture you, perched on top of one of the branches of the trees, staring down at me as I write this letter. If only you were.

Lately, I find myself thinking about when we were young. I miss the innocence and naivety of those days. I wish I could go back and tell myself that those strange feelings I was having were those of jealousy and love. Maybe if I had recognized them sooner, I'd be with you now.

Once I realized my feelings, I thought that not

knowing how you felt about me was the worst it could get. I was wrong. I realized that the day you almost died.

Knowing that you're awake and recovering is what I focus on now. Even though I'm not with you, each day you grow stronger, I grow stronger too. But I'm still incomplete without you.

How do you spend your days? What's filling them with excitement? I wish I were there with you. I regret leaving you every single day.
Drake

Addy,
I know I'm not supposed to write you. Your father says my letters will only hurt you more, which will hold you back in your recovery. I don't want anything to hold you back, especially not me. But I can't stop writing you. So instead I'll put the words that I wish I could say to you on this paper and keep them with me. It's better than keeping them in my head. I already have enough thoughts in there to drive me mad.

I wish I could say that I'm happy you've moved on. But the thought of you with Charles makes me sick.

Why did you choose him? I guess it doesn't matter why. It was your choice to make. I made my choice the day I left. I made the choice to chase a past that doesn't seem to exist, instead of stay in the present and save my future with you.
Drake

The tears are running down my face as I reach for more letters and tear through them. It's like binging on sweets; addicting, but in the end, I know my stomach will sour with the thought of how much pain has been caused and how much time has been lost.

Addy,
King Theoderic agreed to let me see the prisoner from Incarnadine. He said I've done well in my training and will be allowed to help question him in the next few days.

I'm eager to see him and get some answers, but I'm scared too. I'm scared that he'll tell me something awful about my family or about myself. But honestly, what terrifies me most is the possibility that he won't know anything. If that's the case, I'll be left, once again, with no answers.

I also think I might tell King Theoderic the truth. I

trust him and don't think he will punish me for being from Incarnadine. And maybe if he knows the truth, he'll give me more information.
Drake

Addy,
The prisoner is dead. King Theoderic said he killed himself, but there are rumors that say otherwise. If the rumors are true, I can't tell King Theoderic the truth about my past. Though I still think he would help me, I can't take the chance. I don't care much about what he would do to me. But I'm worried about what could happen to you. I'm terrified that you could be punished for lying. If I tell the King about how you really found me, will the news spread to Faygrene? And if it does, what will this mean for you? People in Faygrene would be furious with you for lying about me. Even if the King wouldn't consider me cursed, others will, and they'll punish you for bringing me into their village. I could ask him to keep my secret, but I don't trust anyone, apart from myself, with your safety.

I'll still ask him what he knows about Incarnadine,

and see if he'll give me any information. With that information, I'll try to put the pieces together on my own. But it really doesn't matter to me anymore if I ever remember or not. I'm tired of the constant dead ends, and I miss you. I miss all of you. I miss the life I had in Faygrene.

I wish I could talk to you.

Drake

Addy,

Gregory left today. Right before he left, he asked me if I wanted to leave with him. I couldn't answer him. I couldn't make my mouth form the words to tell him no, but I couldn't go with him. So I walked away and let him leave, without saying good bye. He must think I'm a coward. Maybe I am.

Drake

I stay up all night reading his letters, trying to decipher his words and the emotions they leave inside me. As the sun begins to rise, I find myself reaching for the last one.

* * *

Addy,

I'm on my way home to you. I asked Walter to write Mary and ask her about your relationship with Charles. He just brought me her response. She said that she has no knowledge of you being courted by him and that from what you have told her, you have no interest in him. She also said that, though you've recovered, you're different. You're solemn and not yourself. She thinks that it's because of me. Though it kills me to know I may have caused you pain, her words have also allowed me to feel hope for the first time in months. So I'm coming home. Don't be angry with Mary. Walter promised her he wasn't going to tell me anything.

Drake

I sit on my bed stunned, as I absorb it all. Drake was telling the truth. Which means my father lied to us both. Anger courses through me. I don't know why my father would lie, but I'll find out later. Right now I have to find Drake.

I jump off my bed and throw my black hooded cloak over my chemise. I find my black riding boots, shove them onto my feet, and make my way out the window, landing on the cold ground.

The sun is barely making its presence known, peeking over the horizon with a lazy glance. I head straight for the woods, knowing that's where he'll go. He may not be there yet, but he'll come and I'll be waiting for him when he does.

What am I going to say to him? There are so many things I want to say, but I don't know where I should start. I blow out a nervous breath and watch it form in the air. It's bitter outside and the fact that I'm wearing nothing but a thin chemise under my cloak does little to help keep me warm. I pull the cloak tighter around me and raise my hood. I didn't look in the mirror before I came, but I'm sure that after a sleepless, tearful night, I look far from my best.

I turn the corner and the line of the woods comes into view. Drake is already there, leaning against the wall. His arms are crossed over his chest, his shoulders hunched. He's wearing the same clothes he wore last night.

His head snaps up at the sound of my footsteps and when his eyes find me, I notice the dark shadows underneath them. I want to run into his arms, but something in his expression makes me hesitate, and instead I come to a stop several feet away from him.

His cheeks and nose are red from the cold. He must be freezing, having nothing to cover his arms other than his thin black tunic. His face is pale, causing the dark circles under his eyes to look like bruises. We stare at each other in silence, both of us waiting.

"How long have you been here?" I ask, knowing I need to be the one to speak first, but unsure of what to say.

"I came here last night, after I left Lord Berrenger's."

"You've been here all night?"

"I wanted to be here in case you decided to look for me. I didn't want to risk missing you." There's a tremor in his voice, and I can't help but wonder if it's from the cold or something else. His eyes continue to search mine, and I can't stand the space between us any longer.

I move toward him and wrap my arms around his waist, pressing my body against his and laying my head on his chest. He tenses momentarily, but within seconds he wraps me in his arms, pulling me against him and letting out a breath of relief. Having him here and knowing he loves me fills me with a web of emotions. I want to laugh and cry at the same time. I want to pull his body as close to mine as it can get, leaving nothing between us, and I never want to let go.

I wrap my arms more firmly around him and become suddenly aware of the chill of his skin seeping through his clothes. I remove my hands from his waist and find the opening of my cloak. Then, I wrap my arms around his neck, with the cloak, trapping both of our bodies inside its warmth.

My chemise offers a practically nonexistent layer between my body and his. I can feel every curve and line of his body pressed firmly against mine as we embrace. The buckles of his vest are pressing into my chest, his belt pressing into my waist. The muscles of his strong arms are wrapped around me, his fingers rubbing gentle circles on my back. But it's not enough. I want more.

I lift my head up and turn into him. The ties of his

black shirt are undone, leaving part of his chest and collar bones exposed. I stand on my toes and gently press my lips to the exposed skin. He inhales sharply and as I brush my lips along his chest, he lets out a shaky breath and pulls his arms out of the cloak. Then his hands are on my face. He gently pulls my face back, breaking my lips away from his body. His eyes are ablaze with desire, his cheeks flushed, but I have a feeling it's no longer from the cold.

His eyes travel to my lips and I wait with painful anticipation for him to kiss me. With each that second that passes, the frustration burns more and more painfully, until eventually I can't take it anymore.

"Kiss me," I say breathlessly.

The corner of his mouth twitches and pulls up into a half grin. "No." Amusement is dancing in his voice and sparkling in his eyes. He lets go of my face and takes a step away from me, breaking my hold on his neck. My arms drop to my sides and I cross them over my chest, hating the void his stepping away has created.

"Why not?"

"Because I have already tried that, twice, and you pushed me away both times." There's no pain or anger in his voice—it's light and playful—but it doesn't lessen the guilt I feel.

"I promise I won't push you away this time," I say, my voice coming out in more of a whine than I intended. He raises one eyebrow and his face breaks into a full smile, exposing both of his devastatingly handsome dimples.

"Oh, really? What would make this time different?" His words are still playful, but there's a seriousness to his face and tone as well. He wants a real answer. I take a deep breath and prepare to give him one.

"I read your letters."

"And?"

"And, honestly, I don't know what to say. I know that you were telling the truth, that you thought that I had moved on with Charles, but I'm still so confused. I don't understand why my father would lie to you, to me." My voice breaks and I swallow back the oncoming tears.

He's looking at me intently, no longer smiling. "Isn't it obvious?"

"Isn't what obvious?"

He takes a small step toward me. "Your father wants you to be with someone who can give you a better life than I can. And I don't blame him for that. Part of me wishes I could let you go so that you could have a better life. And I think part of you wants that too."

"How could you say that? *You* make my life better. I don't care about anything else. I don't need anything else but you."

"Then why did you accept Charles's jonquil?"

"Because I didn't think you were an option anymore. Holding on to you was nearly killing me. I wasn't ready to move on, but I had to try." I speak forcefully, wanting him to know how deeply I mean these words. But his face still holds doubt, his body still keeps distance. "Now you don't believe me?"

He runs his hands through his hair, tugging on it as

he lets out a breath. "I believe you, Addalynne, because I can tell that you believe what you're saying is true. Right now you want me. But how can I be sure it's not just a momentary impulse?"

I blanch, feeling stunned that he could actually believe that. "You think I'm that shallow?"

"No, but you turned away from me before I left. We had a chance to finally be together and you refused it."

"I already explained that to you last night. I didn't want to hold you back."

I wait for him to respond, but he remains silent, so I continue instead.

"When I was sick, I remember fading in and out of consciousness, my mind trapped by the pain, by the hallucinations. But when you were there, my body knew. It responded to you: calming me in ways no one else's touch could. I also remember having nightmares, nightmares in which I couldn't find you, no matter how hard I searched. Nightmares in which others kept me from you. You consumed every thought I had, even when my thoughts were uncontrollable. All I wanted was you by my side. When I woke, you were the first person I thought of, the first person I needed. It destroyed me when I realized you had left." I stare straight into his dark green eyes. "You have to believe me, Drake. I only accepted Charles's jonquil because I thought you were never coming back to me."

Drake slowly crosses the distance between us, coming to a stop merely inches away from me. His breath blows lightly across my face and he lifts his hand. He gently brushes it across my cheek, wiping away a tear.

"I'm so sorry I left." His voice is saturated with pain and anger. "I should have never left you. I should have stayed and fought for you, taken care of you. I'll never forgive myself for walking away."

"It's not your fault, Drake. You needed a chance to find answers, and I'm the one that pushed you away. I'm the reason you were able to believe my father. I had given you no reason to believe that I . . ." My words falter.

He searches my face. "That you what?"

"That I loved you."

He pulls in a breath and holds it, sealing us in this moment. When he lets it out, I feel it brush along my skin, sending shivers across my spine. "You say you loved me then, but do you still love me now?"

I can't believe he's asking me this. Can't he tell by the way I've been behaving that I love him? The hint of excitement in his eyes tells me he can, but the desperation and fear in them tells me he needs to hear me say it.

"You asked me in one of your letters if I ever dreamt of you. The answer is yes, I dream of you every day and every night. You were on my mind as much as I was on yours. Of course I love you, Drake. I will always love you."

Those words are all it takes. His face spreads into the most breathtaking smile I have ever seen. In this moment, all the fear, all the pain, all the doubt, completely washes away. He reaches his arm out, wraps it around my waist and pulls me firmly against his chest.

"Now, I'll kiss you," he says, and his smile once again turns into my favorite crooked grin. He leans down toward me, and when his lips meet mine, they are soft and gentle. I wrap my arms around his waist and give in completely, letting every emotion and feeling take over. I no longer have to try to fight against it. He is here and he is mine.

We stay until the sun has risen fully, but still it feels like it's all too soon when he pulls away.

"We need to get you home and get some more clothes on you," he says, while gazing down the length of my body, taking in the thin chemise I have on under my cloak.

"No, not yet. One more kiss," I stand on my toes and try to reach his lips. He places his hands on my shoulders and presses me back down.

"After you've changed."

"Why?"

"Because kissing you while you're wearing that is pushing the boundaries of my self-control."

"That's fine. You don't need self-control." I trace my hands along the lines of his stomach, and feel his body tense beneath my touch. His hands slip from my shoulders and I rise up on my toes once more, smiling with my victory. This time I place a kiss on his neck. A grunt escapes his lips and he reaches his hands into my cloak and runs them along my waist. I press myself against him and trace my lips across his throat while his hands move down the sides of my hips, gathering the material of my chemise in his fists until he reaches my bare thighs. I stiffen at the feel of his hands on my legs, skin against skin, and in that moment of hesitation, he finds his self-control.

His hands instantly drop from my thighs and he pulls them out of my cloak. "I'm sorry," he says as he closes my cloak and wraps it firmly around me.

"Sorry for what?"

"I shouldn't have done that. Touching you that way . . ." His face is feverish, his eyes dark with desire, but I know he won't give in again. I hate self-control. He turns away from me and runs his hands through his hair.

"Drake, look at me." I can't believe he's apologizing. I wanted everything he gave me and more, so much more.

He slowly drifts his gaze back over to my face, a look of shame clearly reflected in his eyes.

"Do I look bothered by what you did?"

"No, but . . ."

"But nothing, Drake. I want you. I want all of you, and nothing you give me will ever be too much." I watch some of the shame leave his face and am relieved when a ghost of his smile returns.

"I won't take advantage of you, Addy. No matter how badly I want to. So please let me be a gentleman and take you home. Besides, people are going to be waking up soon. Do you really want to have to explain to your family why you've been running around in your undergarments?" he asks with a raised eyebrow.

I look down at the ground, a frown weighting my lips. He's right. I have no argument to use against his logic. He laughs and traces his fingers across my face.

"Don't look so sad. We have our whole lives ahead of us to be together." He places his fingers under my chin and tilts my face up to look at him. "And I promise I'll let you try to make me forget my self-control again very soon."

Chapter 16

HER

The rising sun creates a golden landscape across the sky. Drake's lips are gentle against my own, his fingers twirling through my disheveled curls. I could spend my whole life kissing him and it wouldn't be long enough. Much to my disappointment, he slowly pulls away.

"Don't leave," I whisper and wrap my hands around his vest. He gives me a small smile, then places his hands on my waist. He lifts me up and sets me on the ledge of my windowsill. I let my legs dangle off the side and reach out and grab his face, successfully pulling him to me. I kiss him this time, enjoying the height advantage the window has given me. He leans into me, bracing his arms on either side of my body, his hands gripping the frame of the open window. After a few seconds, he again pulls away.

"When I said I would let you try to make me forget

my self-control again sometime soon, I didn't mean today," he says with a grin, his green eyes sparkling in the early morning light.

"I'll be trying to make you forget every day." I try to put on a seductive smile, knowing I'm most likely failing completely. His eyes darken slightly. Maybe I'm better at this than I thought.

"Go inside, Addalynne."

"Only if you come inside with me."

His lips part with an exhale. "No," he says, but the word has little conviction behind it. He runs his fingers through his hair. Then, he looks down at the ground and shakes his head. "I can't," he murmurs, but it's clear he's trying to convince himself, not me. He looks back up, his face flushed. "I want to . . . but I can't."

I should give up and go inside, but I'm not ready to let him leave, and he's so close to breaking.

"Yes, you can. You have been in my chambers plenty of times. Besides, if we hear anyone coming down the hallway, you can just jump back out the window." I fist my hands around the collar of his shirt and pull him to me once more. This time he doesn't let me win. He plants his feet firmly into the ground, his forward motion completely stopping. He gives me a quick, disapproving look before removing my hands from his collar and placing them back on my own lap.

"I promise I'll come back later," he says. "You need to rest, and I need to change and talk to my father."

"Does he know you're back?"

"He knows. But I arrived in Faygrene just as the Ball

was starting and only had time to change my clothes. He was completely shocked when he saw me barge through the door and run for my loft. I was in such a rush that I didn't even try to explain anything to him."

I laugh, picturing what my uncle's face must have looked like.

He reaches forward and gently cups my cheek with his hand. "My only thoughts were of getting to you." I turn my face into his palm and place a kiss inside it.

"You promise you'll come back as soon as you can?" I hate that I'm giving in and letting him leave. But I have to. He needs to see my uncle, and we both need to change. I can't spend the entire day in my chemise, though the thought does have its appeal. Besides, I need to talk to my father, too. I need to know why he lied.

"I won't waste any time getting back to you, I promise." He leans in and places one last kiss on my lips.

I stay on the ledge of the window as I watch him walk away. Once I can no longer see him, I pull myself into my chambers and throw myself down on the bed. I'm exhausted, but I'm too restless to sleep. Thoughts of the conversations that I need to have with my father and with Charles have my head spinning. My mind wants me to get dressed and deal with them now, but my body is trapping me in bed. I roll over onto my side and see Drake's letters scattered on my table and floor. My father and Charles can wait. I reach down, pick up some of the letters and re-read them, letting Drake's words lull me into the first truly peaceful sleep I've had in almost a year.

* * *

* * *

I jump up into a sitting position, my heart racing from the sound of someone pounding on my door. Letters are scattered across my bed, the ivory paper reflecting the light of the midday sun that's trespassing through the window.

"Addalynne, are you in there?!"

So it's my mother making that awful noise. I make my way over to my door and fling it open. Mother's eyes graze over me.

"Have you really been asleep this entire time?" she asks, her eyes widened with disbelief.

"Yes. I didn't sleep well last night. I finally fell asleep early this morning." I don't bother trying to mask the annoyance in my voice as I think longingly of the dream her abrasive knocking woke me from. I can still feel the brush of his lips gently working their way down my neck. The feel of his . . .

"Addalynne, listen to me. I said you have a visitor." It takes me a moment to understand what she's saying. When I do, I instantly regret my sleep. Instead of getting dressed so I would be ready when Drake came, I let myself sleep, and now I'll have to wait even longer to see him.

"Tell Drake I'll be right out." I turn and search for a dress to wear. My hands land upon a green gown that has gold ribbon tying up the arms and neckline; that will help him forget his self control. I turn back around, eager to change, and am startled by my mother, who's still standing in my doorway, staring at me curiously.

"It's not Drake. It's Charles." Her words sound like an apology.

Disappointment and apprehension scatter through me. I pause, unsure of what to do. "Oh. . . Please tell him I might be a while. I need to bathe and change." And think. "He can either wait or I'll come visit him later." Mother nods and closes my door.

I'm tangled with anxiety as I dry myself off and begin to dress. I still don't know what I'm going to say to Charles, and though I played out various conversations in my head while I bathed, nothing seemed right.

After I'm fully dressed, I move toward the mirror and look at myself for the first time since last night. I look more alive than ever, despite the shadows under my eyes. My face is flushed, my eyes shining, and I can't help but smile.

My hair is still wet and dripping down my back, dampening the green dress. I decide to put it in a single, long braid, the only kind I can do myself.

After I finish my hair, I run to Elizabeth's chambers and rummage through her jewelry. Finally, I find a beautiful, triple-stringed, pearl necklace that will fit perfectly around my neck. I fasten it and make my way down the hall.

"He decided to wait outside," Mother says, her eyes on the quilt she's knitting by the fire. "He's still there now."

I nod and with a steading breath, I open the front door.

Charles and his black horse are standing outside the front wall, along the side of the stables. Charles's dark blond hair shines above the navy blue cloak he has draped around his shoulders. My stomach turns. If only I hadn't accepted his jonquil.

He turns at the sound of my footsteps and a smile breaks across his face. "Addalynne! You've kept me waiting."

"I'm sorry, my Lord." I've never referred to him this way before, but I figure a little flattery may help.

"You're forgiven. Your beauty is worth the wait." His face still holds a smile, but there's something in his voice that makes me wonder if he's not as forgiving as he seems.

I come to a stop several feet away from him and cross my arms over my chest, shielding myself from the cold breeze and the discomfort.

He takes a step closer to me. "But I'm confused about what happened last night," he says as he begins to walk around me. "If I remember correctly, I got our wine and tried to find you, but you were nowhere to be found." His tone is measured and interrogative, and I'm left with an engrossing sense of unease.

"I'm sorry. I became ill unexpectedly, so I left the Ball. I should have told you, but I had to leave as quickly as possible." I speak as strongly as I can, forcing myself to keep my head up while he continues his slow circular dance. Finally, he stops directly in front of me and reaches out his hand, placing it on my neck. His fingers slip under my necklace. They glide underneath the pearls, pulling the strings uncomfortably tight around me.

"This is a lovely necklace," he says, his narrowed eyes locking onto mine. My pulse quickens. "Was it a gift?" The way his mouth curls into a snarl when he says "gift" sends apprehension crawling down my spine.

"No. I borrowed it from my sister."

He releases it from his grasp and I take a welcome breath.

"It's lovely on you. Perhaps you'll allow me to purchase you a necklace of your own."

"That won't be necessary."

"Oh, I disagree. It's not only necessary, but expected for my Lady to be properly adorned. And you are my Lady, Addalynne. Or did I imagine you accepting my jonquil last night?"

"No. But I made a mistake. I wasn't myself last night, and I shouldn't have accepted your jonquil. I'm sorry, but your attention would be better directed elsewhere." I try to put as much conviction into my words as I can, but the tremor in my voice is as distinct as the clouds in the sky.

"I see," he says quietly. The carefully masked anger is barely perceptible, but it's there.

I take a step back, wanting nothing more than to get away from him and his penetrating gaze. Finally, he turns on his heel and walks back to his horse. As he pulls himself atop it, he turns back to me. His face once again holds the meticulously crafted, charming smile. "I'm sorry things didn't work out the way I had hoped, but I wish you well, Addalynne."

"You as well, my Lord," I reply, my voice feeble with anxiety.

As he rides away, I let out a breath and slowly make my way back into our home. I'm grateful to find the entry vacant, but when I step through the doorway of my chambers, my gaze immediately lands on Drake. He's standing in the shadow next to the window, his back against the wall, his arms crossed over his chest. He has one leg bent, the bottom of his black boot flat against the wall. His hair is tousled and falling across his forehead and his eyes are narrowed as he stares at me.

I smile and make my way toward him, but something in his expression stops me half way.

"How was your meeting with Charles?" he questions coldly, making me feel exposed and guilty.

"How did you know about that?" I ask without thinking. He raises both eyebrows and blows out a sharp breath of air. Those were the wrong words. I made it sound like I was trying to keep it from him.

"I was on my way here when I saw you talking to him. Tell me *please* why you lied about your reason for leaving him last night?"

"How . . . You were listening?"

"I thought it would be best if I were nearby when you told him about me, in case he got angry. Clearly though, you have no intention of telling him anything about me. Once I realized that, I stopped listening and came here." The anger and hurt in his voice and face make me feel incredibly guilty, but also defensive. I don't appreciate the accusation I see in his eyes.

"I'm sorry I didn't tell him about you. I was afraid it would make things worse, and I assumed he would eventually find out on his own. Besides, if you had stayed a little longer you would have heard me tell him that I'm not interested in him and that it would be better for him to turn his attention elsewhere."

He drops his foot from the wall, the first movement he's made since I walked in. Progress, perhaps. I take one step toward him.

"How did he take it?" he asks, as he studies my face. If I lie to him about Charles's reaction, there's a good chance he'll see right through it. But if I tell him the truth about how Charles made me feel, he'll overreact, and if he so much as says one wrong word to Charles, a man who's considered to be royalty in Faygrene, he could be severely punished. Protecting him is more important than him wondering if I'm lying. I pull myself out of my thoughts and realize that Drake is now standing directly in front of me.

"I know you, Addy. I know when you're worried, and you've bitten your lip so badly it's bleeding." He reaches up and extracts my lip from my teeth. "There's something you're not telling me. *What happened?*"

"Nothing. It was fine. He wished me well."

He drops his hand to his side. "You're lying to me."

"No. I'm not."

"Yes, Addalynne, you are." He turns away from me and walks toward the window. His hands run aggressively through his hair, balling it in his fists, while he stares outside. "We can't keep lying to each other. It only ends up hurting us more in the end." He's right, but I know how protective he is. Besides Charles didn't really do anything—it was more the feeling he gave me, like the strong wind before a storm. And I've always had a wild imagination. I could be the one overreacting.

I watch Drake stare out the window, his hands still fisted in his hair, the muscles in his arms tight with tension. He's angry and hurt, and all I want is for things to go back to the way they were this morning.

"I'm sorry if my actions hurt you. But I'm not lying to you."

"Then why do you seem so anxious?"

"Because I hurt him and I feel bad about it," I lie, hoping this will be a good enough reason to justify my silence, but his body stiffens in response to my words.

"Do you have feelings for him?" he murmurs, pain cutting through his voice.

I move to his side. His eyes are closed, his eyebrows scrunched together. I gently reach my hand up and rub my thumb over the crease in his brows, trying to erase the concern and doubt I see there.

"No. Of course not."

He slowly opens his eyes and turns his head toward me.

I wrap my hands around his fists. With the contact, he automatically loosens his grip, allowing me to place my fingers in his.

"Now can we please move on from this? I love you, Drake. You know that."

He lowers our clasped hands and leans his forehead against mine, his eyes closed. "I've wanted you for so long," he begins, "and every time I came close to having you, you would slip away."

"I won't slip away this time. But you have to promise you won't either."

His nose brushes against mine. "Never," he says, his breath warm and intoxicating on my mouth. His lips touch mine and everything else fades away, leaving nothing apart from this moment and this promise.

Chapter 17

HER

"Addy, we don't have to do this if you're not ready. We can go to the market instead." Drake pulls us to a stop, interpreting my silence as hesitation. His gaze is on my face, mine lingers on the trees. The wind is blowing through the newly grown leaves and the sun is glistening off the tall branches. It's a perfect day to be in the woods.

For the past six months, I desperately wanted to go into the woods again, to return to my place of escape. But every time I looked toward the trees, any shred of bravery I had would cower inside me. Now that Drake is here with me, I finally have the confidence to try.

"No, I want to. I need this." I place more conviction in my voice than I actually feel and swallow back my fear.

Drake nods. "We won't go anywhere near the river," he promises and offers my hand a light squeeze as we continue to make our way toward the tree line.

With one last deep breath, we step into the shadows of the trees. The scent of dirt and sap invades my nostrils, and the sound of leaves and sticks crunching under my feet creates the perfect melody. Everything is at once familiar and comforting. There's no fear. A smile breaks across my face as I take it all in, relishing the feel of the woods around me.

I look at Drake. He's smiling down at me with amusement. I reach up and kiss one of his dimples before wrapping my arms around his waist.

"Thank you," I say, and lean my head against his chest.

He returns the embrace and runs his hands down the length of my back. "For what?"

"For being here. I couldn't have done this without you."

"I'll always be here for you," he murmurs, his lips pressed against the top of my head.

I have two things back in my life that I was sure I had lost forever. I can't imagine wanting anything more than I have now.

"Are you ready to practice?" he asks, after a few minutes of comfortable silence. It's now that I remember the bow and arrows he has strapped across his back. My answering grin tells him, 'Yes,' and he leads me further into the woods, being sure to keep a safe distance from the river.

After several minutes, we arrive at our old practice space, bringing with it a flood of memories—The many days Drake spent teaching me to shoot the bow; sitting among the wildflowers as we ate pie with our fingers, our laughter cutting through the air around us; laying on the trunk of the upturned tree and finding pictures in the clouds—These memories used to take the air from me, but now they're another thing I can have back: untainted and mine.

I smile and watch Drake remove a vial of red paint from his bag and pour some onto his fingers. The way the paint falls, slow and thick, makes it appear as though blood is dripping from his hands. I want to push the thought away, hating the memory it evokes, but I can't.

We still haven't spoken about that day since I told him the truth. Part of me wants to mention it and ask what he was able to learn about Incarnadine from King Theoderic, but I don't know how he'll react. Regardless, it needs to be discussed. As much as I want to, we can no longer pretend his past doesn't exist.

"Were you able to learn anything in Synereal?"

Drake stops walking, and the question hangs between us.

"No." He looks down at his hands and watches the paint drip from his fingers. "I wasn't able to ask many questions. Between the prisoner and the capital's knowledge of what had happened in Faygrene—with the attack on you and the disappearance of Samuel Hunt—the suspicions were too high. I tried to learn about the prisoner, but all the other Schilds told me was that he seemed crazed and that he kept rambling about experiments. How he didn't want to be the King's next experiment. The Schilds tried to question him more about it, and King Theoderic was going to send me in to see him, but then they found him dead. He bit off and swallowed his own tongue."

"But in your letters you said some people, including you, didn't think he killed himself."

He shrugs and walks to one of the trees. His fingers drag along the bark in a circular motion, creating red targets.

"I don't know anymore," he says as he moves toward the next tree. "I don't think King Theoderic would have a hand in killing a man whose only crime was being from Incarnadine." His words are wiped of emotion, leaving no trace of how he feels about what happened. But I can guess.

"Being from Incarnadine is not a crime."

"Maybe. Maybe not. But people have their superstitions regardless."

"So you think someone else could have had a hand in it?"

He finishes marking a third tree, then he wipes the rest of the paint off on some leaves, leaving them bleeding in the sun. "It's possible," he says and turns to face me. "There's a lot of distrust, Addy. More than I would have thought. So I figured that asking too many questions wouldn't do me any favors."

"So you didn't learn anything then?"

He looks away, his gaze on the South.

"I learned about the history of the kingdoms, which was basically everything that's in The Divided Kingdom book that we have here. I learned that the current King of Incarnadine is King Gareth. I listened to the rumors about the different hellions people think exist in Incarnadine. I saw the fear people have about King Gareth challenging our borders, though there's no proof that he's tried or ever will." He takes in a breath and blows it out as he runs his hands through his hair. "It was interesting," he continues. "But nothing helped me. Nothing triggered a memory or spoke of a missing boy."

I walk toward him and place my hand on his cheek, turning him to face me. His eyes meet mine and though he's trying to hide the hurt, I see it, and it breaks my heart.

"I'm so sorry, Drake."

He traces the tips of his fingers along my cheekbone and a small smile pulls on his lips.

"I'm fine. Really, I am. I don't need my past anymore. If it decides to find me, we'll deal with it, but I'm not going to seek it out. This is my home. You are my home."

"If you ever change your mind, I'll help you. We'll search together," I say as I slide my hand to the back of his head and pull him down to me. Our kiss is brief: an unspoken vow.

After several seconds we step apart and Drake nods toward the trees. "First one to hit the center of the circle on the farthest tree wins. The closer ones are for practice."

This is his way of ending our conversation, which is fine with me. There's already enough strain on the day from Charles's visit. Drake walks toward the bow. "Do you want the first turn, or do you want me to go first?" he asks, while picking up the bow from the forest floor. His fingers move meticulously over the bow, checking the string and the sturdiness of the wood. I watch his fingers, thinking of how they feel when they're on me, before trailing my gaze up the length of his arms, where the thin white sleeves of his fitted tunic are rolled up to his elbows. My gaze travels farther, to where his tunic ties low on his chest, exposing the curve of his muscles below his collar bones. I watch those curves disappear into his shirt, and wonder what they look like underneath.

"Addy, are you listening . . . ?" His eyes are on me, a curious smirk playing on his mouth, ". . . or is my presence too distracting for you?"

I look away, blushing furiously. He begins to laugh.

"No. Your presence is not distracting me. I was just thinking about your question."

"And?" he asks, while continuing to laugh softly.

"I want to go first." I march over to him and, without looking him in the eye, take the bow from his hands and turn away.

"How are you going to shoot without an arrow?" he asks, humor thick in his voice. He's enjoying this way too much. I hesitantly let myself turn to face him and see that the quiver of arrows is still slung over his back.

"Give me one."

"No."

"Drake. Give me an arrow *now*," I reply, my last word coming out as more of a growl. This makes him laugh harder. I'm glad he finds me so entertaining.

"Nope. If you want one, you're going to have to get it yourself." His sideways grin pulls up the corner of his mouth.

Fine. Two can play at this game. I look around and see a boulder that's about as tall as my knees, only a few feet away. I walk toward it and place the bow carefully on top. Now that my hands are free, I place them on my hips and stare intently at him. He's still smirking, eager to see my next move. I slowly saunter over to him, my eyes never leaving his. I don't stop walking until I'm directly in front of him, leaving merely a fingernail's length of space between us.

I reach up and place my hand on top of his shoulder. Then, I slowly drag my hand down the length of his right arm, feeling it flex beneath my touch. When my hand reaches his elbow, I slide it under his arm and trace my fingers across his ribs. He inhales slightly, and I allow myself to press firmly against him. Our eyes remain locked, and his uneven breath blows across my face. I struggle to keep my composure while my hand makes its way to the quiver of arrows, feeling the softness of the feathers brush against my fingertips. I wrap my hand around one of the arrows and pull it from the quiver. Then, I slide my arm out from under his and take several steps back.

"Thank you," I say with a wink, before turning around and walking back to the bow, leaving him completely silent. My heart is in my throat, but I can't help but smile at my momentary victory.

I pick up the bow and fit the notch of my arrow into the taut string. I look up and find a tree with a target about twenty feet away; a good starting point. With a deep breath, I raise the bow, take aim, and feel Drake's chest press against my back. His hands slowly make their way from the tops of my shoulders, down along my arms and to my hands, stopping only when his arms are completely draped over mine.

"You're not holding it right," he whispers in my ear as he holds my hands in place, keeping them from releasing the arrow.

"Yes I am," I reply with a traitorous tremble in my voice.

"No, you're not, but I can show you." He nips the bottom of my ear with his teeth, as one of his hands releases the ribbon from the bottom of my braid, allowing my hair to spill around me. I close my eyes and try to clear my mind and body from the intoxication of him. But it's not working.

"I'm perfectly capable of shooting this arrow on my own. Let go of me and move away."

"Are you sure?" He traces the tips of his fingers along the inside of my arm, the sensation travels from my skin to somewhere deep inside of me. I take a steadying breath.

"I'm sure that if you don't let go right now, I'm going to tell my mother that you're interested in taking up knitting. She would love to spend hours teaching you."

"Sounds fascinating," he replies with a laugh. But he removes his arms from mine and backs away from my body.

I focus on the target, pull the arrow back and release it. The arrow soars toward the tree and hits right outside the center of the target.

"Not bad, but you would have done better if you hadn't let yourself become so distracted."

I spin around to face him. "I was not distracted!"

"If you say so. My turn." He reaches his hand out to me, smiling innocently. I shove the bow into his arms and take several steps back. He pulls an arrow from his quiver and loads it into the bow. "Now watch carefully. I'm going to show you how to hit the center of a target." He looks over and winks at me.

No. He's not going to win this one.

As he raises his arms to aim the bow, I raise my left leg and place my foot on top of the boulder. I reach down to the bottom of my dress, hook my fingers underneath the hem, and slowly pull it up, exposing my brown boot and then my white stocking. I don't need to look at him to know he's watching me. I can feel his eyes on me as certainly as I can feel the sun on my skin. A smile pulls at my lips and I continue to lift the dress higher, coming to a stop where my white stocking ends on the middle of my thigh. I adjust the top of my stocking, being sure to keep several inches of my bare thigh visible as I say, "Aren't you going to take your shot?" I hear him blow out a sharp breath seconds before I hear the release of his arrow. The arrow sails toward its target, the same practice tree I aimed for, and lands about five feet to the left, stabbing firmly into the dirt. I drop my foot back on the ground and let my skirt fall around me.

"Not bad, but you would have done better if you hadn't let yourself become so distracted." I say his words back to him as I turn and face him. He has one hand grasped around the bow and his other hand is moving unsteadily through his hair. His eyes are dark, his gaze penetrating.

"You don't play fair."

"I never said I did." I move toward him. "My turn." He places the bow in my hands, then reaches behind himself and grabs an arrow. When he hands it to me, I notice his hands are slightly shaking. Confidence burns through me as I realize just how much of an effect I've had on him.

As I load my bow, I use that confidence and aim for the farthest tree. I release the arrow and watch it sail beautifully toward its mark, striking directly in the center of the circle.

"I won!" I exclaim excitedly, and begin to spin around in circles as I laugh. I've never beaten him before. After a few more seconds, I stop spinning and plop to the ground, feeling dizzy but ecstatic.

Drake crouches in front of me. Before I can say anything, he leans in and presses his lips against mine. He deepens the kiss while he simultaneously takes the bow from my hands and gently pushes me down until I'm lying on my back. He pulls away to look at me, his face hovering inches above mine. His knees are placed on either side of my hips, his hands on either side of my head, holding himself over me. A sly grin spreads across his face.

"I won," he says. And then he kisses me again, and this time it is tender and sweet, but I don't want tender and sweet. I part my lips, and drag my tongue across his lower lip, savoring the taste of his mouth on mine. His body tenses and he inhales sharply, but he responds by pulling my bottom lip into his mouth, his teeth lightly nipping on it. His lips travel from my mouth, making their way to my jaw. His warm breath blows across me, sending chills through my body as his lips trace across my throat. My back arches off the ground, desperate to be closer to him.

He moves from his knees to his feet, elongating himself, and then carefully lowers the full length of his body on top of mine. He returns his lips to my own, and between his kiss and the weight and feel of him pressing against me, I become completely consumed by him. Even with my eyes closed, the only thing I see is his face. The taste of his lips fills my mouth. The scent of him—smoke, mint and leather—invades my nostrils. The only thing I feel is his body and his hands, and every breath, grunt and moan fills my ears.

One of his hands presses roughly into the dirt next to my head while he continues to kiss me. I can smell the earthy scent of the ground as he pushes his fingers through it, but it's his other hand that has my attention now. It's caressing its way across my chest and down my waist. It lingers for a moment on my hip, clenching the material of my dress, but it soon descends farther, stopping midway down my leg. Suddenly, his hand begins gathering up my dress, pulling it higher. Cool air hits the top of my thigh seconds before his warm hand reaches it. His hand grips firmly onto the skin of my thigh, and we both simultaneously moan. My hands fist into his shirt. He lowers his head and gently kisses my chest, his fingertips grazing the inside of my thigh. A shudder rips through me and I close my eyes in anticipation. And then he's gone.

My eyes fly open. *What just happened?* I push my unsteady body into a sitting position and see Drake sitting on the ground several feet away from me. He's leaning back on his elbows, his chest heaving, his face flushed, his gaze fixed on something in front of him. I follow his line of sight—Gregory. My heart falters. Gregory is staring down at Drake, a murderous expression on his face. Mary is standing cautiously behind him, her eyes darting uncomfortably back and forth between myself and Drake.

"Go home, Addalynne." Gregory's voice is quiet and filled with rage, his hands in tight fists.

"Not unless Drake comes with me."

"No. He's staying here with me so we can have a little chat. *You* are going to go back with Mary."

I force myself to rise shakily to my feet and make my way to Drake's side. "No, he's not." I offer my hand to Drake, but Drake doesn't look at me or my hand. Instead, he stays on the ground, a look of shame and guilt on his face.

"Go home, Addalynne," Drake responds, repeating

Gregory's words.

"No! I won't leave you here!"

"Addalynne, you don't want to be here for this. Go home." The implied threat is clear in Gregory's words and tone.

"No, Gregory! I won't let you hurt him! We're together, and you're going to have to accept that!"

"Accept that? I can accept the fact that you're together! What I can't accept is that he decided to drag you in the woods so that he could have his way with you! So that he could dishonor you!"

"He did not dishonor me! Besides, what were you bringing Mary in here for? To pick berries?" Mary gasps, but I refuse to look at her. I know my words embarrassed her and I hate myself a little for saying them, but it doesn't change the truth in them. My words also give me Gregory's complete attention. He's glaring at me with absolute fury. I've never seen him this angry with me. Gregory takes an infuriated step in my direction, and Drake instantly rises to his feet, placing himself between me and Gregory. There's no need. Gregory would never hurt me, but I'm glad it got Drake off the ground. Drake looks at me, but keeps Gregory in his line of sight as well.

"No, Addy. He's right. I should never have pushed it that far." He turns his attention to Gregory. "I'm sorry, Gregory. What I did was inexcusable. I love your sister, but I shouldn't have taken advantage of her in that way."

Taken advantage of me?

He sets his shoulders and takes a step toward

Gregory, preparing himself for whatever Gregory's about to do. Gregory regards him, his arm twitching in anticipation.

"Stop!" I yell, but it's too late. There's a sickening pop as Gregory's fist connects with Drake's jaw. Drake staggers backward, but manages to stay on his feet. I run toward him, and this time I put myself in the path between him and my brother.

"Leave, Gregory!" I scream, the tears stinging the backs of my eyes. Gregory stares at me for a moment, his face still filled with anger. "Leave!" I scream again, before turning to Drake. His lip is bleeding in the corner. I gently wipe the blood from under his mouth, and his eyes find mine. They're distant and filled with shame. He holds my gaze for several seconds, before turning away. I hate Gregory for ruining this day for us, and even more for hurting Drake.

"Let's go, Gregory. Leave them be," Mary says softly. Gregory looks at Mary and his mood noticeably calms. She uses the opportunity to pull Gregory away. I watch them until they disappear into the trees. Then I turn back to Drake and wrap my arms around him, leaning my head against his chest. His body is tense as he stiffly encircles me in his arms.

"I'm so sorry," I say roughly, my voice strained with the effort of trying to hold back my tears.

"You shouldn't be. Gregory was right, and I deserved much worse than that," he says firmly, before pulling himself away and wrapping only his hand around mine.

I look up into his face, and the look I see there

reminds me of a solid door: closed and impenetrable. As we walk back toward the village in silence, I feel nothing but apprehension.

Chapter 18

HER

By the time we reach my home, I'm ready to scream with frustration. He's completely overreacting! I don't know what's worse—his prolonged silence or his murmured apologies.

We approach the front door and Drake tugs lightly on my hand, pulling me to a stop. I glance at him expectantly, my heart thumping loudly in my chest, but whether it's in anticipation of his words or from aggravation, I don't know.

"I want to apologize again about today."

Here we go again. "Will you stop doing that?" I shout and pull my hand free of his grasp.

"Stop doing what?"

I force the next words out, through my teeth, and try to hold back the tears.

"Stop acting like touching me is so reprehensible!" I

fail at holding back the tears and they fall, cold and steady.

His gaze lingers on my tears for a moment before he turns away. "The way I touched you was reprehensible."

His words fracture me. I grasp the cold metal doorknob, desperate for an escape, but his hand wraps around mine, stopping me from turning it. I look toward him, waiting for him to speak, but he says nothing, instead he just stares at me with blank uncertain eyes. Several dismal seconds pass before he removes his hand from mine and steps back. He's not going to fix this. I turn away from him and push open the door. The heat from the fireplace blankets my body as I step inside. I slam the door shut behind me and lean my forehead against it, letting the coolness of the wood calm me while I try to steady my breath and slow my tears. His shadow is visible beneath the crack of the door, hovering on the other side. The urge to go back out to him is overwhelming, but I fight against it.

"I love you, Addy," he murmurs, and then his shadow disappears. I glance out the window and watch him walk away.

* * *

When I hear the front door open, the moon has taken the sun's place in the sky. Mother and Elizabeth must finally be home. Though I'm curious about where they've been, I'm too tired to get up and ask.

The last several hours have been torturous, as I've spent them waiting for Drake to come back. I was certain he would knock on the wooden shutters of my window. He never came. Instead, there's a sturdy knock on my door.

"Come in," I say tiredly, lifting myself off the bed.

Father walks in, an apprehensive look on his face.

"What happened?" I ask as I stand. "Is everyone all right? Where are Mother and Elizabeth?"

"Everyone's fine. Your mother and Elizabeth are at your uncle's, having supper. I told them you and I wouldn't be able to join them. They should be home within the hour." His face puts on a soft smile while he continues to linger in my doorway, his weight shifting from one foot to the other.

"Why aren't we joining them? If we leave now we could still make it in time." And I would be able to see Drake.

"Because, Addalynne, there are some important matters we need to discuss."

I hold his gaze. I have no idea what matters he wants to discuss, but I know what answers I want from him. And though I'm in no mood to argue with my father, it's one more thing that I can get out of the way. I cross my arms in front of me and wait expectantly for him to say what's on his mind.

"Let's move into the study," he says before turning and making his way down the hall, expecting me to follow. Every step I take behind him seems to echo in my ears, and I can't help but fidget with an unraveled string on the sleeve of my green dress.

As I step into the study, my gaze lands on the many familiar books that decorate the wall behind my father's desk. The candlelight from the bronze chandelier that hangs above our heads reflects off their spines, creating spots of light around the room. I have spent so much time in here over the last six months, trying to find an escape within the pages of these books. Now that Drake came back, I thought I would no longer need that escape. I was wrong. I find myself yearning for a book, desperately needing something to get my mind off him.

"Vernold informed me that Charles came to see you today, and you told him you no longer wanted to be courted by him. Is that true?" My father's words seem to reverberate loudly, making it impossible for me to miss them. I turn toward him. He's staring out the window across the study, his back to me. His brown hair is beginning to thin on the back of his head, showing his age where his face does not. His hands are clasped behind him and he's rocking methodically on his heels. He's still dressed in his work clothes, but his black vest and breeches are rumpled from the long day.

"Yes," I reply, and step farther into the study, coming to a stop next to one of the four wooden chairs.

"I suppose I don't need to ask why. But I think you're being foolish."

"*Really?* I'm foolish for trying to take control of my life and right the wrong that you created?" All my frustration and anger tangles together, as sharp as a blade, and takes aim at my father.

Father turns to face me, his brow furrowed. "What wrong did I create? Wanting you and Drake to move on so you could both have a better life? Wanting you to be with someone who could care for you, provide for you?"

"*A better life?* I was devastated when Drake left, and you are the one who convinced him that I had moved on! You are the one who told him not to come back to me! You are the one who hid the truth and his letters from me! I was under the impression that, as my father, you were supposed to help ensure my happiness, not destroy me." My hands clench tightly into fists, my fingernails cutting into my palms.

Father regards me for a moment, and the silence permeates the tension around us.

"This is why I wanted him to leave," he finally says. "I've seen enough to know what this kind of passion leads to and it's not happiness, Addalynne. You and Drake are the ones that hurt each other and this isn't the first time."

"You don't know anything about us."

"I'm your father, Addalynne. At times I know you better than you know yourself. And Drake . . . I love Drake, but he doesn't even know his place in this world. He needs to find solid ground, roots if you will. And you're just waiting to jump from tree to tree."

I open my mouth to argue, wanting to argue, but I don't know where to start. There's some truth to what he's saying, but he doesn't understand that Drake and I complete each other. We're each other's missing pieces.

"You think I destroyed your happiness," Father

continues. "But I was trying to give you a chance at a life that I believe could make you happier. I knew that if Drake were here you would never see past him. You would never see the life you could have with Charles."

"You had no right to lie to us." My voice is low and trembling with anger.

"Maybe I shouldn't have lied, but I saw an opportunity to improve your life and I took it."

I look down at the ground and try to hold back my tears. I want to look like a level headed young woman who's capable of making her own decisions, not a hot tempered little girl who's about to be scolded for spilling stew. But I'm so angry.

"Where are the letters he sent? The ones you took?"

"I burned them."

I sway on my feet and swallow against the lump in my throat. A tear breaks free.

I hear him take a step toward me, but I don't look up.

"I'm sorry, Addalynne. I shouldn't have done that. But I thought I was protecting you. And I realize now how difficult his leaving was on both of you, but I had to try." His voice is filled with remorse, but I have no desire to forgive him. It's because of him that things are so strained with Drake. He didn't succeed in making us move on; he only succeeded in making us doubt not only ourselves, but each other.

"Why Charles?" I ask as I finally let myself look at him. "Why do you want me to pick Charles so badly? And don't say it's because he can provide for me. I don't need to be provided for or taken care of, that's not me and you know it. And even if I did need to be provided for there are plenty of men here who are capable, including Drake. *Why Charles?"* My voice shakes with my question. Father has always supported me in making my own decisions. It's my mother who has fought me at every turn. So if he's trying to push me into something, he has a reason.

Father's eyes meet mine, weary and guarded, before he looks down to the floor.

"Shortly after Charles returned to Faygrene he asked me for your hand in marriage, and I gave my consent."

Blood rushes to my head and the air rushes out of me. *This can't be happening. I can't marry Charles.* I look down at the rug beneath my feet and try to find the anger in me that I had before, but all I find is desolation.

"I won't marry him. I'll run away if I have to," I say quietly. Numb. I try to breathe, but my throat feels like it's being filled with dirt.

"Don't be rash, Addalynne. Imagine the life he could give you. He could take you anywhere you wanted to go, give you everything you ever dreamed of. It's a perfect match for you."

"You're wrong.".

"I don't think I am. However, the choice is ultimately yours."

What? I look up, my body feeling as though it's trying to break the surface of rushing water.

"I told Charles that he had my blessing and that I would do everything in my power to persuade you, but that I would never force your hand."

"I won't be forced into this?" I ask breathlessly.

"No, Addalynne you won't. Your mother and I always agreed that we would not force you into a marriage you did not want. When I agreed to give Charles your hand in marriage, I thought it was going to be the best thing for you, that it would make you happy. I still think that you could be happy with Charles. But if Drake is the one you want, and he asks for your hand, I'll allow it."

I run to my father and wrap my arms around him. He returns the embrace and places a gentle kiss on top of my head.

"All I ask is that you go to the Berrengers' and speak with Charles. Listen to what he has to say and, if you're still certain you don't want to marry him, you may formally refuse him."

"There's nothing he could say to convince me. Besides, I already told Charles to direct his affections elsewhere."

"I understand that. But Charles is under the assumption that you two already have an arrangement. He's waiting for you to warm up to the idea, which he's certain will happen. If you're positive that you don't want to marry him, then you'll have to formally refuse the marriage arrangement."

"Fine, I'll go now." I turn to leave, ready to put this fully behind me.

"No, it's too late. It wouldn't be appropriate. Go tomorrow morning," he says as he sits at his desk, settling in for tonight's work. I nod and leave the study. I hate having to wait, but he's right. Besides, the thought of seeing Charles again already has my stomach in knots.

As I make my way toward my chambers, the front door swings open, and Mother and Elizabeth come rushing in followed by a gust of cold air.

"How was supper?" I ask, heading toward them. I really want to ask, *How was Drake? Did he ask about me? Did he look miserable?* But I can't.

"It was pleasant," Mother replies while hanging her cloak on the wall, her body shivering from the chill of the outside air. Elizabeth's eyes are on me, studying my face.

"You've been crying," Elizabeth says, a frown pulling on her lips. My darling little sister, always too intuitive. I cross my arms defiantly over my chest.

"No, I haven't."

"Yes, you have. I can tell. Your eyes are puffy and your face is red. Did you have a fight with Drake?"

"Did he say we did?" I counter, not wanting to talk about our fight, but curious to know if she spoke with him.

"No, he wasn't there." Her eyes become less questioning and more analytical. She's reading my face like a book and I can do nothing to stop her because all I can think about is where he could have been. The torturous side of my imagination pictures him finding comfort with Jacqueline, but I push the image away, knowing I'm being ridiculous.

"Well, that's not entirely true," Mother says,

thankfully interrupting my self-destructive thoughts. "He wasn't there while we ate, but he did arrive before we left," Mother continues as she walks toward Elizabeth and also begins studying my face.

"Did you talk to him?" I ask a little too forcefully. I watch both of them as they watch me. Their matching red hair and blue eyes blend while I stare at them, my vision relaxing until they become one scrutinizing person.

"Very little. When he saw us, he asked if you were there, and when we told him, "No," he asked us to excuse him, and went straight to his loft." Curiosity is thick in Mother's voice.

I turn around and walk back to my chambers, thinking only of Drake and what he's doing now. As I open my door, Mother's voice floats down the hall.

"He seemed very distraught, Addalynne. You really shouldn't be so hard on him."

I shut my door on her words. *I'm being hard on him?* I'm furious that she automatically assumes this is my fault! Part of me wants to go back out there and tell her the truth. I wasn't hard on him, Mother. In fact, I was very easy, too easy, and apparently he doesn't like how easy I was being, and that's why he's so upset!

I throw myself down on my bed and try to let the anger, hurt, confusion, desire, and frustration fade away. Today has been a cyclone of emotions, leaving me physically and emotionally drained. I don't bother taking off my dress. I simply blow out the candle on the table next to my bed and close my eyes, letting my mind drift to tomorrow. I picture myself confidently telling Charles that I will never marry him, and then spending the afternoon wrapped in Drake's arms. I imagine us picking up from where we left off today, only this time, Gregory doesn't show up and Drake doesn't regret it.

Chapter 19

HER

The early morning light spills into the entry in streaks, making the wood on the door appear as though it's been painted in alternating shades of brown. Father is sitting near the fireplace, sipping on his morning cup of tea and reading a worn, leather-bound book. I grab my black cloak from the hook on the wall and drape it over my shoulders.

"Off already?" Father asks before taking another sip.

"Yes, I want to talk to Charles as soon as possible. Are you going to the Berrengers' today?"

"No, I have chores to take care of here at home."

"Like fixing the hole in the roof of the barn?" My eyebrows raise in skepticism.

He lifts his head from his book and gives me a displeased look. "Now you sound like your mother."

I chuckle slightly at this, but it's half-hearted. My

nerves are too tangled for me to offer a real laugh. I reach for the doorknob, but can't make myself open it. Closing my eyes, I try to still my rapidly beating heart with a calming breath.

"Don't worry, Addalynne. The young lord will understand. He's an honorable man: just like his father."

I glance back at my father and force a smile and a small nod.

The stable is dark and smells strongly of hay. My brother's horse, Sejant, is closest to me. I offer him a handful of hay and a small pat. "Freyja!" I call out and walk to my horse. She stands proudly while I fasten the brown leather saddle to her back. But before I get on, I brush my hand through her golden hair, letting the softness of it calm me. She leans her head toward mine and nuzzles my cheek with her light brown nose. "Let's get this over with, girl."

Once we reach the main road, Freyja breaks into a swift sprint. The force of the wind blows my hood off, the cool air nipping at my face, causing me to squint against its harshness. The heady scent of dirt and smoke drifts over me as people light their morning fires.

Several minutes later, I arrive outside Lord Berrenger's manor and am greeted by multiple guards. They help me off Freyja before tying her to the outer fence.

The manor somehow looks bigger than it did the night of the Ball. The morning sun is shining on it, causing every tower and wall to glow behind the green vines that are ascending the stones.

My hand shakes slightly as I lift it up to the brass knocker. *Breathe,* I tell myself, and rap the knocker against the door. Several seconds later, the large door groans, pulled open by the same servant who was distributing jonquils on the night of the Ball. His light brown hair falls across his forehead as he greets me with a bow. When I step inside, he removes my cloak from my shoulders and then asks me to wait in the Great Hall.

Without the large amount of people, food, and decorations, the Great Hall gives off a cold, desolate feeling. There's one long empty banquet table along the far right wall that a woman in a dingy apron is dusting. I offer her a quiet hello, but she doesn't look up from her work. I turn away and look toward the space where the dance floor used to be, but now there are only four, red, cushioned chairs facing each other around a small wooden table. The large fireplace illuminates the far left side of the space, looking all the more colossal today without the minstrels performing in front of it. The heat of the flames caresses my cheek, and I think longingly of the cool morning air outside.

"Addalynne." Charles's voice startles me and I can't help but jump. I turn and see him standing before me, a curious smile on his face. "To what do I owe the pleasure of seeing you so early in the morning?" He says as he gazes down the length of my body. I wish I still had my cloak on.

With a deep breath, I push out my words. "I'm sorry to call on you so early, my Lord, but there's a matter of importance I was hoping to discuss with you." My fingers fidget with the gold-trimmed sleeves of my black dress and I have to force them to be still at my side.

"Oh, and what would that be?" he asks, taking several deliberate steps toward me.

"My father informed me of our pre-arranged engagement and—"

"Yes. Isn't it wonderful?"

My heart batters in my chest as he takes yet another step toward me. I swallow with difficulty and continue. "It's a wonderful offer, my Lord. I'm deeply honored. However, I must decline the proposal." I want to look away from him as I speak, but I force myself to look straight into his eyes, hoping to project confidence.

"Is that so?" he asks curiously, taking one more step toward me, making the space between us less than an arm's length. He stares down at me with narrowed eyes. "That is disappointing. Perhaps there's something I can do to help change your mind." He reaches forward and brushes his fingers along my cheek. His touch sends chills across my body, and not the good kind.

"I'm sorry, my Lord, but I've thought this through. I can't marry you." I speak kindly, but decidedly. He needs to see that I'm not going to change my mind.

Charles assesses me for a moment, his hand traveling from my cheek down the length of my hair. His hand comes to a stop at the tips of my hair and he twirls it methodically with his fingers.

"Oh, I'm not so sure about that. I'm no fool, Addalynne. I know the reason for your resistance and I assure you, the orphan can easily be taken care of."

I exhale sharply, struggling against the shock of his words. "He has nothing to do with my decision," I lie shakily, but it's no good. Charles sees right through me.

"Do stop lying to me, Addalynne. It's growing rather tiresome. I've seen you with him and am well aware of what took place between you in my garden on the night of the Ball. I considered disposing of him then, but decided to give you another chance. So, here it is. I will not be made a fool twice. You will be mine. I was merely placating your father by letting him think you had a choice. Granted, I suppose you have one, but if you don't want the orphan to have an unfortunate accident, you will make the right choice."

No. I won't let him force me into this! I won't let him take everything away from me now that I just got it back! Besides, he's not a threat. He's a coward. I set my shoulders and look him straight in the eye. "You won't hurt him. You're nothing but a spoiled coward who's unaccustomed to hearing, no, so you're trying to scare me into agreeing. But I'm not afraid of you."

A small smile tilts his mouth. "Oh, but you should be . . . . Sarah, come here please. I'm in need of your assistance," he calls to the maid who has moved on to dust the golden mantel around the fireplace.

She turns toward Charles, her face flushed from the heat. She wipes the sweat from her brow and moves toward us. "Yes, my Lord," she says in her haste and comes to a stop with a slight curtsey before him.

Charles pulls a dagger from his belt and my heart

clenches. He tilts it toward her, the tip facing her.

"Don't." The word leaves my mouth, but it's shallow and quieted with fear.

"Sarah," he tsks. "This is not nearly clean enough. There's still blood on it from your son."

Sarah stares down at the dagger and I finally realize who she is; Sarah Hunt, Samuel Hunt's mother. Samuel wasn't taken by a hellion. Charles killed him. I see the truth in the dried blood on the dagger and in the slow tear falling from the corner of his mother's eye. My stomach lurches.

"He's always leaving a mess, even in death," Charles continues. "And since you can't clean it up anymore, I will just have to find someone else who can." Charles flicks his wrist, slashing the dagger across her throat. My hand flies to my mouth, muffling my screams. I watch, helplessly, as Sarah Hunt's body drops to the floor, her eyes rolling back in her head, a gurgled cough forcing blood from her lips.

Uncontrolled tears fall from my eyes and the room spins around me. Blood rushes in my ears and I have to fight against the dizziness that's overtaking me. Suddenly, I feel someone wrap their arms around me and guide me to one of the red chairs.

Breathe Addalynne. Keep it together. Now is not the time to fall apart. I force breaths in and try to force out the image of Sarah Hunt's face as she fell to the ground.

The room finally stops spinning and I allow myself to look up at Charles, his image blurry through my tears. He's looking down at the dagger as he wipes her blood off with the ends of his black tunic, his head shaking with disappointment. "She was my maid, Addalynne. I actually liked her. So imagine what I would do to the orphan: someone I like less than the dirt beneath my nails."

He looks at the dagger, checking for any remnants of blood. When he doesn't find any, he nods with satisfaction, places the dagger in his belt and steps over her body, as though it's nothing but a rock in his way.

"You're a monster," I spit the words out, watching him until he's standing in front of me. I want to stand, to feel strong enough to face him, but I don't trust my legs to hold me, so instead I stare up at him, feeling helpless as an infant.

"That may be true, but I'm not really one for labels. Besides, I'm not to blame for her death. Her death is on your hands. You thought my threats were empty, but now you know the truth. I may not be a lot of things, Addalynne, but I am a man of my word."

The image of her eyes going dark as her life left her flashes into my mind. *My fault. It's my fault.* He may be the one who killed her, but I pushed him to it.

"What have we here?" Lord Vernold Berrenger's voice bounds into the Great Hall. I glance over at him, my heart hammering. Vernold has always been kind to my family. He has to help me.

Vernold's eyes drift from me, to Charles, to Sarah Hunt's body. I wait for him to react, but he looks at her like a bowl of oatmeal left out too long. "Is anyone going to clean this up?" He asks and my small dash of hope scatters like leaves in a storm.

"What's wrong with you?" I ask, before I can stop myself.

Vernold's eyes meet mine, filled with the same patience and compassion I've seen in him all my life. "What do you mean, my dear?"

"Your son just murdered her. For no reason. And you don't even care."

"Now that's not true," he says as he walks toward us. "I do care. Her blood is staining my floors." He stops behind Charles and places a hand on his shoulder. "Since you're here, Addalynne, I'm assuming you've accepted my son's hand in marriage?"

I look down at my hands, but I feel their stares on me, waiting for me to speak.

Say no. Just say, no. I can find a way out. There has to be a way out. But as much as I want this to be true, I know it's not.

"Does my father know?" I ask instead of answering, because I have to know.

"Know what?" Vernold asks, his voice truly curious.

I finally allow myself to look up and meet his eyes.

"She's as pale as a ghost," Charles says with a laugh, but I ignore him, and keep my gaze on Vernold.

"Does he know what you and your son really are?"

He tilts his head. "And what's that?"

"Murderers!"

"That's not fair, Addalynne. We're not murderers, we're negotiators. We attempt to find reasonable solutions to what we need done and if we can't, then we deal with it."

"You call this reasonable?"

"Yes. Charles made you a fair offer and if you take it, no one else will need to be harmed. And, to answer your first question, no, your father doesn't know about the people we've disposed of out of necessity. He wouldn't understand. Which means our conversation must not leave here. Anyone you tell would have to be eliminated, and though I would hate to do it, I will do what's necessary."

"My father trusts you. *I* trusted you."

"And there's no reason for you to lose your trust," Vernold says, and what's most disturbing is that he seems to truly believe his own words. He places a hand on my shoulder. I want to shake it off, but I can't bring myself to move. "You just can't see past this moment, Addalynne," he continues. "But let me remind you that I'm the man who gave your father a job when he had a starving, pregnant wife at home. I'm the reason your family has risen. Your father didn't come from money. Everything you have is because of what I gave you, and I could just as easily take it away, but I won't as long as you give me no reason to, and you can trust in that."

What's left of my resolve completely shatters. My hands may as well be bound. To fight against Charles would already be difficult, to fight against them both is impossible. And I have no one to turn to for help because I can't risk telling anyone what happened today. I can't risk the lives of my family or Drake, just to save my own.

"If I agree to marry Charles, will you give your word to never hurt Drake or anyone else I love?" I put all the energy I have left into securing their promise. It's the only thing that matters.

"You have our word," Vernold replies with a nod of his head.

"As long as you continue to remain compliant, there will be no problems," Charles adds, and he reaches forward and brushes his hand along my cheek. I don't know what I want to cut off more, his hand or the skin that he's touched.

"Then, I'll marry you," I finally reply and the sound of my own acceptance stabs through me. I close my eyes, willing myself to wake up from this nightmare.

"Wonderful!" Vernold replies. My stomach turns, and I have to swallow the vomit that has risen in my throat.

"Now, may I please be excused?" I ask, a tremor present in my voice while I struggle for a breath of composure.

"Yes," Charles replies. "Do keep in mind though, that I'll be announcing our engagement tomorrow. It wouldn't be proper for you to be seen with the orphan anymore considering you're a betrothed woman. If I or anyone else sees you with him, I will consider it a breach of our arrangement and I will handle the situation."

I simply nod my head and rise to my feet, having fully reached my limit. Tears are forcing their way out of my eyes, and the pressure in my chest is nearly suffocating. I turn slowly and almost stumble out the door, not bothering to retrieve my cloak.

The cold wind bites at my tear-streaked face as I run toward Freyja. I pull myself up and squeeze her swiftly in her sides, setting her into a sprint, not caring where she goes.

Today I have promised away my life in order to save Drake's. Marrying Charles will be torture, but the thought of something happening to Drake is unbearable. He means more to me than my own life, and I'm more than willing to sacrifice mine for his.

Drake's face lingers in my mind. I promised myself a long time ago that I would do whatever it takes to keep him safe. I won't let anything happen to him. The thought of going to Drake and persuading him to run away with me enters my mind like a fire of hope. But as quickly as it comes, a devastating wave of realization crushes it. If we leave together, Charles will hurt my family. I know he will. Life means nothing to him. And we couldn't all leave. He and Vernold will be watching all of us closely until the wedding is finalized. Besides, there are others they could hurt. An image of Mary's smiling face flashes before me. I could never protect everyone.

Knowing what I have to do next rips me apart. I have to tell Drake of my engagement, and I have to convince him it's what I want. If he so much as suspects I'm being forced into this, he'll fight against Charles and he'll be killed. The only way to save his life is to make him hate me. It shouldn't be too hard, I already hate myself.

Chapter 20

HER

It's the middle of the afternoon when I finally get back home. After returning an exhausted Freyja to the barn, I make my way to the front door. Before opening it, I try my best to craft my face into a mask devoid of all emotion. If this is going to work, everyone has to believe that it's my choice. With a ragged breath, I push the door open.

"Where have you been, Addalynne?" My father's reprimanding voice carries easily down the hallway, preceding his heavy footsteps. "I went to the Berrengers', but Vernold said you had left hours before," he continues as he steps into the room.

"I'm sorry. I stayed out riding Freyja and must have lost track of time." I try my best to put life into my voice, but the image of Sarah Hunt's face drifts into my mind and this time, as her body falls to the ground, her face changes, turning to Drake's, and it's his lifeless eyes that stare back at me. I close my eyes and will the image away before it breaks me.

"Next time, tell someone where you are."

"I will," I manage to say as I lean my back against the door and stare down at the bottom of my black dress. The gold ribbon that is sewn along the bottom hem has begun to unravel, taking on a frayed and mangled appearance. "Did Vernold say anything else?" I ask.

"He said that we have a wedding to plan," my father says skeptically and waits for me to confirm or deny his words.

"We do," I reply.

He stares at me expectantly. "Well, what happened?" he asks, after realizing I'm not going to divulge the information myself.

I look up at him, preparing my words. Out of my entire family, he will be the easiest to deceive. If I can't convince him that I'm choosing this and that I'm happy about it, then I'll never be able to convince anyone else, especially not Drake.

"I changed my mind. I'm going to marry Charles."

"I ascertained that, but how did you come to this decision?"

"I did what you said and gave him a chance to speak. He . . . made strong points in favor of a union with him, and I realized that it was an offer I couldn't refuse." The truth of my words presses against me like a corset that's too tight, making it difficult to breathe. My father regards me for several moments, his eyebrows scrunched in thought. He knows I'm holding back, but he's usually not the type to force information. Hopefully, he stays true to form today.

"I hope you're not choosing this just because it's what I chose for you. I know how much you love Drake." He pauses, the expression on his face questioning. But I remain silent. There's nothing I can say in response to his words. It hurts far too much to think about Drake, much less say his name. My father shakes his head slightly. "Just promise me that you're making this decision for you."

"I am. Charles will take me beyond the walls of Faygrene, which is something I've wanted for a long time. And Drake—" Saying his name almost steals my resolve. I take one steadying breath and somehow find the strength to continue. "Drake and I fight. All the time. You were right, Charles is the better choice for me."

"And what of love?" His words are like a kick to the stomach. I'll never be able to get through this with Drake, when it's nearly killing me to have this conversation with my father.

"I have feelings for him. And I'm sure they'll grow into love."

"But you already love, Drake. I'm having a hard time understanding this Addalynne."

"I already explained it!" *Calm down, Addalynne.* "My love for Drake is a childish love. I'll outgrow it. I *am* happy about my decision, Father. Isn't that enough?" I almost choke on the words, but I manage to get them out. *Please let it be enough.*

My father's face slowly spreads into an appeased smile. "Then I'm happy too. All I ever wanted for you was a safe and happy life. And I do believe Charles can give you this and more. I'm very pleased with your decision." His voice is filled with joy and pride, making it impossible for me to maintain eye contact. I force a smile, then let my eyes drift back to the floor.

"Thank you, Father," I respond quietly, and make myself move forward. One step at a time.

"One more thing, Addalynne." My footsteps cease, but I keep my gaze directed on the door of my chambers. "Drake stopped by to see you. I didn't tell him where you had gone. I only told him that you should be home shortly. Obviously, you weren't, and he came back again about an hour ago. He was worried when I told him you still weren't home. I think he went out to look for you. I wouldn't be surprised if he stops by again soon."

My heart actually slows in my chest. Perhaps it's giving out on me. I hope it does. Death would be an easier option.

I don't want to do this now. I don't want to do this ever. But I have no other choice. Charles will be announcing our engagement tomorrow, and I can't let Drake find out that way. Right now, he's probably looking for me in our woods and at least there I can talk to him in private, without my family or Charles's spies prying around.

My father doesn't ask where I'm going when I make my way back out the front door.

* * *

Cold rain splashes on my face and the weight of my dress pulls against me as it becomes thoroughly soaked. The sky is dark, covered by thick grey clouds, and the sound of thunder resounds overhead, providing the perfect background for my inner thoughts. I stop and look for any guards patrolling the perimeter of the woods, but I don't see any. They're probably hiding from the storm.

When I enter the embrace of the woods, the fall of the rain slightly lessens due to the coverage of the thick trees above me. The green leaves catch the water and send it cascading down in glistening drops.

While I walk, I search inside myself and try to find the distress I would expect to feel, but there's nothing except a numbing void, accompanied by the occasional stab of pain in my chest. Maybe this is a good thing. If I can't feel, I'll be more convincing.

I move around a large willow, and the small clearing, where we practice with the bow, comes into view. I squint through the rain. There's a dark figure beneath the branches of one of the trees. The hood of his black cloak is pulled up, his back toward me, but I know it's Drake. All my forward progress stops, and I have to lean against a nearby tree for support. I was wrong about not being able to feel anything. Every part of me is battling against a hurricane of emotions as I look at him. He's my life and I'm about to destroy him. I'm about to destroy us. I don't know if I can do this.

He slowly turns around, and I completely stop breathing. He moves forward, his gaze on the ground, his dark hair falling across his forehead, skimming along a worried crease that is set above his eyes. After several steps he looks up.

"Addalynne." My name passes through his lips in an exhale. I remain motionless as he jogs toward me, closing the distance between us. He wraps his arms around me and crushes me against his chest. I reach forward and almost wrap my arms around his waist, but I stop myself and instead force my hands to my sides, motionless and unresponsive.

I should pull away, but instead I let him hold me, memorizing the feel of his body against mine. This is the last time I will be in his arms. A shudder rips through me at the thought and I have to bite the inside of my cheek to focus the pain somewhere else.

"Where were you?" he asks, his lips brushing along the top of my head.

"I took Freyja out for a ride." I lean my forehead against his chest and breathe in the scent of him. I'm not ready to tell him. I'm not ready for him to let me go.

"I would have gone with you if you had told me," he says quietly, and runs his hands underneath my hair, along the length of my back. "You're freezing."

Am I?

"Where's your cloak?"

At the Berrengers'. "I forgot it."

"Here, take mine." He removes his arms from around me and unties his cloak.

"It's really not necessary," I tell him, but he drapes his cloak around my shoulders anyway. He ties it shut, his fingers grazing along the damp skin of my chest. They linger a little longer than needed and I'm left battling against my own will—wishing he would let go and then wishing his hands would travel farther. I need him, desperately, and I want him more than anything. But I can't have him. Not anymore. I take an agonizing step back and hate it when his arm deplorably drops back down to his side.

"I came to see you today," he says, as he, too, takes a step back and tries to look at my face. I keep my gaze on his grey tunic, watching the relentless drops of rain darken it. I have yet to look him directly in his eyes. I'm not sure I'll be able to get through this if I do. "I wanted to apologize." He reaches out and tucks a wet strand of hair behind my ear before dropping his hand back down to his side. He takes several more steps away from me and begins to pace nervously. "I'm sorry for the way I've been acting, Addy. I know it's been frustrating you, and believe me when I say I've been frustrating myself. It's just that I . . . I want to do right by you. I love you too much to ever do anything that could dishonor you."

"Stop." The word forms on my lips, but it emerges with no volume to it.

"You have to believe me when I tell you how much I want you. I should have never walked away from you yesterday, and I swear to you that I will never walk away from you again."

Yes, you will. You'll walk away from me today, and

I'll lose you forever. I stare at the trees behind him, unable to look at him. I can't let him continue. Each of his words is like its own knife, stabbing into me and scarring me forever. "Stop, Drake," I speak a little stronger this time, but it's still only a whisper and not nearly loud enough for him to hear over the sound of the rain.

"After we leave here, I'm going to go straight to your father and ask him for your hand in marriage . . ."

My eyes flash back to him. He has stopped pacing and his gaze is on mine.

He can't be saying this, not now, not ever. The hope in his eyes is more than I can take, but I can't seem to break from his gaze.

He takes a cautious step toward me. ". . . that is, if you'll have me?"

My heart agonizingly stutters. *Please don't do this to me.*

He takes another step, his eyes searching mine. They're still hopeful, but now there's a trace of fear in them. He lifts his hand and places it against my cheek. "I want nothing more than to spend the rest of my life with you."

All the air has been taken from me, leaving me struggling to breathe as I stare into his face, watching the hope minimize and the fear grow. The rain is falling heavily around us, painting both of our faces and bodies in wet streaks. I'm grateful for it, knowing it's masking the tears that have steadily begun to fall down my face. I close my eyes.

"Addy, *please* say something."

"I'm marrying Charles." Everything goes still and quiet. It's as though I've floated away from my body and have entered a void of darkness. The sound of the rain is gone, replaced instead by a low hum. The feel of the rain is gone as well. In fact, the only thing I feel is his hand against my cheek. I instinctively lean into it, but then it's gone, taking with it my altered reality and grounding me back into the harshness of my fate. Once again I hear the loud drumming of the rain and feel its stinging droplets battering across my face. I open my eyes.

He's standing several feet away from me and he's staring down at the ground, his chest heaving. His rain-soaked hair is hanging around his face, dripping tendrils of water down his neck. After several excruciating seconds, he finally speaks.

"I thought you told him to direct his attention elsewhere." His voice is trembling, fractured. And though I thought my heart was already broken beyond repair, it breaks further.

"I did, but yesterday my father told me that Charles asked him for my hand in marriage, and my father gave his consent."

His head flies up, his eyes fixing on mine. They're burning with fury. "Addalynne, if they're forcing you into this, I'll . . ."

"They're not, Drake. My father told me that, though it had been previously arranged, the choice was mine, and if I wanted to refuse Charles and marry you, I could."

"*Then why?* Why are you choosing him? I asked you if you had feelings for him and you said, "No." You told me that you loved me!"

"I do love you!" I shout before I can stop myself. His face takes on a look of confusion. *No. I have to fix it.* "You were my first love, Drake. I'll always love you, but it's not enough. What I have with Charles is so much more."

"You're lying," he says harshly and he takes a purposeful step toward me.

"No, I'm not. Charles can give me the life I've always wanted. When we were younger, I told you what my biggest fear was: to never leave Faygrene. With you, that fear would come true. With him, I'll get to travel to all of Silveria, and I'll no longer have to imagine what the ocean looks like. *He* can take me there." My words taste like poison as I spit them out.

His face is stunned, as though my words physically slapped him. "I would give you all those things if I could, Addy. You know I would. And I can try. I'll send a letter to King Theodoric and ask if I can bring you to Synereal and I will find a way to take you to the ocean. When you told me about your fear, I promised you we would go, and we will. I'll find a way to give you everything." His voice is unyielding, determined, and I can tell by the set of his shoulders and the look in his eyes that he hasn't given up yet. I'm going to have to go further. I swallow back the nausea and force myself to push through.

"Don't be ridiculous, Drake. You know you could

never afford to take me, with or without the King's permission. Besides, you were the one who once said that girls like me belonged with a lord, not an orphan." I turn the words he once said back on him, using his own insecurities against him. The pure hatred in my voice is palpable, as the anger and animosity I'm feeling against myself seeps into my words. I don't recognize myself anymore and, though I know why I'm doing this, I still hate myself more than ever.

I move my gaze to the ground, unable to look at his face any longer. Knowing I'm hurting him is tormenting enough, but watching the pain rise into his eyes is more than I can bear. I take a deep breath as I prepare myself for my next words.

"And I want someone who doesn't regret it when he touches me." Silence. I listen to each ragged breath he takes while I wait for him to speak.

"You let him touch you?" Disbelief. His voice is infused with pain.

"Yes."

"You let him touch you the way I have touched you?" Anger. Good. Hate me, Drake. I need you to hate me so you can let me go.

"Yes."

"When?"

"When you were gone with the Schild." I feel disgusted, but I force myself to continue the lies. "My father didn't lie to you. I did. I was angry with you for leaving, and Charles was there for me. Mary told Walter that I hadn't moved on, that I was waiting for you, but she was wrong. I had begun to move on with Charles. Mary just didn't know because all of our time together was spent in the privacy of my home. Then, on the night of the Ball, I accepted his jonquil, you *know* that. I have feelings for him, Drake. Deep ones. When you came back, it confused me because I had missed you so much. You even told me on the morning after the ball that you were worried my feelings were a momentary impulse. I didn't believe it then, but you were right. And when I went to see Charles today, I knew he was the one I was supposed to be with."

"You saw him today? I thought you were out riding Freyja." Fury. He's starting to hate me, and though it's what I want, it kills me.

"I lied. I was with Charles for most of the day."

It's excruciatingly quiet for several seconds.

"Did you think about me at all while you were with him? Or am I just disposable to you?" There it is: hatred. I succeeded. I swallow back the lump in my throat, close my eyes, and let the rain wash over me. Thunder claps loudly and the lightning flashes brightly enough to see through my closed lids. I let my eyes slide open. He's staring down at me, his eyes filled with animosity, his body now only a foot away.

"What is it, Addalynne? Now you suddenly have nothing to say?"

I can't move. I can't even open my mouth. I'm nailed in place by his words and the look on his face. There are no words for how this feels—to have the person you love, more than anything in the entire world, completely despise you. But at least I know he'll live.

"I'm so sorry, Drake," I reply numbly. They are the only words my mouth can form. We're both broken now. There's nothing left to say.

"Don't, Addalynne. Just . . . don't apologize, I can't . . ." His voice breaks. He turns around and begins to walk away, but after several feet, he stops. "Let's go."

"What?"

"I'm walking you home. Just because I can't bear to look at you doesn't mean I'm going to leave you in the woods alone." The familiar stab of pain pierces my chest and the nausea rises into my stomach again. I won't be able to hold it off for long.

I silently follow him out of the woods, my gaze set on his back. The complete agony is crushing me, and all I want to do is drop to the ground and give in to the pain, but I have to keep moving. As we approach the end of the woods, Charles's warning echoes in my ears. I stop at once. I can't walk out of these woods with him. I can't risk anyone seeing us together.

"This is far enough. I don't want to make you be near me any longer than you have to. I can make it home safely from here," I say hurriedly, hoping he doesn't sense the panic in my tone. He nods once and steps aside, letting me move past him on my own.

I walk briskly toward my home, fighting against the need to look back.

As I walk, I pull the hood of his cloak up over my face, allowing myself to breathe in his familiar scent. I'm glad I didn't think to give it back to him. Though his scent brings excruciating pain, it also brings a small amount of comfort, knowing that part of him is still with me. After several minutes, I pass inside the gate of our home, and I finally let myself glance behind me. What I see shatters what's left of my heart.

He followed me home. I broke his heart, and he still made sure I got home safely. I watch Drake's retreating form walk several feet and then suddenly drop to his knees. I take a step toward him, but force myself to stop by grinding my fingers into the stones of the wall in front of me, hard enough to puncture the skin. His head falls into his hands and his body begins to shake with his sobs. My fingers rake along the stone wall as I drop to my knees as well. The image of him flashes behind my eyes and my own sobs tear through me. I lie in the mud, finally giving in to all the pain, and though he doesn't know it, we share the moment of loss together.

Chapter 21

HER

The faint light of the fire burns my eyes when I finally allow them to open. It's as though my eyelids have been sealed shut and the weight of them makes me want to close my eyes and sleep forever.

All at once, the past few hours come rushing back. Charles's threat, Sarah Hunt's murder, and the confrontation with Drake plays out in my mind like a nightmare, except this time there's no escape in waking. My body curls into a ball and I wrap my arms around my knees.

"What happened, Addalynne?" My brother's voice echoes in my ears, startling me. I don't react. Instead, I keep my gaze on the flames dancing in front of me. His hand brushes through my hair. "Did Drake hurt you?" he asks, his voice a mixture of concern and anger.

"No." I pull my legs tighter against me. "I hurt him."

Gregory's hand stops moving. "What do you mean?"

I don't want to say the words again. I hate the way they sound and feel when they fall from my mouth, taking pieces of me with them. I wish I could write it down, tell him on paper. Then it wouldn't feel so real.

I close my eyes, wishing I could sleep again. At least there my dreams are my own; at least there I can be with Drake.

"Addalynne?"

"I'm marrying Charles Berrenger." I count to ten, focusing on my breathing. The vomit is fighting its way up. Somehow, I'm able to push it back down.

"You're what? Why?" His anger takes me by surprise. After the way he reacted yesterday, I assumed he didn't want me to be with Drake. This news should make him happy. Regardless, I don't have the strength to deal with his ire.

"Because I want to," I reply blankly.

"If Charles was who you wanted, why did you accept Drake's advances?"

Because I love him. I want so badly to tell Gregory the truth. To beg him to help me. But if I do, it will place him in danger, and I can't take that chance. This is my life now, and I have no choice but to surrender to it.

"Because I was confused. I missed Drake so much when he was gone. And when he came back I guess I just . . . I just got wrapped up in being with him. But in my heart I knew it wasn't right. I had spent a lot of time with Charles when you and Drake were gone and I actually started to fall for him. I just didn't realize how much I had fallen for him until he proposed today."

Gregory scoffs. "I don't believe you. If this was what you wanted, then I wouldn't have found you lying unconscious in the mud outside. I know what it looks like when you've given up, Addalynne, and that's exactly what this is."

So that's why I have dried mud caked all over me. He's wrong though, I haven't given up. I'm fighting harder than I ever have before. I'm just not fighting for myself. "No, it's not. I'm sad, Gregory. I'm sad because I hurt Drake. You know how much I care about him. I never meant to hurt him." I swallow back the lump in my throat. "But it doesn't change the way I feel about my decision. You may not agree with it and you may not understand it, but it's my choice and you will accept it."

Gregory stands and turns to face me. "You go ahead and make your choice, Addalynne, but I don't have to accept it. That's the beauty in choices, we all get to make our own."

I push myself into a sitting position, my hands clenching around my blanket. "So what choice are you going to make Gregory? To keep me from marrying Charles? You have no say in the matter! Father gave his permission and I accepted! There's nothing you can say or do to change it!"

"Maybe. But if I find out that you're lying to me. If I find out that something else is going on here—"

"Oh, stop it Gregory!" I jump to my feet and stand directly in front of him, my gaze locking on his, my heart beating uncontrollably. "If you want to play hero, then go back to Synereal! There's no one here who needs your saving!"

He stares down at me, his gaze piercing, contemplating. I try to focus on breathing, but my breaths feel shallow, blocked. *Calm down. I have to calm down.* I pull in another breath and try to think of the words I need to say, because everything hangs on this moment. If Gregory doesn't believe me, he'll go to Drake. He'll convince him that I'm lying. I can't let that happen.

"I want to be with Charles, Gregory. I do." A shallow breath scrapes my throat and the backs of my knees brush against my bed. *Stay on your feet, Addalynne.* "I can't marry Drake," I continue, letting my desperation fuel my words. "If I did I would be stuck in Faygrene. You know I've never wanted that. For a while, I thought that my love for Drake would be enough to accept a life here, never traveling, never seeing what's out there. But I know now that it's not."

Gregory shakes his head, and I pull in another tightened breath. "Fine, Addalynne. But just know that, if what you're saying is true, you deserve the pain you're feeling, because no matter how much pain you're in, Drake is in much more. You used him. You used him until you found someone who could give you the escape you're always looking for. And if that makes you happy, then go be happy, but leave me out of it."

I turn away from Gregory and pull my lip into my mouth, biting until the pain is sharp enough to distract me from the pain in my chest. The sound of Gregory's heavy footsteps retreating from my chambers takes what's left of my strength, and when the door shuts, I drop back down on the bed, alone with my grief.

* * *

It's too early in the morning when Mother wakes me and ushers me into the bath. Father must have filled her in on the engagement, because she doesn't ask about it. She just says she, "only wants me to be happy," and fills the tub. She then explains that Lord Berrenger sent a message to our home stating that I was to be in the market square at noon for the announcement of my engagement to Charles. It all seems to be happening so quickly, and too soon, I'm being rushed into a carriage that's waiting out front to take me to the market.

"We'll meet you there, and after the announcement, you'll ride home with us," Mother says, before kissing me on the cheek and helping me in.

On the ride over, I look down at the ivory-colored dress I'm wearing while fidgeting with the long sleeves. Charles sent it with a note stating that I was to wear it today. It fits tightly across my bust and is rather low cut, exposing more of me than I'm used to. The rest of the material, starting directly under my bust line, drapes loosely down to my feet. My hair is delicately braided to one side—a detail Charles requested as well. I wonder how many more decisions he's going to be making for me; not that it really matters. He already took the most important one away—the rest are irrelevant.

The carriage pulls up behind the center square of the market and I see Charles. Overwhelming resentment rises in me as I take in the sight of him and the matching color of our outfits. He glances at me and the bells in the market begin to toll. They ring three times, telling the villagers that there's going to be an important announcement. Yes, everyone come watch and cheer for my undoing.

Charles strides over to the carriage and assesses me before wrapping his hands around my waist, pulling me down from the seat and setting me on my feet in front of him.

"I knew that dress would be a wonderful fit on you." His gaze travels to my chest—leaving me thoroughly disgusted—before rising back up to my face. "Do try to wipe the scowl off your face, Addalynne. It's not very becoming on you." He leans down and places his lips against my ear. I can't stop myself from recoiling, but his hands wrap around the tops of my arms, holding me near him. "I hope I don't need to remind you that it is of vital importance for you to appear happy about our engagement. And you *are* happy, aren't you?" It's not a question, it's a warning.

He straightens back up and smiles, releasing his grip on my arms. They pulse slightly as the blood recirculates through them. "Oh, and one more thing." He reaches into his vest and pulls out a long, pearl and gold necklace. He places it around my neck, and though it's delicate it feels like iron. He takes a step back; perusing his purchase. "There. Now you're perfect."

I imagine taking Drake's dagger from my boot and dragging it across Charles's throat, watching as the blood drips down his ivory vest and cloak, turning them crimson. The thought gives me the smile I need to wear on my face when Charles takes hold of my elbow and escorts me into the market square.

Edmund, the Squire, announces us, as we step out onto the stage. I squint against the blinding sun and try to block out the dull hum of Edmund's words, but the word engagement breaks through and I have to remind myself to breathe.

All around me the familiar faces of everyone in Faygrene are cheering loudly, ecstatic smiles spread across their sunburned faces. I wish I could tell them not to cheer, that I'm just another prisoner brought on this stage to receive her sentence.

Sweat trickles down my brow, and my head swims. All I can do to keep from collapsing is focus on the trees that lie far ahead, beyond the outskirts of the village. I stare at the green leaves that sway in the gentle breeze, thinking about the comfort they give me, and try not to faint.

Once I feel slightly composed, I let my gaze drift back to the crowd and I see him. He's standing at the back, leaning against the grey stone wall. He's staring straight at me, his face filled with contempt. I want to look away, but I can't. His face has become my lifeline and, though it tortures me, it gets me through.

As the announcement comes to a close, I reluctantly

tear my gaze away from Drake and turn to leave the stage. Charles's hand is still wrapped around my elbow, and when we round the corner, his grip tightens and becomes increasingly aggressive.

"Give me a moment with my betrothed," he tells his guards, while leading me onto a deserted street near the carriage.

"You call that happy. I'm not convinced," he says as he pulls us to a stop.

"What else do you want from me Charles? I stood there with you, smiling, playing along in your little game."

He pulls me closer. "I want you to convince me."

Panic seeps into my blood, but before I can move he leans down and crushes his lips to mine. Complete revulsion shutters through my body at the feel of his mouth on me. I turn my head and use all my strength to pull away.

Pure rage ignites his face. He raises his arm and brings it down, slamming the back of his hand across my face. The pain is blinding and instantaneous. I stagger sideways and nearly fall, but he roughly grabs hold of my upper arm, keeping me on my feet.

I try to focus my blurred vision on his face, my left cheek pulsing with pain.

"Don't *ever* turn away from me again," he sneers, his voice quiet, but enraged. "You are to be my wife and I *will* have you when I want you. You will be compliant, Addalynne, or I swear to you I *will* kill the orphan."

His words throw me back to my reality, and this

time, when he leans down and presses his lips against mine, I let him. The taste of his mouth and the feel of his hands grazing hungrily across my back makes my stomach turn and tears sting my eyes. He's pulling my body against his, claiming it as if it were his own, and I'm powerless to stop him. I almost cry with relief when he finally pulls away.

He smiles down at me with blood on his mouth. It takes me a moment to realize that it came from me. My lip is bleeding from when he hit me and, as he stares proudly at the cut on my lip, he licks the blood off his own with his tongue.

The sound of footsteps thankfully frees me from his grip, and I watch my family turn the corner, along with Vernold.

"There you two are. We were wondering where you had run off to," Vernold calls playfully, his eyes cautiously falling to my lip.

"My future bride and I desired a few moments alone," Charles says with a bashful smile, putting the full force of his charm into effect. "Unfortunately, we spent most of our time caring to Addalynne's face." He looks at me sympathetically and gently runs his fingers across my jaw. "She tripped on an uneven stone and fell. I tried to catch her, but wasn't fast enough, and she hit her face on the wall." His eyes are fixed on mine the entire time he says this, daring me to contradict him. Fury buries itself inside me, but I hold myself in check, knowing that this is a test I cannot fail.

"I wasn't looking where I was going. I was . . .

distracted," I say with a shy smile.

He raises one eyebrow at me in satisfaction and then turns toward my mother. "She keeps insisting that she's fine, but I'm still worried. Will you take care of her for me, Genoveve? It devastates me to know that she's in pain." His voice and face are masked with false concern and frighteningly convincing.

"Of course, my Lord," my mother replies. She rushes to my side and quickly checks my face, her fingers gently tracing over what I'm sure is a harsh red mark. I look over to Gregory. His eyes are on Charles, his posture stiff. He doesn't believe him.

"I really am fine. I just lost my footing," I lie, hoping to fix whatever doubt may be unfolding in Gregory's mind. Gregory glances at me, his gaze scrutinizing.

"That *is* strange, because normally your reflexes are so fast. I can't imagine that you wouldn't catch yourself before hitting your face," Gregory replies skeptically. Elizabeth moves to stand next to him now, her eyes equally questioning.

"That's because she was fidgeting with her necklace. You know how distracted ladies become with pretty things," Charles replies swiftly. Gregory nods once, but his eyes never leave my face.

"We should be getting home now," I say as I look down the street, searching for my escape.

"Yes, we need to be returning as well." Charles thankfully agrees. I turn and walk toward the carriage with Charles's arm looped through mine. As much as I detest the thought, I know I have to say a proper goodbye in order to not add to Gregory's suspicion. When we reach the carriage, I rise on my toes and place a kiss on Charles's cheek. When I pull away, he reaches out and wipes the blood from my lip. He dredges it across his fingertips as he smiles down at me and then turns and walks toward his own waiting carriage. I climb into ours with the rest of my family, hoping that I convinced Gregory and Elizabeth, but their stares accost me the entire way home, showing me that they're both filled with doubt.

Chapter 22

HER

Several weeks pass with no mention of suspicion or doubt from Gregory or Elizabeth. They watch me cautiously, their eyes haunting my every move, but never vocalize their thoughts. I'm thankful for this, but I'm also feeling more alone than ever. I have no one to confide in. No one to find comfort with. My days are spent mostly in my chambers, lying in silence as the time passes. I only leave for a few hours a day, when I have to walk the market with Charles, or have a meal with him at his manor. He calls it courting; I call it imprisonment.

This morning I'll be going into the market on my own for the first time since before the Ball. Charles left two days ago. He's pretending to investigate the disappearance of the Hunt family. They haven't disappeared. Their unmarked graves haunt the forest behind the manor: four mounds of fresh dirt. But I can't tell anyone, so instead I listen to the rumors, to the fears of the villagers. "Taken by a hellion," they say. So Charles and his father are off to play hero, to pretend to try and rid the town of their monster. At least his fake quest frees me from mine.

As I remove my chemise from my body, I play out the different scenarios of what could happen, but the truth is I don't know what to expect from my trip to the market. When I've been in the market with Charles, I've seen Drake, but he always turns and leaves before I can even get a decent glimpse of his face. I'm scared of how he'll react to seeing me without Charles on my arm. What if he turns and leaves again, or ignores me completely? Or worse, what if he tries to speak with me? I don't know what I'll do, but I'm pushing aside all my fear, all my caution, in hopes of getting one look at him. If I can just see his face, I can get through whatever comes next.

I look down at my bare body and study the dark bruises that now decorate my arms, ribs, and waist. Ever since the day of our announced engagement, Charles has found ways to punish me in places that aren't visible to others. The largest and most recent bruise stares back at me. It's a grapefruit-sized collage of black, blue, purple, and green that rests on top of the left side of my ribs. Every time I breathe I feel a sharp stab of pain. I'm certain at least one rib is cracked. It happened three nights ago, after supper at his manor. He moved in to kiss me and I impulsively turned my cheek. He didn't appreciate my defiance and threw me against the table.

I'm still glad I refused him. In a way, I wear the bruise as a small victory.

My entire body aches in protest as I carefully pull on a clean chemise and then my green dress. But I'm actually growing accustomed to the physical pain and even find myself grateful for it. It provides a distraction from the incessant heartache and emotional pain, which is worse.

Apprehensively, I move to the mirror. The dress fits more loosely than the last time I wore it, but it still evokes the memories of that day. I let my mind drift there now—to the woods with Drake. I close my eyes and remember the feel of his hands running along my arms as I held the bow. I can almost feel the weight of his body pressed against mine, and the tingle of his lips on my mouth and neck. I stay in the memory for a while, letting my mind conjure up the lost moments.

The feeling of emptiness is crushing when I reopen my eyes and stare at my face in the mirror. My eyes are vacant, like glass, providing only a reflection and nothing more. Dark circles shadow the skin beneath my eyes, strikingly obvious against the paleness of my face. I pinch my cheeks in an attempt to give my face some color, but it only makes me look worse. I give up. It doesn't matter anyway.

I grab my cloak, which I eventually retrieved from the Berrengers', and make my way out the front door. In my head I go over the list of items I told Mother I would purchase—ribbon for Elizabeth, carrots for tonight, and mint leaves.

* * *

Though it's still early in the morning, the market is bustling with people. At first I'm surprised by the amount of villagers present, but then I remember why— they're preparing for my wedding. I almost forgot that it had been promoted from a small village affair to a full out extravaganza in Synereal. Apparently Charles asked King Theoderic if we could get married in the capital, since that's where Charles lived for the past fifteen years. King Theoderic agreed, saying the capital could use something joyful after all the fear that has been brought on from the hellion's attack, the disappearances, and the prisoner from Incarnadine. King Theoderic invited our entire village to attend, and he's even going to host this year's Tournament of Knights in the days leading up to the ceremony. I've been told it's all "very exciting" though that would not be the word I'd choose. Nightmare? . . . No, it's worse than that. Even though I'm going to finally see the capital, I feel nothing but dread. I have one week left with my family in Faygrene and one week of travel with them before I will completely belong to him.

Stares come at me from all directions as I make my way through the crowd, making me feel uncomfortable and exposed. I miss the days when others took little notice of me, when I was just Addalynne Troyer, a girl who was a little odd, but definitely not significant. Now I can't help but cringe when people automatically clear a path for me.

I pull the hood of my cloak up, partially to conceal myself from the wind, but mostly in hopes of no longer being recognized.

"Addalynne!" a girl's voice calls out. So much for not being recognized. I turn and find myself face to face with Jacqueline. "I'm so happy to see you!" she says while wrapping her arms around me and pulling me in for a hug. My hands drop stiffly to my sides as the shock and revulsion of her embrace incapacitates me. Finally, she lets go and takes a step back, considering me speculatively.

I should turn and walk away, but my curiosity at what she could possibly want holds me in place. Or maybe I'm just craving more punishment.

"You're looking a little pale," she says with a fake drawl of concern, "not that you ever had much color to begin with," she continues with a laugh.

"What do you want, Jacqueline?"

"You're irritable, too. Is it the stress from planning your wedding? You know I may soon know what that's like myself." I don't bother pretending to know or care what she's talking about. Instead, I turn away. No amount of curiosity is worth this. "Oh, don't go yet, we have so much to talk about!"

We do?

She hooks her arm in mine, stopping me. I turn back toward her and a conniving smile breaks across her face. "I wanted to tell you how happy I am that you're marrying Charles."

I untangle her arm from mine. "Thank you." I try to

leave, but she grabs hold of my arm again.

"Don't you want to know why?" She asks and her voice somehow becomes even more annoying.

"No." Irritation burns through my voice. I try to pull free from her grip, but it's like iron, and my injuries make it impossible to pull hard enough to get loose.

"Well, I'll tell you anyway. You marrying Charles made Drake realize how much better off he is with me, although I'm certain he would have realized it eventually. You merely . . . expedited things. Now, he couldn't be happier, and between you and me, I think he's going to be asking for my hand very soon." She drops my arm, gives one last smile, and then walks away.

The impact of her words twists the knife that seems to have found a permanent haunt in my heart. I want to say something, but all I can do is watch her retreat as I struggle for composure. My body sways slightly, and I realize I haven't been breathing. I look down at the ground and force ragged breaths through my lungs while I try to take my mind away from the thoughts that are branding into my brain.

Once I feel strong enough, I lift my head and see the only thing that could once again shift the ground from underneath me. Drake is leaning against the eastern wall of the market, about fifteen feet away. He has a grey cloak draped around his shoulders, the hood shadowing his face, but I can still see his eyes, and they are set on me. All at once, everything else goes away, and it's just us. There are no bustling of feet, no voices, no market. I tell myself to move, to leave before I do something I'll regret, but his presence is binding me in place. Ripping out my own heart would be easier than tearing my gaze away from him now.

Instead, he severs the line between us himself, his gaze shifting to the side. As soon as he looks away, everything else comes flooding back in. It's like a door being suddenly opened, allowing people and sounds to come rushing through all at once, completely overwhelming me. But what I see next is like a scene pulled directly from my nightmares. I watch as Jacqueline sashays toward him. Once she's within arm's reach, he pulls her into his arms and kisses her the way he used to kiss me, his hands tangling in her hair, her body pulled tightly against his. I thought things couldn't get worse. I thought I couldn't feel more pain. I was wrong.

Finally, he pulls his mouth away from hers and looks over her head, at me, his expression impenetrable. I want to look away from him, to make it seem like what I just saw didn't fracture me into a million pieces, but I'm completely immobile.

Suddenly, someone bumps into me. I stumble and, though I manage to stay on my feet, the sharp movement sends an excruciating shot of pain through my cracked rib. I gasp in agony, my hand clutching my side, my body hunching in pain. Tears fill my eyes, but I force myself to straighten out my body. I drop my hand back down and look at Drake. His blank mask is gone, his expression now strained with confusion and concern. He takes Jacqueline's arms from around his neck and moves toward me.

No. I can't let him approach me. There are too many people around, and I know that at least one of them is ready to report back to Charles. I break into a painful run, pushing myself as fast as I can. He calls my name and runs after me, but I turn the corner and am thankfully able to lose him in the large crowd.

My first instinct is to run home, but I can't go home, not yet. Drake might go there to look for me and I can't risk seeing him again. Instead, I wander around for a while, staying in places that I'm easily concealed, places where he won't find me. When enough time passes, I finally go home.

I stumble through the doorway, ready to collapse with exhaustion, and find Elizabeth sitting by the fire, knitting a red quilt.

"I'm sorry, Elizabeth, but I wasn't able to get your ribbons. Also, please tell Mother that I wasn't able to get the carrots or the mint," I say breathlessly as I pass her and head down the hallway toward my chambers. The sound of footsteps follows me, and when I try to shut my door, Elizabeth is there to stop it. "What is it, Elizabeth?" I ask tiredly.

She makes her way into my chambers, shutting the door behind her. "What happened to you, Addalynne?" she demands.

"Nothing. I'm just tired. Now will you please leave and let me rest?"

"No. Gregory and I know that you're keeping secrets from us and I want you to tell me what they are." She crosses her arms, stubbornly waiting for my response.

"I don't know what you're talking about."

She raises one delicate eyebrow in disbelief. "Then let me explain. You don't eat. You hardly sleep. You rarely come out of your chambers, and when you do, you float around like a ghost. You're miserable, and don't try to tell me otherwise because, so help me, Addalynne, I can't hear another one of your, 'This is my choice and I'm truly happy' speeches."

I have never in my life seen my sister this angry. All I can do is stare at her while I try to find something to say, but words evade me. After several seconds of silence, Elizabeth marches toward me and wraps her fingers around my wrist. By the time I realize what she's about to do, it's too late. She pulls up the sleeve of my dress, exposing the bruises that lie beneath. Closing my eyes, I brace myself for her reaction. She gasps with shock as she takes in the least of my injuries.

"Addalynne, what has he done to you?" she whispers in horror. Her fingers gently brush along my arm, and when I finally allow my eyes to open, her face is wet with tears. "I knew it," she says, dropping my arm. "The day of your announcement, he hit you didn't he?" I still can't bring myself to answer her. I stare into the crack of the door, wishing I could slip through it. "Why are you letting him hurt you? Why are you marrying him?" she yells, her anger reaching a new level. She seems much older than her eleven years, and in this moment, I'm the one who feels like the child. "Answer me, Addalynne!"

"Because he said he would kill him, Elizabeth! He

said he would kill Drake!"

Elizabeth stares at me, her mouth open in shock.

I can't believe I told her. After everything I've been through, everything I've agreed to, to keep him safe, to keep them all safe, I go ahead and ruin it. Still, I can't help but feel a minor sense of relief at getting it out there, at having at least one person know the truth. But the relief doesn't outweigh the panic. "You have to swear to me, Elizabeth, swear to me that you will *never* speak a word of this to anyone. *Do you understand me?* If anyone finds out about this, he *will* kill Drake. *Please* promise me, Elizabeth, *please!*" I beg her, my heart thrashing in my chest.

"Addalynne . . . I . . ."

"Swear it, Elizabeth!"

"I can't, Addalynne! I can't let you do this! *He's hurting you!*"

"I can handle it, Elizabeth! It's only a few bruises. I can live with that, but I won't be able to live if something happens to Drake! You have to swear that you won't say anything!" I clutch her hands in mine, desperate, begging her to keep my secret. After several agonizing seconds of silence, she finally speaks.

"I swear, Addalynne, but do you honestly think that this is what Drake would want? How do you think he would feel if he knew you were doing all this just to protect him? He loves you, Addalynne. He would rather die than let you be hurt."

"Then we have that in common," I murmur quietly,

thinking about her words. Of course he would be angry, but I am the one who has to make the choice and it's an easy one to make. I would choose his life every time.

"You can leave! You and Drake can leave; go somewhere Charles can't hurt either of you!"

"Do you think I haven't thought of that? We can't leave. Charles would come after you and Mother and Father and Gregory and . . ." My breath is coming in short bursts, and I know I have to stop before I completely fall apart. "It's not possible, Elizabeth. This is the only way."

"How can I stand by and watch him hurt you?"

"Because if you say anything, it will hurt me more."

"Will you at least consider telling Drake the truth? Or perhaps Gregory . . ."

"No, Elizabeth. They can never know, and neither one of us is going to tell them. You're my sister. I'm trusting you to keep this secret for me, and in return I'll no longer lie to you."

She studies me contemplatively before her features slightly soften, but the sadness and pain she's feeling flows through her. "Fine. I'll keep this between us," she promises, while wrapping her arms around me, and pulling me into an embrace. "But you have to promise me you'll try to find a way out."

"All right, Elizabeth."

She pulls back and locks her eyes onto mine. "I mean it, Addalynne." The tone in which she says this reminds me so much of my mother, and I feel even more like a lost child.

"I *will* try, Elizabeth. I promise" And I will. If there's a way out that won't risk the lives of those I love, I *will* find it.

She nods and offers me a pained smile. "I'm going to go to the market to pick up the ribbons, carrots, and mint. We don't want Mother to start asking questions. I'll be back soon," she says before kissing me on the cheek. After she leaves my chambers, I take off my dress, leaving me in my chemise, and lie down on my bed, praying that I can trust her to keep my secret.

After a while, my eyes close. As I drift into sleep, images of Drake wrapped around Jacqueline flash in my mind. I jump off the bed and grab Drake's cloak and letters out from underneath. I wrap Drake's cloak around me, pretending the feel of his cloak against my bare skin is really him. I lie back down. As I breathe in his scent and read his words, I can almost believe he's still mine.

* * *

The sound of footsteps in my chambers draws me from my diluted sleep. I open my eyes and squint against the harsh light of the late afternoon sun, my head throbbing. There's a figure moving about my chambers, picking papers and clothes off the floor. My first thought goes to my mother, but then I realize that the person has soft blond curls falling down her back and across her shoulders.

"Mary?" My voice grates in my own ears. Mary

jumps at the sound, as though I'm the one who has come into her chambers and startled her. I pull Drake's cloak tighter around me, trying to cover my bruises. I should have never changed out of my dress.

"Addalynne, good. You're awake," she replies breathlessly as she continues to lift my green dress off the floor.

"Leave it. I'm going to wear it tonight."

"You are?" She turns it over in her hands, likely looking at the wrinkles and scuff marks. I wasn't actually planning on wearing it, but I only wore it for a few hours and it's already out, so I may as well.

"Yes."

"Very well," she replies skeptically, and lays the dress across the back of the chair. Finally, she turns to face me, her eyes cautious, watching me like she's waiting for me to burst into flame.

"What are you doing here, Mary?" I ask, not entirely with irritation, but these days, my voice seems to have a tinge of irritation lining each word. She fidgets with her fingers as she walks toward me and sits on the edge of my bed.

"I came to check on you. It's been a while since I last saw you."

Great. Now I feel guilty. "It has. I'm sorry, I've been . . . preoccupied."

"I know. There's no need for you to explain." The way she says this makes me wonder how much she knows.

She rises to her feet and moves across the floor,

retrieving a silver jar from the desk. When she returns, she sits next to my arm. She gently reaches down and grabs hold of my wrist. It's barely exposed under the cloak so she uses her other hand to move the cloak aside. My first instinct is to pull away, but there's no surprise, anger, or judgment on Mary's face when she looks down at my bruises. Still, I don't know how I'm going to explain them.

"Drake isn't interested in Jacqueline," she says softly, while she begins to rub a strong smelling ointment on one of my bruises.

Why is she telling me this? I want to ask her, but I don't trust my emotions enough to speak.

"I think he has a hard time even tolerating her," she continues.

"Then why is he with her?" The question leaves my mouth without my permission.

She glances at me, her brown eyes kind and comforting. "Because he's a man whose pride has been injured. Nothing makes a man more illogical than a wounded ego." She looks back down at my bruises and rubs the ointment on another one. "I believe he's with her for no other reason than to illicit a reaction from you. He wants to see if you still care." She pauses, as though she's waiting for me to confirm or deny my feelings. She should know me well enough to know I'll do neither.

"What makes you so sure? Maybe he's with her because she's willing to give him things that I . . ." I trail off. There's no right way to finish that thought. *Things that I wouldn't give him* . . . that would be entirely untrue. I would give him everything. *Things that I couldn't give him* . . . That's closer to the truth. There's nothing I can give him anymore. Regardless, the thought of what Jacqueline would be willing to do with him has me sickened. Will he be concerned about her honor, as he was with me, or will he give in to her?

"He doesn't look at her the way he looks at you," Mary replies, her words pulling me away from my contaminated thoughts. "Every time he looks at you, it's like . . . I don't know how to describe it . . . I suppose it's similar to the way a man who's been trapped underground all his life would look upon the sky. The way he looks at Jacqueline . . . It's like . . ." her face scrunches with disgust. ". . . looking at the bottom of your boot after you've squished a cockroach." A laugh escapes me. She glances up at the sound and smiles softly. "You know, Addalynne. I've always admired you." Her brown eyes are completely sincere, but there's a slight trace of sadness to them.

"Me? Mary, you're a much better person than I am. If anyone should be admired, it's you. Your ability to put aside your own feelings in order to be there for someone you care about—it's not something I'm always able to do."

"Oh, I wouldn't say that. You don't disclose much, Addalynne, but I know you enough to know that almost everything you do is for the people you love. You're one of the strongest people I know, and one of the most loyal." She looks back down at my arm and then pulls the cloak back over it. "The ointment will help the bruises fade faster. I'll leave it here in case you need more. And you don't have to tell me how you got them. I'm not about to pretend I understand why you're marrying Charles and I'm not going to ask you to explain it to me. I know it's not a decision you made lightly. And I know you wouldn't be doing it if you didn't have a very good reason for it, so I'm not going to question it. But I want you to know that you *can* talk to me. You can tell me anything. I want to be here for you, if you'll let me, and I swear to you that everything you tell me will be kept in complete confidence."

Her words bring a mixture of guilt, relief, and appreciation. I feel completely torn. I believe her and desperately want to tell her the truth. But I can't burden anyone else with this. Elizabeth knowing is bad enough. I won't pull Mary into my nightmare.

"Thank you, Mary, for everything. You've been a great friend to me, and sadly, I'm not sure I can say the same about myself. I want you to know that I trust you completely and I wish there was something I could tell you, but . . ."

"There's not," she finishes my statement. I turn away from her. I hate disappointing the people I care about. "If you happen to change your mind, you know where to find me."

She stands, causing the bed to rise slightly with the absence of her weight. I wish she would stay. It's nice having someone to talk to, especially someone who's not going to question my motives or my choices. But I can't ask her to. There is, however, something I can ask her before she leaves, something that has been weighing on my mind.

"Mary, has Gregory mentioned anything to you . . . about me?"

Mary is halfway to the door, but she stops and turns to face me, the skirt of her grey dress swaying at her feet. "He hasn't mentioned much, but he has seemed . . . distracted and agitated lately. When I asked him why, he said he was worried about you. He didn't offer any more information, and you know me, I'm not one to pry." She smiles apologetically. "I can ask again though, if you'd like?"

"No. That's all right." That would only add to his suspicion.

She nods and then turns again, but as her hand reaches the door knob, she pauses. "This afternoon, when I arrived, he seemed . . . out of sorts. Before he left, he asked me to check on you. I asked him if you were all right. He said no and told me that I would see for myself what the matter was when I saw you. I think we both know what he saw."

My bruises! He must have come into my chambers while I was asleep and saw my exposed arm. My insides twist with dread as I think about what must be going through Gregory's head, and worse, what he's going to do about it. "Do you have any idea where he was going when he left?"

"No. I asked him, but he wouldn't tell me."

Think, Addalynne, think. He couldn't be going to the

Berrengers'. He knows they're away, but that doesn't mean he won't go straight to Charles to demand answers as soon as they return. I have to talk to him before then. I have to persuade him to let go of any suspicion he may have.

"There's something, though, something I think I heard him say as he walked out."

"What was it?" I ask breathlessly.

"I could be wrong, but it sounded like he mumbled something about Drake being an ignorant bastard."

No! He can't be going to Drake! If he tells Drake about his suspicions . . . No . . . this can't be happening . . . I have to stop him!

I push myself off the bed and run for the door. Mary steps aside and lets me through, her face filled with bewilderment.

"Addalynne, where are you going?" she calls, while trailing me to the entry. I ignore her question and run for the door.

"Addalynne, don't be absurd. You can't leave in this state."

I pull open the door and run outside.

"For goodness sake, Addalynne, you're not even wearing shoes."

She's right. The rocks cut into my feet as I run, but I don't care. If I can only make it to Freyja, then I can ride the rest of the way.

But Mary's hand is now firmly holding my shoulder. I try to pull away, but my body is weak, and she's able to spin me around to face her.

"Addalynne, please listen to me. I know you can't tell me what's going on, but it's clear that there's something you're trying very hard to keep secret. Now, think about what you're about to do. If you go riding into the village in your chemise, searching for Gregory and Drake like a mad woman, you're only going to confirm their suspicions."

"You don't understand! I can't let him tell Drake!"

"No, I don't understand, but I can help you. I'll go to the village and find Gregory and I'll try my best to keep him away from Drake. That will give you some time." She's right again. If I go like this, it will only prove that there's something terribly wrong. Mary is my only hope for stopping Gregory.

It kills me to let her go in my place, to stay here and wait, with only my thoughts to torment me. But I have no choice, so I nod my head in affirmation.

"I'll do my best," she says, running past me.

"Take Gregory's horse!" I call back, watching her run toward the barn. Seconds later, she exits the barn atop Sejant. I wrap my arms around myself and watch them ride toward the village, praying with everything in me that she'll get there in time.

Chapter 23

HER

I run the brush along Freyja's mane, trying to let the feel of her hair and the sound of the strokes calm me. It's not working. I wasn't careful enough, and now the only chance I have of keeping Drake safe is if Mary was able to stop Gregory. If she got to him in time, then I can figure out something to tell him, even if it has to be the partial truth. But it's been almost an hour since she left, and the fact that Gregory still hasn't come home has me dizzy with trepidation.

At least Charles isn't here. I have to fix this before he returns.

The sound of the lock latching into place on the stable door alerts me to someone else's presence in the barn. Startled, I spin around.

"Drake," his name falls from my lips and the brush slips from my fingers, clattering to the ground.

I take in the totality of him as he lingers near the heavy wooden doors, the look on his face determined, yet vulnerable and pained. His face is flushed, his eyes sparkling with what I can only assume is anger. His white tunic is streaked with dirt, his black breaches dusted brown. Mary was too late.

He closes the distance between us and comes to a stop with merely inches separating us. I press my back against Freyja's sturdy side and look up at Drake. His eyes are burning right through me. I look away, setting my gaze at the hem of my navy dress, focusing on the way it grazes against the hay at my feet, while I try to catch my breath.

My heart is beating so intensely that I can hear it drumming in my ears. It's as though it's trying to break free, to jump out of my body and dive into his, returning to where it knows it belongs.

His fingertips brush against my cheek, and my body ignites with need, his touch as familiar as my own name. I close my eyes and focus on the path of his fingers as they move toward my ear and push my hair behind it. His fingers continue to trace down my neck and then to my collarbone, where they linger.

"I've been such a fool," he says quietly, and then his hand drops to his side, taking with it the first warmth I've felt in weeks. "I need you to talk to me, Addy. I need you to tell me what Charles is doing to you." The pain in his voice is crushing, but there's harshness to it when he spits out Charles's name.

I take a deep breath and raise my head to look at

him. "I don't know what you're talking about."

His expression doesn't change. Instead, he reaches forward and gently places his hand on my left side, on top of my cracked ribs. He doesn't apply any pressure, but his touch shows me just how much he knows. I swallow against the lump in my throat and try to think of something to say, but Drake's words come first.

"I've been blind, Addy, and I will *never* forgive myself for it. If I had been more aware, I could have stopped him. I could have kept you safe. But I'm not blind anymore. This morning, I saw the pain you were in, and then Gregory told me . . ." his voice breaks. "I don't deserve your forgiveness, but I do need your honesty." His words are oxygen, and my body craves them—craves the love that is pouring from them; love that I never thought I would receive from him again. I don't want to lie to him. I want to tell him how much I'm hurting, and let him heal each wound with his touch. I want to convince him that there's nothing to forgive because none of this is his fault. But wanting these things is irrelevant. This isn't about what I want; it's about keeping him alive.

I set my shoulders and look him straight in the eye, trying to appear strong, when internally I'm turning to ash. "I know exactly what Gregory told you and I can assure you he's mistaken. He's not happy about my engagement to Charles, and he's looking for any reason to put an end to it, even if it means creating one."

Drake drags his hands across his face and a humorless chuckle of pure aggravation escapes his lips. When he drops his hands and sets his gaze back on me, there's a perceptible trace of anger in his eyes.

"Okay, Addalynne, I'll play along. Let's pretend that Gregory's wrong about the bruises on your arm. What about what I saw this morning in the market? I know you were in pain. Don't try to tell me that I imagined it."

"No, I am injured, but it's because I fell off of Freyja, not because Charles—"

"Stop, Addalynne! Stop lying!" His chest is rising and falling heavily with his breaths and his face is flushed. He's furious and devastated, and it's entirely my fault. I want to wrap my arms around him and quiet all his anger, all his fear.

I slide my body sideways, stepping away from him before I give in to what I want. I walk toward the window and look outside, fixing my gaze on the swaying willow tree. It's planted firmly in the ground, and no matter what storm comes its way, it keeps hold of its roots and its position.

"I'm not lying, Drake. I told you the truth. It's not my fault if you can't accept it." I force the words out, but every strand of my body is fighting to give in.

His hand wraps around my hip and he slowly spins me around to face him. He looks down at me with hurt and desperation as he places both hands on either side of my head, trapping me in place. With every inch of space he closes between us, my cover slips. And he's so very close to me now. I have to escape his gaze and his proximity if I'm going to get through this. My current position offers nowhere to move to, making it impossible to escape him. But I can avoid his gaze. I look down at the ground, removing him from my line of sight.

"Look at me," he demands, but I keep my focus on the hay at my feet. *"Look at me,"* he pleads, and his fingers brush across my cheek, sending the deepest longing through my body. He runs his fingers under my jaw and gently lifts my face. My resolve is almost completely gone, and the determined look in his eyes tells me he knows it.

He's not going to let this go. He may not know everything, but Gregory has filled him with enough suspicion to make him pursue answers. Neither he nor Gregory will stop until they know the absolute truth, not anymore. And if I don't tell him, he'll go to Charles for answers. *I failed him.* My heart breaks with the realization.

I let myself look fully into his eyes, knowing I no longer need to pretend, and let my fingers run across his cheek. As I touch him, his eyes close and we simultaneously exhale. Giving in and letting my fingers graze across his skin sends an overload of feelings and emotions through me. Desire, longing, heartache, comfort, fear—I wonder how much a person can take before they reach their limit and shatter.

He places his hand on top of my own, cradling it against his cheek.

"Please, Addy. I need to hear the truth *from you.* I need you to tell me what he's doing to you. All these lies *—they're killing me."* His eyes slowly open. There's so much pain and fear in them.

"Drake, seeing that look on your face and knowing that I'm the one who put it there is torture. But the worst part is that there's nothing I can tell you that will make any of this better for either of us. If I tell you he's hurting me, it won't change anything. Nothing I tell you today will stop any of this from happening." Confusion passes over his features. I pull my hand from under his and drop it back down to my side. "I love you, Drake. But I still can't be with you. I have to marry Charles."

"Because he's forcing you to marry him?" He waits for my confirmation, his body trembling slightly, pure rage storming in his eyes.

"Yes." The word leaves with my breath. I did it. I told him the truth. A paralyzing amount of dread numbs my body, but I push it back and focus on this moment and the fact that we're together.

Drake pulls me into his arms and holds me against his chest. I return the embrace, memorizing the feel of his heart beating against me, his breath caressing the top of my head.

"Addy, you don't need to be afraid. He can't hurt you, not anymore. I won't let him come near you. And whatever he said, whatever he threatened to do to you if you didn't marry him—"

"He didn't threaten *me*." I pull back slightly and look into his face. If only it had been that simple. A threat on my life I could handle.

"Then, how . . . I don't understand."

I take a deep breath in preparation for my answer. I'm worried about his reaction, but I've come this far already. There's no going back, not anymore, not ever. "He threatened you, Drake. He said he knew you were the reason I was refusing him and that he would kill you if that's what it took to get you out of the way. I had no other choice but to agree to marry him." My voice breaks with my confession.

I wait for him to respond, but he remains silent, his eyes vacant, his face a blank mask. Whatever thoughts are running through his head are being meticulously concealed from me, which is absolutely terrifying. He removes his arms from around me and takes a step back. He drops his head into his hands and drags them across his face.

"Why didn't you tell me the truth? Why did you lie to me?" he asks quietly, his hands still covering his face.

"Because the only way to keep you safe was to make you believe I was choosing him."

He turns his back to me and takes several steps, his hands fisting into his hair.

"That day in the woods, I wanted to die." I continue. I have to make him understand. "I'll never forgive myself for the things I said to you, but you have to understand that there is no other way. They *will* kill you, Drake! Charles killed Sarah Hunt in front of me just to prove a point! The Hunts aren't missing, he killed them! If I refuse Charles, if the truth about the Berrengers comes out, what will stop them from killing you and the rest of my family? I have to keep all of you safe!" Tears burn their way down my cheeks. Drake's hands drop to his sides and he turns back toward me, his eyes alight with ire.

"Lord Berrenger adores your father. He would never let any harm to come to your family. And I don't care about my safety, I care about yours! I would forfeit my life a thousand times over to keep you safe! You will *not* marry him to save *me*!"

"I will do whatever it takes to keep you alive!"

"And what kind of life would that be, Addalynne? Standing idly by, knowing he's hurting you? I'll kill him before he has a chance to even look at you again, much less lay a hand on you." The look on his face is murderous. Everything about him tells me that if Charles were in Faygrene, he would be riding straight to his manor to drive a blade through his chest.

"You can't, Drake! His guards are always with him. You'll never be able to get him alone."

"I don't need to," he sneers as he begins to pace. "There are plenty of times that I've seen him with only one guard. It will be easy." I can practically see the plan forming in his head. I need a new way to reason with him.

"And what happens if you fail? Do you think that he'll stop and leave me be? Of course he won't! He'll take me anyway, and he'll only hurt me more as further punishment. Are you really willing to take that risk? You'll be dead, and I'll be his, and there will be absolutely nothing that I or my family will be able to do about it. Plus, if you do manage to kill him, his father will have his guards kill you, and then he'll hurt me as punishment. Killing Charles is not a solution!"

He finally stops pacing and turns to face me.

"He's next in line to be the Lord of Faygrene, Drake. We have no chance of standing against him."

He turns away from me, his hands curling into fists. He knows I'm right. A blacksmith and a woman have no chance against a lord. I'm relieved that I seem to have silenced his argument, but the broken set of his shoulders devastates me. I move toward him and place my hand on his back.

"Just know that every moment I'm with him, I'll be thinking of you. I may have to be his wife, but I will always be yours." He turns around and his eyes stare into mine. Pure heartbreak is reflected through them, and the tears instantly return to my eyes. He reaches up and wipes a tear from my cheek.

"I won't let you do this, Addalynne. Don't ask me to let you do this." His voice fractures with emotion, and there's nothing I can say to make it better. He knows the truth now and, though he's resisting, he knows there's nothing that can be done.

I reach my hands up and place them on either side of his face. The thought that this is most likely the last time I will ever be alone with him courses through me, like lightening burning through my body, causing excruciating pain, but also giving me the strength I need.

"Drake." His name leaves my lips in a painful moan, showing him how much I need him. I have to remind myself to breathe when he leans down and presses his lips firmly against mine.

The feel of his mouth on mine brings life back into

me. Having him here with me and being able to hold him is more than I could have ever hoped for, but it's fleeting. This moment will end and I will lose him. The taste of salt mixes with our kiss, calling my attention to the tears that are streaming down my face. He must notice them too because he pulls back slightly. He regards them for a moment before leaning in and pressing his lips against them, wiping each tear away with a brush of his lips.

He continues to kiss his way down my cheek, to my jaw, his lips passing over it and brushing down my neck. As his lips reach the curve of my neck, his hands move to the sides of my waist. He walks us backwards and then he gently lifts me off the ground, using his body to pin me between himself and the wooden wall of the barn. A gasp escapes my lips and I wrap my legs around his waist, exulting in the feeling of having his body this close to mine, but still desperate to be closer.

He returns his mouth to mine and continues to kiss me, his lips warm and urgent. I respond just as passionately, trying to take all of him in, my hands alternating between tangling in his hair, and pulling on the collar of his tunic. His hands travel from my waist down to the sides of my thighs. He pauses for a moment before grasping his hands under my thighs and backing us away from the wall. He holds me while I move my mouth down his jaw and to his neck, the stubble scraping against my lips. A grunt escapes his mouth and he drops to his knees.

I return my lips to his, and he gently lies us down

onto the ground, the hay snapping under the pressure of our bodies. My heart is erratic as I wait to see how long this will last, how far he's willing to go. I want to give him everything, and I can only pray that he won't stop.

As he lays his body on top of mine, I push all thoughts of Charles away. I refuse to let the thought of him ruin this moment. He may be taking my future, but tonight belongs to Drake.

Drake's lips move across my throat, his warm breath sending chills across my body. Suddenly, he pulls away, leaning his body onto his left arm, his eyes finding mine.

"I love you, Addalynne. I love you more than I thought it was possible to love someone. You're my best friend, but you're also so much more. You're the reason that anything in my life makes sense, because, despite everything that has happened, you have been my constant. Even when I thought I couldn't have you, I kept parts of you within me, and I could feel you in every breath, in every thought. I don't know what the future holds, but I know we *will* find a way to be together. Nothing will keep me away from you. Not anymore. I just . . . I need you to know how much I . . ." A subtle blush colors his cheeks and he glances away for a moment, letting out a frustrated sigh. "I'm rambling," he says, followed by a small smile. I smile back and he reaches down and brushes my hair from my face. "I want you, Addalynne." My heart skips a painful beat when I realize what he's implying.

"I'm yours, entirely. Nothing will ever change that." My voice shakes with my response.

He seems nervous but determined when his lips return to mine. Our kiss has a new sense of hunger and desperation to it. My back arches off the ground and he slips his hands underneath me, his fingers fumbling with the ties on my dress. My heart is beating so fast that I'm certain it's going to give out on me. I can feel his beating just as quickly and, after several more seconds, he slowly pulls my dress and chemise down with trembling hands.

The blood burns underneath my skin, flowing rapidly and spreading across my face and chest as he stares down at my body. It takes me a moment to realize that he has gone completely still, not even a breath passing through his lips. I open my mouth to ask him what's wrong, but then I see that his gaze is locked on my bruises. His hands fist tightly in the fabric of my dress, his knuckles turning white, the anger building in his eyes. It stays there, burning through him for what feels like a century, while I wait with painful anticipation for his reaction, praying that our night hasn't been ruined.

Slowly, he loosens his grip on my dress and lowers his head down, hovering right above the bruise on my ribs. He gazes at it for a moment before pressing his lips against it. The sensation of both intense pleasure and dull pain sends a shiver through my body, and my eyes flutter closed. His lips linger there for several seconds before moving on to each one of my bruises. Every kiss he places on my skin evokes a tremble, and my body shifts underneath him, the anticipation overwhelming. I want him so much. I need him. I need all of him.

Finally, after each mark of anger has been covered by one of love, he brings his mouth back up to my lips. With trembling hands, we remove the rest of the fabric that lies between us. Drake stills above me, questioning me with his eyes. He wants to know that I'm sure, that I still want this. I answer by trailing my fingers along the lines of his chest, watching them travel lower, passing over the ridges of muscle on his stomach.

"You're so beautiful," I say reverently.

His breath blows shakily across my face. "I'm nothing compared to you." His fingers graze across my cheek and his lips find mine.

Together, we become one person, completing each other in a way I never knew possible. And, in this moment, we can almost pretend that there's nothing but the two of us, nothing separating us, nothing threatening to pull us apart—even if it's only for one night.

Chapter 24

HER

The chilling evening air seeps its way into the barn. I pull my knees to my chest and wrap my arms around myself while I watch Drake fasten the ties of his breeches. His dark hair is sticking up in disarray, and I blush as I remember how it felt when it was tangled in my fingers and when it brushed along my skin as he kissed my body. He finishes with the ties and moves over to his tunic, which is still lying on the floor. His skin looks silver in the dim light of the evening, reflections and shadows alternating across his body. He shakes his tunic out, allowing pieces of hay to drift gracefully to the floor, before pulling it over his head, making me instantly miss the sharp curves and definitive lines of muscle on his chest and stomach.

His gaze meets mine and he offers me my favorite crooked grin. There's a shy innocence to it, though, making him even more tempting.

Slowly, he walks over to me and drops to his knees behind me. I turn my head to the side and watch him out of the corner of my eye as he begins to tie up the back of my dress. His fingers lightly graze my back when he pulls the ties closed, sending shivers through my body.

"Are you cold?" he asks. Before I can respond, he pulls my body backward into his arms, cradling me in his lap.

"Not anymore," I tell him quietly, and plant a single kiss under his jaw.

He leans down and kisses me, gently at first, but the kiss deepens with every passing second. My heart accelerates and my hands tangle in his hair. He pulls away enough to whisper, "We should go inside."

"Go inside?" What does he mean, 'go inside'? My family is home.

His lips graze across my face. "Yes. It's probably almost time for supper. I can stay, if you'd like." The feel of his lips moving on my skin distracts me, making me forget momentarily why this could never happen.

"I . . . No . . . you can't, Drake. You know you can't."

"I thought . . ."

"What? That this changed things?" I pull myself out of his arms and turn to face him. He stays sitting on the ground, his elbows resting atop his knees, his expression guarded. "I love you, Drake, but this doesn't change anything. I still have to marry Charles, and everyone still has to believe that it's what I want. I can't go in there with you. It will only raise their suspicions." His expression turns to one of anger and pain. I can't look at him. Instead, I begin to pace, the repercussions of my actions seeping like poison through my veins. "No. I won't do it. You have to leave. We've already taken too many risks."

"You are *not* still marrying him!" he shouts furiously, while pushing himself to his feet. "And if you think I'm going to sit back and let you—"

"There's no other option, Drake! We've been through this! I'm not discussing it any more!"

His hand wraps around my wrist, putting my frantic pacing to a stop, but I keep my eyes on the ground. "There doesn't need to be any more discussion. You have made your decision and I have made mine."

What decision has he made? To kill Charles? To fight against this, even though it will only lead to his death?

Tears fight their way up, tightening my throat and burning my eyes. "I will not be seen with you," I say as I turn my back to him, willing myself not to cry. Not yet. Wait until he leaves.

He drops my wrist and turns away from me. I listen to the sound of his retreating footsteps, followed by the groan of the unlatching wooden lock. Lastly, the barn door slams shut, sealing me inside with only my own heartache for company. At least heartache is a companion to which I've grown accustomed.

Supper passes in uncomfortable silence. The only words spoken are, "Where's Gregory?" asked by my mother. Father's response is a shrug. Elizabeth sends a troubled glance in my direction. I push my carrots around with my bread and wait to be excused from the table. Surely Gregory's with Mary. They can be together with no fear of repercussions.

After eating enough to satisfy my mother and father, I ask to be excused, and push myself back from the table, not bothering to wait for an answer.

"Hold on, Addalynne," Father calls. "Shouldn't we discuss our upcoming travels to Synereal? We leave in five days."

"Yes, I'm well aware. What is there to discuss?" I reply as calmly as I can manage while turning around to face my family. Seeing their faces staring back at me makes my heart constrict with the realization that my days with them are numbered. I've been so focused on losing Drake that I haven't thought about my family. Once Charles owns me completely, I'll lose them too. Time with them won't be something he'll grant me. The thought leaves me feeling as though I'm staring down a narrow tunnel, watching the infinite darkness move precariously closer, my days trickling down to the moment I lose everything.

"First off, are you prepared?" Father asks, his voice drifting over me, returning me to the familiar walls of my home. I blink several times, allowing myself to focus on his face and his question.

Prepared? I'll never be prepared. I feel Elizabeth watching me and I know she's internally screaming at me to tell the truth. I chance a glimpse in her direction and see all the doubt, fear, and anger I'm feeling staring back at me through her eyes. I should never have burdened her with my reality.

"I'm not sure I know what you mean by 'prepared?'" I stall.

"Have you begun to pack?" Mother replies tenderly, offering me a comforting smile.

"No, but I still have time." And I have to hold onto it with everything in me.

"And I'll help her." Elizabeth's voice surprises me, but I'm grateful for her offer. She succeeds in helping me placate my parents, and I retreat to my chambers.

Before I close the door, my father shouts, "And don't forget! The carriage we'll be traveling in isn't very large! You mustn't bring too much—only your necessities!"

"And your wedding dress of course!" Mother adds as I push the door shut. *My wedding dress?* More like my wedding shroud. Charles is choosing it and will be bringing it with him when he returns from his fake quest tomorrow. I wonder what lie he'll tell the villagers. I imagine him riding into town with a fake hellion head on a spike. I shake my head and push the image away. I don't want to think about Charles or the impending wedding anymore.

I take off my dress and pull on my wool stockings before settling myself under my fur blankets. Even with the fire burning strongly, I feel ice cold. I pull the blankets over my head and try to sleep, but my emotions are racing in a hundred directions. My only comfort comes from thinking about Drake. I have never felt as complete or safe as I did when wrapped in his arms, feeling his body moving with mine. Now that moment feels like a huge contradiction. Still, I'll never regret it. I may be marrying Charles, but I belong to Drake completely. I close my eyes and think of every freckle on his body, every curve and line of his muscles. I think of his eyes, dark and ignited with passion; his dimples as he looked down at me, smiling. I remember the way he held me and kissed me, and in no time at all, I'm no longer cold.

A strange creaking sound interrupts my thoughts, which are now floating somewhere between a dream and reality. My brain is too foggy with near sleep to decipher if it's real or not, so instead of fretting about it, I let myself slip back into darkness.

Another creak, followed by footsteps. I'm awake. I throw the covers off my head and try to look around, but my chambers are bathed in darkness, the fire having burned out, making it impossible to see.

"It's me," Drake whispers. My heart skips a beat and I turn toward the sound of his voice. I can barely make out the shape of his shadow next to my bed—a black form, blocking out a portion of the grey wall behind him. "I had to see you." His shadow moves closer and then lowers, the weight of his body pressing down on the bed.

My eyes begin to adjust to the darkness and I can finally see him. He reaches forward and runs his fingers across the length of my cheek, setting my body ablaze with desire.

"Drake, I . . ."

"Addy, wait." His finger touches my lips, quieting me. "I need to say something. I'm sorry for leaving the way I did. It wasn't fair of me to be upset with you, but I cannot *bear* to hear you speak of marrying him."

"It's not easy for me either, Drake. It kills me to speak of marrying him, but there's no other way."

"There is. There is another way," he says decidedly, leaning in, and bringing the tip of his nose against mine.

My breaths are coming fast and unevenly as I try to form words. "Drake . . ." is all I get out before he quiets me again by pressing his lips to mine. His hand moves to the back of my head and he tangles his fingers into my hair, pulling my face tightly against his. Parting my lips with his own, his warm breath blows into my mouth, sending a yearning more intense than any hunger through my body. To my disappointment, he all too quickly pulls his lips away and leans his forehead against mine.

"Trust me, Addy," he whispers, before leaning down and kissing me again. He pulls back slightly, "You have to trust me." He returns his mouth to my lips. This time he deepens the kiss and elongates his body on top of mine. My body automatically arches into him and I wrap my arms around his neck, desperate to be closer. He lowers himself farther, his weight pressing me into the bed, awakening every nerve in my body.

Our kiss is urgent and unyielding, and my side of the argument is slipping further and further away with each passing second. I force myself to think clearly, trying desperately to remind myself why my side is vital. His lips move to my neck and I'm able to find my words.

"I trust you, Drake, but I can't let you do whatever it is you're planning."

His mouth lifts slightly. "You don't know what I'm planning," he contradicts, his voice low and hoarse. Then his lips return to my neck, causing me to exhale roughly before forcing more words out.

"No, I don't, but I'm sure it involves something that will likely get you killed."

He pulls away again, a coy smile playing on his lips. "Actually, it's much more thought out than that," he replies breathlessly, before crushing his lips against mine. I give in for a moment, but after several tempting seconds, I grab his face with both hands and push it away from mine. Keeping my hands on his face, I stare into his eyes. They're filled with desire and determination. He speaks before I do. "I promise you that I'm not going to get myself killed. I want a life with you, Addy, and I can't have one if I'm dead. Gregory and I have a plan, and it *will* work, but it's going to take your cooperation." His words and tone show his resolution, and a spark of hope illuminates within me.

The thought of being able to have a life with Drake and to never be touched by Charles again is more desirable than anything I could have imagined, but I need to know how realistic it is. If I allow myself to hope, and it's not a true possibility, it will kill me. "You're certain this plan of yours will work?" I ask tensely, running my fingers through his hair.

"Yes. When we go to Synereal, Gregory and I will meet with King Theoderic. Though we were only in the Schild for a short time, he grew fond of us. Besides, he already asked Gregory to report any strange occurrences in Faygrene back to him. And he believes the Hunts were taken by a hellion. He'll want to know the truth, and he'll listen to us. Then he'll agree to speak with you. All you'll have to do is tell King Theoderic about Charles and his father. You have to tell him what Charles has done to you, and what he did to Sarah Hunt and the rest of her family. The King will detain Charles and Vernold while he sends Schilds to search Lord Berrenger's manor. When they find the Hunt's graves, he'll formally arrest the Berrengers. Then I *will* find a way to kill Charles." His voice is filled with malevolence as he vocalizes his plan. His expression is severe, his eyebrows drawn together, forming a harsh line, while he waits for my response.

"I want nothing more than to believe this plan will work, Drake, but I'm scared."

"I know you are, but you don't need to be. Not anymore. We can do this. We can beat him."

There's still a river of fear with a shoreline of doubt running through me, but he's right. I have to trust that we can do this. It's the only chance we have.

"All right. We'll try it."

His answering smile is radiant and, without hesitation, he crushes his mouth against mine. I move my hands to the blankets that are pressed between us and try to push them down. He realizes what I'm trying to do and lifts his weight off, helping me remove them. Once they're successfully on the foot of the bed, he repositions himself to hover over my body.

His weight rests on his forearms and his mouth travels down to my neck. He shifts his weight to one arm and his other hand travels lower, his body moving slightly while he fidgets with something at his waist. After several seconds, his body stills, and he leans to the side, gently placing his sword and sheath on the floor. His lips return to my mouth and his hand to my waist. His fingers graze down the material of my chemise, before slipping underneath and moving up the length of my stocking. A shudder rips through me as his hand reaches my bare thigh. He grips my thigh firmly with his hand and his kisses become more forceful, taking my breath and all coherent thought from my mind. His hand releases my thigh and continues to make its way over my hip and to my stomach, causing a deep fluttering within me. His fingers rub along the skin of my waist and a moan escapes my lips. The sound brings a new round of urgency to him and, within seconds, he removes my chemise and throws it to the floor.

He inhales sharply as he gazes down at my body. I take this moment to let my fingers fumble with the strings of his grey cloak, but they're shaking too badly, and he has to help me untie it. After successfully removing it and his tunic, I reach out and place my hands on his stomach, letting them graze along the hard lines of muscle. His mouth finds my lips, but I'm acutely aware of his hand tenderly traveling to my chest. My back arches toward him in response, giving him permission. Suddenly, he pulls away and stares down at me with an intensity that stops my heart.

"He will not have you, Addalynne. And he'll never hurt you again."

"The only thing that can hurt me is losing you," I reply, my heart clenching at the thought.

"You'll never lose me," he swears, before leaning down and returning his mouth to mine. This time our unity is intensified with the newly found addition of hope.

Chapter 25

HER

The cracks in the wooden shutters allow the sun's light to break in. My head is resting on Drake's bare chest. His arms are wrapped firmly around me, holding me securely against him. I close my eyes and listen to his heart drum in my ear, slow and steady, its rhythm provides an instant calm to my frayed nerves.

After a few minutes, his heart rate increases. I lift my head and see him staring back at me. His eyes are bright with excitement, yet they hold a dreamy sleepiness. His hand traces tenderly across my back, his mouth pulling up into a lazy dimpled grin.

"Good morning," I whisper.

"The first good one I've had in weeks," he replies as he grabs hold of my hand and presses my palm to his lips. "No, that's not accurate. It's the best morning I've had in my entire life," he murmurs into my palm, his eyes sliding closed.

"I wish it didn't have to end."

His eyes open and he stares intently at me. "It doesn't. We will be together, Addy. I swear it." He reaches forward and brushes a tear from my face.

My heart is breaking at the prospect of what's to come. His plan has to work. If it doesn't . . . "I can't marry him, Drake. I can't," my voice breaks when the words that have been tormenting my mind for weeks finally escape the prison of my lips.

"You won't."

"I will if it means saving you."

"You will not sacrifice yourself to save me," he says firmly. "Besides, you won't have to. The plan will work. You have to have faith in it."

"I have faith in you."

"Have faith in us."

I press my lips against his, trying to show him with my kiss how much faith I have in us. After several seconds, the rising sun caresses my shoulder. I push him away. "You have to go."

Disappointment eclipses his face and he regretfully pulls himself out of bed. "We have four more days to get through. Then we'll be together when we travel to Synereal," he says while tying his breeches and pulling his tunic over his head. I reach down and grab hold of his grey cloak.

"I thought I was traveling with my family," I reply, while wrapping his cloak around my bare chest.

"You are, and that includes my father and me." He

glances at me and offers me a crooked smile.

Knowing we'll have that time together makes the thought of the next few days bearable.

"We'll be able to use that time to formalize our plan," he continues, while stepping into his boots. "The King won't make you marry Charles once he hears of the laws he's broken." He spits out Charles's name with feral animosity. "Four more days," he says again, this time mostly to himself, as he places his sword in its sheath.

"But during these four days I can't be seen with you," I remind him. "You have to understand that. And we both need to be patient."

He turns to face me. "I can agree to that. But you have to promise me that you won't be alone with him." His tone is severe, his eyes hard, but there's a hint of fear in them.

"I'll try, but I can't promise. He's controlling this game, not me."

"Addalynne . . ."

"I'll be fine, Drake. He can't do much to me considering he has to present me to the King. He's smart enough to know that I need to be presented in one piece." As I speak, I watch him become increasingly aggravated by my words. He drops to the edge of the bed and places his head into his hands, his body stiff with tension.

"He can't do much?" he practically growls. "If he touches one hair on your head, I *will* kill him. So do us both a favor and promise me you won't be alone with him."

"Fine, I promise." I tell him what he wants to hear, though I know they're empty words. The look on his face when he lifts his head out of his hands, tells me he knows they're empty as well. "I'll try, Drake. You know I will." His eyes soften slightly, but he still looks worried.

"I know you will, Addy. And I want you to understand that when I get frustrated and angry, it's not with you. None of this is your fault." He runs his thumb along my cheek.

"Four more days," I say, as hopeful as I can manage. I wish there was something more I could say to calm both of us, but there's not.

"Four more days," he repeats determinedly, before leaning down and placing a gentle kiss on my lips. After pulling away, he rises to his feet and slowly makes his way around to the window. He pulls the shutters open, but instead of climbing out, he turns back to me, a mischievous grin playing on his lips. He moves toward me and leans across the bed, planting one more kiss on my lips as his fingers hook underneath the fabric of the cloak. Swiftly, he pulls it off me, leaving me completely exposed. "I'll be needing this now," he says with a smirk. He backs away to the open window, gazing lazily over my body before turning around and jumping out.

* * *

Readying myself for the day is tedious, considering what the day has in store. Charles is coming back, and knowing I have to see him makes my skin crawl. I search among my dresses for my most unflattering one. Finally, I find it—dark brown, high neckline, billows out from right under the bust. It's perfect. Next, I go to the mirror to check my hair. Charles prefers it curled or braided. I'll leave it straight. Now that I'm ready, I lie back on my bed and breathe in the scent of Drake that still lingers on the pillows and blankets. His scent makes my chest ache. I already miss him, and he hasn't even been gone an hour. Four more days.

"Addalynne," my mother lightly calls and slowly opens my door. "Oh, good. You're dressed." She steps fully into my chambers and shuts the door behind her. "Charles is here," she whispers. My stomach responds by tying up in knots.

"I'll be right out," I say with a controlled smile that takes all my strength to maintain until she leaves. Once the door shuts, I roll over and close my eyes. One . . . two . . . three . . . I count to one hundred, trying to delay the inevitable, as well as calm myself. It's no use. Familiar waves of nausea return to my stomach.

I make my way into the entry of our home and find my family standing around the fireplace. Charles is speaking with my father about business at the manor, his rich navy cloak fastened around his shoulders by a round silver pin. When he sees me, his mouth curls up into a smile. I force one on my face as well, but it feels like a grimace.

"Addalynne!" He walks toward me and pulls me into his arms. It takes a moment for me to remember that I should be embracing him as well, instead of letting my arms hang limply at my sides. I return the embrace and let him hold me against him while he tells me how much he missed me. Yes, I'm sure you've been very lonely without me to throw around.

Charles finally steps away from me, taking only my hand in his, and continues to ramble on to my parents about how he found what he thought was a promising trail, but unfortunately uncovered no sign of the Hunts or the hellion. Surprise, surprise.

"What are those?" my brother interrupts Charles's lies. Charles looks at Gregory, and Gregory motions with his chin toward a pile of wooden boxes by the door.

"Those are gifts for your sister," Charles responds and pulls me toward them. "They're the dresses I bought for you, including your wedding dress." He looks at me with a curious smile, gauging my reaction. I wonder how angry he would become if I were to vomit all over his pretty navy cloak.

"Thank you, Charles. I can't wait to see them. Especially my wedding dress," I reply, my voice strained with false sweetness as I paste an artificial smile on my face.

"You're most welcome," he says before placing a chaste kiss on my forehead. "Unfortunately, I have to be leaving. I have much to attend to." He turns to face my parents. "However, there's something I need to discuss with you first."

"Of course," my father replies. "What is it?"

Charles's face takes on a look of despair. "My father

has fallen ill and will no longer be traveling with me to Synereal."

My father's eyes widen in surprise and concern. "What's wrong with him?"

"He over-exerted himself on our trip, and is now fighting off a terrible fever. And, though I'm saddened that he won't be there for our wedding, I refuse to delay. However, due to the change in plans, I've decided that I would like Addalynne to accompany me on the travels to Synereal instead. With the hellion's attack on Addalynne, and the recent disappearances, I want to be sure that my future bride is safe by my side. I will likely lose my father soon. I can't risk losing her as well."

His words leave me breathless, causing my vision to shift out of focus. I can't be forced to accompany him. I'm supposed to travel with my family and Drake. We're supposed to have that time to be together, to make our plans. I force myself to breathe through the panic, desperate to maintain a state that can at least pass for complacency.

"*We* can keep her perfectly safe. *We* are her family and she belongs with us on these travels." Gregory's voice rings through my ears, trembling with his anger. He pushes himself off the wall and takes several steps toward Charles.

Father shifts uncomfortably and clears his throat. "What Gregory meant to say is that we are all deeply saddened to hear about your father. He's a great friend, and we'll be praying that he makes a full recovery. However, Gregory is right. You don't need to worry about Addalynne while she's with us, my Lord. She'll be perfectly safe." My father's voice is filled with remorse as he speaks, his body hunched with sorrow.

"I do believe that you would keep her safe, Robert, but I'm more comfortable having her with me and my guards. I hope you understand." Charles's words are firm. He has no intention of discussing the issue further. He's only informing my family that I will be accompanying him, not asking.

"Also, I have business to attend to along the way," he continues. "So Addalynne and I will be leaving in two days."

It feels as though I have drifted out of my body and am watching myself stand stoically by Charles while my world once again comes crashing in around me. *This can't be happening.* I was barely going to make it through four more days. Now . . . now I can't . . .

"I understand your desire to keep her safe, but do understand our hesitation." Gregory's cynical voice draws my attention away from my self-pity. "You're not married to her yet. Traveling alone with her isn't proper, and my sister's reputation will be at stake." Gregory's voice is firm and persuasive. He may have said the only words that will get me out of this.

Charles's eyes are slightly squinted, his lips pursed, as he ponders Gregory's words.

"Perhaps you're right," he says. The relief floods into me. "I must be going now," Charles continues, "It was wonderful to see you all." He nods toward my family, and then he sets his gaze upon me. "Addalynne, I would like to dine together this evening. Even though my father is ill, my head guard, Henry, will be there to chaperone," he lies, obviously trying to pretend to be a gentleman in front of my family. "I'll send for you at dusk." The look in his eyes when he addresses me sends a sense of foreboding through me. Being alone with Charles is awful enough, but now it's worse. Now it also means I'm breaking my promise to Drake.

* * *

The dresses are beautiful. Of course they are. But they're contaminated. They reek of his touch, his influence. I can't stand them. I lift up the blue one, the one my mother suggested I wear this evening. It's made of deep blue satin and has a squared and low neckline, followed by what appears to be a rather fitted bodice leading to a long, full skirt. The sleeves are long and billowy, flowing down past my hands.

It's not only beautiful—it's stunning, emphasizing my curves bringing out the color in my lips and cheeks. My dark delicately braided hair appear as black as a raven. If only it were Drake I was wearing it for and not Charles. I study the matching blue ribbon that Mother weaved through my hair while she braided it. The pattern is delicate, but erratic as it crosses over and under. It's supposed to be flowing with the hair, but I can't help but feel as though it's trying to escape.

* * *

The ride over to the manor is extremely short, and, all too soon, one of the guards is taking me by the arm and escorting me inside. I find Charles waiting in front of the oversized fireplace. His back is to me and the light around him dances frantically, a duet of orange light and black shadows. From this distance, with him dressed entirely in black, the fire seems to be consuming him.

"Don't linger by the doorway, Addalynne. I truly detest that little habit of yours," he comments, while continuing to stare into the flames. All my senses are screaming at me to turn and run right back out the door. Instead, I slowly make my way toward him, my gaze on my elongated shadow. For some reason it gives me comfort, making me feel less alone, less vulnerable.

I come to a stop several feet behind him, close enough to feel the sweltering breath of the flames, but far enough to evade the chill of his proximity.

"Tell me, Addalynne. How did you spend your days while I was away? Did you do anything of interest?"

Panic grabs hold of me. *Does he know? How could he know? We were so careful.* He turns to face me, his eyes interrogative, as he waits for my response.

"I ran errands in the market for my mother and caught up on some reading. Nothing of much interest," I respond blandly.

He studies me, deciding whether or not to believe my words. A sedated smile spreads across his face and a single chuckle escapes his lips. "Well, I promise you'll have an interesting evening tonight. In fact, I have a surprise for you, but it will have to wait until after supper. Shall we?" He motions his arm toward the banquet table that has been set up for our meal. The table is decorated with bouquets of purple tulips and golden candles. There's an array of roasted lamb, breads, and fresh fruits and vegetables. If I weren't so disgusted with the company, I might actually enjoy this meal. Instead, I push my food around in uncomfortable silence while we eat.

"You know, Addalynne, throughout my life I've learned a lot about people." Charles finally fills the silence, his voice carrying easily across the elongated table. I glance up and see that his eyes are set on me. They look black from this distance, with little sparks of fire dancing in their centers, reflecting the flickering flames of the candles that decorate the space in front of him. "I've watched them go about their daily lives and watched them squirm under my subordination. It's easy to rule someone. All you have to do is find out what controls them. For some it's money, for others power and social standing, and for others it's love or fear. And in all actuality, I have come to believe that love and fear often go hand in hand. Take you, for instance. Your love for the orphan causes you to fear any harm coming to him. It's what allows me to control you. If you didn't love him, I wouldn't be able to use him against you."

"I don't love him."

He chuckles darkly, slowly spinning the stem of his goblet in his hand, his eyes never leaving my face. "Nice try, Addalynne, but I know you love him. It took me almost no time to figure that out. Your love for each other was glaringly obvious from the first day I saw you in the market. It's interesting to me that neither of you realized it at that time and yet I did. Don't take it personally though. I'm much better at reading people than you are." He stops spinning the goblet, his eyes narrowing, observing my vacant reaction to his words. "It doesn't bother me that you love him. I don't need a relationship built on love—only obedience. And it's so much easier to make you obedient with him around."

I swallow the bile that has risen into the back of my throat, burning its way back down with its bitterness. He speaks of my love for Drake as though it amuses him. Of course it does. It's amusing because it gives him control over me, and there's nothing I can do about it. He's right about people. If I didn't have anyone in my life whom I loved, I wouldn't have anything to fear.

"If you're done pretending to eat, I would love for you to accompany me into the study," he says, before swallowing what's left of his wine and rising to his feet.

"If you're done speaking, I would love to," I reply contemptuously as I, too, rise to my feet. I'm sure that will earn me a slap, but the irritation in his eyes makes it worth it.

He raises one eyebrow. "Careful, Addalynne. You don't want to anger me right before I give you your surprise, now do you?" A taunting smile plays on his lips. I don't want to give him the satisfaction of my silence, but I can't form any words. The thought of a surprise from him has me quieted with apprehension.

I follow him into the study, my fingers growing cold.

I've never been in here before, but I'm not surprised by the nauseating extravagance. The grey stone walls of the study are mostly covered by tapestries of black cloth and gold trim, each one adorned with the Berrenger family crest; a winged lion. On the left wall there's an oversized mirror, trimmed with gold. Inside the glass of the mirror, the reflection of a large fireplace dances. I turn toward the fireplace, on the wall to my right, and let my eyes graze over the golden mantel. It has the same winged lion from the crest carved intricately into it, its wings elongated and wrapping around the side of the fireplace. In the middle of the study there are several wooden chairs adorned with gold velvet cushions, and a single wooden table on which several dimly lit candles sit. The study is so overrun with detail that it takes me a moment to notice the grey-haired man who is standing in the far right corner, under one of the tapestries.

The man is dressed in a long, black and white, floor length surcoat, and as my gaze goes to the golden pendant he's wearing around his neck, Charles speaks. "This is Prestur Medriack. He's here to marry us."

Chapter 26

HER

Charles's voice storms in my head, his words repeating themselves disjointedly until I find my voice.

"But we're to be married in Synereal." My words are breathless, desperate.

"Yes, but today your brother made me aware of the complications with that particular plan. He was right. It's not proper for you to travel with me when we're not yet married, and I must have you with me. So I called upon my good friend, Prestur Medriack, and asked him to travel from Tacitus and marry us. Luckily for us, he was able to make the short journey immediately." Charles's face holds the smirk of success.

I close my eyes, unable to look at him or the Prestur. "We should wait for the King. *You* are the one who asked him to host our wedding, and he's gone through a lot of trouble preparing for it. We can't cancel on him now. We have to wait for the King!"

Charles's cold hand grasps my shoulder and he spins me around to face him. A pleased sneer affixes on his face, his eyes engulfed with amusement. He's enjoying every moment of destroying me. It's as though a single stitch is holding me together and I can feel it pulling, shredding. I'm seconds away from becoming completely undone.

"King Theoderic will understand. Besides, he'll still be able to hold a celebration in our honor after the tournament. Nothing has to be cancelled, just modified."

I jerk my arm out of his grip, and turn, preparing to run, but Charles's guard, Henry, is standing in the entrance of the study, blocking my only exit. I turn back toward Charles, my heart frantic. "I promised I'd marry you and I will, but not tonight. Not without my family and their consent." I look over my shoulder, at Prestur Medriack, silently pleading for his help. If he's anything like the Presturs that run the temple in Faygrene, he'll help me. He gazes at me apologetically, but then he turns his back to me. Charles's fingers grip my chin, turning my head to face him.

"Your father already gave his consent when he said, 'Yes' to my offer of marriage. And you, you behave as though you have a choice in this. I'm not asking you to marry me tonight; I'm telling you that you will." He wraps his hand around the top of my arm and squeezes while leaning his face down to mine. "Be careful how much you try to oppose me, Addalynne." His warm breath blows across my face, reeking of stale wine as he speaks low and forcefully. "Although I'm entertained by your spirit, I'm still eager for it to be broken. Now be compliant and tell me how much you want to marry me tonight." He straightens himself back up and stares down at me expectantly.

"No," I snarl.

"Henry, gather the other guards and head straight to the Waltons'. I need you to pay a visit to Drake Walton."

"NO! No, please! I'll marry you tonight! Just leave him alone!" Tears are raining down my cheeks, and my fingers are grasped firmly around the collar of his black vest. *"Please!* I'm begging you! Don't hurt him! I'll do it! I'll marry you!" The room tilts and sways around me. I try to breathe, but each breath sends a stab of pain through my chest. I didn't think hearts could actually break, but I feel mine crushing with each passing second.

Charles continues to stare down at me silently, and Henry has already begun to walk away.

"Please! I'll do anything you want! Just don't hurt him!" The edge of my vision is darkening, but I can still see the gratified smile that slowly spreads onto Charles's face.

"Henry!" Charles calls out to his guard who enters the study at once. "On second thought, leave the Walton boy alone . . . for now."

"Yes, my Lord," Henry replies, before bowing and exiting.

"You just bought him his life. Next time I won't be so forgiving," Charles says scornfully. Then he looks toward the Prestur. "We're ready."

With those words, I am undone. At least I saved Drake, knowing that is the only thing keeping me breathing.

As we drop to our knees and the Prestur begins the ceremony, I close my eyes and hold on to the thought of Drake, pretending it's him I'm tying my life to. I envision the life we could have had together, if only we'd had more time.

* * *

I have to stop again, my stomach convulsing with pain, while I vomit into the bushes. I can still feel his touch on my body, as though it has seared a brand on my skin. The memory of it makes me wrench in disgust, my body heaving until there's nothing left to expel. I sink down to the ground and try to dig my fingers into the earth, but it's solid and impenetrable.

My fingers scratch rhythmically on the surface of the dirt while I watch the sun rise through the heavy clouds, creating a luminous ceiling of silver and gold. I try to find comfort in its beauty, but all I feel is misery and sickness. *How could this happen?* In all the time I spent preparing for this and telling myself it was what had to be done, I must have never really believed it was going to happen. Deep down I must have thought there would be a way out. And yesterday . . . yesterday I honestly believed Drake had found one. We had a plan. A plan that should have worked. Now everything is gone. My life, my future, my hope—everything. I belong to him now, and he has made me his in every way.

My stomach turns and I again dry heave into the bushes, the bile burning my throat. The pain of it all brings me to tears. I held myself together during the ceremony. I held myself together when he took me to his chambers. I held myself together when he finally let me leave this morning. I can't hold myself together any longer. I lie on my side and bring my knees to my chest, letting my tears fall sideways down my face, watering the dirt with my sorrow.

Once the sun surpasses the tree line, I know it's time to either pick myself up and make my way home or move elsewhere. People will be waking soon, and I can't be seen this way. I push myself up and contemplate my destination. It's a simple choice. I can't go home, not yet.

I head for the tree line and find a tree to take perch in. Up here, in the tall branches, I can almost pretend that I'm separated from it all. I can almost pretend that nothing exists beyond myself and the trees.

I let an hour pass, waiting until it's late enough in the morning that my family should have already left for the day.

Slowly, I make my way to our front door, listening for any sign of stirrings inside, but there's nothing. Besides, the smoke from the fireplace is dark and dwindling. I let myself in, relieved that no one is here to question me about why I didn't come home last night.

Though Charles probably sent a note with some excuse so they wouldn't come looking for me.

Lingering near the doorway, I close my eyes and inhale the scents of home—smoke and lavender. I will miss this. It's familiar and comforting, unlike the smell of my own skin, which is still penetrated with Charles's scent.

I heat some water and create a steaming bath. As I submerge myself, the shock of the hot water sends stinging shots of pain across my chilled body. Once the shock wears off, I scrub at my skin, trying desperately to erase his touch. I scrub my skin raw, but no matter how hard I scrub, I still feel him on me. I choke back a sob and drop my face into my hands, my tears uncontrollable. *Stop crying! Stop crying!* I repeat this mantra over and over, but it does no good. I can't stop, and I hate it! It makes me feel weak! I bite the inside of my cheek, hoping that the physical pain will numb the emotional one and stop my tears.

Once my skin is sufficiently red and the water is noticeably cold, I pull my body out of the tub and try not to look at the water. If I look at it and think too much about why it's now a light shade of pink, I'll start crying again, and I finally made myself stop. I throw on my navy gown, not bothering to dry before changing, and drip my way down the hall, my footprints creating a lonely trail behind me.

Pushing open the door to my chambers, a sudden movement startles me. Drake is standing in front of my chair, his hair disheveled, a worried crease between his eyes. I go completely still, my heart pulsing unevenly.

"Where were you?" he asks hesitantly. I don't respond. I can't. Not yet. Instead, I take in his appearance, noticing the creases in his white tunic and the dark circles under his eyes. I don't know how long he's been here, but it's evident that he hasn't slept. "Addy," he says wearily, taking several slow steps toward me, my sapphire hairpin gripped in his fist. "What happened?" There's pure panic in his eyes, and I know he's reading the pain on my face. *"Talk to me,"* he pleads, as he gently takes my face in his hands. Staring into his eyes, I break down completely, my body shaking with sobs.

He pulls me against his chest, holding me firmly against him. *"Please,* Addy. Tell me what happened." The tremor is thick in his voice, and I can feel his heart beating erratically. I try to calm myself enough to get the words out, but just thinking them brings on another round of hysterics. It takes me several minutes to feel composed enough to speak.

"He forced me to marry him."

Drake's body stiffens and his breath completely stops. "You mean he's *forcing* you to marry him."

"No, Drake." I pull my head away from his chest and stare up into his eyes. I hate the fear I see in them, and the fact that I'm about to confirm it. "I married him last night. I'm his wife now." I speak the words quietly, wishing, as soon as they leave my mouth, that I could take them back and make them untrue. His chest rises and falls with his labored breaths, and his eyes are blank, as though they're seeing something that's not really here. Suddenly, he pulls away from me and walks toward the fireplace, where he begins to pace frantically, his hands fisting through his hair.

"*No.* You couldn't have married him. We were supposed to have time. We were supposed to stop it from happening!" His words are filled with desperation, as though he's trying to convince me that I'm mistaken, that it didn't really happen. All I can do is stare at him with tears falling down my face. *"Why?"* He stops pacing and turns to face me. "Why did you do it? You should have refused him!"

"I tried! Believe me, Drake. I tried everything! I begged, I pleaded! And lastly, I refused! But ultimately, I had no other choice!"

"Why?"

"You know why!"

He laughs without humor and closes his eyes, his fists pressing against his temples. "How many times did I tell you not to marry him to save me?"

"And how many times did I tell *you* that I would do anything to protect you! I won't let him hurt you!"

His hands drop to his sides and his eyes open. They're filled with fury. "You think this doesn't hurt? This is killing me!" The fury leaves his eyes, replaced instead with emptiness. "What you've sentenced yourself to, and thus sentenced me to . . . It's worse than death."

His words deplete me. I'm so tired. I'm tired of the pain. I'm tired of hurting him. It seems to be all I ever do. If only he never loved me, then the only person I'd be destroying would be myself. That I could live with.

I move to sit on my bed, my legs no longer able to hold me, and drop my head into my hands.

Flashbacks of last night start to replay in my mind. I try to push them away, but all I can see is the golden canopy of Charles's bed and his face looking down at me. All I can feel are his hands grabbing me, his body holding me down. Suddenly, I feel a hand gliding across my back and I instinctively flinch and recoil. It's then that I remember where I am and that it's Drake touching me, not Charles. I lift my head and see Drake standing above me, a look of absolute horror on his face.

"Addalynne did he . . ." he begins, his voice unsteady, and my body goes numb.

I drop my face back into my hands, but I can still sense his movement as he crouches in front of me.

Please don't ask this question, Drake.

"Addalynne?" His voice breaks with a fear so deep that I can feel it radiating off of him and mixing with mine, until it becomes its own entity.

I try to open my mouth to say the word we both don't want to hear, but I can't bring myself to do it. I can't say it out loud. He needs to know the truth, though, so I nod my head.

Something shatters. I look up, startled by the sound. Drake has risen to his feet, his face is livid with anger, his body heaving. All that's left of my sapphire hairpin is a pile of glass and silver shards lying in front of the wall.

We stare helplessly at each other for several seconds before he turns and makes his way toward the window.

"Drake!" I yell, but he ignores me and continues to push open the frame. "Where are you going?!"

"You know where."

I run to the window and grab hold of the back of his tunic. It rips when I try to pull him to me, and I fall to the floor. "You can't do this!" I cry as I push myself back up. He stops moving forward, but he doesn't turn to face me. *"Please don't do this!* It's done, Drake. Nothing will undo it, and going over there will only get you killed."

"That would be better than this."

My breath catches in my throat. "Don't say that."

He slowly turns his head to look at me. The pain in his eyes is palpable and there are tears gathering at the bottom of them.

I drop to my knees and curl in on myself as the sobs take over. Within seconds, I'm in his arms. He lifts me off the ground and cradles me against his chest as he walks over to the bed. He sits down and holds me on his lap while I continue to cry.

"You don't have to stay and comfort me," I say between my sobs. "I don't deserve it. Just please don't go there."

"Why would you say that?" His fingers slide under my chin and he turns my head to look at him.

"Because, this is my fault. You must hate me for letting this happen. But believe me, I hate myself more."

"Addalynne, you have done *nothing* wrong. *None of this is your fault.* Do you understand me? *None of it. He* is the one who has hurt you. *He* is the one who has taken you. And I *will* kill him for it." The look on his face is murderous, his voice broken.

My brain is foggy with exhaustion, making it impossible to form an argument. Instead, I close my eyes and lean my head against his chest. He presses his lips to the top of my head and we cling to each other for what might be the last time.

I feel myself slipping into unconsciousness. I try to fight against it, but I don't have the strength. After several minutes, I give in, letting myself be comforted by the warmth and safety of his arms around me.

Chapter 27

HER

My eyelids are heavy with drowsiness. They flutter in and out of sleep for several seconds before finally committing to stay open.

The first thing I notice is that I'm in my chambers, on my bed, with blankets tangled around me. The fire is lit in the fireplace and my hair is a mess. Sunlight spills through the window. I sort through the images replaying in my mind, trying to determine which are real and which are dreams. Living by the ocean with Drake, somewhere that no one can find us—a dream. The pain of knowing that it's not real and never will be leaves me heart sick. Marrying Charles—the memory sends stabs of agony through me. It's horrifying and completely real.

I force my mind away from him and instead try to focus on the last thing I remember before waking: *Drake.* He was here. Wasn't he? Yes, I know he was. But if he was here, then where is he now? I must have dreamt it, but it feels like a real memory. I fell asleep in his arms right after he said . . . Terror settles like ice in my blood —he went to kill Charles.

I jump out of bed and run toward the window. Before I can open it, I notice a folded piece of parchment trapped in the shutters. I grab it with trembling hands and unfold it.

Addy,
I have to do it. I refuse to sit back and let him get away with what he's done to you. If anything happens to me, do NOT blame yourself. This is my choice and it's one I should have made weeks ago. I love you, Addalynne. I'll do anything to make you safe.
Drake

My fear is overwhelming and immediate, causing the blood to drain down my body, numbing me and making it impossible to breathe.

Pull yourself together, Addalynne. Think. You have to think. You have to do something. Before I have more time to think about what that "something" is, I throw on my boots, push myself out the window and land on the ground. I run to the barn and pull myself onto Freyja, not bothering to use a saddle. Giving a swift kick into her side, I push her to run faster than she ever has.

The wind whips my face as we ride, I squint against

it, making the last turn that will lead to the manor. All of a sudden, the bell in the market begins to toll. I pull Freyja to a stop while I count the rings. One . . . two . . . three . . . four . . . five . . . six—*please keep going. Please don't stop at six.* I wait with bated breath for another toll, but nothing comes. A *prisoner* . . . it's him. I know it's him. I turn Freyja around and head to the market, praying I'm not too late.

Dozens of people are lining the streets when I arrive at the outskirts of the market. I jump off Freyja and run, pushing my way through the crowd, not stopping until I'm directly in front of the stage. I'm terrified that it's going to be him, but at the same time I feel a small sense of relief at the thought. If it's him, it means he's not dead, but that could change very quickly.

Commotion on the left side of the market draws my attention. There are at least half a dozen guards dragging a prisoner toward the center. His hands are tied behind his back with a brown rope and there's a potato sack over his head, but I know it's him. I recognize his black riding boots and the bottom half of his white tunic, which is now splattered with blood. The sight makes me sick, but at least he's alive. I have to keep him that way.

The guards escort him up the stairs of the stage and move him to the center. They pause for a moment, allowing the shouts of the people to envelop the air around them. Their heads rise with contentment, and then they force Drake to his knees and pull off the sack.

Seeing his face takes the breath from me. A bruise is forming around one eye, and blood is trickling from cuts along his brow and his bottom lip. He's looking down, his shoulders slumped in defeat.

Charles approaches the stage and moves unhurriedly to stand behind Drake. Charles has been cleaned up, but he didn't get away unscathed. His left cheekbone is red and slightly swollen and his lip has been split down the middle. But most importantly, there's a bandage on the side of his throat with a faint line of blood seeping through.

My attention goes back to Drake just as his gaze lands on my face. His eyes widen with shock, but soon turn to defeat and sorrow. "I'm sorry." He mouths the words to me. But I know he's not apologizing for trying; he's apologizing for failing.

"People of Faygrene!" Charles's voice resounds, silencing the crowd. "This prisoner has been brought forth to be sentenced! His charges are trespassing and attempted murder! The sentence shall be either imprisonment or death!" All around me there are murmurs and gasps. Blood rushes through my ears, and I have to fight to listen to the rest of his words. "He tried to murder me in a jealous rage! If I weren't so forgiving, I would have had him killed immediately! However, I somewhat pity the boy, and though his fate still rests in my hands, I have decided to let you, the people, speak for him! If anyone would like to tell me why this prisoner should be allowed to live, the time to do so is now." He looks down at me as he finishes his speech.

Whether it's in warning or in expectation, I don't know.

"I will speak for him, my Lord," a familiar voice calls from the back of the crowd, but I don't turn like the others. I keep my eyes on Drake. Drake looks to his adopted father and his eyes become increasingly pained.

"State your name for the people."

"Geoffrey Walton, my Lord. Your prisoner is my son." Uncle's voice is nearer now.

"*Your son?* I was under the assumption that this boy was an orphan."

"There was a time when he was an orphan, my Lord, but he has not been one for several years. I am his father."

I allow myself to glance in Uncle Geoffrey's direction and watch him drop to his knees in front of the stage. His greying hair is covering his face, but I don't have to see it to know the look it holds.

"Please have mercy on him, my Lord," Uncle continues. "He's a good boy with a kind heart. I don't know why he tried to harm you, but I swear on my life that he will never try it again. Please release him, and if he ever comes near you, I'm willing to be held accountable and punished accordingly."

Charles offers Uncle Geoffrey a soft smile. Others will view it as kindness or pity, but I see it for what it really is—joy at witnessing someone else's weakness. "Your appeal is touching, Walton. However, releasing the boy is not an option. He's lucky to be alive, and if his luck remains, his life will be what he leaves with today, not his freedom." Charles looks away from my uncle, and gazes out at the crowd. "Is there no one else?"

I open my mouth to speak, but I'm unable to find words. I have to say something. I have to save Drake. But what can I say that will save him? I have to walk a thin wire if I'm to speak. If anything I say upsets Charles, he will kill Drake.

"Perhaps the prisoner would like a moment to speak," Charles says with mock benevolence as he looks down at Drake. "Do you have anything you would like to say?" Charles leans toward Drake's head. I press against the stage, straining my ears to hear Charles whisper, "Now is the time for you to beg me for your life."

Please, Drake. Please ask him to let you live.

Drake sets his shoulders defiantly, refusing to speak.

"Very well," Charles says quietly before straightening his back and continuing to address the crowd. "My people, as you can see, this prisoner has no remorse for his actions! I know now what needs to be done!"

The crowd is still and silent around me. I struggle to remain standing, my legs weakening with each passing second.

Charles turns and nods at the executioner, who moves toward the stage, sword in hand. *NO!*

I push myself up on the stage and run to Charles's side. I drop to my knees, my fingers wrapping tightly around Charles's hand. "My Lord, I beg of you, don't do this!" Charles studies me, his face carefully composed, but he holds up a hand to halt the executioner. I take a deep breath, and then extract the words that I pray will save Drake. "All I ask is that you show compassion for someone less fortunate than yourself and instead of executing him, imprison him. That will still bring him suffering for what he's done to you, but it will be merciful. And others will be reminded of him if they ever think to do the same." Charles's face is a blank mask as he looks upon me, meticulously trying to give nothing away. "He's my friend," I continue. "And if you love me as much as I love you, you won't kill him. That won't serve to punish him. It will only give him an escape, and leave me as the one punished. *Please,* spare his life."

Charles assesses me in silence, enjoying every second that passes, knowing that each one elapses in torment. Right now he holds both mine and Drake's lives in his hands, and that power makes him glow with pride.

"You say death won't serve in punishing him. Tell me then, what would be a sufficient punishment for him? As long as I find your chosen punishment to be appropriate, I'll let him live." A smile spreads across Charles's face.

My stomach and heart clench with anxiety. This is just another game to him, to make me sentence Drake, to make me be the one to decide how Drake will be hurt. Imprisonment won't satisfy Charles. He'll want more than that. Charles will want me to show the crowd that I'm loyal to him, not Drake. He'll want no one to walk away from here thinking that I'm in love with Drake.

"What have you decided?" Charles asks.

"Flogged. He should be flogged." I speak, but I can't bring myself to look at Drake. To sentence him to pain is unbearable.

"Agreed," Charles says joyfully. "And what of his imprisonment?"

Stay strong, Addalynne. "For trying to kill you, my Lord." *Stay strong.* The sentence has to be harsh. Charles won't accept it otherwise. And I *will* find a way to get him out. "Imprisonment for life."

Charles smiles, and I imagine taking the executioner's sword and stabbing it through his heart . . . and then my own.

"I'm pleased that we could come to a reasonable solution," Charles says before turning back to the crowd and informing them that the flogging will begin momentarily.

My vision tilts in front of me. I feel faint and violently ill. Still, I manage to make my feet move forward, walking shakily toward the stairs, but I'm shaking so badly that my feet get tangled in my dress. I hear Drake call my name seconds before I trip on my skirt and fall down the stairs, slamming into the hard ground.

* * *

I wake in a daze, my head pounding. I lift my hand up to my forehead and my fingers graze against a cloth bandage.

"Oh, good. You're awake." I turn at the sound of Charles's voice, and find him sitting in the chair next to my bed. There's no delight in his voice, face, or eyes.

Only contempt. Maybe he's starting to hate me as much as I hate him. No, that's not possible.

"What happened to Drake?" I ask, my voice wrought with vulnerability and fear.

"He's alive," Charles says regretfully. "But he is as you might expect after a flogging." He smiles slightly with these words. I do my best to force away the hurricane of images they bring to mind. "I must say though, I'm terribly disappointed that you missed the action," Charles continues. "Once you fell, he began screaming your name and fighting frantically to break free of his bindings to get to you. We had to start his flogging immediately in order to subdue him. He resisted for a while, but finally lost consciousness after thirty-two lashes." He stares at me observantly, waiting for me to express the emotions that are clawing inside me. But I won't give him the satisfaction of seeing me break. "Tell me, Addalynne, how does it make you feel to know that the entire time he was being beaten, he kept calling your name?" I turn away and look out the window. But all I can see is Drake and his limp, bloodied body.

"What do you want from me, Charles?"

"Well, I could tell you that I want you to love me, but that would be a lie. All I want is your obedience, which I have somewhat obtained, but not fully. I don't trust you, Addalynne. I don't trust you or the orphan. And I won't trust you until you have proven yourself to me many times over." The chair groans as he rises to his feet. "Rest now. We have a long journey ahead of us and we'll be leaving early tomorrow morning." I listen to his footsteps retreat as he heads toward the door. "Oh, and wear the yellow dress I brought you," he adds before closing the door behind him.

I turn to my side and wrap my arms around my knees. Closing my eyes, I think only of Drake. He's in a cell now, possibly bleeding to death, and I'm stuck here, unable to do anything to help him. I turn and reach for the dagger under my bed. Twirling it between my fingers, I watch the light dance across it.

It would be so easy. I could end it all if I wanted to. End all of my pain, all of my suffering—but I can't. It would give me an escape from this hell that has become my life, but it would cause more suffering for everyone else I love, especially Drake. He's taken a public flogging and been imprisoned, all because he tried to save me. If I were to take my own life, it would kill him. Besides, I can't give up. I place the dagger back under the bed and close my eyes. I have to find a way to save him. I have to.

Chapter 28

HER

Sleep is elusive, not that I desire it anyway. There's no comfort in dreams when time is against you. I pace madly in front of my window, debating. I have to see him. It will be risky, not that I care about the risk it presents to me; it's the risk to him that concerns me.

I taste the blood as it trickles into my mouth, pulsing from the skin on my lip that I just bit into.

"Addalynne." Mother's soft knock and voice interrupts my self-mutilation. I don't turn to face her when she walks in. That would be too distracting. Instead, I stare helplessly out the window, watching the spring storm build outside, feeling much like a prisoner myself. "I'm sorry about Drake," she continues quietly, her voice closer. "But I don't understand why he would have gone after Charles that way."

Don't you? Surely you're not as naive as you seem.

"Unless there's something you've been keeping from us."

There it is—suspicion. Still, I can't let it continue.

"No, Mother. It was just a misunderstanding," I reply emotionlessly.

"Just a misunderstanding, Addalynne? He tried to kill your husband. And that's another issue in itself. Why did you marry Charles without your father and I being there? How could you do that to us? We're your parents. We deserve to be present at your wedding or at least notified of it."

"You were notified of it. You were notified of it nine months ago, when you and father agreed to the arrangement."

"Don't be sharp with me, Addalynne. Besides, I had nothing to do with that. That was your father's bidding, not mine."

"Regardless, Mother, why does it matter?"

"Because I have dreamt of your wedding since the day you were born. I have imagined what it would be like to watch you walk down the aisle on your father's arm, to watch you tie your life to someone who will love and protect you."

My throat constricts. My dreams aren't the only ones that have been killed, and now I feel guilty for taking part in a forced wedding ceremony.

"Why couldn't you wait, Addalynne? There was to be a beautiful wedding in Synereal! Why couldn't you wait?"

"I'm sorry." My voice breaks on the only words I can find. I keep my gaze on the storm outside, watching the white clouds form a blanket for the sky and send heavy snow down to cover us as well. It's late in the year for a snowstorm. Maybe the sky is mourning with me.

"That's all you have to say?"

I turn to face her, my patience having fully run out. "What else is there to say, Mother? It's done! Charles decided this, not me. He didn't want to wait. I did not choose this, and nothing can change it now, so scolding me does little good. Besides, how can you question me about this when Drake's in a cell, injured and alone? Shouldn't he be on your mind? Why aren't you more concerned about him?" Her face is blank with shock at my outburst. I turn back around and again face the window. Guilt creeps its way back up. "I won't talk anymore about Charles or my marriage to him. Now please, leave." I speak sharply, hoping my words will drive her away.

I get my wish, but at the sound of the door shutting, my heart breaks. I don't want to hurt my mother and I don't want to leave her tomorrow. Right now I feel as lost as a child after a nightmare and I want nothing more than for my mother to walk back into my chambers and hold me in her arms. Instead, I grab a lantern from my closet, ignite it with the fire, and pull on my cloak before climbing out the window.

I'm a tornado of contradictions. I wander aimlessly, but with purpose. I'm determined, but lost. I have to find Drake, but I can't reach him. I know that going there is foolish, but I have to try. Still, how will I get to him? It's too risky. If the guards see me, it could bring more punishment to him. But how can I leave him there? If I were the one in prison, he would find a way to see me.

Even if it could possibly mean risking my life?

No, he wouldn't come then. Maybe I shouldn't go.

No, I have to. I *will* find a way to see him. I'll use my authority as Lady Berrenger and insist on seeing the prisoner. Yes. That will work. The thought of referring to myself as Lady Berrenger has my insides turning, but power has its advantages.

I walk with more conviction toward the village, holding the lantern with one hand as I use the other to pull my hood covertly around my face. The wind is bitter and the snowfall is heavy, creating a cloak of white beneath my feet, the flakes falling hurriedly toward their destination. The air smells of smoke as the villagers burn the little wood they have left to keep warm. It's only been dark for an hour, but the temperature has already dropped drastically, making it well below freezing. I think of Drake in a cold, dark, prison cell. Will they light a fire for him, or will they let him freeze? I know the answer. I have to get him out.

I reach the market, dragging my feet through the thick snow, and find it deserted. Everyone else has already found shelter from the storm, which I'm thankful for. Having no one else here means there's no one to stop me or distract me. I move faster, cutting through the center square, and head for the eastern wall. Behind the wall I can see the vaulted roof of the temple and, to the right of the temple, the cracked, ivy covered bricks of the prison.

I cut down the street that leads to the temple, and hands grab me from behind. Before I'm able to scream, another hand covers my mouth. It's calloused and cold. I struggle as I'm pushed up against a wall in the corner of the street, and my attacker stares into my face—Gregory. He pulls his hand away from my mouth and gives me a disapproving look.

"What are you doing here, Addalynne?

"I could ask you the same question."

He lets out a frustrated breath and shakes his head slowly. "Go home."

"No. I have to see him, Gregory. I have to make sure he's all right." I try to move around him, but he steps in front of me, blocking my path to Drake.

"*Make sure he's all right*? Of course he's not all right, but he still has a chance, as long as you stay away." His words feel like a slap across my face and I can't help but recoil at them. "I'm sorry, Addalynne. I know you're hurting, but your being there will only make things worse for him. Besides, they'll never let you see him."

"They will if I insist on it. I'm the Lady of this village now. They have to do as I ask."

"Not if the future Lord of the village told them not to let you see him. And don't think for a second that Charles didn't think of that. I can guarantee you that not only did he tell them not to let you see Drake, but he probably told them to expect you. Your determination to be the martyr has become predictable, Addalynne. That's how I knew to keep watch for you."

"You can't expect me to sit back and do nothing while Drake rots in a cell." I try to push my way around him, but it's no use.

"That's exactly what I expect you to do." He blocks me again, his eyes set and determined. "For once in your life, Addalynne, I'm asking you to trust me."

"I do trust you."

"No, you don't. You don't trust anyone but yourself."

"That's not true!" I can't believe he would say that. Of course I trust him.

"Oh, really. So you not telling any of us the truth about Charles, and deciding to deal with it on your own, was your way of trusting us?" he questions, his voice pained, his eyebrow raised skeptically. "Admit it, Addalynne, you won't let anyone help you. You insist on fighting these battles alone. But you don't have to. I have a plan. But it won't work if you're here. Your being here could jeopardize everything."

I try to find holes in his argument, but I can't. He's right. I did push everyone away when I needed them most, but I only did it because I had to. And I have to do something now. "No, it won't. I can help, Gregory. Tell me what your plan is."

"No."

"Gregory, *please*. I can't lose him. He'll die down there if I don't help him."

"And how do you think you're going to help him? By going down there and insisting on seeing him? There are two ways that could play out. One is the off chance that they actually let you see him. If that happens, you'll go down there and find him beaten and humiliated. Do you think he wants you to see him that way? He's broken right now, Addalynne. You're the last person he wants to see him that way. Besides, if you get down there, what will you do? How will you get him out?"

"I . . . I don't know . . . I just . . . I have to see him. He needs to know that I'm not giving up."

"He knows that, Addalynne, and he's not giving up either, but you going down there won't help him. Now, the second scenario, the one that's most likely, is that they tell you, "No," that Lord Charles Berrenger has forbidden you to see the prisoner. Then they'll tell Charles that you tried to see Drake, and Charles will have him killed. *You know this*. You know how Charles works, and you coming to see Drake will be the last act of defiance he takes from you."

Cold tears sting my cheeks as the reality of Gregory's words sink in. He's right. Of course he's right. But I can't just go home and wait. Gregory's face softens as he looks down at me. He reaches his hand up and brushes my tears away before pulling me into his arms.

"I'm sorry, Addalynne. I know how much you want to help, but *please* trust me. Drake is like a brother to me, and I will get him out of there. Uncle Geoffrey and I have a plan. We will save Drake, and then all of us, including you, will work together to save you. Don't forget how much I love you, Addalynne. I'm just as willing as Drake to do whatever it takes to keep you safe, and part of that is making sure that you have him in your life. Now please go home. I can't help him if I have to worry about you."

I nod my head in agreement, knowing that if I open my mouth to speak, I'll break down completely.

Gregory walks with me in silence back across the market. Once we arrive on the road to our home, he stops. The snow is coming down harder now. We can barely see our home in the distance, but the smoke from the chimney makes it visible. I listen to his footsteps retreat as he heads back toward the market.

"Please be careful," I say, turning toward him. "I can't lose you too."

He stops and turns around to face me. His cheeks are flushed from the cold and his dark brown eyes are assuring. "You won't lose me. And I swear to you that I will get him out," he vows, before turning around and disappearing into the falling snow.

Chapter 29

HIM

The ground is cold beneath my bloodied cheek and smells of damp earth. If it weren't for the pain, I would think I was dead and buried deep underground. *I failed her.* I'm always failing her. And now I'm stuck here, and she's out there . . . with *him.* If I get out . . . no . . . *when* I get out, I will finish this. I will finish him.

I open my eyes, determined to find a weakness in my cell. Glancing toward the metal bars in front of me, I see a scuffed pair of brown boots resting on the mixture of dirt and hay outside my bars. I follow the tattered leather up to the worn and dirt-stained cloak that is draped around a hunched back, leading to a familiar face.

"Sir Alsius?" My voice is harsh in my ears, and I'm reminded that I haven't had a drop of water since Genoveve came to me hours ago.

He regards me with quiet curiosity, a knowing

disposition in the set of his shoulders.

"You have interfered with your destiny, and now your path is unknown," he says calmly. "Though, you may still find your way, if you learn to follow the signs, instead of trying to be a changer of fate. But . . ." he continues with a tilt of his head, "how does one follow what's meant to be, when one was born to challenge the stars?"

I push myself into a sitting position, my teeth grinding in pain, the movement causing my already-torn skin to pull farther apart underneath the bandages and ointment Genoveve placed there. Sir Alsius isn't the last person I want to see, but he's definitely toward the bottom of the list. I don't have the energy or the clarity of mind for someone who winds his words around the truth.

"I've never had patience for riddles that seem to have no other purpose than unnerving me," I tell him, my voice labored. "You once told me that I was from Incarnadine . . ."

"I never told you that. You place your own understanding on my words."

"You may have not said those exact words, but it's certainly what you implied. And now you're here again, offering no answers, only creating more questions. I know where I came from, and I can see in your eyes that you do too. My life is ruined. I've lost everything, and I don't know where to go from here. So if you have some answers for me, tell me now or leave."

A cloud seems to stir within Sir Alsius's grey eyes, as

though a storm is awakening within him. Perhaps there's always a storm in his mind and that's why his words have the clarity of a fog.

"You and I are of the same land, and you and I are both bred of heartbreak. Be thankful you have no memories. I would give anything to be rid of mine."

I push to my feet, my hands grasping the cold metal of the prison bars. "For years you have kept your knowledge from me. I'm begging you, tell me what you know."

"The things you truly want to know, I don't have answers for," he continues, his voice barely above a whisper. "My story alone won't help you. It's true that I came from Incarnadine, and it's true that you did as well. I could see the difference within you the moment I laid eyes on you. It's as though a dusting of magic that comes from Incarnadine hovers over you, and only those who know it, only those who have seen it before, know how to recognize it."

"Why didn't you tell me the truth years ago? Why did you hint at it, but then try to hide it just as quickly?"

"Because I was being honest when I said that it wasn't safe there, and it would be equally unsafe for you here if anyone were to find out where you came from."

"I know how superstitious the villagers are. But Addalynne's family . . . my family, they wouldn't care if —"

"They are not *your* family. They are *her* family, and they would protect her before they would protect you."

"But they don't need to protect her from me. I would

never hurt her."

"No, not on purpose. But they wouldn't trust you anymore." For a moment his eyes soften with pity. "I know you want to place your trust in them, just as my family wanted to place trust in the people who took us in when we fled from Incarnadine."

"Why did you flee?"

He looks down. "That's a story for another time." Several seconds pass and when he looks back up, it's clear that his mind is no longer in this prison. "Believe me when I say that, though these people may show you love, though they may lead you to believe you can tell them anything, once they hear the truth, they will turn on you . . ." He looks past me now, and his voice drops to a blank murmur. "When we fled Incarnadine and crossed the Glass River into Silveria, we found ourselves in the village of Doneria. At first we told the villagers that we had come from Kallimonia, and they welcomed us. After about a year, I thought that it would be safe to tell my companions the truth. I was young and wanted to tell them about the magic and hellions I had seen. But those words were fatal, and the villagers turned on us. They thought us to be unnatural, as they believed everything from Incarnadine to be. We tried to convince them that there was no darkness in our hearts, but they wouldn't listen.

"When we tried to flee, they captured us, but I managed to get away. I ran along the Glass River, the sound of my family's screams a fading trail behind me." Sir Alsius falls completely silent, his gaze fixed over my shoulder. The torture in his eyes tells me that, though many years have passed, he remembers that day more vividly than any other he has lived. Without warning, his unsettling stare snaps back on me. "I made a home for myself in the woods for several years," he continues, "surviving as only an animal could. And then, when I was old enough, I came here. I again told the villagers that I had moved from Kallimonia, and I've maintained that story until now. I know you believe that the people here are different. But people are the same in their core, and they all fear what they don't understand."

I wait a few seconds before I speak, giving his story the silence and respect it deserves, letting its sorrow seep into the already tortured air between us. "I'm sorry for the loss of your family," I finally begin, "and I understand why you say it's not safe for me to tell the truth about where I come from. But I don't understand why it's unsafe for me to return to Incarnadine."

"The reasons behind the danger there are meant to be discovered by you, not disclosed by me. It's in your path to find the truth."

"How? How am I supposed to find the truth if I'm not meant to return?"

"I told you you weren't meant to return when you were just a boy, and that was true then. You were too young to be burdened with the path that laid in front of you. But it has always been in your destiny to find your way back. You have a hand to play in the war that is yet to come, that much is certain, but what side you will stand for is not. The problem is that your course seems to have been altered. It used to be laid out before you, a fire in the dark to light your way. But now that fire is gone and your path is unclear."

"Why? What changed it?"

"You did. You changed your course when you saved Addalynne. She was not meant to be saved. If she had died, as she was supposed to, you wouldn't be here. You would be where you were meant to be—hunting the hellion that killed her, avenging her death in the Faenomen Forest, and then finding your way back to your true home. That was your path, but you ventured from it."

My eyes flash to his, his words burning away my patience. "If my path was formed with Addalynne's death, it's a path I don't want. I will choose her every time."

He stares at me with an aggravating mixture of pity and disappointment. "I wish you could see how much she weakens you. Your love for her fills you with fear and doubt. If you stay by her side, you will be more consumed with her than with what needs to be done, and her presence will change everything."

"You're wrong!" My fingers tighten around the prison bars, causing blood to seep from the gashes in my knuckles. "She is not my weakness."

"Yet here you are—beaten and imprisoned. Is this not because of her?"

Blinding fury rises within me. I drop my hands from the bars and take a step back. "Leave."

"I pray for our sake, you return to your course."

"The only course I want is the one with Addalynne by my side."

"Then we may all be doomed."

"Leave, now." I sneer, resisting every urge I have to reach through the bars and strangle him.

"There's that anger. I hope you learn to control it before you go back."

With that, he turns and leaves, and as he slowly walks up the stairs of the prison, I sink down to the ground, my head falling into my hands. I don't know how long I stay this way, my mind a war of chaos. But eventually something pulls me from my collapsing mind —the sound of a gurgled cry, followed by the clatter of a fallen sword.

Chapter 30

HER

I have to remind myself to blink. My perpetual staring into the flames of the fire has successfully dried my eyes. They sting as I close them. *Where's Gregory?* He should be back by now! It's been hours since I returned home and it's already well past midnight.

Rising, I begin to pace. I can't stand this! I should have never let Gregory convince me to come home. I could have helped! And now . . . now all I can do is wait, completely helpless.

What if they were captured? They could both be dead. My heart beats manically in my chest. I reach my hands up and fist them in my hair as I drop back down to the floor. I stay there, steadily rocking, pulling on my hair until it hurts, until everything hurts.

* * *

* * *

Voices . . . I hear them whispering outside my window. I lift my head out of my hands and stare into the darkness. The fire has burned out, leaving nothing to be seen around me apart from the shadows. I strain my ears, trying to push past the sound of my pounding heart. More voices, clearer this time. I push myself off the floor and run to the window. When I push open the shutters, I find a pair of familiar green eyes staring back at me. I forget how to move. I forget how to breathe.

Drake grabs the window frame and pulls himself inside. His muffled grunt of pain snaps me out of my shock, and I wrap my arms gently around his chest and help guide him into my chambers. Once he's in, he drops his gaze down to me. The intensity in his face leaves me breathless, and before I have a chance to speak, to move, his lips are on mine. His arms wrap around me, pulling me flush against him. Reaching up, I tangle my fingers into the hair on the nape of his neck. His kiss is urgent and consuming, making me almost forget about the pain and fear surrounding us.

As his lips travel down to my neck, I realize that I can taste a hint of blood. His cut lip flashes in my mind and I'm reminded of the lashes he received. I reach my hands up to his face and push it away from me. It's difficult to see him in the dark, but I can still make out the passion and desperation in his eyes.

"Stop, Drake. We can't do this," I speak softly, rubbing my fingers across his cheek. "You're hurt."

"I'm fine," he growls and his lips return to my neck. I pull his face away once more.

"No, you're not." He stares at me with irritation before taking several steps back. "I need to check your wounds." I reach for his black tunic, but he moves farther away.

"You don't have to. They're already healing."

"Drake . . ."

"Besides, it's too dark in here. You wouldn't be able to see them."

"Then I'll restart the fire." I move toward the doused flames, but he passes me and crouches in front of them first.

"I can do it," he says, reaching for a new log.

"No, Drake. Let me."

"Addalynne, I'm capable of starting a fire."

"But you're hurt."

"I'm fine," he repeats and throws the log roughly into the hearth. "It's only a few lashes."

"Then let me see them." I crouch down behind him and grab hold of the back of his tunic. He stands up and moves to the other side of my chambers. I let out an impatient breath and finish fanning the growing flames. Rising to my feet, I turn to face him. He's standing next to my bed, his arms crossed stubbornly in front of him.

Suddenly I'm left feeling as though all the air has been taken from me as my emotions completely overwhelm me. I'm so relieved to have him here, safe and free. But he's closed off. He won't let me help him, and that leaves me frustrated and helpless. Then there's the fear of what's to come. Surely he can't stay here. If Charles's guards aren't already looking for him, they will be soon enough. The first tear trails its way down my cheek. I try to hold back the rest, but it's no use, and within seconds I'm back on the ground, my arms wrapped around my knees, sobbing uncontrollably.

Within seconds, his fingers are gently pushing aside my hair and brushing against my cheek. He moves his fingers under my chin and lifts my head to face him. He's kneeling next to me, his body fully illuminated by the fire dancing behind him. The bruise near his eye is darker and there's an angry welt on the side of his forehead that I hadn't noticed before. I come to a kneeling position as well, bringing my body to face his. I swallow back the oncoming hysterics and caress his face with my fingers. He closes his eyes and lets out an unsteady breath. When they reopen, they reflect sorrow and frustration.

"I'm sorry I pulled away from you," he says, while reaching up and grabbing hold of my hand. He brings it to his lips and kisses my palm before bringing our hands down and holding them against his chest. "But I *am* fine." He must see the disapproving look on my face. "Well, maybe I'm not fine, but I'm healing, and faster than I would have expected. You know better than anyone how skilled your mother is at dressing wounds."

Why is he talking about my mother? My eyebrows scrunch together, and a chuckle escapes his lips.

He runs his fingers along my brow line. "I take it she didn't tell you."

"Tell me what exactly?"

"Your mother came to see me. She told me she reminded the guards that the Lady of Faygrene would be very angry if I died. So they let her give me bread and water, and clean and dress my wounds. She also gave me something for the pain."

What? How can that be? I would have known if my mother had gone to see him. I would have seen her leave. "But . . . when? She was here all day. I don't . . ."

"She came right after I was taken down to the cells. It was probably while you were unconscious." His fingers move to the back of my head and he gently brushes them along the welt I have forming as well. "Are *you* all right?" Concern strains his face and voice.

No. I feel horribly guilty. I accused my mother of not caring about Drake, and she had already gone to him. Why didn't she tell me? "Yes. I'm a little sore, but the headache's gone."

"I was so worried about you."

"Worried about me? You had just been flogged and thrown in a prison cell and you were worried about me?"

"Of course I was."

I wrap my hands around his neck and pull his head to me, pressing my lips securely against his. He responds tenderly, but the urgency from earlier has been replaced by a hint of hesitation.

"What's wrong?" I ask, pulling away. I wait for him to speak and watch as he opens his mouth, but then he quickly closes it again. "What is it, Drake? *Tell me.*" He looks into my eyes, a regretful expression on his face, but still he won't speak. Dread seeps into my blood. "They're coming for you."

His head nods in affirmation.

How could I be so foolish? I can't believe I let him stay here this long! "You have to leave." I rise to my feet, pulling him with me.

"I can't leave you." He shakes his head. "I won't leave you."

"You have to, Drake. You can't stay. They'll find you, and this time they will kill you. You have to leave." I gently push him to the window and see Gregory and Uncle Geoffrey pacing outside. Gregory moves toward the window.

"We have to go, Drake. The other guards will be arriving at the prison cell any minute. We don't have much time." Gregory looks at me. "I told you we would get him out," he tells me with a smile before walking back to his horse and pulling himself on top. He grabs the harness of Drake's horse, Bear, and motions with his head for Drake to come.

"Come with me," Drake says, grasping my face in his hands, his eyes frantically searching mine.

"I can't."

"Yes, you can. You have to. I won't leave you here."

"I can't go with you, Drake. It will make things worse than they already are."

"You expect me to leave you, knowing that you'll have to travel with him to Synereal. Knowing that he'll hurt you and force himself on you," his voice breaks on the word "force" and fury and anguish build in his eyes.

"He won't hurt me, Drake. He's smarter than that. I told you before; he has to present me to the King, and he can't present me to him if I look beaten or harmed in any way."

"No." He moves away from the window and tears through my chambers, frantically grabbing random pieces of clothing.

"What are you doing?"

"Packing."

I move toward him and grab hold of his hands. "Drake, stop." He stills, his sight set on the items he has thrown onto the bed. "You know I can't go with you. If I do, he could hurt my family. I can't risk that and neither can you." His eyes slowly move up to find my face. I hate the fear I see in them, but it's soon replaced by determination.

"Then they'll come, too. We'll all leave tonight."

My entire body aches with desire at the thought, but it would never work. His hopeful expression breaks my heart. "No. It would take too long. You would never be able to get away in time if you had all of us with you. Charles and his men would find us and we would all be punished or killed."

He opens his mouth to respond, trying to find an argument, but he knows I'm right. His gaze falls to the bed and he pulls his hands from my grasp. "How can you ask me to leave you?" The anxiety in his voice is palpable, branding a searing pain on my heart.

"Because it's our only option. You can still help me, Drake. You can get to the King first and tell him everything I told you about what the Berrengers have done to me and to the Hunts. By the time Charles and I arrive, King Theoderic will be ready to detain him. Then I will tell the King what I've witnessed. He'll have to arrest them."

He turns his back to me, his head dropping into his hands. I place my hand on his shoulder, feeling the tension in his muscles. "We can't fight against Charles here, Drake. He has too much power. We need King Theoderic on our side. It's our only chance." I'm not sure this plan will work, but it's something to hope for. Besides, the only way I'm going to be able to convince him to leave me is if he honestly believes that it's the only way to save me.

"I can't. Don't ask me to do this, Addy. Don't ask me to leave you with him."

I move to stand in front of him and take his hands in mine, removing them from his face. His expression is filled with despair.

"You have to. If they find me with you, my punishment will be much worse than anything he'll do to me during our travels. You can give us a chance to beat him, Drake. You can give us a chance to be together, without fear. But you have to leave now." He stares down at me for several seconds before turning away and slowly walking toward the window. I follow him silently, and as he reaches the open window, he turns to face me. Our eyes lock and both of us cling to the sight of each other, the same thought seemingly running through our heads; Will I ever see you again?

The wind blows in, rustling his hair. He leans down and presses his lips against mine. My heart clenches with the contact and even more when he pulls away.

"Wait." I reach under my bed and grab hold of his black cloak. He needs it more than I do. "Here, take it. It's yours anyway," I say shyly as I hand it to him. He offers me a sad smile and wraps it around his shoulders.

"I love you," he says before climbing out the window.

"I love you." I lean my head out and place my lips against his once more. After I pull back, he rubs his hand along my cheek and places a kiss on my forehead.

"I *will* see you soon," he murmurs against my skin, before turning around and running to his horse. He pulls himself up and gives me one last glance before galloping off into the dawning horizon, my uncle and brother by his side.

Chapter 31

HER

I pull myself away from the window and turn to face my bed. Lying in front of me is a multitude of fabrics. I gently drag my fingers across one of the dresses and, in my mind, I see Drake frantically gathering my belongings in his haste to make me leave with him. If only I could have. I would give anything to be with him now, to know he's safe. But I know, deep through to my core, that leaving with him would have resulted in Charles taking his anger out on my family. I made the right choice, the only choice, but it still devastates me.

At least his frantic packing accomplished one thing. I have yet to pack for Synereal, and am supposed to leave in a few hours. Drake's diligence has given me a small start to the tumultuous task. I turn toward the large trunk that is leering at me from across my chambers, my hands on my hips, contemplating how to fill it. Charles is expecting me to pack the new dresses he bought for me, including my wedding dress. He reminded me that, although we're already married, I'm still to wear it at the Ball that will be thrown in our honor. *Our honor.* As though honor is a word that can be associated with our marriage.

The thought of our marriage sets my body prickling with equal amounts fear, anger, and disgust. I push the unwanted thoughts away and move toward the trunk, reaching for the gold latch.

The sound of rapid pounding causes me to jump, my fingers flying to my chest.

"Under orders of Lord Berrenger, we demand you open the door at once!" the guard's boisterous voice echoes down the hallway from the front door. My pulse races while I remain paralyzed in the confines of my chambers. They have nothing to find here, but I'm terrified, knowing they won't be far behind Drake.

"What is the meaning of this?" my father's voice calls out. The door groans loudly, followed by the incessant march of footsteps. The sound of their heavy boots on the stone floor tells me there's at least a dozen of them.

"Where's the orphan?" It's Charles's voice I hear now. The undercurrent of rage is clear in the harshness of his tone.

"Is your father aware of you barging into my home at this ungodly hour?" my father responds angrily.

"My father is dead." Charles's voice is clipped and aggressive. There's no sorrow.

I blow out a breath, and move closer to the door,

listening carefully for my father's response.

"How? When?" Father stutters, devastation dampening his voice.

"The fever took him last night."

"I'm sorry to hear that, Charles. Your father will be greatly missed."

"Yes, he will. Now tell me, Robert, have you any idea where Drake Walton may be?"

"The last I heard he was in a prison cell. Am I mistaken?" My father's voice is still saddened, but there's a surprising amount of harshness to it.

"That's where he was, however, he's no longer there. He broke out in the middle of the night, killing several of my guards. Now we both know this would be impossible for him to have done on his own. Tell me, Robert, where's your son, Gregory?"

My breath pushes past my lips in shaky, short bursts.

"He's on his way to Synereal. He left with Geoffrey Walton. Geoffrey needed help trading some merchandise along the way and, since his son was in prison, he asked Gregory to go in his place." I try to wrap my head around my father's words. Would he lie for Gregory and Uncle Geoffrey? Was he part of their plan as well? "He left me a note explaining his departure. I can retrieve it if you'd like." *A note.* Gregory really did think of everything.

"Don't you find it strange, Robert, that your son and Geoffrey Walton left suddenly, on the same night that Drake Walton broke out of his cell?"

"A coincidence, I'm sure."

"If I find that you're lying Robert, your entire family will be held accountable and punished accordingly, regardless of my relationship with Addalynne."

"If you find proof that I'm lying, you can punish me, not my family. But I'm not lying to you. If Drake broke out of his cell, my family did not help him do it."

Silence fills the air for several seconds, and then the sound of footsteps moving about breaks through it.

"In that case, there's no harm in my men and I looking around, is there?" Charles replies with his usual air of false politeness.

"None at all."

"Excellent. Now if you'll excuse me Robert, Genoveve."

Footsteps move closer to my door, causing me to take several steps back. I watch with consternation as my door opens and Charles steps into my chambers. He kicks the door shut with the heel of his black riding boot and faces me. His black cape is slung across one shoulder of his white tunic and a black velvet roundlet hangs low around his head. His dark, narrowed eyes take me in.

"Where is he?" His voice is hushed, but sharp as a blade.

"I haven't the faintest idea."

I set my shoulders as he swiftly closes the distance between us, my body tensing in preparation. His hand wraps tightly around my arm and his hot breath blows across my face, his eyes black with fury.

"Do not lie to me, Addalynne. I know you have seen him." He leans down and brushes the tip of his nose along my neck. "You reek of him." I pull my arm away and take a step back.

"I have not seen him, and I don't know where he is. But even if I did, I would never tell you."

His eyes narrow, the fire casting an orange glow across half of his face. "Do you think that just because the orphan is temporarily out of my reach, I can't still hurt you?" A soft chuckle escapes his lips and he slowly shakes his head. "He's not the only weakness you have." He moves closer to me. I step back, trying to keep distance between us, but my back hits the wall and he's upon me, bracing his arms on either side of my head. "Tell me, how is that darling little sister of yours?"

I pull in a violent breath, while the room seems to tilt around me. "Don't you dare threaten my sister. I have done *everything* you've asked of me. You will not touch her." I speak as forcefully as I can, trying desperately to sound firm, when internally I'm barely holding on to solid ground.

"I never said I would." The corner of his mouth turns up into a sadistic smile. "Oh, and I assure you that my guards will find the orphan, and when they do, they'll bring him to me and I will kill him . . . slowly, while you watch." He leans down and aggressively pushes his lips against mine. The urge to bite his mouth is overwhelming, but I fight against it, as I always do. He pulls back and moves his lips to my ear. "There's nothing you can do to prevent it now," he whispers before turning and walking toward the door. "Be ready to leave within the hour." His departing words precede the sound of the door slamming shut behind him.

* * *

The emotional heaviness of my family standing next to me presses against me like the weight of a thousand mountains, consuming and suffocating. I can feel their gazes on my face, waiting for me to speak, to start my goodbyes. Instead, I stare at the ground, telling myself repeatedly that I will get through this. Once I leave with Charles, my family will be out of his reach, and I will be the only one he can hurt. Then, with any luck, when we arrive in Synereal, Drake will be there, and King Theoderic will be well-informed and waiting to detain Charles. This thought brings a smile to my face, and I cherish the small amount of hope I feel coursing through me. It's not much, but it's enough to get me through.

"Addalynne, are you sure you have everything you need?" Mother asks, her voice hesitant. I look toward her. Her eyebrows are drawn in a worried line, and her hands are fidgeting with the hem of her cloak. She looks younger in this moment, more vulnerable than usual, standing there with concern hovering over her. I think about how she went to the prison and helped Drake. She risked potential punishment for him, and I know she did it for me as well. The emotions blow through me, as though I'm only partially solid, and I run to her, my arms wrapping around her waist. Her body stiffens momentarily, but she quickly loosens and embraces me tightly. I lean my head against her shoulder, my face pressed into her neck, breathing in her scents of lavender and vanilla.

The first tear trickles its way down my cheek and onto her cloak. She leans her head against mine and slowly begins to sway, rocking us back and forth, soothing us both, comforting me. In this moment I wish desperately that I was a little girl again, lighthearted and carefree, running around the woods without a worry in the world. There was no darkness pressing in on me then, no burdens to carry.

I feel the presence of another hand on my back. I lift my head enough to see my father, a sad smile forced on his face. I lift one arm and wrap it around him, pulling him into our embrace. Within seconds, Elizabeth makes her way in and we stay there, holding each other. No words are spoken, but through our tangled embrace we show every apology, every forgiveness, and every goodbye.

The sound of the carriage and horses approaching causes us to slightly pull apart. What I see in front of me leaves me dismayed. There are five guardsmen riding on horseback, surrounding the carriage. The carriage itself is being pulled by four of Charles's solid black horses, followed by the carriage driver, perched on top of his wooden bench. This is normal, to be expected. It's what comes next that holds my attention.

Behind the driver is the enclosed wooden carriage. But this is no ordinary carriage—this carriage is at least three times the size of the one I'm used to riding in.

There are three windows running along the side of it and the dark brown wood is carved with intricate spirals. It's as beautiful as it is disturbing.

Several of the guards dismount and give us gracious nods before gathering my belongings and piling them into the back. The wooden door of the carriage opens and Charles gracefully jumps down, wearing the same clothes from early this morning. He stands stiffly in front of one of the large wheels, his eyes drifting over my family before stopping on me.

"Addalynne, we need to leave. Surely you've had enough time to say your goodbyes." I'm taken aback by his words. He has never spoken to me like this in front of my family. This tone of voice has, until this moment, been reserved for me alone. He arches one eyebrow and folds his hands behind his back. "Were my words unclear?"

My father pulls away from us and turns to face Charles. "There's no need to speak to my daughter that way, Charles." Father's voice is reprimanding, and I find myself cringing in response, afraid of how Charles will react.

"I am the Lord of this village now, Robert, and you'll do well to remember it. I may speak however I wish, and you will address me properly, as 'Lord Berrenger.'"

My father stiffens in anger. I untangle myself from my mother and Elizabeth, and place my hand on my father's shoulder.

"It's fine. He's just upset over the loss of his father," I whisper. Father looks at me, his brown eyes weary. I offer him a reassuring smile, and after several seconds, he gives me a small nod. I rise on my toes and place a kiss on his cheek. "I love you," I tell him before turning toward my mother and sister. There are tears in their eyes, forcing me to choke back my own. "I'll see you soon," I tell them in a voice that oozes forced merriment. Elizabeth eyes me speculatively, but turns her head away, biting her lip in what I'm sure is an attempt to not say something she knows will only make things worse.

I turn and make my way toward the carriage. As I approach the open door, I set my gaze on Charles. He's looking down at me, his expression unreadable. Just as I'm about to pull myself into the carriage, he turns and grabs onto my waist, lifting me into the coach.

Navy, velvet drapes hang along the top of the windows, and the bench is covered with a thick, fox fur blanket. I sit down slowly and see, from the corner of my eye, that there's another window inside the carriage. This one opens into the part of the carriage that extends behind us. I rise to my feet, in a slight crouch, and glance into the opening. What I see robs me of my breath. Lying in the back of the carriage is a wooden coffin, the lid upturned, revealing the ashen face of Vernold Berrenger. Charles moves to take his seat next to me. A smile curls along his face as he reaches through the window and snaps the lid of the coffin shut.

Chapter 32

HER

I try to keep my mind off the fact that we're traveling with a dead body, but it's impossible. I can't stop my thoughts from drifting to the coffin behind me. Lord Berrenger's pale face is plastered in my mind—the transparently thin lids of his eyes, the blue veins that were beginning to darken across his face and neck, the mouth that was slightly opened, as though he was about to take one final breath. Repressing a shudder, I look out the window, trying to replace the pictures that are decaying in my mind with the trees I see around us.

We have been traveling for several hours and are now deep into the woods. The suffocating presence of Charles's body radiates toward me. I slide down, crushing the left side of my body against the door of the carriage. Traveling with him in such an enclosed space is as uncomfortable as I thought it would be. However, I didn't expect his silence. He hasn't spoken one word to me. This is fine; wonderful, in fact. It lets me try my best to pretend he's not here.

I try to resist the urge, but my curiosity gets the better of me and I find myself looking at him. His back is stiff, his arms crossed in front of his chest. He's no longer wearing his hat and his hair is standing around his head in a knotted mass of gold. He's staring out the window on his side and his fingers are drumming impatiently on his arm. He must feel my gaze on him, because he suddenly turns his head to face me, his eyes locking onto mine. I fight the urge to look away and instead continue to hold his gaze with my own, telling him with my eyes that he doesn't scare me. Hopefully, he can't hear the rapid pounding of my heart.

"Stop the carriage, Dawson. I want to stretch my legs," Charles calls to the driver, his eyes never leaving my face. I look away first, hating myself for it, knowing it made me seem weak and intimidated.

The carriage pulls to a stop and I push the door open and jump out, landing among the trees. I inhale deeply and relish the scent of the woods around me. The smell here is different, cleaner, away from the villages and the burning fires.

Charles walks up behind me, making me hate him even more for ruining the solitude of the woods for me. "Let me guess. You're thinking about the orphan. Wondering where he is and if you'll ever see him again." His voice carries a whimsical dreaminess to it, mocking me.

"Actually, I was thinking about how your body would look, hanging from one of these trees."

He laughs humorlessly, and his hand travels down the length of my sleeve. His fingers reach my wrist and he grabs hold of it. I try to pull away, but his grip is firm and unyielding. He pulls my body around to face him and his free hand presses into my lower back, holding me against him. I have to tilt my head back to look into his face. He's smiling down at me, excitement dancing in his eyes.

"You pretend you're not afraid of me. But your rapid pulse gives you away," he says, lifting my wrist. I pull away again, and this time he lets me. His laughter follows me as I turn and walk back to the carriage. I slam the door shut and pull the navy velvet drape across the window.

I shut my eyes and lean my head against the door, while I try to control my breathing. I'm overcome with anger and humiliation, but neither will do me any good —not right now. I need to be in better control of myself if I'm going to outplay Charles in his game.

After several minutes, the carriage shifts with the weight of Charles's body, and the carriage lurches forward. We continue on, traveling well into the night. It's very late when the carriage stops, and the guards begin to assemble tents, making our camp for the evening. I lean back against the seat, my eyes shut, my foot tapping apprehensively while I wait.

"Your tent is ready, my Lady," one of the guards says through the window. I let my eyes open slowly and take a deep breath before climbing down the carriage steps and onto the scattered leaves of the forest floor.

The light of the moon is reflecting on the branches and reaching down to the ground. I'm instantly reminded of that night in the woods with Drake, when we were both so young. I remember the way he wrapped his arms around himself, desperate to remember who he was. I remember the way he held my hand, looking for comfort, the vulnerability painted so clearly across his face. I take my mind from that day and picture him now, somewhere under the same sky, the same pale moon reflecting off his skin. In my mind, I imagine his face holds the same vulnerability and fear that it held that night. The pain the image brings is consuming. I take in a ragged breath and tell myself that he's all right. He has to be.

"This way, my Lady," the same voice says, and I cast a glance in his direction. The guard is standing in the flickering light that is spilling out of the opening of a square-shaped ivory tent. I cross my arms in front of me and rub my hands along my arms, trying to repress the chill that has begun to seep its way through my body. With a deep breath, I move toward the tent.

I step inside and squint against the light from the fire that's burning in the center, reflecting off the ivory cloth. To my left, there's a table with a few berries, parchment, a quill, and a jar of ink. To my right, there's a metal wash basin, and directly ahead of me, on the opposite side of the fire, there's a bed made from several fur blankets. I tear my gaze away from it, my body shuddering.

Footsteps approach from behind me. "Leave us," Charles says. I glance over my shoulder. Charles is standing in the open archway of the tent. The guard behind him bows slightly and then walks away.

Charles steps toward me, and my heart beats violently. His chest presses against my back and his hands grip the tops of my shoulders and move down my arms. They reach my elbows and then begin their ascent back up. As his hands once again reach my shoulders, he spins me around to face him. My stomach lurches. He brings one hand to the small of my back, pushing me against him while the other hand travels to my face, cupping my jaw.

"Let go of me," I speak through clenched teeth.

"Now why would I do that?" The right side of his mouth curls into a smile. Pressing my hands against his chest, I shove him as hard as I can. He stumbles backward, and I break into a run, desperate to get around him. He steadies himself and lunges for me. His arms wrap around my waist and he lifts me off the ground, holding me pinned against him while he moves us farther into the tent.

"Let go!" I scream, and kick back at him with my legs. Pushing down on his arms, I scratch and claw at him. But his grip remains firm, and when we reach the blankets, he throws my body down. The blankets do little to soften the impact of the hard ground, and the harshness of the blow leaves me gasping for air.

I blink through the pain and see him, standing over me, excitement fully ignited in his eyes. Turning onto my stomach, I push myself onto my knees and crawl forward. But his foot finds my back, and he kicks me flat onto the ground. His foot presses down, right between my shoulder blades, and a sharp cry of pain escapes my lips. He lifts his foot and I fight for air, my back searing in agony. Before I have a chance to move, his hands wrap around one of my arms and he rolls me around to face him. He's kneeling over me, his cheeks flushed, his eyes storming with a mixture of fury and anticipation. He must see the fear in my eyes because he laughs once and then leans down toward me. His tongue traces its way across my neck. Revulsion shudders violently through my body, and then I remember my dagger.

This is that moment—where I fight back or decide to give in. Deep down I know I don't have much of a chance. Fighting back will probably only prolong my pain, my torment. But to give in again? I can't. Besides, Drake and my family are out of Charles's reach. I'm the only one Charles can hurt now. Knowing this gives me the final breath of motivation.

I move my leg up cautiously, and slowly reach my hand down toward the dagger. Charles is too busy pulling at the ties of my dress to notice my movement. My heart slams in my chest as my fingers slip under my skirt and find the top of the hilt, which is protruding from my boot. I wrap my fingers around it just as he begins to undo the tie on his breaches. Pulling the dagger out, I raise it in the air and bring it down toward his neck, but he moves and the dagger slashes across his cheek.

His body jerks up, his hand flying to his face. Blood pools around his fingers and drips down his arm. I'm temporarily paralyzed with both astonishment at what I've done and horror that I missed my mark. He stares down at me in shock, but soon the shock is replaced by absolute fury. I lift my hand and drive the blade back toward him, but this time he's ready for me, and he catches my wrist. His fingers wrap around my wrist and he twists it until we both hear the bone crack. I scream with agony, and the dagger drops to the ground. Clutching my wrist against my chest, the pain sears through me. He lifts me up by the shoulders and slams my head back down onto the solid ground. He slams my head one . . . two . . . three times more. My vision bursts before my eyes, a shower of sparks erupting in front of me, before going black and leaving me swimming in darkness . . .

Somewhere in the distance I hear the sound of my dress ripping. I will myself to open my eyes, but my body won't listen. I fall back under . . .

Something warm drips onto my face. This time I'm able to open my eyes long enough to see Charles above me, his blood raining down on me. My eyes flutter and I try to roll onto my side, but his weight crushes me down, pressing me firmly onto the ground. I fade away again . . .

* * *

Pain. Pain tearing through my body. Trapped. I can't move. I can't breathe.

Chapter 33

HER

I splash the cold water on my face, blinking against its harshness, my one useable hand trembling slightly. I look down at it and watch the water trickle its way down my fingers and back into the metal bin in front of my bare knees. I take one end of the fur blanket that I have wrapped around me, and dip it into the water. Bringing it up to my face, I begin to scrub, profoundly aware of every splotch of dried blood that's painted onto my skin. The thought makes the vomit rise into my throat. I scrub harder, determined to remove every remaining sign of him from my body. I continue this for several minutes, until I'm certain none of his blood remains. I pull the blanket securely around me, clenching it in front of me with my left hand. My right hand is cradled against my chest, pulsing in a pain that has at least settled to a dull throbbing. With trembling legs, I rise unsteadily to my feet and suppress the groan of agony that wants to accompany the movement. Every single part of my body hurts.

I look across the tent, at the desk, which now holds a steaming cup of tea, next to my bloodied and torn yellow dress. How much longer will this last? Is this going to be my life now? I can't bear the thought. I can't exist this way, stumbling through a life that's worse than hell. If our plan fails, I will find a way to kill Charles myself.

"My apologies, my Lady," a panicked voice calls out from the front of the tent. I turn in the direction of the voice. There's a guard standing inside the entrance, his back turned toward me, his feet shifting uncomfortably. Though I can't see his face, I know it's the same guard from last night, the one who escorted me from the carriage. At first I'm confused by his reaction, and then I remember that I have no clothes on and am only partially concealed by the blanket. I try to find any feelings of embarrassment, but there are none. A guard seeing my bare legs and shoulders is the least of my troubles. I search my mind for his name, but come up with nothing. The only guard I've heard Charles address by name is Henry. This, of all things, bothers me.

"What's your name?" I ask quietly. He stiffens slightly, clearly surprised by my question.

"Rowan, my Lady," he responds hesitantly. "Again, I'd like to apologize. I wasn't aware . . ."

"It's all right, Rowan. You don't need to apologize," I tell him, my voice a grating whisper. It's strained and raw, like the harshness of metal being carved into a blade. I think of the tea on the table and move slowly toward it. "Were you the one who brought me this tea, Rowan?"

"Yes, my Lady. I hope you find it to you liking," he replies shyly. I move to reach for it, but realize that to do so, I'll have to let go of the blanket.

"Rowan, I'm afraid I need a favor from you."

"Anything, my Lady."

"Would you please retrieve my trunk for me?"

"Certainly, my Lady," he says, hurrying off in the direction of the carriage.

I push the yellow dress to the ground, watching it fall in a tattered heap of realities and nightmares, and perch myself on top of the desk, letting my legs dangle off the side as I wait. In no time at all, Rowan returns, carrying my trunk in his arms. His eyes are squeezed shut as he moves forward into the tent, his black hair falling down across his forehead. He's young, probably not much older than me. I watch him try to lower the trunk to the floor, feeling around with his hands for a good place to put it. As he sets it down, a chuckle escapes my lips, and blush spreads across his cheeks in response. I instantly feel guilty.

"Thank you, Rowan," I say emphatically, hoping I didn't embarrass or offend him.

He keeps his eyes shut and bows slightly. "We'll be leaving soon, my Lady," he says, before exiting the tent.

It's difficult, but I manage to dress myself in a light blue gown. When I'm fully clothed, I reach for the tea.

It's not as warm now, but the earthy, mint liquid is soothing on my throat. I close my eyes and let my mind fall to Drake. The thought of him is overwhelmingly painful. My fingers tighten around the cup in my hand and my breaths quicken. *Please let him be alive.* These words repeat over and over, but eventually, my thoughts slip further and I can't help but wonder how he'll react when he sees me. Surely he'll know what has happened. He'll see the injuries and the look on my face. I won't be able to hide it, and it will destroy him. The cup falls from my hands and clanks noisily as it bounces against the rocks on the ground. I clench my good hand around the edge of the desk, squeezing tightly. *You can't break now. You have to push through. You knew this was going to happen.* Still, the difference is that I told myself I would fight him. I took comfort in the thought. And I tried. I tried to fight him. I failed.

The following days go by in a self-sedated blur. There's a block forming in my mind in an attempt to push out the reality that exists around me. Every day is filled with traveling, and every night follows the same pattern—Charles comes to me, I still try to fight, I still fail.

On the third day, I tried to run away. That earned me a snapped finger to go with my already broken wrist on my right hand, which is now swollen and discolored. Rowan tried to bandage it yesterday, but Charles struck him and told him that if he tried to help me again, it would be the last thing he'd do. I still remember the way Rowan looked at me, a broken apology in his grey eyes.

If only I had my dagger. I wouldn't merely lash at him, like before. This time I would drive it straight through his heart. But it's gone. He took it. The thought tortures me. It was the last thing that I had of Drake's. I need it. I know Charles hasn't destroyed it. He'll keep it and use it against me when it will hurt me most. He knows who gave it to me, and that dagger holds significance for him, too, though what it means to us is very different. I have to get it back.

The forest is just as thick in the area we're now passing through as it is back home, but there are more flowers and shrubs growing here. The air is also lighter, warmer: a complete contradiction to the frigid heaviness that exists inside the carriage. I try to ignore the fact that Charles is several inches away from me and that his dead father is decaying behind me. But this last fact is harder to ignore, considering the heavy stench of death that has spread through the air in the carriage. Despite the open windows, the distinct scent of rotting flesh hangs around me like a cloud. I bring my hand to my face and drape it over my nose, desperate for a clean breath.

Outside my window, something glistens in the distance. My heart beats faster as my gaze trails along the pristine surface of water to the fog that stands behind it: The Glass River. A tremor of fear trickles its way down my spine at the sight of it. I want to ask why we're headed toward the Glass River, but the only people in the carriage with me are Charles and his dead father, and I don't want to talk to either of them. I rise slightly and lean farther out the window, glancing around for Rowan, but he must be on the other side. Without warning, the carriage tilts on the uneven ground, tipping me back into my seat.

"This is far enough, Dawson. We'll travel on foot from here," Charles calls out, making his voice loud enough to be heard over the shaking of the carriage. Being this close to the river and the Faenomen Forest has my stomach tied up with apprehension. I haven't been this close to the river since the day I was attacked. The memory brings back terrifying flashes, and I find myself rooted in my seat.

Several minutes later, my door is pulled open. Charles is standing on the ground in front of me, impatience written across his face. The stitches on his cheek are jagged and glisten moistly under the sun.

"Get out," he says roughly. I hesitate, my gaze returning to the fog. His patience expires and he reaches in and wraps his fingers around my broken wrist. I cry out in pain as he yanks me from the carriage, making me stumble and fall violently to my knees. He releases my wrist and I clutch it against my chest. Tears fight their way up, but I try desperately to blink them back. I refuse to let him see how much he's hurt me.

I begin to rise shakily to my feet and a set of hands gently grip my shoulders, supporting me as I stand. Glancing over my shoulder, I see Rowan. His lips are taut, his forehead drawn into a hard line while he stares into my eyes, likely seeing the tears that are seconds away from spilling over.

"Are you hurt badly, my Lady?" he whispers. I try to speak, but I'm afraid if I open my mouth, I won't be able to hold off the tears. Instead, I slowly shake my head, no. He looks down at my wrist and reaches forward to check it. I turn and move away from him, again shaking my head, no. I don't want him to receive more punishment for trying to help me.

Just then, a large, thick set man slips his arm underneath mine. I glance up, startled by the contact, and realize that it's Henry. His light blue eyes, outlined by a dark set of lashes, are set on me. I've never been this close to him before and I find myself distracted by his thick, black eyebrows that are peppered with grey hairs. The skin on his face, that's not covered by his grey beard, is lined with several light scars and a few wrinkles, looking like a worn piece of leather.

"This way, my Lady," he says, walking us forward.

The Glass River is merely yards away, and crossing over the top of it is a fallen tree. The trunk is massive and extends easily to the southern side. As we get closer to the tree, I realize that it's been carved out, turning the overturned tree into a natural bridge. It takes a moment for my thoughts to catch up with what I'm seeing, and once they do, my heart thrashes. I plant my feet firmly into the ground, refusing to move forward. *This can't be real. We're not crossing the Glass River.* Henry pulls on my arm once, but soon realizes that I'm not going to budge. He bends down in front of me, and I'm abruptly swung off my feet and thrown over his shoulder.

"Put me down!" I shout, finally finding my voice. Henry obeys and drops me harshly onto my feet. I stumble, but manage to keep from falling. "Don't ever touch me like that again!" I yell, not actually feeling overly offended by it, but trying to find something to say that will let me express the anger and uncertainty I'm feeling. Henry doesn't apologize, he just stares at me with a look of pure boredom on his face. Charles moves toward us and stands next to Henry.

"You are not the one who gives orders," Charles says, taking several steps toward me. I move backwards and the back of my legs brush up against the trunk of the upturned tree. "Now you can either cross the bridge on your own or Henry will carry you. You choose." He moves around me and steps onto the surface of the tree. Henry walks toward me once more.

"I'll walk," I assert, and then turn around to face the bridge. It looks as though someone tipped the tree over, cut it in half and then continued to hollow out the middle, leaving only a curving shell of tree, forming a makeshift bridge with walls on both sides. I step cautiously onto the tree and notice that along the floor and sides, there are hundreds of intricately carved designs. They're not designs I've ever seen before, with their harsh lines and graceful curves, but there's a purposeful pattern to them. Henry nudges me none too gently from behind, and I make myself move forward. Walking across the bridge, a nervous anticipation mingles with my fear. I'm about to step onto the southern side, into the Faenomen Forest, into Incarnadine. I always dreamt of what this would be like, but now that it's real, I'm not sure I want to know.

The wood under my feet groans with every step I take. The closer I get to the fog, the more it seems to thicken, fully obstructing my view of the southern side. I glance around and find that I'm covered in mist, my visibility extending to only a few feet in each direction.

The end of the bridge approaches and the thickest part of the fog stands in front of me, as firm and heavy as a white wall. I reach my hand out and press my fingers into it. They disappear into the heavy cloud, and a cooling tingle spreads across them. With a final breath, I shut my eyes and step forward. My entire body erupts in chills that prickle across my skin. It feels as though bristles of hay are poking into me at the same time that ice is being poured down my body. I keep moving forward, my arm outstretched in front of me, my eyes still closed. Finally, the tingles subside, and my feet press onto the soft dirt of the ground.

I slowly let my eyes open and look around me. Everything is so . . . ordinary. The southern side looks exactly the same as its northern counterpart. The trees are the same, the dirt is the same, the rocks are the same, and the fog is now gone. I look back to the northern side and realize that I can't see the river. The fog is there pressed up against it, still forming a compact wall of mist. But now the fog is pressed up against the side of the river that we're on, obstructing our view of it. The rest of Charles' guards descend off the bridge, Rowan appearing last. His eyes meet mine for a split second before he quickly averts his gaze.

I turn around and face the Faenomen Forest. Charles is inside the tree line, glancing around anxiously. All at once, the sound of horses approaching echoes through the trees. Henry walks up behind me and wraps his arms securely around me, confining my arms to my side while pushing me forward. The sound of horses grows louder. *Something's wrong.* Henry's not just trying to keep me walking; he's keeping me from running.

Turning my head to the side, I bite down as hard as I can on Henry's arm. He yells in surprise and his arms loosen their grip enough for me to pull away. I break into a run, but within seconds, a stab of pain shoots through my scalp as I'm yanked backwards by my hair. I lose my footing and stumble painfully to my knees, the rocks and dirt tearing open my skin. Henry stands over me. He releases my hair and slams the back of his hand across my face, knocking me to the ground.

"No! Not her face!" Charles shouts, running forward. Charles's hands wrap around my arms and he pulls me to my feet. He places one arm around my back as he holds me up, supporting my weight. My head is pulsing rhythmically and my vision is shifting in and out of focus. I can barely make out Charles's face looking down at me while he turns my head from side to side. "Dammit, Henry! You've bruised her cheek and busted her lip! You'd better pray they recognize her enough to still honor the agreement!" Charles is speaking, but it's diluted, as though he's speaking through water. "Come on, Addalynne, pull it together," he says, dragging me forward. I try to make my legs move, but they stumble slightly. Charles groans impatiently, and then another set of arms wrap around me.

"I can carry her," Rowan says. Charles pauses momentarily, but then concedes and lets go of me. I stagger slightly, but Rowan is there. In a swift, gentle motion, he sweeps me up and cradles me against his chest.

"I'm sorry," he whispers while walking forward, heading deeper into the trees.

"For what?"

"For not helping you." He's staring straight ahead as we come to a stop, and I realize I can no longer hear the horses. I turn my head to the side. Around a dozen armored men are standing about fifteen feet away from us, their black horses waiting behind them. Their armor is the color of the deepest black and they have black capes that are lined with red trim attached to their shoulders. They're standing firmly in a row, their arms folded stiffly behind their backs.

In front of them, a strange creature that looks like a cross between a wolf and a dragon is pacing. Its tail is thick and covered in brown scales, ending in a long, pointed tip. Its body and legs are covered in silver fur, its feet ending in paws with sharp black nails. Its face is also covered in fur and resembles a wolf, but its mouth is long, snouted, and scaled. Its lips are pulled back, revealing razor sharp teeth, and as it breathes, several gusts of smoke and fire burst forward. I repress a shudder and let my gaze travel down the line.

Standing at the end is a man who's at least seven feet tall, but as I look closer, I realize that he's not a man. Though male in form, his skin is made up of what appears to be tree bark. He's wearing no armor and is only clothed in a pair of dark brown breaches covering most of his legs. His feet are bare and extend slightly outward, resembling roots, and his hair is made up of twirling green leaves and vines that drape their way down his back. He's as magnificent as he is terrifying. Standing next to him, providing a startling contrast, is an ordinary girl, dressed in men's clothing. She looks to be around my age, and has beautiful brown skin and long black hair. Her eyes dart toward me. They're a vibrant green and remind me instantly of Drake. The pain their likeness evokes snaps me back to the reality that's facing me, and I force myself to concentrate on what's happening.

Charles is speaking with one of the armored men. The man has removed his helmet, and his russet-colored hair covers the top of his head and curls around his mouth in a full beard. He glances toward Rowan and his blue eyes land on me.

"She can't walk?" he asks Charles.

"She can walk. She was well cared for. As you asked."

"Then what's wrong with her?"

"Unfortunately, she had a minor accident. She . . ."

"Bring her to me," the man says sternly, cutting off the rest of Charles's words. Rowan stays planted where he is, his heart beating rapidly against me. But it's Charles who speaks.

"I want to see my mother first."

His mother?

"You're not in a position to be making the demands here, Berrenger. I want the girl brought forward." He looks at Rowan and I. "Now!" Rowan staggers forward and sets me gently on my feet. My head is still aching, and I can feel the blood dripping down my chin from my lip, but at least my thoughts and vision are clear. "What happened to you, child?" he asks, his voice hard, but curious.

"I was struck down," I reply emotionlessly, refusing to lie for Charles anymore.

"I see. And why was that?" he asks, his gaze landing on my injured wrist.

"Because she was disobedient," Charles replies for me, his voice eerily fearful. I have never seen him afraid, and it leaves me terrified.

"Well, my little raven, I can't blame you for disobeying him. He seems to be a difficult man to tolerate," he says with a smile. "However, I do hope you learned your lesson, because I don't take well to being disobeyed either. And neither does King Gareth." His smile fades, his voice spilling caution. I pull in a breath and try to make sense of what's happening. The man turns his attention to a small black carriage, nestled within the forest and guarded by several more armored men. "Bring him," he calls. One of the armored men turns toward the carriage and helps a man climb out. From the way he moves; slow and painfully, I assume he's elderly, but the man's body is completely covered in a floor-length green cloak, the hood pulled up to conceal his face. The armored man guides the elderly man toward me, stopping only when they are inches away. I take a hesitant step back and bump into Rowan's chest. I still can't see the elderly man's face, as it's shadowed so sufficiently by the hood of his cloak, but I can feel his eyes on me.

"Yes. She is the one I saw. The one King Gareth needs." His words leave me chilled. How am I the one he saw? Saw where? And why would their King need me?

But before I can even muster the courage to ask him to explain his words, the elderly man walks back to the carriage, disappearing into its confines.

"The King will be pleased," the red-haired man addresses Charles.

"Then you'll return my mother to me?" Charles asks, anxiety drowning in his voice.

The man turns toward another one of his armored men. "Obsidian, tie the girl to one of the horses and bring Berrenger's mother." Obsidian moves toward us, and Rowan wraps his arm around my waist.

"No!" Rowan shouts. "You can't do this! I won't let you give her to them!" Rowan pushes me behind him and draws his sword.

"You won't let me?" Charles replies, his voice filled with equal amounts intrigue and anger. I look around Rowan's arm and see Charles moving toward us.

"Stay back," Rowan says, a tremble in his voice, as he points his sword at Charles.

"Rowan, don't do this," I plead and try to move around him, but he holds his stance and repositions himself firmly in front of me, his blade shaking in his hand. "Rowan, please!"

Henry comes from the side and kicks Rowan's extended arm, causing the sword to fall from his grasp. I run for the sword, but am grabbed from behind by another one of Charles's guards. He holds me firmly against him, my arms trapped at my side, helplessly watching the scene unfold before me.

Henry has Rowan on his knees, his hands wrapped around a chunk of Rowan's hair, his knee pressing into his back. Charles is standing in front of Rowan, but he's looking at me as he reaches into his cloak and extracts my dagger. The sun bounces off the emeralds, sending streaks of green light through the forest. Charles smiles and then looks down at Rowan. My own scream rings in my ears as Charles swiftly drags the blade across Rowan's throat. Rowan's body falls to the floor, his blood spilling around him. My body falls limp in the guard's arms. Shutting my eyes, my tears begin their descent.

I feel the presence of someone standing in front of me and let my eyes re-open. Charles is looking down at me, a stretched smile on his face that causes his stitches to pull and release drops of blood. "I want to thank you, Addalynne. It's because of you that I'm getting my mother back today." He leans down and places his lips to my ear. "I hope they enjoy you. I know I did." I look down, sickened, and see the splatter of blood on his white tunic, and my dagger twirling in his fingers:

Rowan's blood staining the blade. Charles grabs me by the arm and shoves me forward into the waiting hands of the armored guard, Obsidian.

Obsidian walks me toward his horse and pulls a rope from under the saddle. He ties the rope to the stirrup, then begins to wrap the other end of the rope around my wrists, causing blinding pain to shoot up the arm of my broken wrist.

"Mother!" Charles's scream breaks in, distracting me from my pain and my imprisonment. I turn toward him and watch as an armored man places the body of a woman at Charles's feet. Charles drops to his knees, his hands pulling her motionless head into his lap. The elegant curls I remember seeing as a child are now a tangle of weeds. "Mother, wake up!" he cries, sounding like a lost child, and though I despise him, I can't help but pity him as I watch him try to wake his mother from an endless sleep.

Slowly, Charles staggers to his feet, drunk with despair, and his hand withdraws his sword from its sheath. He points it at the red-haired man. "You broke our agreement!" he shouts, tears streaking his face.

"I did no such thing," the man replies blandly.

"You did! You promised that my mother would be returned to me if I brought her to you!" He points the sword toward me when he says the word "her," his hand shaking violently.

"And I kept my promise. I returned your mother to you."

"She's dead!"

"Yes, she is. I never said that I would return her to you alive, only that I would return her to you."

Charles charges at the man, but before he can reach him, he is slammed backwards by an invisible force. He falls down, his sword flying out of his grasp.

"I don't want to kill you, Berrenger, but if you come at me again, I will have your head."

"I want Addalynne back. You broke our agreement," Charles says, but there's little conviction behind his words.

"You can't have her back. She belongs to us now. But I can give you something to remember her by." The man walks toward Charles and pulls him to his feet. His fist connects harshly with Charles's face and, as Charles stumbles backward, the man reaches out and snaps Charles's wrist. Charles falls to the ground, screaming in pain. "Now go home," the man says, before turning back toward his horse, leaving Charles sobbing on the ground, his dead mother next to him, and his men standing around him in paralyzed shock.

Chapter 34

HIM

"Drake Walton! It's wonderful to see you again!" The corners of King Theoderic's blue eyes wrinkle as he smiles at me through his grey beard. Grey marble steps lead up to the raised throne on which he's sitting. The throne itself is composed of ornately carved wood and silver that depicts the battle fought between the kingdoms. A blue rug runs from his thrown, down the stairs, and across the throne room to the double wooden doors at the entrance. It's on that rug that I stand now. "I wish I could say you look well, however . . ." he continues, gesturing at the fading bruises that shadow my face and the dirt that stains my clothes.

"Your Grace, it's an honor to be in your presence. I apologize for my appearance, but I had to see you as soon as possible. Thank you for agreeing to meet with me," I reply with a bow.

"There's no need to apologize, Walton. Though your arrival is earlier than expected. Does this mean you have come to rejoin my Schild?"

"No, your Grace. My presence is not because of the Schild, and as of yet, I have no plans to rejoin."

"That is unfortunate. Tell me then, what can I do for you?"

I recount the events of the past few weeks and tell him everything that Charles and Lord Vernold Berrenger have done. He listens patiently, and when I finish, he sits silently for several seconds, processing my words. I wait anxiously for his response, praying to the gods that it will be in my favor.

"If these things you speak of are true, then the Berrengers will be arrested and the title of lord taken from them. However, though I believe you, I can't act until I speak with the girl. She is the one who witnessed the murder of Sarah Hunt and she is the one who Charles abused. This means that she is the only one who can file a formal complaint."

This is the answer I expected, and though I understand it, it still aggravates me.

"I understand, your Grace. All I ask is that as soon as they arrive, you allow me to take her away from them and keep her safe."

"Once they arrive, I will remove her from them and speak with her. I assure you she will be perfectly safe. And once she confirms what you have told me, I will detain the Berrengers and conduct a further investigation. I also grant you temporary amnesty. As long as Addalynne and the investigation collaborate what you have just told me, I will state that you acted in defense of your village, and the Berrengers will no longer have grounds to take you into custody or have you punished."

"Thank you, your Grace." I bow and then excuse myself from his presence. There's a slight sense of relief, but knowing Addy's out there with *him* keeps me infested with panic and anger.

I exit the Great Hall and one of the Schilds escorts me to where Gregory and my father were asked to wait. They're leaning against the ivory, outer-stone wall of the castle, and their eyes question me as I approach. I quickly fill them in before the Schild proceeds to lead us to the chambers that King Theodoric had set up for us.

We walk in heavy silence through the corridors of the castle. It's quiet, almost too quiet, making the sound of our footsteps echo and pound in my head. By the time we get to Gregory's chambers, I want to break something. Gregory says something about coming by my chambers later before closing the door behind him. The Schild continues forward, knowing my father and I will follow.

"Would you mind giving us a moment?" my father asks the Schild when we reach my chambers. The Schild nods and allows us to step inside the room before shutting the door behind us.

I walk to the four post bed and sit on the edge, my head dropping into my hands.

"How are you feeling?" Father asks.

"Angry. Helpless. Scared. How would you expect me to feel?" I answer sharply though I know I shouldn't.

The bed shifts beside me, and the weight of his hand settles on my shoulder.

"I expect you to feel those things, but I also expect you to feel hope."

"Hope?"

"Yes, hope. This nightmare is almost over, Drake."

"It's not over until she's here, safe, with me. How can I feel hope when she's with him? Do you have any idea what he could be doing to her?"

"Yes, I do. But I try not to think about it, as you should."

"How? How can I do that when each sickening thought in my mind is competing with the next?"

"Because you can't control what's happening to her right now. And focusing on that will only trap you in fear and sorrow. Believe me, son, I've been there. I tormented myself for a long time with thoughts of things that I couldn't control, and it lead nowhere."

My mind drifts back to my adoptive father's past, to the time when he lost his wife and unborn child. If anyone understands pain, it's him.

"How did you survive . . . losing her?" I ask. I have never asked him about his wife because I know how much it hurts him to speak of her. I only know what happened from what Addy has told me and from the passing remarks he has made about her. But I can't keep the question inside any longer. I need to know how he got through it, because the thought of facing another minute without Addy seems as impossible as turning water into fire.

I drop my hands and look at him.

"I survive because I have other people in my life whom I love: you, Genoveve, Robert, Gregory, Elizabeth . . . Addalynne." Her name is a knife in my chest. "I live for all of you, and you make surviving bearable. The pain never goes away, not really, but you learn to breathe around it. Some days it's easier. Others . . . others it chokes you like a block of ice expanding in your throat, cutting off your air and freezing your blood." He shakes his head slowly, as if pushing the thoughts away. "But you won't have to experience this. You *will* get Addalynne back."

"You can't possibly know that." I shake my head and push myself off the bed.

"I may not know with certainty what the outcome of this will be. But I know you. And I know you won't give in to the anger, helplessness, and fear that you feel. There was a time when I gave in and let those emotions control me. But then I found hope. *You* brought me hope. Hope that I could be happy again. And from that hope I learned to take control, to act. And you and Addalynne are the same. The determination and conviction that you both have will save her and bring her back to you. That should give you hope. And it does. The hope is inside you. It's what's keeping you from giving up. That's how I know you won't lose her."

I walk to the balcony, and stare at the never ending forest surrounding Synereal. She's out there now.

Hopefully making her way to me. Hopefully keeping Charles away from her, but deep down I know how small the chance of her arriving unscathed is. He's probably hurting her as we speak. "Maybe you're right. But I can't feel it. I can't find anything inside me apart from the absolute terror and rage."

"It's there. Believe in yourself and you'll find it."

I turn to face him and our eyes meet. That's when I see it—fear. It's written in his eyes. "Try to get some rest," he says, and then he exits the room, leaving me in solitude.

* * *

"Stop pacing, Drake. You're making my head hurt," Gregory mumbles grumpily. I shift my gaze toward him, but don't falter in my strides. He's sitting on a wooden bench that's near the heavily draped canopy bed of my chambers. His elbows are resting on his knees, his head in his hands. He's anxious. *Anxious.* Is that what I am? No. I don't know what I feel right now. Fear, anger, concern, dread, guilt, anxiety, confusion, restlessness— every possible negative emotion is in me, burning me alive.

Where is she? It's been five days since I spoke with King Theoderic, and the rest of Faygrene, including the Troyers, arrived two days ago. Today is the opening day of the tournament. But they still aren't here.

Uncertainty gnaws in my stomach, and I move to the

exterior balcony. I stop and grip my hands tightly around the wooden railing. Far down below, the outer streets of the city wind around the castle. They're lined by ivory stone walls, and from this distance, they resemble spirals. People are scrambling about, preparing for the tournament that will begin with or without the guests of honor.

I should have never left without her. If only I had insisted she come with me, then I would have her here, safe by my side. Instead, I'm here without her, my mind reeling with possibilities, endless scenarios that all end with me losing her. I can't stay here.

"We have to look for her," I say, loud enough for Gregory to hear me across the room.

"Drake." He pauses, letting out a long breath. Here it comes—the voice of reason. "We wouldn't know where to start. We have to be patient. I'm sure the business Charles spoke of is just taking longer than planned. They'll be . . ."

"Do not say they'll be arriving soon!" I shout while turning to face him. His head raises out of his hands, his face hardened with irritation. "You know as well as I do that something's wrong. We can't sit here and *do nothing!* She needs us! *Your sister* needs us!"

"Don't speak to me as though I don't care about Addalynne!" he shouts, rising to his feet and moving toward me. "And don't think for one-second that I wouldn't do anything to find her, to make sure she's safe!" He steps onto the balcony, his eyes burning with rage. Good. He should be angry. We're the ones who are supposed to protect her, and we left her with a predator. "You're not the only one who loves her, Drake. I have loved her and vowed to protect her since the day she was born. Don't you see that I'm also going crazy with thoughts of her being injured, or worse?" His voice breaks, and I have to turn away from him, setting my gaze back on the people moving about the streets. "I would already be looking for her, Drake, if we had a clue where to begin, but we don't, and leaving won't do us any good. We have to stay until we have more information."

I hold my tongue. Any argument would be futile. I know he's right, but it still infuriates me. My hands wrap tighter around the wood, squeezing until I feel a piercing pain in my hand. I lift my hand up. There's a jagged piece of wood sticking out of it, its sharp tip impaled in the center of my palm. I watch the blood trickle down, and then Gregory grabs my hand, pulling it toward him. He rips out the wood, and more blood pours out, spilling faster. I watch in silence as Gregory wraps my hand with a white cloth and curses at me for being such a "reckless fool." He shouldn't be surprised; recklessness seems to be what I'm good at.

* * *

"Try to get some sleep." That's what Walter Cromwell said when supper ended in the Great Hall. He's still a member of the King's Schild and has been trying to keep Gregory and me informed on any news. There's been none, but he promised to retrieve me if anything changed.

Try to get some sleep. His words would be laughable if humor were even a remote possibility.

I look at the nightclothes that have been left on the bed for me and throw them to the floor. I'm not going to change. I need to be ready to leave at a moments notice. I lie on my back and twirl my dagger precariously through my fingers. Looking down on me is a sheer, light blue fabric, draped over the tall wooden posts of the bed. Blue has always been my favorite color on Addy, bringing out the fairness of her skin and the subtle blush in her cheeks. I imagine how she would look, lying with me on this blue bed, and a flood of desire burns through me. But my next feeling is one of nausea. How can I think of her in that way when I don't even know if she's alive? My only thoughts should be of finding her; my only feelings should be of worry, not lust. Still, I can't turn it off, and the desire mixes painfully with the worry, guilt and anger. I squeeze my eyes shut and focus on breathing, telling myself repeatedly that I will find her.

I move through the crowded streets of the market, disquiet humming through my body. I look around me, searching, desperate. My feet take me farther, heading out of the village and toward the line of the woods. Movement. *Something blue melts back into the trees. I sprint into the woods and run through the trees, looking frantically beyond the trunks scattered around me. Something rustles behind me. I turn and my breath solidifies in my throat. It's her. Her long hair spills over her shoulders, falling around the curves of her body that are hidden behind a blue dress. Her amber eyes meet mine; they're frighteningly empty, lost. "Addalynne!" I run toward her, but she turns away from me, moving inhumanly fast through the woods, disappearing through the trees. I try to follow her, and she again comes into view, but this time her back is turned toward me and she's facing the Glass River. "Addy!" I run toward her, reaching for her. She turns back and gives me a haunting smile before plunging into the water. I reach the bank and jump, only to be slammed back to the ground. A shimmering veil hovers in front of me, trapping me here. Through the translucent rippling, I see her. She has emerged from the river and is standing on the southern side, in Incarnadine. I scream for her to come back, but my voice echoes off the clear wall and vibrates back into my own ears. I continue to yell her name as I pound, kick and punch at the invisible barrier that's blocking my way. I watch her move farther and farther into the Faenomen Forest, until I can no longer see her.*

"Drake!" I fly into a sitting position, my hair matted to my forehead and neck with sweat, my hands trembling. Looking around frantically, I see blue blankets tangled under my feet. I blink rapidly, waiting for the trees to come back, for her to come back. Confusion sifts through my mind, tangling my reality with the vividness of the dream, and with a painful clench of my heart, I remember where I am.

"Drake!" a voice calls again, and I realize that Walter is standing in the open doorway of my chambers. I try to find my voice, but his presence and the memory of my dream have left me speechless. "They have arrived." *Addy.*

I jump off the bed and sprint out the door, only partially noticing the apprehensive look on Walter's face. I race down the stairs and don't stop until I'm skidding to a halt inside the Great Hall.

The King's Schilds and the Berrengers' guards are gathered around who I can only assume are the Berrengers and Addy. *My Addy.* I push my way through the masses, approaching the front of the congregation, but hands wrap around my shoulders, stopping my progress. I try to shake off whoever has a hold of me while I search the scene in front of me, but their grip only tightens. It's not necessary because what I see immobilizes me. Charles is speaking with one of King Theoderic's Schilds. He looks badly beaten and has a four-inch-long, stitched gash on the side of his face. But that doesn't matter; all that matters is what I see behind him. It's a wooden coffin, and Addalynne is nowhere in sight. My eyes glaze over in a dizzyingly dark haze, my vision narrowing in on the wood. It's as though I can see her through it, her face pale and lifeless, her lids closed over her eyes, sealing them off from me forever. *She can't be dead . . . this isn't real.* My hand trembles and I reach for the sword on my hip. *Not her . . . I'll kill him . . .*

*please don't let this be happening . . . wake up . . . wake up,
Drake . . . this is just a nightmare . . . wake up . . . I'm
going to kill him.*

Somewhere in the recesses of my mind, a voice
whispers in my ear. I try to block it out, but one part
manages to get through to me.

"Not her . . . Vernold . . . died before they left." *Not
her . . . not her.* The words begin to register and I'm able
to focus on who's speaking them and who's holding me
back—Gregory. *It's not her . . . she's alive . . . she's alive.* I
remove my hand from my sword and shake Gregory off.
Gregory's grip reluctantly loosens, and I once again
search for her, but she's nowhere.

"Where is she?" I shout, my voice livid with anger,
my gaze fixing on Charles. He turns to me, his eyes
widening, partly in surprise, partly in amusement.

"Well, what have we here? Arrest him."

My hand reaches toward my sword as several of his
guards approach me. I welcome them forward, eager to
kill every one of them.

"Stop!" King Theoderic's voice booms as he enters
the Great Hall. Everyone simultaneously drops to the
floor in a bow. I do as well, but my sight remains fixed
on Charles and his men, my fingers dancing along the
hilt of my sword. "You have no authority here, Lord
Berrenger. Besides, Drake Walton has been temporarily
pardoned. His arrest will be mine to make if I deem it
necessary," he continues while we rise to our feet.

"Your Grace, this boy is my prisoner!"

"Not anymore," King Theoderic asserts while walking toward Charles. He stops several feet away from him.

"Your Grace! I implore you to see reason! The boy tried to murder me! He—"

"I have been fully informed of what transpired between you and Walton, among other things." King Theoderic interrupts Charles. "Now, I need to have a word with your Lady. Where is she?" Charles's face flashes with momentary panic before concealing itself in a mask of pained calculation. Anger burns through my blood as I wait in torment for his words.

"While we were traveling, we were attacked by woodland nomads. They killed one of my guards and rendered me unconscious. When I awoke, she was gone. They took her."

I run at Charles, my body colliding with his and taking us both to the ground. His head slams into the cold marble floor and I pull out my dagger, placing it against his throat.

"What did you do to her?" I shout while pressing the dagger against his skin. A single drop of blood trickles out and Charles's eyes narrow into slits. Commotion spreads around me, but I don't care. All that exists in this moment is me, Charles, and the dagger between us. Without warning, hands grip my shoulders. I struggle as they pull me off him, but there are several men holding me, and within seconds, they have my arms behind my back and my body restricted. My chest is heaving, my breaths coming in ragged bursts. I turn my head and see

Gregory. The tip of his sword is pressed against the chest of Charles's right hand man, Henry. Henry's sword is also drawn, the tip hovering directly over Gregory's heart. They are halted in a fatal stalemate. One quick move by either one of them will end in death.

"That's enough!" King Theoderic shouts. His face is flushed with anger as he looks from me to Gregory. Gregory and Henry slowly lower their swords and step back from each other, their eyes stationed menacingly on one another's retreating forms. Charles has risen to his feet and is standing with his arms crossed arrogantly over his chest.

"One day it will be just you and me, and no one will be able to save you," I speak venomously, glaring at Charles. King Theoderic turns and heads straight toward me, stopping with only an inch of space between us, our eyes level with each other. I don't look away. Instead I hold his steady blue gaze with mine, watching the anger twitch behind his eyes.

"I said, that's enough, Drake," he speaks sternly. Leaning closer, he places his mouth near my ear. "Stop testing my boundaries. I bent the law by pardoning you once. I cannot pardon you twice." He turns away from me and moves toward his throne. "Please see Mr. Walton and Mr. Troyer to their chambers." He takes his seat and lets his eyes settle on me. "Your families will join you shortly." With a single nod, Gregory and I are escorted out of the Great Hall, while everyone else, including Charles, remains.

Chapter 35

HIM

"He's lying! How can King Theoderic not see that? She wasn't taken by woodland nomads! He did something to her!" I shout furiously, my hands tightening into fists in my hair. My head is pounding and my vision burns around me in an anger-induced haze.

"I'm sure he suspects that, Drake. But without proof, he has no other choice than to accept Charles's version of what happened." My father addresses me, but I don't turn to face him. "Not without any witnesses to speak otherwise."

"That's because the only witnesses are Charles's men. They'll never contradict him," I counter.

Genoveve, Robert, Elizabeth and my father have now joined Gregory and me. My father fully informed Genoveve and Robert about Charles before they came to my chambers. I can feel their eyes on me, pitying me. I don't want their pity, though—I want their resentment. They should be as angry at me as I am at myself for not keeping her safe.

"What I still can't wrap my head around is why she didn't tell us the truth from the beginning." Robert voices his thoughts, his words etched with pain and regret. "Had I known, I would have never allowed this to happen."

But I did. Robert's words are like an arrow to the stomach, causing me to exhale sharply. I sense him approach and soon feel his hand on my shoulder.

"That's not what I meant, Drake. We all know that there was nothing you could have done. You need to stop blaming yourself. This was my fault. I arranged it, and I should have been the one to stop it."

"You couldn't have, Father.," Gregory responds solemnly. "There was nothing you could have done to convince Addalynne to tell you the truth. This is my fault. I knew something was wrong, but I didn't act on it until it was too late."

I watch the clouds passing overhead, my hands resting on the balcony. I can't look at them, not while they assign blame on everyone but me.

"You and Drake did everything you could, Gregory. You devised a plan to help Addalynne, and tried to keep the rest of our family safe," Genoveve says to Gregory, her voice hollow. "You were paying attention to what mattered." There's a tonality to her voice that sounds like Addalynne. It crushes me. "We should have seen it, Robert. How could we have been so blind? We knew she wasn't herself. We knew something was wrong. Yet we looked the other way, our sole focus on the fact that she was going to be the Lady of Faygrene. We told ourselves that this was going to be best for her and that she would be happy. What we should have done was see what was staring us in the face—what these kids were able to do, but we were not."

I hate that she's grouping me into the category of people who knew and saw what was best for Addalynne. The only thing I knew was how best to anger her: by courting Jacqueline. If Gregory hadn't cornered me and told me of his suspicions, I would have been as ignorant as everyone else.

"I'll never forgive myself for letting her down, for not being there for her when she needed me most," Genoveve continues, her agonized voice speaking the same thoughts that torment my own mind.

"There's no reason for this conversation," my father halfheartedly shouts. A crow flies across the sky and lands on one of the balconies across from me. It stretches out its wings and carefully scans the ground. I watch its movements, while my father's voice continues to drift through my ears. "What's done is done, and Addalynne wouldn't have had it any other way. She would sacrifice herself a thousand times over to save any one of us. We all know that. And as much as we detest that quality in her, it will never change. All we can do now is figure out a way to find her and bring her back home."

Part of my mind traces the idea that she may have run from Charles, but I quickly push it away, knowing that if she had, she would have come here. She would have found us. Besides, something's wrong, I can feel it, as firmly as I feel the stones at my feet.

"Charles is leading the expedition to look for her," Robert comments. This gets my attention. I turn around, and their eyes fall to me, waiting for my reaction.

"Tell me you've been misinformed." My words come out in a near growl, my fingers clenching so tightly into fists at my sides that my nails pierce through the skin on my un-bandaged hand.

"I wish I were. They're gathering a group now and will be setting out at dawn."

"He's not going to try to find her!" I shout, while telling myself that Robert is wrong. Somehow he misunderstood. Sending Charles to look for Addalynne is as beneficial as sending a thief to reveal the whereabouts of his stolen jewels. "Maybe he's telling the truth. He did look distraught," Robert says quietly. I'm too stunned for words. After *everything* we have told him, he's still blinded by his loyalty to the Berrengers. I glare at him, hatred building inside of me. I know it's misplaced, but I can't contain the resentment his words have created. His face floods with shame and he looks down at the brown rug beneath his feet. Setting my sight on the door, I move past them, ignoring them when they call out to me. There's only one person I want to speak to right now. As soon as the door shuts behind me, I run.

"Why are you letting him lead the search for her? He

should be rotting in a cell for what he's done!" I shout, while pushing open the large wooden doors of the Great Hall. King Theoderic is seated on his throne with a cluster of Schilds around him. He looks up at me, offering me a reproachful and tired look. The Schilds, on the other hand, have turned to face me, blocking my path to the King. Right, protect him from me, but send Charles after Addalynne.

"It's all right, men. You're dismissed. I would like a private word with Walton." They bow toward him and quietly retreat. He returns his gaze to me. "I cannot imprison him with no evidence."

"I have given you plenty of evidence."

"Drake, your word, as much as I value it, is not evidence. You're not even a witness. Charles insists that the story about the Hunts being taken by a hellion is true. He claims that he even led the search for them, but found no trace other than some bloody clothes near the river. As far as Addalynne's injuries are concerned, he claims she fell off her horse. He believes that you have created these allegations, and convinced others of them because you're jealous that Addalynne chose him. And I must admit, on the surface, you could very well pass as a young man who lost the love of his life to another. Young men will do anything when they're blinded by their jealousy."

I stare at him incredulously. "Do you honestly think I'm making all this up because I'm *jealous*? What about Addalynne's sister. She told you what Addalynne said to her and she told you about the bruises she saw on

Addalynne's arm. Is she jealous too?"

King Theodoric lets out a breath. "I believe both of you, Drake, and I know you're not acting out of jealousy. But you have to understand how it looks to those on the outside. I can't arrest him just because I trust your word more than his. As much as I believe you and Elizabeth, my hands are tied, and without Addalynne here to say otherwise . . ." he shrugs slightly. "I'm sorry."

His words are sincere, but they do nothing to suppress the rage clawing inside me. "So instead you'll let him pretend to look for her? *He's lying!* He did something to her! I know he did! How can you let him lead the search? He won't try to find her! He'll only lead them on a fool's chase!" I pace frantically, unable to stay in one place.

"I'm not so sure about that, Drake," he says quietly. I stop moving and set my eyes on him.

"How could you say that? After everything he's done."

"Because Charles is a proud man and proud men take honor in their property. Ever since he married Addalynne, she has belonged to him." I flinch at his words, the truth in them further ripping an already gaping wound. "He wouldn't let her go so easily. Besides, if you could have seen the look in his eyes when he spoke to me, there was real pain there. In this case, I feel as though he may be telling the truth."

I shake my head in disbelief.

"You're welcome to accompany him on the search, Drake. I'm sending several men with him and they'll ensure that neither of you try to harm each other."

A humorless laugh escapes me. I close my eyes and drag my fingers across my face. I would love for him to try to harm me. I would give anything for the opportunity to fight him again, because this time, I would kill him. But I refuse to follow him. "No. I won't go with him. He has no intention of finding her." I let my eyes open, my empty gaze focusing back on King Theoderic. "I'll go on my own." I back away from him and turn toward the exit.

"Do you think that's wise?" he calls out before I have a chance to leave. I turn around to face him again.

"It's my only option. I can't sit around and do nothing, but I refuse to go with him. I have a better chance of finding her on my own."

"I understand your decision," he acknowledges. "I am unable to send Schilds with you because the ones I have left are needed here, to protect the city, but I can at least send Walter, if you wish. I know you're friends."

"No. Send Walter with the others."

A look of confusion passes along his face. "Since you don't believe Charles will actually be looking for Addalynne, why send Walter with him? Wouldn't it better serve you to have him accompany you on your search?"

"No. I need someone I can trust regarding Charles and his men."

"You can trust any one of my Schilds."

"Not as much as I trust Walter. We grew up together, and he cares for Addalynne. In the off chance that I'm wrong and Charles is looking for her, then Walter will be there to help Addalynne if they find her. He won't let any harm come to her. And, he'll also be able to tell us what Charles does."

"You're certain of your decision?" he asks hesitantly.

"Yes. Gregory will go with me—he'll be enough."

King Theodoric nods. "I admire you, Drake, for your fierceness and your loyalty. When you find Addalynne and return her here, I'll hopefully be able to do more for you, starting with annulling her marriage to Charles."

I savor his words. Though they sound like a lost dream, I pray with everything in me that one day soon he'll be able to honor them. After a bow, I make my way out of the Great Hall. As soon as I'm through the doors and in the corridor, I break into a sprint, heading straight for Gregory.

Chapter 36

HIM

I look around me, observing the heavy shadows of the trees. It's nearing dark. Another day gone. Another day without her.

Three days have passed since we started trailing Charles, Henry, and the King's Schilds. At first I was completely opposed to this idea. Now, I'm still uncertain of it, but I'm hoping it will end up being worthwhile. Gregory's the one who insisted on following Charles. He argued that we had no idea which direction to head in. I argued that the opposite direction of Charles would be the best place to start. Next, Gregory pointed out that if we followed Charles, we might overhear him confiding in one of his men about Addalynne's whereabouts. This point helped me to consider his plan. Then he said that if the opportunity presented itself, he wouldn't stop me from killing Charles. This made me agree to his plan.

But now I'm growing impatient.

Gregory and I have lingered in the woods, skirting around Charles and the other men, trying to watch and listen for any clues to Addalynne's whereabouts. The fact that we can't get too close makes this problematic. But we told Walter about our plan before we left, and he has been reporting back to us with information or, more accurately, with a lack of information. Apparently, Charles has done nothing but feign ignorance about where she might be. All along he has stuck to his story about the woodland nomads.

I shift uncomfortably on the branch I'm sitting on. It's pressing painfully into sensitive areas that should never spend this much time in a tree. I let out an impatient groan and glance at Gregory. He's sitting in a tree next to mine and looks equally uncomfortable. He must feel my eyes on him, because he turns to look at me as well.

"This is the last night I do this. If we don't get any new leads by tomorrow afternoon, we're going on our own," I whisper.

"Agreed."

I lean my head back on the trunk and let my eyes close. I think about Addy and all the hundreds of days we spent together sitting on the branches of the Grey Tree. I remember the first time I climbed it with her. Her face was scrunched in determination as she ascended higher and higher. Even then I felt an immense amount of fear at the thought of her falling. I always tried to position myself close enough to catch her if necessary. As the years passed, I realized how good she was at climbing, but the protectiveness never seemed to fade. I was always worried about her getting hurt. Blowing out an aggravated breath, I drag my fingers across the wood. I was there to protect her from the most unlikely dangers, but I failed when it came to the real ones.

A rustling noise underneath me draws my eyes open. I glance to the ground and see two figures walking away from the camp; Charles and Henry. Adrenaline sears through me. Keeping my eyes on them, I tear off a piece of bark and quietly toss it at Gregory. It bounces off his cheek, and he turns toward me in irritation. I place one finger in front of my lips and point the other one in the direction of Charles and his number one confidant. Gregory's face purses in thought and then he offers me a conspiratorial grin. We simultaneously climb down our trees and move silently through the woods, trailing our targets.

My fingers twitch toward the sword at my side while we follow them farther into the woods. They come to a stop in a small clearing, about twenty feet away from us. Behind them lies a narrow stream. They're standing close together, speaking in hushed tones. From this distance, I can't make out what they're saying, but I'm sure it's about her. I take a subtle step in their direction and Gregory's hand wraps around the sleeve of my black tunic, halting me. I look back at him and he gives me a single shake of his head, no.

"I'm going closer. It's our only chance to hear what they're saying. If they see me, then we'll fight," I say with a shrug, offering him a sideways smile. A frown of disapproval pulls on his face, but he lets go, and I continue forward, stepping cautiously toward them. Faint whispers drift to my ears, and I take my place behind a bush that's several feet away from them. Crouching down, I listen carefully to every word they speak.

". . . another week at most and then they'll be ready to give up," Charles says. My heart pounds in anticipation of their next words.

"How can you be so certain? I hardly believe her family will give up their search after a little over a week, or the orphan, for that matter."

"The orphan will die as soon as we return. King Theoderic can't protect him much longer. And as far as her family goes, they can continue to search to their hearts content. They'll never find her. She's too far away by now."

Blood rushes to my head, making my ears ring. Every part of me wants to run straight for him and plunge my sword into his chest.

"That she is," Henry agrees, humor staining his voice. He'll die too. "Should I go hunt down something for us to eat?" Henry asks. I tense in preparation of Charles's answer. If Henry goes, I'll have my chance with Charles—one on one. There will be no one to help him this time.

"I suppose. I've grown sick of the dried meat the King's Schilds have been eating. Bring it back here, though. I don't want to share with the rest of them."

"As you wish, my Lord."

I glance back at Gregory, and he gives me a knowing nod before moving through the trees, trailing after Henry. Rising to my feet, I move around the bush and step into the clearing. Charles is crouched down at the edge of the stream, cupping water in his hands. When he hears me approach he rises abruptly to his feet. His hand wraps around his sword and he draws it out at the same time that he turns to face me. Shock registers on his face, but it's soon replaced by a slanted sneer. I take several more steps toward him, my hand wrapping tightly around the hilt of my sword.

"Well, well. I should have known you would follow me. Congratulations on surprising me. You should be proud. That never happens." He takes a step toward me with his sword extended, pointing at my chest. We begin to move sideways, circling each other.

"I have many surprises planned for you," I say, while I plan my misdirection. My father always taught me that if you can get your opponent to fall for your misdirection, you can gain the upper hand.

"Is that so? As many surprises as I had for Addalynne?"

I halt momentarily, his words rattling me. He uses the moment of hesitation to his advantage and runs forward, slashing diagonally. The tip of his sword barely misses the front of my chest as I leap backwards. His movement sends him slightly off balance and I use the opportunity to bring my sword around in a downward swipe aiming for his arm. He raises his blade up at the last second and the clank of metal vibrates loudly, blocking my sword. I raise my foot and kick him squarely in the chest. A grunt of pain escapes him and he stumbles slightly, but manages to right himself. Our eyes lock and our circular pacing resumes.

"Someone taught you well, Orphan. Was it that pretend father of yours, or the measly time you spent in the Schild?"

"I didn't realize you knew so much about me. I suppose I should be flattered that you find me so interesting."

"I make it a point to learn all I can about my opponents. Perhaps you should have done the same, then maybe you could have saved her."

His words inflict more than I want him to know. Instead of responding, I watch his sword while I think of my next move: one that will silence him permanently.

"Nothing to say now?" he says with mock disappointment. "How unfortunate, but I know how to make you speak. Tell me, orphan, how many times did you lie with Addalynne before we were married?"

My eyes flash to his face. *He knows.* The thought sickens me, knowing it brought her more pain. At least I also know that, regardless of where she is, he will no longer be able to hurt her. I let this thought mollify me, but I still refuse to speak. I won't give him the satisfaction.

"Still nothing to say? That's fine. Regardless, I know you were with her. And though I may not know how many times, I can guarantee it's nowhere near the amount of times I had her." A feral smile spreads across his face and my stomach twists. He's lying. He's trying to get in my head. "My favorite thing about her is how ferociously she always fought back. Oh, and that little beauty mark on her right hip."

I lunge at him, an animalistic growl escaping from me as I dodge sideways to avoid his sword and slam my body into his, throwing him down to the ground. Both of our swords fly out of our hands from the impact. I straddle his waist and bring my fist down onto his face. The image of Addalynne's body, bruised and broken, flashes in my mind. I use my other hand to place a second blow, shattering his nose. He cries out in agony, but responds by reaching around to my back and digging his fingers into my scabbed over lashes, re-breaking the skin. I groan as my body stiffens in pain. He uses the distraction to toss me off of him, and my shoulder slams into the ground. He climbs on top of me and lands a punch on my face. I blink against the sting of it and notice that one of his wrists is bandaged. I reach for it, but before I'm able to grab hold, he punches me again. My vision blurs, but I can still make out the smile on his face. I picture Addalynne trying to fight him off and him smiling this same smile, thinking he's won. The thought gives me the adrenaline I need and I slam my elbow into the center of his chest. He coughs, sinking forward as I roll sideways, tossing him off me.

Rising to my feet, I run for my sword while trying to push the images of him forcing himself on Addalynne out of my mind. My feet slip on the dirt and I drop to the ground, my hand wrapping around the hilt of my sword. I push myself onto my feet and run for him. He's staggering to his feet, but his sword is back in his uninjured hand. I yell as I slice the sword in an upward motion. He tries to move, but the tip of my blade scratches across his chest, leaving an open gash in his shirt and skin. He stares down at the blood in shock as it trickles out. It's not a fatal wound, but it will slow him down. I thrust my sword forward, aiming for his heart, but he clanks it away with his own. Raising my arm, I bring the hilt of my sword down across his face. His body spins around and then falls to the ground. He rises onto all fours and spits out a mixture of blood and several teeth. I run toward him and land a kick directly into his ribs, hopefully shattering several, two for every one he broke of hers. He yells out in pain and falls back onto the ground, his fingers loosening their grip on his sword. I kick it out from under him and send it skidding several feet away. Placing my foot on top of his back, I keep him down on the ground. I can feel the rise and fall of his rapid breaths underneath my boot. I toss my own sword to the side and pull the dagger out of my belt. Using my foot, I flip him over onto his back. I lower myself on top of him and stab my dagger into one shoulder and then the next, letting his screams of pain ignite my adrenaline. I raise the dagger up, now saturated with his blood, and place it over his neck. It's not time for him to die yet.

"Where is she?" I demand. He spits at me, his blood and saliva landing on my cheek.

He laughs an amused and ragged laugh. "As though I would ever tell you," he replies with a cough. I use my sleeve to wipe his spit off my face and my gaze lands on the stitches on his cheek.

"She gave you that cut," I say, and I can tell by the contempt in his eyes that I'm right. I feel a swell of pride as I think of her, fighting back and cutting his face open. That's my Addy. I place the tip of the dagger on his opposite cheek and drag it down, creating a matching line. He growls in pain, his eyes widening with their first traces of fear. "Where . . . is . . . she?" I ask slowly, leaning toward him, my face only inches from his.

"It doesn't matter where she is. You'll never find her. They have her now," he speaks with a slur, the wound on his cheek making it difficult for him to form words.

"Who has her?"

He laughs, a sick, raspy sound. Blood is pooling around his head and matting into his hair, staining it red. "You're going to kill me no matter what I say. Besides, I would never give you the satisfaction of telling you where she is. You may kill me, but you're the one who will spend the rest of your life constantly wondering where she is, always asking yourself if you could have done more to save her." His words strike me more than any physical blow could. Knowing he's about to die isn't good enough. He deserves much worse than death.

If only Addalynne could be here now, watching me drain the life from him. I picture her, smiling down at me, and I freeze, the image of her in the woods bringing back flashes of my dream—Addalynne running through the woods, crossing the river, staring back at me from the bank of Incarnadine.

Everything shifts, becoming instantly clear: the final piece falling into place. And though I don't know how or why, I know that it was more than a dream. "She's in Incarnadine," I say as much to myself as to him. He tenses underneath me and I lock my eyes onto his. They're filled with surprise, telling me I'm right. My body surges with equal amounts of hope and dread. I press the tip of the dagger against his neck. "Any last words? Now is the time for you to beg me for your life," I repeat his own words from the day of my arrest back to him. He continues to stare at me, refusing to speak. I picture Addalynne one last time, and then slice the dagger across his throat. A gurgled cough escapes his lips and the blood flows from his neck. Looking at his eyes, I watch the life fade from them.

Once I'm certain he's dead, I push myself to my feet and drag his body across the ground to the stream. It's not large at this sect, but it's big enough to carry a body in its current. I move behind him and shove his body forward with my boot until it splashes into the water.

From the corner of my eye I see Gregory run into the clearing. He's disheveled and covered in dirt and blood, but thankfully seems unharmed. His gaze falls on me and his face noticeably relaxes. Then his gaze trails to Charles's body, which is floating downstream. We both watch as his body drifts farther away, bumping into rocks. A blood trail follows its lead, sanguinating the water with crimson curls.

"Tell me you got information from him *before* you killed him?" Gregory says with frustration.

"I take it that you got none from Henry," I reply, a small smile tugging on the corner of my lips.

"No. Grimy bastard wouldn't say a word."

I nod my head in understanding and stare toward the south. Sir Alsius's words drift through my mind; *It has always been in your destiny to find your way back.*

"She's in Incarnadine."

Gregory's response is a silence so deep it seems to take the air with it.

I turn toward him. His face is pale and his hands are tightened into fists, but I can still see them shaking. He closes his eyes. "Tell me your wrong," he says, his words pained and breathless.

"I know it's not ideal Gregory, but we know where she is now. *We can find her.*"

He opens his eyes. The pain in them is consuming. "Drake. I know you want to believe that. But she's gone."

"No, she's not," I say, shaking my head. "She's just in Incarnadine. We will find her!"

Gregory shakes his head and drops down to his knees. He sits back on his heels, his hands gripping his thighs, his chest rising and falling with his breaths. I want to punch him.

"Why are you acting like this?" I shout.

He doesn't answer me, he just stares out, his eyes glazed over in despair. My heart pounds in anger. "Gregory!" I shout, but he doesn't even spare me a glance. "We need to leave now, Gregory. If we leave now we can be half way to the Glass River by tomorrow night."

"She's gone, Drake," he says again and this time a tear trails down his cheek.

"Stop saying that!"

"Why should I?" he shouts and pushes to his feet, his anger finally finding him. "It's the truth Drake! If she's in Incarnadine, she's probably already dead, and even if she's not, Incarnadine is three times the size of Silveria. We'd never find her!"

"She's not dead." My words push through my clenched jaw, my anger barely contained. "But it's true that she's in a dangerous place and every minute we waste arguing here is a minute that she could get hurt."

"Or killed. If she hasn't already been."

I take a step toward him, my hands tightened into fists. "If you say that she's dead one more time, I'm—"

"You'll what Drake? You'll fight me too? Are you going to fight everyone you come across for the rest of your life, hoping that one of them will lead you to her?"

"If I have to."

"Well, that's very rational. Good plan," he says with a humorless laugh.

"At least I'm not giving up on her!"

His punch is unexpected and momentarily blinding. I stagger, my hand clutching my cheek.

"I'm not giving up on her," he snarls. "But I know a lost cause when I see one."

I drop my hand from my face and look at Gregory.

He no longer looks angry, just defeated.

"If you want to get yourself killed in Incarnadine, then go ahead," he says, his voice emptied of emotion. "But I won't follow you. I have my family and Mary to think about. I can't abandon them to go on a suicide mission in Incarnadine. If I thought we had any chance, *any chance at all* of finding her, I would take it. But there's not." He walks toward me and places his hand on my shoulder. "I know you don't want to accept that Drake. But if you want to live, if you want to see your father again, then you'll come back home with me." He drops his hand and then walks away, not waiting to see if I'll follow. He knows me well enough to know that I won't.

Chapter 37

HIM

The sound of footsteps behind me causes me to glance back, but all I see around me are the trunks of the trees and the dark green shrubs—a deserted forest. Turning back around, I continue to walk, but I hear them again. I whip around and see the tail end of a cloak darting behind a tree. I move quietly toward it and extract the dagger from my belt. As I approach the tree, I see the toe of a black boot sticking out from behind it. I move to the side of the trunk and reach my free hand forward. Wrapping my hand around the collar of my pursuer's neck, I pull him around to face me.

"It's me. It's me," Walter says in a hushed, but frantic tone. I release my grip from around his cloak.

"Why are you following me, Walter?"

"Where are you going?" he counters.

I place the dagger back into my belt. "Did anyone

ever tell you that it's rude to answer a question with another question?"

"Well, then you're being rude yourself, aren't you?" he replies with a chuckle.

I raise my eyebrow in annoyance. "I don't have time for this, Walter, so if there's a reason for your being here, please tell me or be on your way."

He nervously runs his fingers through his light brown hair while glancing to the treetops above us. "I went to tell you and Gregory that Charles and Henry were missing. But then I saw that Gregory was asleep next to both of your horses and you were gone. I tracked your footsteps to another tree and then to a clearing. I found a large blood stain, which I'm now guessing belongs to Charles, and then I found more tracks which led me here, to you. It's a good thing that it rained recently right?" he finishes with a laugh, but when I don't respond the smile leaves his face. "Where are you going, Drake?"

"Don't worry about it," I say as I move around him. I can't handle another person telling me that she's dead and that I should give up. "Go back to camp. Charles is gone and there's no need for you to look for Addalynne. I will find her." I continue to move quickly through the forest, hoping he'll turn back around. But I'm not that lucky.

"So you did kill Charles?"

"Yes."

"Good. That bastard needed to die."

A small smile forms on my lips, but I push it away

with a shake of my head. I'm not here to talk to Walter. "Good bye, Walter."

"I'm coming with you."

I stop moving and turn to face him, my body rigid. "No, you're not." I place my hand against his chest, stopping his forward motion.

"What are you going to do, Drake, fight me?" he asks, reminding me of what Gregory said, and making part of me want to punch him in his freckled face anyway. Instead, I drop my hand and let out a frustrated breath.

"You can't come with me, Walter. I'm sorry, but you need to leave."

"If you don't let me come with you, then I'm going to tell the Schilds where you are and convince them to come after you."

I place my head in my hands, tugging at my hair. "Why do you want to come with me, Walter?"

"Because, you're my friend and a fellow Schild."

"I'm not a Schild."

"No, but you used to be, and we're still bound by our oath to protect each other. Besides, no matter how strong you are, you shouldn't do this alone. You may find yourself needing help, Drake, and you owe it to Addalynne to have someone to help you. Two are always better than one."

I know he's right, but after Gregory refused to come with me, I convinced myself that it was better to go alone anyway. Less footsteps to cover. But I don't think Walter's going to give up, and I don't have time to waste arguing.

"You're not going to leave, are you?" I ask exasperatedly, dropping my hands back down to my sides.

"No."

"Fine," I growl, and continue to move forward. "But I won't slow down for you, and you will do everything I say. Is that clear?"

"Yes. I give you my word," he replies excitedly, hurrying to catch up to me. He has to jog to make his slightly shorter legs match my pace. "Do you mind telling me where we're going?"

"Incarnadine." I don't look at him when I say it, but I hear his breath, a distressed intake. But his footsteps don't falter.

As the sun begins to rise, I look toward the south, the sky above tinged with red, and find myself plagued by the irony of it all. Addy was the one who jumped into the river that day, saving me and bringing me from Incarnadine. Now I have to do the same to save her. I will finally go back to the place that has held the keys to my past, in order to find my future. My entire life rests in its uncertain grasp, and it's up to me to put my life back together, by bringing her home.

Acknowledgments

Eight years ago I sat down and started writing a story about a boy and a girl who loved each other more than anything, but were forbidden to be together. (Is it obvious that I grew up obsessed with Romeo and Juliet and Wuthering Heights?) This first dive into writing became chapter 23. From that moment, Addalynne and Drake climbed into my heart and never left. I outlined their story and after about six months, Masked was complete. What would follow would be years of editing and rewrites; queries and speed bumps. This entire process wouldn't have been possible without so many people in my life.

Thank you times infinity to . . .

Martine Bowers for reading every chapter as soon as I wrote it and for helping me edit this book and bring it to life. You are always there for me to bounce ideas off of and to offer encouragement, advice, and a laugh. You are not only my writing partner but my best friend of 22 years! Yikes!

Kate Brauning for not only editing this book and other ramblings of mine, but for answering my millions of questions and offering invaluable guidance.

Jennet Grover for being the first editor to look at this book and tell me I had a shot. Your belief in me helped me see this through, and for that I am forever grateful.

Bianca Barela for writing an incredible poem for my book. To read more of her beautiful words go to www.biancabarela.com

DiDi, my amazing cover artist who worked tirelessly all the way from Indonesia. Thank you for designing such a breathtaking cover! If you ever need any graphic designs or cover art done for you, contact Didi at wahyudi.trend@gmail.com

Lisa Ortiz for being my friend and my fellow fantasy fiction lover. You are my favorite person to obsess over stories with. Thank you for obsessing over mine with me and for your endless support.

Danielle Webb for helping me hone in on my writing skills with our cowritten butterfly tales. Your friendship means the world to me.

Maura Casados of Maura Jane Photography for your friendship, support, and for being the amazing photographer that captured my author photo.

Minuet Sandifer for your encouragement, friendship, and for helping me navigate the maze of marketing.

Margie Baca for all the laughs, tears, and name searches. Oswey!!! You were one of my first readers and fans. I will always be grateful to you!

Rose Clark for being a fellow nerd and one of my best friends. Thank you so much for your support and assistance in all areas of my life.

Sue Liming and Karen Drysdale for your friendship, guidance, encouragement, and endless laughs. You helped me through many stressful times and I'm so thankful for you both.

Karen Shepherd and Jeanie Williams for believing in me and helping me navigate my writing career.

My mother and father in law, Paulette and Mike, for welcoming me into your life when I was just a teenager and instantly treating me like your daughter. Your support over the many years has been invaluable to me. I love you both.

My sister, Jennifer, for your support, advice, courage, and work ethic. You have always been an inspiration to me and have always been there for me; from the times I would climb into your bed when I was a scared five year old to now when I call you for advice as a scared mother. I love you!

My nieces: Danielle, Loren, and Natalie for filling my life with so much joy; and to Danielle and Loren for reading my work and supporting me. (Natalie, you can read it when you're older.) Danielle, thank you for helping me navigate through many choices and letting me play you song after song that reminded me of my book.

My grandma for supporting me from day one and for reading every word I wrote. Your love for your family and the endless love you've always shown me has meant the world to me. You and Grandpa were one of my first examples of a great love story. I love you both so much and I wish Grandpa were here every day.

My mom and dad for teaching me about unconditional love,

laughter, and imagination. You are the most amazing parents and gave me an incredible childhood. Watching you dance together in the headlights and seeing how much you still love each other year after year is what turned me into the hopeless romantic I am. Thank you, Mom for reading and rereading every chapter and talking me through every heartbreak and victory. And thank you, Dad for always offering advice, jokes, and encouragement. I couldn't do anything without you both! I love you more than I can say!

My husband and best friend, Kyle, for teaching me what true love feels like. Without you this wouldn't have been possible. We were kids when we fell in love and through every obstacle that came our way, we held on to each other. I could not have written about love if I didn't experience it from you. Thank you for your love, your friendship, your encouragement, and your patience when I'm obsessing (which is pretty often). I love you! You are my person, my soulmate.

Lastly, to my daughter, Layne. You bring endless light and love into our lives. Watching you find the beauty in every moment has been such an inspiration. It was you who motivated me to find my passion again. I want you to learn to follow your dreams and overcome obstacles, which means I have to do the same. So here's to dreams followed and obstacles overcame. I hope you all enjoyed reading this book as much as I enjoyed writing it.

52954351R10280

Made in the USA
Lexington, KY
27 September 2019